SPECTRUM

The works of Alan Jacobson

NOVELS

False Accusations
The Hunted
The 7th Victim *
Crush *
Velocity *
Inmate 1577 *
Hard Target
No Way Out *
Spectrum *

*Karen Vail novels

SHORT STORIES

"Fatal Twist"
(featuring Karen Vail)

"Double Take"
(featuring Carmine Russo & Ben Dyer)

For more information on Alan Jacobson's novels,
including reading group guides, videos, and
interviews, please visit www.AlanJacobson.com.

SPECTRUM

A KAREN VAIL NOVEL

ALAN JACOBSON

OPEN ROAD

INTEGRATED MEDIA

NEW YORK

Author name block text is set in Caudex. The Caudex font is copyright © 2011 Hjort Nidudsson.

Author photograph by Corey Jacobson

Copyright © 2014 by Alan Jacobson

978-1-62467-271-2

This edition published in 2014 by Open Road Integrated Media, Inc.
345 Hudson Street
New York, NY 10014
www.openroadmedia.com

>For MARY ELLEN O'TOOLE,

known in my circles as "the real-life Karen Vail." It seemed fitting that I dedicate Vail's origin story to Mary Ellen, who, for the past seventeen years, has provided me with invaluable insight into the challenges and triumphs she experienced as one of the first female FBI profilers. Mary Ellen is a renowned and talented behavioral analyst, author, educator, and lecturer, and her fingerprints are all over the Karen Vail novels. But more importantly, she's a special person, someone whose friendship I'm fortunate to have had for so many years.

Mary Ellen, this one's for you.

SPECTRUM

"The only motive that there ever was was to completely control a person, a person that I found physically attractive, and keep them with me as long as possible, even if it meant keeping (only) a part of them."

Jeffrey Dahmer, serial killer who murdered
and dismembered seventeen boys and men

"The knife of corruption endangered the life of New York City. The scalpel of the law is making us well again."

Ed Koch, mayor of New York (1978–1989)

"On the 22nd of April 1625 the Amsterdam Chamber of The West India Company decreed the establishment of Fort Amsterdam and the creation of ten adjoining farms. The purchase of the island of Manhattan was accomplished in 1626. Thus was laid the foundation of the City of New-York."

Monument in Battery Park

1

>KENNEDY AIRPORT
AMERICAN FLIGHT 425
QUEENS, NEW YORK
PRESENT DAY: JULY 17

Something was wrong. FBI profiler Karen Vail felt it more than she knew it, but there were times in her career when intuition was all she had to go on. And this was one of those times.

Seated next to her on the Airbus A319 due to take off for Dulles International was her boyfriend, or very significant (and sometimes underappreciated) other, Roberto Umberto Enrique Hernandez, his right arm and hand encased in a hard plaster cast. At six foot seven, he was more than a little cramped in the seat. But Vail did not seem to notice.

"I know that look," Robby said. When he did not get a response, he said, "That look. I've seen it before. You're worried. And still pissed off."

"Good evening, ladies and gentlemen." Unlike Vail's demeanor, the flight attendant's voice was calm, almost uninterested. "Welcome aboard. This is a full flight, so we need everyone in his or her seat as soon as possible so we can close the door and push back from the gate."

Vail looked over at Robby—and noticed him for the first time since they left the homicide squad. "Yeah, I'm pissed off. Frustrated. Hurt. But what's bothering me most is that I might've made a mistake. I'm not sure. I can't be sure. And it's killing me."

"So you said. Twice. On the way over here."

Actually, it was five times. Weren't you listening?

"What's changed in the last fifteen minutes?"

Vail closed her eyes. "We're sitting on a plane about to leave town. And I know that once that door closes, I'm not coming back."

"The way you and Russo left things, I don't think you'd want to go back even if we got off the plane right now."

Vail thought about that. *Robby's probably right, but how can I just go home? I pissed off one of the biggest supporters I've ever had in my career. My mentor, the guy who put his reputation on the line for me.* She opened her eyes and examined the bulkhead. *Am I right? Am I wrong? Am I missing something?*

She had thought that she was too close to this case, was not seeing it objectively. Maybe it would've been better to hand it off to another profiler. But that would mean the NYPD would have to make an official request to the Behavioral Analysis Unit, and she doubted that was going to happen now.

At the moment, there was no time to take a step back and reassess. She was still in New York and they had a suspect in custody.

Vail watched the stewardess talk with the gate attendant. *What should I do? Stay or go?*

"Maybe I didn't approach it the right way," Vail said.

"Wouldn't be the first time."

She looked at Robby, her brow knitted in annoyance. "Thanks."

"Just saying. Yeah, it's possible. But I don't think it matters now."

"I still feel like I should go back."

"Karen, I don't think that's a good idea."

Since when did that ever stop me?

Robby nodded toward the front. "Either way, I think the train has left the station. They're about to close the door."

"I can't do this," Vail said. "I can't just leave. I can't live with that." She yanked open her belt buckle and bolted for the exit.

"Karen, wait!"

But Vail did not wait. She ran down the aisle, her FBI creds dangling from her left hand. "Don't lock that door!"

The flight attendant spun around, her face knotted in confusion—and alarm. "What?"

Vail shoved her brass badge into the woman's face. "FBI, I need to get off the plane."

"But—I'm sorry, miss. I just locked her down."

"It's *agent*. And I don't care if you just closed the door. Open it."

"I can't. It's against FAA—"

"I'm not interested in whatever regulation you're going to quote. Open the goddamn door or you could be responsible for—"

"Is there a problem here?"

Vail turned—a second flight attendant had come up behind her. She glanced down at his name tag. "As long as she lets me out, Ed, no. There's no problem."

Robby cleared his throat, now lined up behind Ed. Robby gave Vail a dubious look. She ignored it and turned back to the woman.

"I'm going to call the captain," Ed said.

Vail pulled out her BlackBerry and offered it to Ed. "I've got a better idea. Why don't you call Douglas Knox? He's listed on my speed dial under 'FBI director.'"

VAIL AND ROBBY caught a cab and headed back into the city. She had already placed a call and left a voice mail, but instead of putting the phone away, she started dialing again.

"Now who are you calling?" Robby asked. "For that matter, where are we going?"

Vail paged through the numbers on her device. "I'm calling Russo."

"I don't think that's a good idea, Karen."

"You keep saying that."

"Maybe you need to start listening."

Vail turned to Robby and stared him down. Then she hit a couple of buttons and her BlackBerry connected. After four rings, it clicked to voice mail.

"He's not answering, is he?"

Vail clenched her jaw, then redialed. On the third ring, Russo answered.

"What."

"We need to talk."

"I'm done talking. Go home, Karen."

"I was. But I can't. I feel the need to see this through. And when I feel something, feel it strongly, I can't walk away."

"We *are* seeing it through. The BAU has done its job. Now it's our responsibility. Go home."

Vail felt Robby's eyes fixed on her face. She turned away, toward the side window.

"I—I want to help."

She heard muffled sounds—a woman asking Russo a question and then him giving orders to someone—a driver?

"Karen, I don't have time for this. I'm on the way to a scene. I'll get back to y—"

"Hang on a minute. Another vic? One of ours?"

There was a long silence.

"Russo, is there another vic?"

"Yes."

VAIL WALKED INTO the apartment in the Battery Park City high-rise, Robby bringing up the rear.

The crime scene detective, Ryan Chandler, had just arrived and was setting up shop. He looked surprised to see Vail, but then reached into his kit and tossed booties to her and Robby.

They slipped them on and continued into the room. Russo had arrived a while ago and was talking with Detective Leslie Johnson at the far end of the room. Russo looked up and saw Vail. His expression was a mix of—she wasn't sure. Embarrassment? Relief at her presence? Annoyance? No matter. This was not about her or Russo; it was about the victim in the other room and their shared imperative to catch the offender before more women turned up dead.

Robby came up behind her and murmured into her ear, "Staring at each other isn't going to get you anywhere."

"Right." Vail walked over to Russo and asked the obvious question: "Is this the same offender?"

"I thought you might want to answer that one for yourself."

"Looks like the same killer to me," Chandler said.

She turned to survey the apartment. It was a nice spread, well appointed, everything in its place. Not unlike the other crime scenes.

Vail started in the living and family rooms, getting to know the woman. She glanced at unopened mail on the coffee table and took the victim's name to be Katherine Stavros.

Greek. Big surprise there.

Vail found the medical examiner, Max Finkelstein, and conferred with him on the time of death.

"Bottom line," he said, "the guy you got in custody's good for this."

His answer clearly pleased Russo, but Vail was less than satisfied. She moved on to a wall that abutted the kitchen, where framed photos were prominently displayed. Vail looked them over and took in the story they told about the victim's life. Katherine seemed to have traveled a great deal: there were several exterior shots of her in various cities with male and female friends. Many of them looked like the kind of pictures posted to Facebook, iPhone candids of people having fun, sharing a beer or standing on a bridge with a city skyline behind them.

There were posed portraits as well, with what appeared to be family members—parents and great-grandparents, perhaps. Judging by their strong features and olive complexions, Katherine had Greek DNA in her cells.

Vail's phone rang.

As she started to turn away, her eye caught something. She leaned in closer, then lifted the frame off the wall and examined the photo—

Wait, what the hell?

Vail was trying to work it through her brain as she reached for her Black-Berry.

And then it hit her.

Oh my god.

2

>ASTORIA. QUEENS
SUNDAY. JANUARY 6. 1973

The bowling ball careened down the Astoria Lanes alley, spun left, and hooked into the pocket. All ten pins leaped off the polished wood lane and fell back with a satisfying crash.

"Strike!"

Livana pumped her fist and grinned broadly. She turned to see Basil's reaction, but he still wasn't back from the café. Her joy faded as quickly as it had risen. *He will never believe me!*

Livana had taken up the sport only a couple months ago. Despite her initial resistance to the loud, smoky environment, she had come to enjoy the Sunday night outings when she, Basil, Cassandra, and Dmitri would bowl a few lines—Dmitri spending more time in the arcade with the pinball machines than on the lanes—and then grab a large pizza, Cokes, and egg creams for dessert.

Their longtime friend Fedor and his ten-year-old son, Niklaus, had started joining them three weeks ago. Livana and Fedor's wife, Ophelia, had met in the hospital in Greece, when they gave birth two days apart. Ophelia's baby died a week later from an unforeseen birth defect, but she got pregnant several months later with Niklaus.

Livana helped Ophelia through an extremely difficult time, and their friendship was cemented by the tragedy.

The two women had much in common, and the families started getting together regularly. Upon moving to the United States, they made time to go to the movies, to Flushing Meadow Park for picnics, to Shea Stadium for Mets games—or to Fedor's backyard for summer barbecues.

When Ophelia died of a massive coronary, her heart having been damaged by rheumatic fever she had contracted as a child, it hit both families hard. Together, they found strength to survive the void left by her death.

"Cassie," Livana said to her eleven-year-old daughter, who was writing in her diary, "Let's go find your father."

They left the lanes and headed for the café, passing the arcade on the way. She peeked in and saw a couple teenagers playing a game of foosball and a few others slapping at controllers on pinball machines.

Livana continued on but slowed a bit when she heard shouting emanating from the café—and then a loud crash of breaking glass. She ran the last thirty yards, rounded the bend and saw, through the doors, her husband kneeling over a man lying on the floor, his face bloodied.

"Basil!" Livana rushed in and rushed over to him. She glanced at the man on the ground, at Dmitri and Niklaus a few feet away, and then turned to Basil. "What happened? What's going on?"

"He started it," Basil said.

Livana took her daughter's hand. "Cassie, go back to our lane and wait there for me." Cassandra's gaze was fixed on the blood covering the man's face. Livana gave her a shove in the rear. "Take Dmitri. Go on, get out of here!"

Cassandra and her eight-year-old brother left the café as Livana knelt beside the injured male. "Nik, go to the front desk where we got the shoes. Tell them to call an ambulance."

Niklaus was staring at the downed man.

"Quickly!"

Livana's tone jolted him out of his trance and he ran out as a woman entered from the kitchen. "Just called one. And the police."

Livana felt her stomach knot up. *Basil, what have you done?* She pressed her fingers against the man's neck and checked his pulse. "He's unconscious but alive. I need something to keep him warm. Give me your sweater."

"My sweater?" Basil asked, his voice rising. "That jerk started the fight."

"Just give it to me!" she said, gesturing angrily for Basil to hurry. "We have to keep him from going into shock."

Livana laid the wool garment across his body, then rose and frowned at Basil in disgust. "This was supposed to be a family day."

"What's going on?" Fedor asked.

Livana looked up to see Fedor standing there, his eyes moving about the room as he took in the scene. "Where are the kids?"

"They're fine. Where were you?"

"I went to the bathroom." He rubbed his abdomen. "That Italian we had last night is still bothering me." He took a step closer and appeared to see the body for the first time. "Whoa, what happened?"

Livana turned toward the injured man and instinctively put a hand over her mouth. His face was sliced badly, and it was all she could do to keep from vomiting.

"TELL ME WHAT HAPPENED," Livana said, standing outside the café as the paramedics attended to the man they identified as Gregor Persephone. Fedor stood at Basil's side, an arm around his friend's shoulder. Fedor had started to talk, but Livana shushed him. "I asked my husband a question. And he seems to be having a hard time answering."

Basil looked at her but didn't speak.

"The police are going to be here any minute. You're going to have to tell them. You may as well tell your wife, no?" She waited a minute, then said, "This is so unlike you, Basil. I don't understand. I'm so disappointed." Still nothing. "That man looks like he's hurt real bad."

"I was just defending myself." Basil sighed, then rubbed his face with two bloody hands. "I ordered our pies and was drinking my beer. The waitress went back to put the order together. Then this woman comes up to me and—well, she starts coming on to me."

"How?"

"She's dressed in this tight shirt, and she's got all this makeup on, fake nails, and she touches my face, says she's never seen me here before. I told her we just started coming. Then she touches my—she starts rubbing my crotch."

"What?"

"I grabbed her hand and told her I was here with my son and I'm married and she gets all mad and slaps me in the face, starts screaming at me. Then that guy comes up to me—"

"What guy? Gregor?"

"You know him?"

"Everyone knows him. He's your boss's son. How could you not know him?"

"I—I've seen him around. But I've never talked to him, and he doesn't work at the factory. He's my boss's son?"

"Sir."

They all turned to see two NYPD officers standing near them.

"Which one a you's Basil?"

"Me."

"You really had to ask?" the other officer said to his partner. "The one with blood all over his hands and face."

"Yeah, whatever. Better to be sure." He turned to Basil. "I'm Officer Kennedy, this is Officer Morgan. We need a word with you." He nodded his chin at Livana. "And you? You the wife?"

"Yes."

"We'll need to talk with you too." Kennedy pointed at Fedor. "You see the fight?"

Fedor shook his head. "I was in the bathroom."

"You know either of those guys?"

"Basil. He's my best friend."

"Take a seat." Kennedy indicated an area several feet behind him. "You two," he said, pointing at Basil and Livana. "With me."

Jethro Tull's "Living in the Past" was playing on a jukebox as they walked upstairs and then outside to a trash-littered alley. The officer pulled out a spiral notepad.

"So how'd this whole thing start?"

Basil shook his head, seemingly at a loss for words. "I really don't know. This woman just starts coming on to me. She touches my crotch, I grab her hand and tell her to stop. Then she slaps me, starts screaming at me, something like, 'Get the hell away from me, you pervert,' and this guy's suddenly there, pushing her aside. He says, 'You came on to my wife?'"

"'This guy'—you mean Gregor Persephone?"

"Yeah. I've seen him around the neighborhood, but I've never talked to him."

"You sure you've never talked to him before? This isn't from something that happened a week ago, a month ago—"

"I never talked to the guy. Ever."

"Ever talk to his wife? About anything?"

"I don't remember ever seeing her before. And I'd probably remember."

"Why's that?"

Basil shrugged. "If you saw her, you'd know." He must have seen the cop's questioning look, because he added, "She's real pretty."

Livana turned away, shook her head.

"So," Kennedy said, "then you can't say for sure. About talking to her before."

Basil took a deep breath and then exhaled, the vapor trailing off into the cold air. "Look, let me put it this way. I've never made a pass at another guy's wife. I'm married. Happily. So it don't matter who this woman is, or what she looks like. Even if I did talk to her once—which I don't think I did—I'd never come on to her. I'm not like that."

"You're a good-looking guy and all. But you're saying this woman you've never spoken to just walks up to you, touches you—grabs your crotch? A woman you say you don't know?"

Basil shrugged. "That's about it."

Kennedy looked at him. "Does that sound right to you?"

Basil spread his arms at his sides. "I'm just telling you like it happened. Maybe she had an argument with her husband and was trying to make him jealous, and I was the lucky idiot who was in the wrong place at the wrong time."

Kennedy offered a slight nod, like that would not be the first time he had seen such a thing happen. As he jotted a note, he said, "What happened after that?"

"I told him, 'You got it all wrong, it was your wife who came on to me. And I told her to leave me alone.' He called me a liar and pushed me. I told him I was there with my kids and I didn't want no trouble. He pushed me again and said I shoulda thought a that before I came on to his wife. I wanted to walk away, but he hit me in the jaw." Basil brought a hand to his face and palpated the welt.

"Go on."

"After I got back up off the floor, he tried to hit me again. But I got him first."

"Then what?"

"Then . . . I don't know. We fought. I was just tryin' to keep from gettin' hit. I yelled at him to stop, but he was nuts. Like he really believed I made a pass at his wife."

"Basil." Livana shook her head in disappointment, as if scolding him.

"What? What was I supposed to do, just let him keep hitting me?"

"Who else saw what happened?" Kennedy asked.

Basil rubbed his arms to ward off the chill. "No one else was there. Well, the woman behind the counter, I guess, but I think she was in the back getting our pizzas. Or maybe she was hiding. Gregor's wife left, or something, I don't know. I don't where she was. But I was a little busy."

"That it?"

"The kids were there. My son Dmitri and his friend Niklaus. Fedor's son."

"Did they see what happened?"

"They were playing around, chasing each other. But once that woman started screaming, yeah, they probably saw it."

"Can't you leave them out of it?" Livana said, "They're just kids—"

"First things first," Kennedy said. "We're not done. What happened to Mr. Persephone's face?"

Basil hesitated. "His face?" he stammered.

"Yeah. It was bloody, all cut up."

"I, uh, I grabbed a Coke bottle, I swung it at him, smashed it across his face. He went down. Knocked him out, I guess, when his head hit the floor."

Kennedy waited for more, then scribbled another note on his pad. "Anything else you want to add?"

Basil's eyes roamed the dirt-strewn street before coming to rest on the cop. "That's it, I think."

Kennedy reached over and yanked open the fire door. "Wait inside while I sort this out."

As they descended the stairs into the warmth of the bowling alley, Livana grabbed his hand and pulled him to the side. "What are you not saying?"

Basil looked up at the cop, who was now about twenty yards away. "What do you mean?"

"There's something you didn't tell the officer."

"I told him everything I know."

Livana examined his face a moment, then said, "I'm going to check on the kids, make sure they're okay." She shook her head in disgust, then headed off to find the children.

WHEN LIVANA RETURNED, the officers were standing behind Basil, handcuffing him. Fedor appeared to be objecting, to no avail.

"What are you doing?" she yelled.

Kennedy grasped Basil by the arm and turned him around. "Taking him in for more questioning."

"But you're arresting him. He didn't do anything wrong!"

"This ain't right," Basil said.

Kennedy frowned. "Your husband assaulted the other man. Whether or not it was justified, or self-defense, or whatever, I don't know yet."

Livana looked at Fedor, then back at the officer. "Maybe—maybe someone else saw what happened. Did you talk to everyone here?"

"I don't need you tellin' me how to do my job. I talked to everyone there is to talk to. And there's a discrepancy as to what went on before you walked in. We'll sort it out at the precinct."

"I told you what happened," Basil said.

"But Mr. Persephone has a different story. So does his wife. And the woman behind the desk doesn't remember hearing what you heard. Like I said, we gotta sort this out. Not gonna do that inside a loud bowling alley."

"I'll take the kids home," Fedor said. "You go along, make sure Basil's okay."

Livana headed back to the lanes to gather their coats, frustrated at how a family outing ended on the brink of disaster, all stemming from a stupid incident that ensnared her husband.

But she could not know that this night, and the events that were to come, would forever alter their lives.

3

›230 EAST 21st STREET
Manhattan
Wednesday, July 5, 1995

K aren Vail could not get comfortable. Her stiff new uniform was not tailored to fit a female body, or at least not *her* body. But she could stand some discomfort because Vail had graduated from the police academy at the top of her class.

Although some of the guys had a problem with that, she did her best to shrug it off. *It's 1995, assholes. Get over it. This isn't your grandfather's NYPD. A woman can be smarter than a man.*

Seated next to her in the Ford was a seasoned homicide detective, Sergeant Carmine Russo. It was unusual, if not unheard of, for such an assignment, but Vail had remarked to one of her instructors, Deputy Inspector Isidore Proschetta, that it was her career goal to become a homicide detective, and it'd be really great if she could find a detective who'd take her under his wing, show her how things worked. Proschetta liked her—he told her to call him by the nickname his best friend had given him during his academy days: Protch. Her instincts told her that Protch wanted her to get on top of his *crotch*, but she kept him at a safe distance, so it hadn't become an issue. Yet.

Regardless, she figured Proschetta said something to someone, pulled a few strings, hummed a few bars, played his organ or someone else's—she didn't care—because he somehow got her this gig with Russo. In department parlance, she had a "rabbi," someone who looked after her interests and helped advance her career. She wasn't complaining; she wasn't even planning to bring it up. In essence, she was not going to look under the gift rabbi's yarmulke.

"Your uniform," Russo said. "It looks very crisp. Very new."

"Thank-you, sir."

"Yeah, don't thank me. You shouldn't be wearing it. You should be in plainclothes."

Vail swung her gaze toward Russo. "Plain—uh, no one said any—"

"It's okay," Russo said. "Tomorrow, no uniform. Got it?"

"Got it. Sorry."

Russo turned right onto 30th Street and glanced over at Vail. "You know how this works, right?"

How what works? Policework? "Uh, I'm not sure."

"You finished at the top of your class so they gave you a temp assignment as part of your field training. Deputy Inspector Proschetta did you a huge favor and put you in homicide. That's a big deal, okay? Don't screw it up."

"Yes sir. I won't."

"So what do you think?"

Vail sat up straight in her seat. "I think I'm excited. First day on the job. Dream come true."

"Dream, huh? Don't examine that fantasy too closely, Vail. This isn't a walk in Central Park. It's tough work. A thousand decisions a day. You try to do the right thing but sometimes it's not totally clear what the 'right thing' is. Things are muddy, the law is muddy, and sometimes you end up knee deep in a pile of horseshit. You follow?"

"Yes sir. I do." *I'm not sure, but I think I get the idea.*

Russo glanced over at her and then nodded. "Good. You know where we're headed?"

"No idea, sir."

"Crime scene. Homicide."

Homicide. Holy shit. My first homicide? First day on the job?

Vail lifted the mic off its mounting bracket and fumbled with the handset. It dropped in her lap but she recovered it by the coiled cord. "Should I call it in?"

Russo shifted his gaze between the road and Vail's escapades with the radio. "First of all, you push the button on the side. Don't release it till you're done talking."

Jesus Christ. This is embarrassing. Maybe it would've been better to ride with a patrol cop. He'd be more forgiving.

"Second of all, no, you don't need to call it in. Central knows where we're going. I told them before we left. You wanna hit the siren, or should I?"

Vail gave him a look. *I may be grateful for this assignment, but I'm not going to act like a kid.* "Sirens don't excite me, sir. Have at it."

He reached down to a small box between the seats and flipped a switch. The whoop whoop sounded and, damn, if it wasn't a rush. *Hell with what I just said. Sirens do excite me.*

"And don't call me sir," he said above the wailing din. "I'm not your grandfather. Call me Russo. Or sergeant."

"Call me Karen."

"Yeah, well, we'll see about that. For now, you're Vail. Or officer."

So much for being friendly.

Russo navigated through a congested area of the city where construction had brought the flow of cars to a near standstill. Blasting their siren had little effect; there were limits on how fast you could move in a traffic jam. There was simply no place for anyone to get out of the way. Finally they pulled up to a fire hydrant and shoved the gearshift into park.

"You're blocking a hydrant?"

Russo turned to her, his face contorted with disappointment. "Don't tell me you're one of these newbies who does everything by the book. Are you? Tell me now, because you can wait in the car and I'll arrange for a fuckin' patrol cop to come by and pick you up."

Well shoot me now and put me out of my misery. I just spent a couple of months memorizing all the rules—for what? So that I know which ones I'm breaking when I'm out in the field?

"I'm fine. If you wanna block a hydrant, not for me to say. You're the boss."

"Yeah, remember that the next time you try to bust my balls."

Keep your mouth shut, Karen. Just get out of the car.

They met the first-on-scene officer.

Russo nodded toward an area behind the cop. "What do we got?"

"Young woman. ID's missing but she matches the description the landlord gave us."

"Detective Thorne get here yet?"

"Nope. Only the medical examiner and Crime Scene Unit." He turned to face a CSU detective wearing gloves, booties, and white coveralls coming toward them.

"How's it going in there?" Russo asked as he approached.

"It's goin'. Still processing but you can go in."

"Borelli, right?" Russo asked.

The detective's face brightened. "Me in the flesh."

"Good to see you again." Russo and Vail stepped into the brownstone, Russo talking ahead of him even though Vail was behind him. "There are never any curb spaces around here. Which means I gotta double-park. And if I do that, on that narrow side street, no one can get around me. So I block the hydrant. An FD engine needs to hook up, he can hook up. It ain't ideal, but it is what it is. Got it?"

"Got it. You're the boss."

"Don't keep saying that. You can think it, but I don't want to hear it."

"Whatever you say, sir."

He stopped and turned to face Vail.

"Sorry. *Russo.* You're not my grandfather."

Russo frowned, then continued on down the hall to another officer, who was standing outside a bedroom. They walked in just as a photographer's flash illuminated the area.

"Oh, wow." Vail hadn't meant to say it; the words just kind of tumbled out of her mouth. *Gotta watch that. Think before you speak, Karen. You're already on his shit list.*

The murder scene was not like anything she ever imagined. Actually, she hadn't imagined anything—she had only viewed slides the instructors projected during class. Ahead of her was a dead body—a "DOA" they called it in class. A *real* DOA.

It was chalky white, the facial expression frozen in time. *I shouldn't think of her as "it." Doesn't seem right. She's a person, not some inanimate object.* "Does she have a name?"

The ME's assistant consulted his notes. "Carole Manos."

Vail knelt in front of the woman, who was sitting up in the bed, back resting against the headboard. Legs spread, dress drawn up and exposing her underwear. Her face was slashed and gashed, deep folds of flesh folded back at the margins. A chunk of jagged glass was sticking out of the right side of her neck. "Why did this happen to you, Carole?"

"You're not expecting her to answer you," Russo said. "Are you?"

Vail tilted her head. "I—I don't know. I mean, the body can kind of like talk to us, right? Tell us a story."

"When she tells you who the villain is—or better yet, how that story ends—let me know."

Another man in the room, broad in the shoulders, back to them, laughed heartily. He turned around and winked at Russo.

Vail gave the guy a disdainful look as she felt her face flush, then turned to Russo. "Well, I mean, we gotta start somewhere."

"We've already started. This here's the medical examiner. Max Finkelstein."

What's protocol? Shake his hand? She opted for a safer nod of acknowledgment. Cool. Detached. Like a seasoned cop. *Right? How am I supposed to know?* Best to just nod. No one could fault her for that approach. *Besides, I already got off on the wrong foot with him.*

Finkelstein tilted his head and looked at Vail over his reading glasses. "First day on the job?"

Shit. Is it that obvious?

"Indeed it is," Russo said, turning to Vail. "Guess we should turn this into a little learning experience. First-on-scene secured the area, determined the pretty friggin' obvious that it was not a death by natural causes. I was called, then the medical examiner and the Crime Scene Unit. So what are you thinking?"

Vail bit her lip. *What am I supposed to be thinking? I just got here. And—oh, yeah. It's my first day on the job.*

"I'm thinking that this isn't gonna be a walk in Central Park." She smiled.

Russo looked long and hard at her before a grin cracked his face. "Fast learner. Good, I like that."

Borelli walked in, a kit in his hand.

"Any latents?" Russo asked.

"Lots," he said. "Problem is, are any of them our killer? It's gonna take awhile to print the deceased's family and friends, match 'em up against what we've got in the apartment."

"Elimination prints," Vail said.

"Listen to the rookie," Russo said. "You're good at regurgitating the textbook, aren't you?"

Borelli chuckled. Finkelstein appeared to ignore them and go about his business, recording his findings on a form attached to his clipboard.

Vail felt her face flush in embarrassment. She tucked her chin down and knelt beside the body. Hiding.

"Cause of death?" Russo asked.

"COD looks to be suffocation," Finkelstein said. "Strangulation, to be precise. Can't evaluate the ocular capillaries for microbleeding because the eyeballs are, well, destroyed. But the marks on her neck are quite severe and traumatic. Excuse me." With a gloved hand he pushed aside Manos's auburn hair, revealing red abrasions and purple bruises.

A low groan emerged from Russo's throat. "Yes, indeed. And the cut marks?"

"Sharp object. What kind, I don't know yet. The hunk of glass protruding from her carotid is an obvious possibility, but I can't say at the moment."

"Stray hairs or fibers?"

"None," Borelli said. "At least, none we found. So far."

"What do you make of the way she's posed?" Vail asked. She gestured at the woman's left hand, which was palm up and fisted, with the index finger curled slightly.

Russo pursed his lips. "No idea. Never seen anything like that before."

"Looks like she's saying, 'Come here.'" Vail stood, then leaned in a bit while maintaining a careful distance from the body. "How'd the killer make the hand stay like that?"

"You're just chock full of questions," Finkelstein said, not bothering to take his gaze off his work. "What we need are answers."

"Questions are good," Russo said. "Sometimes you gotta ask the questions to know what you need to know. You know?"

Finkelstein looked up. He squinted at Russo and said, "Yeah. I think."

"What about the time line?" Vail asked. "When was she last seen?"

"Now *that* ain't my job," Finkelstein said.

Russo pulled out his pad. "That's for us to put together. You, Vail, will help talk to neighbors, do a canvass, write up a background on who Carole Manos was. Did anyone have a beef with her? Was she dating anyone? Is there an angry boyfriend? Who was the last person to see her alive? Did she owe anyone money? Was she involved in any shady stuff that made her path cross known criminals? Ask around, see if the neighbors saw anything."

"Should I do that now?"

"Not just yet," Russo said. "Tox screen?"

Finkelstein readjusted his glasses. "I'll get you the results ASAP."

"Was she raped?" Vail asked.

"Good question," Finkelstein said, pointing an index finger at her. "We'll know more once we get her on the table, get a good look. But there doesn't appear to be any bruising."

"Not much to go on," Russo said.

Vail nodded slowly. "I told you it wouldn't be a walk in the park."

VAIL STEPPED INTO her rented "apartment," the basement of a house in Rosedale, Queens. Rosedale had been marsh and farmland before the area was developed with basic duplex houses that shared a common wall. For some three decades, it was an Italian and Jewish middle-class, blue-collar neighborhood that bordered Long Island's higher income Valley Stream on one end and the racially depressed Laurelton and Springfield Gardens on the other.

Vail was aware that during the past dozen years Rosedale had been experiencing white flight; once blacks began buying in the neighborhood, whites started selling—all out of fear that their home values would drop precipitously.

It now had a large Jamaican population. A friend had recommended the area, and as long as it was safe and uneventful, it would serve as an address where she could throw her stuff, a short-term, very affordable arrangement until she made enough money to get her own place, even buy something. Doing it this way, she would be able to put cash in the bank and have a cushion if the need arose. A rookie New York City cop's salary barely covered the bills.

Her basement home was a modification that many homeowners made to bring in a little extra revenue. By installing an unpermitted exterior door, a few cement steps, and a bathroom, the subterranean floor became an apartment with its own separate entrance. For Vail, it suited her needs. Except for the persistent smell of mildew that irritated her nose every time she came home. The owner had told her he would take care of it. That was three months ago.

She tossed her purse onto the bed and switched her shoes for a pair of Adidas sneakers, then headed down to 243rd Street, the small town where the neighbors shopped at Key Food, got their hair cut at Fino's and their bicycles repaired at Abel's.

Vail walked into the Pizza King, where music was playing on the radio behind the counter.

"Hey Vinnie," Vail said as she took a seat on a stool. "This that new one from U2?"

"Yeah," the Italian man said as he twirled pizza dough in his hands. "It's got some weird name, like, 'Hold Me, Thrill Me, Kiss Me, Kill Me.' I picked up the CD in Green Acres last week. Goody's last copy." He maneuvered the flexible soon-to-be-crust over his forearms. "Want me to get you a slice?"

"Do I really need to answer that?"

Vail pulled out a pack of Marlboros and started to tap on it.

"Thought you quit," Vinnie said.

"Going to. Haven't yet." She took a long look at the cigarettes, then shoved them back into her pocket.

The smell of fresh mozzarella cheese and tomato sauce sent a rumble of hunger rippling through her intestines. She grabbed the red chili flakes and started to sprinkle liberally when a man sat down beside her.

"You like your pizza kinda spicy."

Vail glanced over at him: a good-looking man, about her age, square jaw, innocent face, dressed in tight Levis and a polyester shirt splayed open down to the third button.

"I like a lot of things spicy," she said as her eyes studied his face.

"Really. You like Italian?"

Vail held up her slice. "This *is* Italian."

"No, I mean real Italian." He used his hands for emphasis. "Eggplant parmigiana, fettuccini alfredo, linguini and clams, insalata, antipasti."

"I like all that."

"Maybe I can buy you dinner sometime. I know a place. In fact, I know a place in the city. We can catch a show, then have a candlelight dinner."

"Really." She did not know who this guy was, but her defenses were down. She was about to agree to a night out in Manhattan with a man she met thirty seconds ago. "I'd be lying if I said it didn't sound nice. But I don't know you or anything about you."

"That makes us even."

"Then let's remedy that," she said, holding out a hand. "Karen Vail."

"Deacon Tucker."

He took her fingers gently in his—and the contact made her shiver. She pulled her hand away. Something told her this was moving too fast—even though the attraction was palpable.

"And what does Deacon Tucker do?"

"He's a numbers guy."

"Uh-oh. You mean like you gamble? You run numbers?"

Deacon laughed heartily. "That's funny. No, I work in the accounting department for National Overnight Delivery in Sheepshead Bay. They're sending me to night school. To become a CPA."

"So you're cutting classes right now?"

Deacon's grin broadened. "It's four days a week. This is my night off."

"They must like you if they're paying your tuition."

Deacon shrugged. "Like I said, I'm good with numbers. What about you?"

"Me?" The opening guitar licks of "Good" by Better Than Ezra started playing on the radio and snagged everyone's attention—giving Vail a few seconds to think. A friend of hers had once told her men were intimidated by women who carry guns. But she wasn't going to poison this relationship with a lie. She looked him in the eyes and said, "I'm a cop."

"Whoa," Deacon said, leaning back on his stool. "Does that mean I have the right to remain silent?"

"Anything you say may be held against you."

"Hey, that's the case in any relationship, you know?"

They both laughed.

"This pizza," Vail said, "doesn't seem so appealing anymore. It's cold and, well, it's just *pizza*."

Deacon pushed the paper plate aside. "That place, the one in the city. Wanna go?"

"You know, Deacon Tucker," Vail said with a sheepish grin, "I do."

4

›ROSEDALE, QUEENS
Thursday, July 6, 1995

The morning came earlier than she would've liked. In truth, the previous evening went later than she should have let it. But she did not regret one minute of the time she spent with Deacon. He was funny and bright, and they ended up leaving the restaurant in Little Italy thoroughly stuffed, then going over to Serendipity for chocolate milkshakes. They stayed until closing, and then Deacon drove her back home.

She thought of inviting him in, but she figured it was best to leave the evening on a high note and not move things along too fast. They planned to get together again on Saturday for a Mets game. She had been to Shea Stadium once as a young teen for game six of the 1986 World Series when her friend's father had scored tickets from a business contact. The atmosphere was electric, and the Mets won in dramatic fashion, forcing a game seven showdown.

Vail arrived on time at the Manhattan South homicide squad, located on the C Deck of the 13th Precinct, adjacent to the police academy—her old digs. The building, a flat-faced 1960s tan brick eyesore, sat in the desirable Gramercy Park residential neighborhood.

Heeding Russo's admonition, Vail came dressed in plainclothes: a short-sleeve blouse and stretch pants. She found Russo immediately, though he appeared to be on the way out as she made her way in.

"We're leaving," he said. "Go upstairs, put us out in the movement log. We're gonna go interview an old homicide witness in the South Bronx."

"Right. Will do." *Movement log?*

Vail walked upstairs and surveyed the area. There was a desk off to the left with a large bound book. She stepped up to it and tried to read the scratch that was supposed to pass as intelligible English.

Is this a movement log? What does a movement log look like?

"You need something? Haven't seen you before."

Vail swung around, as if she had been caught with her hand in the cookie jar. *Don't look intimidated, Karen. Make eye contact.* "Karen Vail," she said, offering her hand to the woman. "I got a temp assignment with Sergeant Russo."

"Oh, you're Vail."

Crap, is it good that she knows my name? Or incredibly bad?

"The sergeant wanted me to put us out in the movement log," Vail said, parroting her boss. "We're going to go interview an old homicide witness in the South Bronx."

"I'm Maggie Beltran. Lieutenant Maggie Beltran. That's not the movement log. Follow me."

Beltran led her to the book, Vail made her note, and thanked the lieutenant.

"I remember my first day," Beltran said. "Butterflies, not knowing the lingo. I get it. It's nothing like being in the academy, is it? Just keep your head, stay within yourself. You'll be fine. Okay?"

Vail grinned. "Okay. Again—thanks."

She met Russo downstairs and he proceeded outside to the detective car.

"First order," he said, "we stop by the ME."

"I thought we were going to interview a witness."

"That's a wink-wink thing," Russo said. "Basically it means we're going to be out of the squad for a while. Like I said, we're headed over to the ME, see if he found anything on the body. Yesterday's vic."

"Carole Manos."

Russo stuck his key in the door and twisted it. "Yeah. Manos." He looked at her across the hood of the car. "Problem?"

"I just think we should call her by her name."

"Do whatever you want." He settled his large frame behind the wheel and turned over the engine, gave Vail a quick look. "I remember when I started, all idealistic, fresh, wanting to do everything right. Please everyone. Make the world a better place." He threw his right arm behind Vail's seat and swung his head around as he backed out of the spot. "After a while I settled for making the city a better place. Then getting through the day without getting shot. Trying to help someone in need. Or trying to set things right in a domestic dispute. When I made detective, it was all about trying to catch the bastard who did the deed."

"You saying the job's ruined you?"

Russo gave her a hard look. "That's not what I'm saying." He made a few turns, seemed to be composing his thoughts. "Reality sets in. You see the job differently, you see people differently. It affects you, changes you. Seasons you. You learn to cut through the bullshit, who to trust, who's being honest, and who's jerking you around. Who's worth your energy and who's not. What things you can change and what things you can't. It's a hard lesson. Take my word for it—don't fight it. Accept it when the lessons come. A lotta guys can't, and they start drinking too much. Only way to deal with it."

"You?"

Russo shrugged. "Maybe. I don't know anymore. Not usually on the job. But at night, my days off . . ." He frowned. "Don't know. Anyway, just trying to save you the grief. Job screws with your head if you're not careful."

They pulled up to the medical examiner's office and took the elevator down to the autopsy room and body storage facility.

Max Finkelstein was dressed in a blue gown over green scrubs, with a paper hair cap and reading glasses perched on his crooked nose. Vail figured he had been a boxer when younger; the prominent, misshapen left brow and distorted bony features suggested someone who was in a physical sport—who either was not very good at it, or went up against men who were better than he was.

"Hey, doc," Russo said. "Talk to us."

"Vic was not assaulted."

"Carole Manos," Russo said.

"Yeah." Finkelstein gave him a confused look. "Carole Manos."

"Officer Vail here thinks we should use her name."

"Really." Finkelstein squinted at her over the tops of his half-glasses. "And what else does Officer Vail think?"

"A lot," she said. "But for now, that'll do."

Finkelstein stared but did not speak.

Russo cleared his throat. "So Miss Manos was not sexually assaulted."

Finkelstein tore his gaze from Vail and refocused on the corpse. "Right." He pulled back the sheet covering the body. "Strangled, as I thought. That was cause of death. The slashes across the eyes were postmortem. So was stabbing the carotid."

"Anything else?" Vail moved closer to Manos's head. "What about the cuts? You said it looked like a knife but you weren't sure."

"Glass." Finkelstein stood opposite Vail and set his hands on the stainless autopsy table. "Broken glass, to be exact. A piece of jagged glass."

Vail examined the cuts from a closer vantage point. "Why?"

"Why what?" Russo asked.

"Why would he use a piece of glass if he could use a knife? I mean, you use a piece of broken glass, you have to find something like a bottle and break it, which makes noise. A knife—there's no noise. Noise is his enemy. Right?"

Finkelstein and Russo shared a look of agreement.

"So, I'm just wondering. Why do that? It's more dangerous for him."

"Maybe he didn't care about getting caught," Russo said. "Or he knew no one would hear or worry about a bottle falling and breaking. I mean, really, what's gonna happen? Someone's gonna hear a bottle break and call the police?"

Vail bit her lip. *Good point. Still, it just seems like there's something there with that. What, though, I don't know . . .*

Russo patted her on the shoulder. "Nice try. Keep thinking like that."

Vail examined his face. She wasn't sure if he was patronizing her or if he really meant it. She *did* think it was a nice try, so she would take his comment as a compliment.

"Oh," Finkelstein said. "The drawing."

"What drawing?" Russo asked.

"Come over here." As they moved around the table, Finkelstein turned on a spotlight above and angled it over Manos's face. He rotated her cranium, then parted her hair. "See that?"

"Looks like . . ." Vail tilted her head one way, then the other. "An X. Or a cross. With letters in each of the quadrants."

Russo leaned in. "An E on the left, an I on the right, a D on the top. And a lowercase d on the bottom."

Finkelstein handed them a color enlargement of the image. "Figured you'd need this."

"That's just weird," Russo said as he studied the photo. "What do you make of this, rookie?"

I've got no idea. Say something, take a shot . . . "Obviously these letters mean something to the killer. Otherwise he wouldn't have taken the time to draw them."

Russo nodded slowly. "Good point. I'll accept that. I wouldn't have called it obvious, but I'm glad it's obvious to you." He nudged Finkelstein. "Thanks, doc."

As they headed back to their car, Vail asked, "Was he a boxer?"

"Max?" Russo laughed. "Hockey player. Almost went pro but he blew out his shoulder and opted for something safer. Cutting up dead bodies. Not like they're going to swing a stick at your face."

As they pulled away from the curb, Vail asked, "Where we headed?"

Russo kept his gaze on the road ahead, his eyes scanning both sides of the street. "Thought I'd show you a seedier part of town, give you a taste of some of the shit that rubbed away that green rookie stuff behind my ears."

He pulled over in front of a pay phone. "Notify the borough we're going up to the Bronx."

Vail got out and did as instructed, then returned to the car. Their excursion accelerated her heart rate, focused her attention, and sharpened her vision as if she had just woken from sleepwalking and wandered into a war zone.

There was no mistaking this section of the South Bronx for an upper-class neighborhood. Graffiti littered storefronts—those that still had intact glass—and metal rolltop doors covered businesses that had since closed.

Fires burned in dingy, dented metal garbage cans on several streets. That was an improvement over the blocks of buildings set afire in the late 1970s, when the structures were stripped of plumbing, wiring, scrap metal, and other commodities before being turned to ashes so the owner could collect insurance money. At one point, the police stopped investigating the blazes, and firefighters were so busy that they often had no time to return to their stations before they were dispatched to another burning high-rise. A perpetual pall of smoke hovered over the city for years.

And amid all this, violent crime surged, with murder, rape, and aggravated assault dominating police ledgers. Drugs, gangs, and prostitution stained what had been a vibrant community until the 1950s.

"Used to be quite the place," Russo said. "Times change. Neighborhoods change."

Vail looked around, taking it all in. She had heard of the South Bronx's reputation as a low income, high crime slum, but other than that, she only knew it was a place to avoid visiting. And she now found herself wearing a badge and driving its streets, a target if ever there was one. She squirmed in her seat.

"Colin Powell was born here," Russo said. "Al Pacino was raised here. And Jennifer Lopez. Know that?"

"Nope."

"Hip-hop music was born in the South Bronx, too."

"Don't like hip-hop."

"Just saying, it's not all bad. A lot of the people who grew up here found a sense of community."

He turned down a street and cruised past a stripped out car on cinder blocks, a shell of its former self. Russo shook his head. "Place was once called Morrisania. Know why?"

"Couldn't even venture a guess."

"Most of the land was once owned by the Morris family."

Is this a test? Vail turned to Russo and shook her head. "Should I know them?"

"Nah, I didn't know who they were neither. My social studies teacher told me one day. Don't remember why, but we were looking at some book with these old black-and-white pictures. And she pointed to this one blurry photo and said it was Lewis Morris." He looked at Vail.

"Still got nothing."

"One of the signers of the Declaration of Independence. Another member of his family—brother or cousin, don't remember—wrote part of the Constitution. Anyway, they owned most of the land here at one time. Some of their descendants still have property here. Not that it's something to be proud of. I mean, look at this place. It's a real shithole."

That it is. Hope he's not planning for us to get out of the car.

"Cross Bronx Expressway," Russo said, hanging a left. "That's what did it. Cut right through the area, killed property values. People moved, businesses closed. Rents fell, landlords abandoned their properties, the place went to shit. They've been trying to fix it up—new apartment buildings, houses, stuff like that—but it's got a long, long way to go. Gotta get crime under control."

"Sounds like you did some time here," Vail said as they cruised by a colorful graffiti-blanketed wall.

"Did time is right." He snorted. "I was born here. Also started my career at the four-one."

"Fort Apache?"

"The one and only." The police station, then home of the 41st Precinct, had a storied past and dated back to 1914 when it was a small town outpost whose ground floor consisted largely of horse stables. "I'm proud I served there, like a notch on my police belt."

"Or a badge of honor."

Russo chuckled. "You could say that."

The radio chirped. It was garbled but Russo understood it. "That's near here." He craned his head and looked at the buildings to orient himself. "No, not *near* here. It's here." He swung the car against the curb and shoved the gearshift home.

"Let's go."

Go?

Russo moved swiftly around the front of the car, hand on his Glock.

Vail followed. She thought the call involved an "officer needs assistance" code, which would explain why Russo's service pistol was now in his hands, tight against his body and pointed ahead.

He led the way into a derelict brick building that should have been torn down years ago.

Russo grabbed his radio and informed Central that he and Vail were responding to the call.

She mimicked Russo, removing her handgun and following him through a rusted metal door that squealed loudly as he pulled it open.

As they made their way through the corridor, darkness enveloped them, save for rays of errant light streaming in through holes and fissures in the walls. Illicit drug detritus—spent syringes, burned metal spoons—littered the cement floor and crunched under her heel.

Russo stopped beside an object on the ground. Vail pulled a penlight from her belt and pointed it toward the lump—not a lump, a *body*. A uniformed cop, blood pooling around his head.

"Shit," Russo whispered. He felt for a pulse.

"Is he d—"

"Still alive. Call it in, 10-13. Officer needs assistance. And get a bus over here forthwith." He rose from his crouch, a scowl on his face and a tightness to the grip on his Glock that he didn't have before.

As Vail pulled her radio, she noticed the officer's name tag: L. Shaunessy. *Holy crap, he's from my class.* He was a good guy—and now look at him. *Son of a bitch.*

She reported it, provided their location, and then wondered what she should do: stay with the downed officer or accompany Russo. She decided that there was nothing she could do for Shaunessy. He was unconscious and his fate was now in the hands of the responding paramedics. Assuming they got here in time. She had to admit, it didn't look so good. Russo, on the other hand, was in danger and could use her help if the perps were still in the building.

"Hang in there," she whispered near Shaunessy's left ear, then set off in search of Russo. She moved more quickly than she had been taught, but she wanted to meet up with him as soon as possible. Whoever had shot Shaunessy had no qualms about killing a cop.

A moment later, she heard shouting, scuffling, the sound of a heavy metal item striking cement—and a gunshot. *Shit. Whose gun? Russo's or the perp's?*

Vail stopped, trying to localize the noises.

She moved forward, and just as she was about to turn the bend in the dark hallway, a figure jumped out at her. Another cop. *Asshole. I almost shot you!*

As she collected herself and let the adrenaline dump clear her system, she whispered, "Did you just discharge your weapon?

"Nah, wasn't me."

Vail leaned in closer. "Your partner's down, back there," she said, indicating the hallway with a tilt of her head. "I called a bus. My sergeant may be in trouble. We've gotta find him."

Before he could respond, two more shots echoed loudly and the officer stiffened. Vail caught him as he fell forward onto her, and she pulled him back the way she came, using the bend in the corridor as a shield. She set the man down—Costello by the name on his uniform—and felt for a pulse. Slow and thready. In shock, no doubt. She ripped open his shirt, looking for an exit wound, and saw two.

Vail keyed her radio again and reported another officer down. "Sergeant Russo missing and possibly being held hostage." She received an acknowledgment. When she requested an ETA for backup, she was told there was no ETA. And then she remembered: when an officer called a 13, the response was supposed to be immediate.

Unfortunately, since it was broadcast over her radio's speaker, the perps were privy to Central's response.

Then: scraping noises, frantic—yet muffled—pleas, followed by what sounded like a punch, a groan, and then footsteps. Several sets. She set Costello against the wall and peered around the hallway corner.

All she could make out was two men dressed in army camouflage wearing flat-billed Yankees ballcaps and toting what looked like automatic weapons. As she pulled back, a barrage of rounds erupted, blowing holes in the cinderblock all around her. The echo was deafening. She dropped and retreated down the corridor—

But the shooting stopped as abruptly as it had begun. Vail headed toward Costello and settled her backside against the damaged wall. She listened a second, then inched forward and peeked around the edge—where she saw the backs of the men dragging an unconscious Russo between them. And what looked like a trail of blood.

If Russo's injured, waiting could kill him—assuming they don't kill him first. But if I follow, I've got no cover. One of them turns and lets loose with his cannon, it's all over.

Vail followed anyway. Because if she remained where she was and waited for backup, who knows where they'd take Russo. Or they would save themselves the hassle and just kill him. They downed two cops without hesitation, so Russo's life meant little to them. At the moment, if she kept up pursuit with the pending arrival of reinforcements, Russo was their insurance policy for getting out of there alive. But once they succeeded, Russo's value would bottom out like a bankrupt company's stock.

They were about thirty yards ahead of her, but she was reluctant to close the distance. She walked gingerly, hoping to avoid the rattle of an errant piece of metal or other condemned-building debris—while attempting to maintain a visual on Russo.

She again spied two men, one on each side of Russo. If there were others, she didn't know. But at the moment, considering their armaments, that was enough.

A bright light appeared at the end of the corridor—they had opened an outside door—and led Russo through. He struggled, but the guy on the right jammed the barrel of his compact submachine gun against Russo's head and he succumbed to their wishes. He stumbled out into the glare and the door slammed shut behind them.

Damn it. They could go in any direction and there'd be no way for me to know. The minute I push that door open, if they're still nearby, they'll realize I've been following them, and they'll turn its metal skin—and me—to Swiss cheese.

At least Russo was upright and moving under his own power.

Vail waited a beat, then ran down the hall, adrenaline pumping her heart faster than it ever had in her life.

mouth bone dry
short of breath
lightheaded

As she attempted to head down the center of the corridor—it was difficult to see the walls and she did not want to miss a curve—she pulled her radio to update her status. But the two-way flew from her sweaty palm and bounced along the hard cement, one, two, three, or four times. The last impact did not sound good as the device appeared to shatter into pieces. Vail stopped abruptly, fear constricting her throat.

Shit, shit, shit. How could I be so stupid?

Karen, stop it. Stop it. Think. Breathe.

Vail stood there in the darkness, chest heaving. She moved forward slowly, reached out and found the door, rested her left hand on the knob. The Glock was in her right fist and she was determined not to let the pistol suffer the same fate as the radio. She tightened her grip, slowed her breathing, and pressed her ear against the metal surface . . . listening for auditory clues to their location.

But she heard nothing. *Are they right there, on the other side, waiting for me?*

She knew ESU—the Emergency Service Unit, New York City's SWAT team—would be arriving soon. How much time had passed? A minute? Two?

But they would be surrounding, and infiltrating, the wrong building. She could pull back and join with the team when they arrived. They could then deploy in the correct area, hoping that the perps had not already put Russo in a car and fled before they could set up a perimeter.

What's the right call here? If I don't pursue, are the guys in my precinct gonna think I was afraid, that I let down my sergeant, just to avoid a fight? My career, my credibility would be gone before I'd earned any.

So what was the right call? *How the hell do I know?* The police academy had not taught her how to handle a complex situation in a dilapidated area of the South Bronx, with a sergeant taken hostage at gunpoint by well-armed criminals who had already gunned down two cops.

Vail was only a couple of hours into her second day on the job, so she had no experience to draw from. The best she could do was keep a cool head, take what she thought was the smartest course of action, and hope it didn't get Russo, or herself, killed.

And that meant she needed to know which way they were headed. She carefully pushed the door open slightly, dreading a scrape or creak. Daylight crept in as the crack widened until she could see about forty-five degrees ahead and to the left. There were two buildings on either side of her and an alley, broken bottles, condoms, jagged chunks of cement, a used tire, and rusted pipes.

And a playground—that was a school directly ahead. *Summer, no kids around. Thank God.*

As to what mattered—Russo or the perps—she saw . . .

Nothing.

Vail leaned into the door and it seemed to stick. She shouldered it and it swung out another ten, fifteen, twenty, thirty, and then sixty degrees. She poked her head through, hoping she would be able to withdraw quickly enough if shots came her way.

A second later, she had a decent view of most of the immediate area—charcoal gray storm clouds brooded overhead—but there was no sign of the men. Or Russo.

Vail moved clear of the building and stood there, realizing she had no cover and no way of defending herself if the perps revealed themselves.

How is this helping Russo?

Off to her right, down the alley, she heard a noise. A homeless person? A rat? Or her suspects?

Vail moved off, no longer concerned about making noise—she was now fully exposed—and ran for the nearest building. She made it and leaned against the rough bricks, burn marks extending up the side; to her left was the mouth of the alley.

Peering around the edge of the wall, she saw the men nearly a block away, at the end of the narrow passageway—near an entrance to the school building. She looked down and saw a trail of blood droplets extending in that direction.

One of the men lifted his M16 and aimed it at the lock and squeezed off a few rounds. He dropped it at his side then yanked open the door and pulled Russo inside. The other perp brought up the rear.

Vail craned her neck—the school was three stories, and looked to be in significantly better condition than the building she had just vacated.

Again, she was faced with the impossible decision of whether to maintain her pursuit or fall back. If she were the one in there, she would want her partner to keep coming. Right now, she was Russo's only lifeline. Radio or not, outgunned and outmanned, she wanted him to know he was not alone. And if the wound was worse than it appeared, hanging back and waiting could endanger his life.

Damn it, stop thinking and start doing.

As she made her way toward the school, she realized that her view of the situation was based on emotion, not logic. If she was taken hostage as well, what good was she to Russo? Would he feel better knowing that he was not going to die alone? Not likely. And what first aid could she render?

But ESU's going to the wrong location. Even if they figure it out, will Russo still be alive?

Seconds later, Vail arrived at the door where the perps had shot away the lock. She grabbed her badge and pulled it off her belt, then set it down on the ground, just outside the school's side entrance—if ESU came this way, they would likely see it and surmise that she was inside.

Vail pushed her red hair behind her ear, which she pressed against the warm metal door.

Yelling. Yelling at Russo to shut up.

Good, that's a good sign.

The area sounded clear, so she carefully pulled on the damaged knob while keeping her handgun tight against her body. She pivoted her feet and yanked the door open.

Vail found herself looking at an empty stairwell. She stepped inside and pulled the heavy fire door closed behind her, silently. Moving into the main corridor, she found administration and staff offices on the right, with the auditorium entrance on the left. It looked vaguely similar to the public school she had attended in Westbury.

Fifty feet or so away, a sliver of fluorescent light spilled into the hallway.

Vail headed in that direction and heard voices. Russo was explaining that they were not going to get away, that a dozen cops would be surrounding the building in a matter of minutes. Standard psychological warfare. The stuff she had just learned in the academy. She had no clue if it really worked, but it must if they taught it in class, right?

How am I supposed to know?

The corridor was relatively clean, though the flooring had not been mopped or waxed recently. The tile was dull and streaked with dried dirt. Dark rooms lined both sides of the hall. She peered into one: a classroom. Desks sat piled up for summer vacation. The janitorial crew had not yet been in to do their annual cleaning.

She moved on, headed closer to the voices.

A moment later, Vail inched up to the door and put her ear against dry, cracked wood that needed sanding and a fresh coat of varnish. Given the pressure on school budgets, she doubted that would be happening anytime soon.

The talking had stopped, but there was movement. *Now what do I do? Knock?*

While she mulled that question, she sensed the presence of someone behind her—and then felt a machine gun barrel sticking into her back.

"You wanna live, don't move," a man said into her left ear. "Don't even fuckin' breathe."

Vail did as she was told and stood rock still while the perp reached around and pried the pistol from her hand. He again shoved the machine gun into her spine, harder this time, like he was trying to bore a hole right through her. Then he grabbed her hair and yanked back. She was reduced to a position of weakness, unable to resist in any meaningful way.

Whoever this guy is, he's done this before. Ex-military?

The man knocked three times quickly, and the wood door swung open revealing a rectangular room, three times as long as it was wide. A staff room used by teachers. A couple of old metal desks sat along the perimeter; errant water-stained papers littered the floor, and peeling paint covered over by cork boards with yellowed notices occupied the walls.

A newer Coke machine stood in the corner to Vail's right, beside a desk with a black telephone console containing multiple line buttons. All were dark—meaning, not surprisingly, no one else was in the building. That was probably a good thing, even though it would've been useful had someone heard the gunshots and dialed 911.

But that phone . . . *It could be my line out of here.* Vail chuckled nervously at her moment of silly humor under these circumstances.

Sprawled prone on the floor, wrists secured with NYPD-issued handcuffs, was Carmine Russo. A tourniquet was fastened around his left bicep, his sleeve soaked with blood.

He lifted his head, disappointment registering on his face. "Jesus Christ. What are you doing here?"

Good to see you too. Sir.

"Get in," the man said, giving her a shove.

Vail winced and did as she was told.

Where the hell's our backup? Will they even find us? What would they do with handguns against machine guns?

Still, right now she would welcome some armed assistance, even if they were overmatched.

Vail cleared her thoughts, turned on her cop brain, and did as she was taught: assess the situation, take in as much information as possible about the layout and the perpetrators.

There were two of them, so no surprises there. They were dressed in camo pants, the brown-toned kind the military used in desert-based maneuvers. *These guys might be Gulf War vets.* One of them had an elaborate tattoo winding around his right forearm and bicep while the one who had manhandled her sported dreadlocks.

Vail eyed the phone on the wall. *I don't suppose they'd give me a chance to make a mercy call. Or would they?*

The door slammed behind her. The image of Shaunessy and Costello haunted her thoughts. *These guys were not into taking hostages. What's more, they have no hesitation about killing cops. There are two of them and two of us. What's the right play here?* Wait for a window of opportunity? Or engage them now, try to overpower one of them and get his weapon? Or start talking, try to reason with them? Negotiate.

Not one of those options sounded like a winning strategy.

"What do you want?" Vail asked. *Get 'em talking. See if there's some common ground I can establish. Start there.*

"Shut the fuck up, bitch," the guy with dreadlocks said.

So much for common ground.

"Is there something I can help you get?"

"We killed two cops, ain't nothing you can help us with."

Actually, they're not dead yet. But maybe it's better they think they are. "So you need a way out of here. Out of the country."

"And you gonna help us get that."

"You guys are running the show. I'm trying to negotiate. I help you, you help us. Let us go."

"Vail," Russo said. "Don't be stupid."

"You," the tattooed man said, "a goddamn cop. You gonna get us a way out of the country?" He laughed, then waved the tip of his machine gun. "Get down on your knees."

That's a killing position. Never a good thing for a hostage.

"I'm a cop, yeah. Second day on the job, actually. But that's not how I'm gonna help you. It's my sister."

The man walked in front of her, dreadlocks bouncing, a deep frown twisting the left side of his mouth. He tilted his head back and examined her face. "Yo sistah."

"She works for INS."

He apparently knew INS stood for Immigration and Naturalization Service because his eyes widened slightly.

"They control border crossings," Vail said, in case her negotiating partner did not know that crucial fact.

"I'm listening."

"Cops are on the way," Vail said, letting some urgency permeate her voice. Truth was, it was adrenaline. And fear. But it would pass as urgency if she quickened her speech. "We don't have long. You want me to call her, see if I can work this out? She owes me. And she's my sister."

The two men shared a look. The one with the tattoos reached over to the phone. As he handed Vail the receiver, his partner lifted the machine gun and again shoved it into her back.

"That doesn't feel very good."

"Not s'posed to. Make the call. Be quick."

Vail tried to steady her hand as she dialed. A few seconds later, the phone started ringing—and was almost immediately answered.

"This is Karen Vail for Maggie."

The officer at the other end hesitated, then said, "Maggie? Lieutenant Beltran?"

"That's right. Quickly, please."

The perp pushed the barrel deeper into her spine. "Yo, be fast. Cops comin', remember? You get us shit, you ain't *got* shit." He laughed, feeling clever.

"I remember," Vail said. Seconds later, the line was answered.

"Beltran."

"Yeah, Maggie, this is Karen. Listen, I don't want you to trace this call, because I'm calling from a place you can't know about. But I need a favor." *Translation: trace this call. I need help!*

"Vail. What the hell? Are you with Sergeant Russo?"

"I am."

A pause. "Is everything okay?"

"No, Maggie, no. And don't interrupt me with stupid questions." *I sure hope she doesn't kick me off the force for insubordination. Assuming we get out of this alive.* "I just need a favor from my little sister, okay? I need to get a couple friends across the border but it can't be reported. Totally off-book. Can you do it? For me?"

"You and Russo are in trouble."

Don't be so dense. Yes, we're in trouble! "You know I wouldn't ask you if it wasn't important."

"Listen, Officer Vail. We know where you were when the sergeant called in. Are you still there?"

"No. That's why I'm calling."

"Which way did you go from there?"

"North, get them something on the northern border." She looked over at the tattooed man, who nodded.

"Canada's cool," he said.

"Yeah, Maggie. North, into Canada."

"We're tracing this call, so don't hang up. It's gonna take some time. We've got a map here, and I'm trying to figure out where you are. You close to your original location?"

"Yeah, exactly. I need this done fast."

Beltran mumbled something to another person in the background. "We see a cluster of potential buildings. Can you give me some kind of description?"

"Hurry the fuck up!" the gunman said, emphasizing his words with jabs of the barrel.

Vail swung her eyes over to Russo, whose gaze was riveted to hers. "Look, Maggie, I don't have a lot of time. Dad's not in a position to help, so that's why I called you. Well—that and you've got the connections that can make all this right. I need you to do this. And I need you to get it sorted out now. Can you do that for me? You owe me."

"I understand," Beltran said. "ESU's been deployed. But it's gonna take time. And they'll have had no time to prepare, they've got no idea of what the interior of that building's like, where you are, or even the location of the tangos. They need all that to make a successful hostage extraction. You follow what I'm saying?"

"Yeah, I got all that, Maggie. But I don't want to feel like I have to *teach* you everything. I have to give my friend a decision. All I wanna hear is yes, you're gonna be able to help us out."

"How many tangos are there?"

"I've been on the phone with you for two minutes. I need an answer."

"Okay, two men. Armed?"

"Big-time. I'd owe you big-time."

"Goddamnit," Beltran said under her breath. No matter—Vail heard it. And it didn't make her feel any better.

"Can they be reasoned with? Will negotiation work?"

"No, that's never gonna happen."

"Gather as much information on your perps as possible."

Vail shifted the phone away from her mouth and looked at the man with dreadlocks. "She needs your names. For the passports."

They both shifted position, looked at each other, then the one behind her said, "Teabag Jackson. Sawbones McGrady."

Vail turned slightly and eyed the man. "You're shitting me, right? Teabag and Sawbones? We can't put that on a passport. The INS would never take it seriously."

"We might be able to get something," Maggie said in her ear. "We're gonna run those names. Good thinking, Vail."

McGrady pursed his thick lips, then said, "Garfield Jackson. Stacey McGrady."

Vail scrunched her face. "Garfield and Stacey? Now I know why you go by Teabag and Sawbones."

"Hey, fuck you, bitch."

"Got 'em," Beltran said. "Running their sheets. Don't piss them off, you hear me?"

Yeah, they may shove a loaded machine gun in my back. Don't want that.

"How big's the room you're in?"

"Narrow and long," Vail said. "But listen, we've got a small window of opportunity. Jackson and McGrady are ready to go."

"The trace hasn't gone through yet. Keep talking. I don't have a twenty on you."

"They want to go north, like I said. Don't make me school you on what you should already know." *Will she get what I'm saying?*

"That's it," Jackson said. "Time's up. Gimme that phone." He yanked it from her hand as McGrady pulled Vail's hair, arching her back again.

"Yo," Jackson said into the receiver. "Listen up, Maggie. Yo sis here is in some trouble. Yo need to do what she say, or yo may not see her again." He shook his head. "Just gotta get us into Canada. Can you do that? Yes or no, I'm not playin' games wich you." Jackson nodded. "Good. We gonna be on the move. I'll call you back in two hours. When I do, I want the address where we can pick up those passports. And some money, we want some money." A smile teased the corners of his lips. "Yeah, that be good. Now don't fuck with me. Remember yo sis is here with me. I know how to kill real good, you hear me? Won't be pretty."

Vail closed her eyes. *How the hell are they gonna get us out of here?*

"Yo gots thirty seconds," Jackson said to Beltran, then handed the phone to Vail.

"Maggie?"

"We've got it narrowed down to three buildings. We see a school, is that what you were trying to tell me?"

"Yes, yes."

"Just heard from ESU. SWAT team's eight minutes out, maybe less. Two patrol sectors were at the other building, they'll be there in seconds. They won't engage unless necessary. Be sharp. Put as much distance between you and Russo and the tangos as possible. If Jackson and McGrady are near you when SWAT arr—"

Jackson grabbed the phone back.

"Maggie," Vail yelled. "Stop. No!"

But apparently Jackson heard enough, because he brought the phone handset back and slammed it against Vail's temple, twice, dropping her to the cold, gritty cement floor.

5

>ASTORIA, QUEENS
TUESDAY, JANUARY 23, 1973

During a three-day period, police questioned those who had been at the bowling alley when the altercation occurred. Basil remained in custody but refused to talk to the detective assigned to the case.

After meeting with a public defender and getting arraigned on charges of assault with a deadly weapon, he was released on his own recognizance because he had no record and had been a model citizen since coming over from Greece.

ON THE WALK HOME from the courthouse, Basil and Livana passed a candy store with stacks of the *New York Times* out front, weighted down by large rocks. The newspaper headline announced the death of Lyndon Johnson. But it was a subhead that caught Livana's eye: the Supreme Court declared abortion legal in a case called *Roe v. Wade*. Being Greek Orthodox, she found that development troubling and feared it would start a tidal wave of people killing their babies. But at the moment, she did not allow such concerns to poison the relief she was feeling following her husband's release.

Two blocks from their apartment, one of Basil's colleagues at the fur processing factory where he worked passed them on the sidewalk.

"Michael," Basil said. "Good news—"

But before he could complete his sentence, Michael spat at Basil, the thick goop landing below his right eye. Basil turned and stared at Michael's back as the man kept walking. "What the hell was that for?" He swung back toward Livana as he wiped away the muck. "Son of a—"

"What happened?" Dmitri asked.

"Nothing, sweetheart," Livana said, placing a hand on his shoulder and redirecting him down the sidewalk, toward their house.

"That man spit on Daddy," Cassandra said, struggling to turn around to get a better look. But Basil gathered her up in his arms and held her tight.

"Some people aren't very nice," he whispered in her ear.

THAT EVENING, FEDOR and Niklaus joined them for dinner. Basil related what had happened in court, explaining that since he was not considered a danger to others, the judge released him to go home until the trial.

"I've got a good feeling," Fedor said. "This madness is all going away, very soon." He hesitated. "But there may be another problem."

"Like what?" Livana asked.

"People are very upset. Gregor grew up here. We've only been in the US five years, so they've taken sides. Against you, Basil. I told them you're my best friend, that you'd never do something like this, that you didn't start the fight, that you were just defending yourself. But they don't want to hear it. They believe what they want to. And Gregor's saying you made a pass at his wife and when he confronted you about it, you punched him."

"Not true," Basil said.

"True or not, doesn't matter."

They were interrupted by the phone ringing. Livana walked over to the pink wall-mounted handset and answered it. "We're almost done with dinner, can he— Yes, okay, all right. Hang on." Livana held out the receiver and Basil took it. "It's Gus. He needs to talk to you."

Livana knew what was coming. Gregor was the owner's son. Basil put his son in the hospital.

"What do you mean?" Basil's shoulders sagged. "No, wait. Gus, that's not what—" Basil held the receiver away from his face and looked at it, then hung it up slowly. He stood quietly a moment, then turned to Livana and Fedor, who were staring at him.

"He fired me." Basil sat down heavily at the dinner table.

Cassandra squeezed past Livana and climbed into his lap and gave him a hug.

Basil took a drink of water, his hand shaking as he brought the glass to his lips. He finished and then wiped his mouth with a sleeve. "He said Gregor's blind, that he can't see no more. Is that true?"

Fedor swallowed deeply. "That's what I heard last night when I was at the beer garden. But you were just defending yourself. I would've done the same thing."

"Blind?" Basil bit his lip. "I should've walked away. If I didn't fight with him, none of this would've happened."

"No." Fedor threw his napkin down. "He started the fight. It was his fault. His!"

"Fedor," Livana said calmly, "please sit."

"Doesn't really matter, I guess," Basil said. "I can't take it back. What is the saying here? I can't unring the bell."

Livana removed her apron and handed it to Cassandra. "Put this in the laundry. And take your brother to his room and help him get ready for bed."

"You too, Nik," Fedor said. "Go help. We're going to leave soon."

As Cassandra shuffled Dmitri out of the kitchen, Niklaus bringing up the rear, Basil covered his face with both hands and rubbed his eyes. "I have to find a job."

"I'll ask at the alarm company," Fedor said. "Maybe they need someone. You're good with your hands."

"All my life, I've tried to do the right thing. It was my idea to go bowling, to have fun as a family. And then this . . ."

Fedor picked up his plate and rose from the table. "Sometimes bad things happen even when you do the right thing."

Basil looked at his friend. "That makes no sense."

Livana, standing behind Basil, draped her arms over his shoulders. "No it doesn't," she said as she planted a kiss on his balding head. "But it's often true."

6

>ASTORIA. QUEENS
WEDNESDAY. JANUARY 24. 1973

Basil and Livana turned off Ditmars Boulevard and headed up 31st Street, walking along the elevated subway platform. Basil wore a fur hat with earflaps pulled down low and a scarf covering his face to disguise himself. His public defender told him to avoid confrontations, as they would only create complications when the time came for him to press his case with a judge and, potentially, a jury. Given the neighborhood's visceral reaction, Livana felt it was better for him to avoid being seen in public.

"What happened with Fedor?" Livana asked as they turned right at the corner. "The alarm company."

"His foreman said no. Their customers would boycott the company. He said it wasn't worth the risk."

"But Fedor told him what really happened, right?"

"He knows Fedor, trusts him. Believing him is not the problem. It's what the *neighborhood* believes happened, not what really happened."

"I'm sorry." Livana took her husband's gloved hand. "Did you thank him for trying?"

"Of course."

After passing a Laundromat, she tugged on his arm. "What about unemployment? Can't we collect money from the government until you find something else?"

"Gus paid me cash, remember? He didn't want to pay taxes, so I was off the books. I can't file for unemployment."

Livana shook her head. "You should never have agreed to that."

"I didn't have a choice. When we moved here, I needed a job. I know furs, Gus was a furrier. He said this is how he did it. Take it or leave it."

Two men approached from the opposite direction, eyed Livana, and then studied Basil's covered face as they approached. One shouldered Basil hard, nearly spinning him around.

Livana gave Basil a tug, righting him and admonishing him with a stern look not to even think about engaging them in an argument.

"Bastards."

"This was a bad idea. Even if you wear that stuff, people see me and they know it's you."

"How can I look for job if I can't even leave my house?" Basil asked.

Livana searched his eyes, conflicted at the illogic of trying to find work when he could not even show his face in public. She did not answer him because, frankly, there *was* no answer.

"Let's go home," she said quietly.

ON SUNDAY, THE FAMILIES put on their finest clothing and walked to St. Catherine's Greek Orthodox Church several blocks away. It was cold but sunny, and they were going to the one place where they could feel safe: their house of worship, where differences were put aside and all was forgiven—even if only temporarily.

As they neared the building, the familiar tiled mosaic came into view: a representation of "The Feast of the Holy Theophany of Our Lord God and Savior Jesus Christ," a scene that commemorated the baptism of Christ and the divine revelation of the Holy Trinity.

People were entering the chapel when two men spotted Basil half a block away. They headed toward them, their arms outstretched.

"Where do you think you're going?" the brown-suited man asked.

Basil put his hands out and stopped Livana and the kids behind him. Fedor took Niklaus's hand.

"We're going to church," Basil said.

"Not this one."

"Says who?" Fedor asked. "You have no right to stop us from—"

"You're not welcome here anymore," the man said to Basil, not bothering to look at Fedor. "Go home. Or go worship somewhere else."

"We're members of this congregation," Livana said. "And we're taking our children inside." She stepped forward, but the men blocked her path.

Basil started to object, but Livana grabbed his forearm. "No, Basil. People are watching. The last thing we need is another . . . altercation."

"But this isn't right. All we want to do is pray with—"

"I know," she said. "But now's not the time. It's still too soon."

"What's the matter?" Cassandra asked.

"Nothing, Cassandramou," Basil said, drawing her close.

Livana took Dmitri's hand and turned to Fedor. "You and Nik go in. We'll see you back at the house."

"I don't want to go," Niklaus said.

"If you're not going, we're not going," Fedor said, stepping forward and standing nose to nose with the man closest to him. "You guys are making a big mistake."

"So are you. Choose your sides carefully." They backed away in the direction they had come from.

Basil and Fedor exchanged a glance, then turned and headed home.

7

>ASTORIA. QUEENS
Thursday. February 15. 1973

Unable to find a higher paying job, Basil began delivering *Newsday* around the neighborhood. Every morning, the production truck dropped off stacks of newspapers, which he folded neatly and tightly so they would be easy to toss. He then took off on his rusted Schwinn bicycle with a sack slung over his back and a ski mask covering his face.

His delivery route brought in some money for groceries—and it did not require him to interact with anyone. He and Livana hoped that, over time, emotions would calm and he would be able to return to life as it was—or at least find decent work, provide for his family, and keep to himself.

In the ensuing weeks, Basil and Livana met with the public defender, who explained that they been assigned a date for a preliminary hearing to determine whether there was sufficient evidence to proceed. It would be, in essence, a minitrial.

The hearing moved swiftly, both lawyers sparring with one another as well as the judge. Finally Basil's attorney requested a dismissal on the grounds that the prosecution had insufficient evidence to convince a jury that the defendant was guilty of assault.

Over the protestations of the prosecutor, the judge agreed and rapped his gavel, providing a sense of great relief to Basil and his family.

THE FOLLOWING MORNING, sporting a renewed spirit and a sense of relief he had not felt since the incident, Basil put aside his disguises and went out into the community to look for work. But he and Livana soon learned that having the case dismissed in criminal court did not register similarly in the court of public opinion.

When he walked into the house, Livana knew by the forward roll of his shoulders that his quest had not been successful.

She rose from the couch and met him at the door. She gave him a firm hug, and he wept on her shoulder. Tears flowed from her eyes as well. Basil was a tough-minded and proud person, and he had always faced adversity with a stubborn fixation on finding a way to get what they needed.

This was different. Being shunned by the community was unlike any other challenge he had ever faced, a kryptonite of sorts that struck to the very core of his weakness. After being abandoned as a child, he treasured the sense of belonging. Having it stripped from him, without a way to restore it, to apologize, to make amends, tore at him.

Livana knew all this. And yet she was clueless how to help him other than to offer support. It was insufficient, but she did not know what else to do.

A week later, Livana had just returned from picking up Dmitri and Cassandra at school. Basil had finished folding the last of the weekend ad inserts and stuffing them into his bicycle sack when the doorbell rang. He ran into the house through the backdoor, shouting, "I got it," as he passed Dmitri, nearly knocking him into the refrigerator.

Basil had submitted a number of job applications on the outskirts of Astoria, hoping to have better luck farther from home. Last night he told Livana he was certain he would be receiving a call any day.

Was someone coming to the door offering Basil employment? Possible, but Livana doubted it. In fact, no one had even ventured to their house since the incident, so the hairs on the back of her neck now rose, as if her inner radar were sending off warning signals.

The man at the door was dressed in a suit and had a respectful demeanor, easing her fears.

"Good afternoon," the man said. "Mr. and Mrs.—"

"Are you here about a job?" Basil asked.

He smiled wanly. "My name is Emil Tazor. I'm an attorney in town." He paused, seeming to wait for Basil to make a connection.

Livana approached the door. This man was not an employer offering her husband a job—or even an interview. Her stomach contracted.

"I'm a friend of Gregor and Alysia Persephone," Tazor said, "and I represent them in a civil lawsuit against you and your family."

"No," Basil said. "The judge dismissed the case against me."

"That was criminal court. This is a civil action. The Persephones want you to pay their medical expenses."

Basil reached back for the wall behind him and steadied himself. "But I lost my job. I—I deliver newspapers now." He said it with disdain, as if embarrassed.

"I understand. But you have to take responsibility for your actions. You blinded Mr. Persephone, and he's got bills for surgery and hospitalization, medical testing and specialists he had to see in the city. If it was up to me, I would be suing you for thirty-five years of lost wages and pain and suffering. But they only want their medical bills covered."

Basil swallowed.

Livana looked at her husband, then at Tazor. "But it wasn't—Basil didn't start the fight. Why should we pay anything?"

Tazor kept his gaze on Basil. "The fact is, you swung a jagged bottle at my client's eyes with the intent to harm him. And you did. You ruined his eyesight. He'll never work a decent job the rest of his life, he'll never see his children grow up." His eyes flicked over to Dmitri and Cassandra, who were standing off to the side, watching the interplay between their parents and the attorney.

After a moment's pause to allow the couple to absorb this, Tazor said, "I'm offering you an opportunity to come out of this relatively unscathed. Mr. Persephone's medical bills have climbed over five thousand dollars—"

"Five thousand dollars," Basil said. "We don't have that kind of money."

Tazor frowned. "If we sue you, it will cost you at least that much to hire a lawyer. You'll end up losing the case. *And* your money."

Basil stared at him, his eyes glazing slightly. "We don't have five thousand dollars."

Tazor looked him over, seemingly to assess the veracity of Basil's declaration. "The court will need to verify this, review your bank statements."

"I'll show you whatever you want. We don't have that much."

The lawyer's jaw muscles twitched. "How much do you have?"

"A little over four thousand. That's our life savings. And after losing my job, we need ev—"

"That will have to suffice. But it's your decision. Here's my information," Tazor said, reaching into his suit coat. He was out the door a second later, leaving Livana standing there looking at the attorney's gold-embossed business card.

Basil sank to the floor, his voice barely above a whisper. "But it wasn't my fault."

BASIL STARED AT LIVANA. She shifted her eyes away, across the room, not wanting Basil to see the fear that she was sure showed on her face.

Basil cleared his throat and said, "I have to go to the bank."

Livana gathered her apron in her hands and played with the material. "That will leave us without any money."

"We'll have enough for food. The newspapers."

"So where will we live, huh? If we can't pay our rent—"

"I don't know, Liv!" He grasped strands of hair and massaged his scalp. "You think we shouldn't pay?"

Tears streamed down Livana's face. "We don't have money for a lawyer. We can't fight this."

"We should just pay and be done," Basil said. "Put it behind us."

"Will the *neighborhood* put it behind them?"

"I don't know." He sighed and let his head drop back against the wall. "But I feel like it's the best thing to do. It shows that we took responsibility, tried to make it right. That has to count for something."

Dmitri climbed into his father's lap; Cassandra stood in front of her mother until Livana spread her arms. Then she stepped forward and buried her face into Livana's chest.

Basil closed his eyes. "I worked so hard to give us a safety net. Now it's gone. Because of a stupid fight."

"Go," Livana said. "Before the bank closes. Then we'll have to figure out where we're going to live."

8

›THE SOUTH BRONX
Thursday, July 6, 1995

"Fuck you, you bullshit me!" Jackson unholstered his Colt .45 pistol, as shiny as it was menacing, and shoved it up against Vail's forehead.

"Now hang on," Russo said. "Her sister really does work for INS. Give her the two hours, like you said you were gonna do."

"Nah, man. She was talkin' to *SWAT*. I heard her say SWAT!"

"No," Vail said, holding her head, which was leaking blood from a jagged scalp wound. "Maggie said SWAB, not SWAT. With a 'b.' It's an acronym: special ways to access borders. It's a way INS agents take people across the border when they don't want the newspapers and TV cameras to see. Special operations. That's why I yelled at her. I think SWAB is too risky for you two."

Jackson looked long and hard at Vail. "So if I call that number back they gonna answer the phone 'INS,' right?"

Vail looked at Russo, who maintained a poker face.

"No," Vail said. "Not right. She works *for* INS, not *at* INS."

McGrady raised his M16 to the base of her skull. "Yo be talkin' shit."

"I'm not." Vail swallowed, trying to disguise her fear. "Maggie works on a task force to stop the smuggling of immigrants across the border. That's why she works special operations. She's out of the 13th Precinct. That's who'll answer the phone. I'm telling you the truth. Go ahead and call. You'll see that what I'm telling you is right. They'll answer '13th Precinct.' Call 'em."

Jackson looked at McGrady, who shrugged. A long moment later, Jackson said, "You best be tellin' it the way it is, 'cause if I see a big old SWAT truck—with a goddamn *T*—pull up outside, I'm gonna unload on you."

Our SWAT team's part of ESU, but what does the truck actually say, SWAT or ESU? She thought SWAT was more of a West Coast term, but she could not remember. Vail licked her lips. "I'm telling you the truth. I'm not worried."

Bullshit, I'm worried as hell.

"WE SHOULD GO," McGrady said. "We can't take a chance. If she set us up, we deal with her later. But we gots no reason to stay here."

Vail shared a look with Russo. *I can think of a reason.*

"Let's go," Jackson said. "Up." He yanked on the handcuffs and Russo groaned in pain. He stumbled to his feet and they shuffled out of the room into the hallway. "Out the back."

Vail tried to position herself so that she could make eye contact with Russo because the moment the officers—or ESU—arrived, they would have to make a coordinated break, or their captors would certainly kill them. No matter how she parsed it, this was going to get ugly in a matter of seconds, and their chances of coming out of it alive were poor.

They proceeded down the hall, Jackson beside Vail and McGrady bringing up the rear, next to Russo. They moved in an organized fashion, almost rhythmically, as if marching to orders.

They passed a corridor that led off in a perpendicular direction, but the perps bypassed it and continued straight ahead.

They had gone thirty yards when two NYPD officers appeared at the end of the hall.

"Police, don't move!"

Vail hit the ground, waiting for bullets to puncture her flesh. But Jackson was busy bringing up his machine gun, aimed at the cops, while McGrady locked his forearm across Russo's neck and swung him around in front as a human shield.

Then both perps squeezed off a cacophony of automatic rounds, forcing the cops to retreat back around the corner.

"Take the rear, let's move," McGrady said, grabbing a handful of Vail's blouse and nearly dragging her along as they ran, back toward the room they had left two minutes earlier.

But before they had gone a dozen yards, ESU officers filled the opposite end of the hall, moving in unison behind a large handheld ballistic tactical shield.

The men shifted position and started shooting again until McGrady's M16 jammed. He cursed and tossed it aside, then pulled out the Colt and squeezed off a couple of rounds.

Vail had dropped to the ground once again, and covered her head with her hands. *Not gonna help much—but it makes me feel better.*

The cops froze and inched backward as Jackson emptied his magazine. He paused, pushed Russo up against the wall, face first, and jammed his elbow into the back of the sergeant's neck as he located his spare clip and shoved it into his machine gun.

"Keep moving," Jackson said, repositioning Russo in front of him and pushing him forward.

"If you want out," Russo said, "put down your weapons and I'll call them off."

McGrady swung the butt of his pistol into Russo's kidney. "Shut up old man. Long as we gots you, nothin' gonna happen to us."

Probably true. Their demeanor, the way they handle their prisoners, these guys are definitely ex-military. Not the brightest bulbs, but disciplined.

"Drop your weapons," the lead ESU officer yelled down the hallway.

Jackson squeezed off another burst of rounds in response. They were several yards from the perpendicular corridor.

Is that their plan? Is there a plan?

As they neared it, Vail figured that ESU probably had that exit covered too. What little she knew of tactical ops was that teams increased their chances of success by approaching a suspect from multiple angles. *And if I'm right about their military training, Jackson and McGrady have to know this, too.*

Before it became an issue, Jackson's magazine ran dry and McGrady couldn't have had more than a few rounds left in his Colt.

The sudden silence was almost painful—and welcome. Until Jackson pulled a pear-shaped object from an external pocket on his camo pants. Vail knew what it was, or rather what it looked like: a hand grenade.

"Stay back," Jackson shouted. He seemed to be hiding the bomb, but she shifted her weight and got a better look. *Yes indeed. That's a grenade.*

"We're leaving with your man here," McGrady said. "Don't come after us or we'll kill him. You hear me?"

One of the ESU officers, crouched behind the shield, yelled, "We hear you. We just want to talk. Let's start with a clean slate. We'll give you a clear path out, but you've got to work with us."

"We ain't gots to do nothin'. I told you. Stay back and your man here lives. Even stupid pigs can follow those orders."

"Get down," McGrady said, kicking Vail in the ribs and sending her to her knees. "Don't get up till I tell you to."

"Take her too," Jackson said.

"Nah, man, we don't need her. She just slow us down."

Vail lowered her torso to the floor and waited for the gun to fire. She didn't believe they would just let her go. She was a witness. Then again, there were now several other cops who could identify them, so killing her served no purpose.

Thank-you, God.

Jackson pulled the pin from the grenade and tossed it down the hallway. The tiny piece of metal tinkled slightly as it bounced—and then disappeared.

Crap.

Jackson backed away with Russo in tow.

"Release your hostage," the officer said. "We'll give you a way out, a car—"

"Soon as we free," Jackson said, "soon as we free. Then we talk."

They're not gonna release him. He's their ticket out of here. And once they get away, who knows where they'll go—or what they'll do. Maybe even shoot him. Just like they did with Costello and Shaunessy—who have to be long dead by now.

As they backed away toward the opposite end of the hallway, keeping an eye on the ESU officers, Vail scooted left on her stomach. She stretched out her arm and palmed the spent M16 machine gun.

When Jackson and McGrady turned in the other direction, she got to her knees and hurled the weapon at them. It struck McGrady's feet and he stumbled. Jackson turned, his face crumpled in anger, and brought his handgun toward her.

Two shots exploded in the hallway.

McGrady dropped to his knees, a bullet hole in his forehead. Another shot struck Jackson in the face and he went down as well.

Vail ran toward the grenade, which had dropped on the hard flooring and bounced knee-high. She snatched it up and in one motion tossed it backhanded down the nearby corridor.

It careened down the narrow hallway—one bounce, two bounces, three, four—and then exploded.

THE CONCUSSIVE FORCE shook the floor and knocked Vail to the ground. Shrapnel flew toward her, whizzing by her face, shattering glass, and sending small projectiles through the air. A piece of hot metal lodged in Vail's thigh.

The burn eluded her for a second, and then the intense pain set in. ESU officers flew past her, kicking away the weapons from the reach of the downed men. Another two helped Russo to his feet.

Vail rolled to her side, tried to push herself erect, and then gave up. Finally a man clad in a tactical uniform helped her stand and led her down the hall before getting called away by his commanding officer to clear the adjacent rooms.

Outside, across the street, Vail saw an ambulance idling at the curb, its colored lights swirling.

"Vail!"

Her hearing was muffled, especially in her right ear, but she made out her name. She turned and saw Russo seated on the rig's rear bumper. Vail limped over and winced as she lowered herself beside him. One paramedic was taking vitals while another tended to his bullet wound.

"Your sister really work for INS?" Russo asked.

Vail flinched again when she twisted her leg to check out her thigh. "Nope. Don't have a sister."

Russo chuckled. "You did good. I'm impressed. And I owe you."

Vail did not know what to do with that, so she simply said, "Thanks, sir—I mean, Russo."

"I'm serious. You showed me a lot in there. You're gonna make a great cop. You can think on your feet, you can think outside the box. That's an important trait we don't see a lot of in rookies, especially not one on her second day on the job. You've got balls."

Vail lifted her brow.

"You know what I mean."

"I appreciate that." Vail winced as a medic probed the foreign object in her thigh.

"I'd go through a door with you any day, Karen."

"Go through a door?"

Russo winked. "Give yourself some time on the job. You'll understand."

9

>ASTORIA. QUEENS
FRIDAY. FEBRUARY 23. 1973

asil emptied his First Astoria savings account and walked to the home of Gregor and Alysia Persephone. Livana met him with the kids a few paces from the front door. They exchanged a long look.

"Why'd you come?" Basil asked as Cassandra took his hand.

Livana's eyes found the ratty canvas Mets bag he was clutching against his abdomen. "Is that our money?"

Basil tightened his thick forearm around the satchel. "Yes."

Puffs of vapor escaped his mouth. Livana knew it was not so much from walking to the bank and back as from the stress of living one step away from being unable to feed and house their family.

They stood looking at one another in silence, until Dmitri said, "I'm cold."

Casandra tugged on Basil's arm. "Me too."

Livana wiped away a tear and said, "We have to give something to someone, sweetie. It won't take long."

Livana took the bag and stepped up to the door. She felt that it would be less threatening, and seem more genuine, if the offer came from a woman—someone who had not been involved in the fight. Basil told Livana he had no opinion on the matter. He merely wanted to give them the money and leave.

As much as he felt it was the best thing to do, he did not want to see Gregor, let alone his wife, Alysia, the instigator and source of his family's troubles.

With Basil standing just behind and to her right, Livana knocked—and then waited. A moment passed . . . followed by footsteps on a wood floor, and then the door was pulled open. Alysia looked at Livana, then at Basil, the confusion clear in the scrunching of her brow.

"Sorry to bother you, Mrs. Persephone," Livana said. "Your attorney, Mr. Tazor, told us about your husband's medical bills and he said we should give you five thousand dollars to cover the expenses . . ." She cleared her throat.

But before she could continue, the door opened wider, revealing Gregor. He was wearing a pair of sunglasses and seemed to be looking above Livana's head, not quite placing where her voice was coming from.

"Anyway," Livana stammered, "we don't have that much, but we brought all the money we have. It's a little over four thousand. I—Basil and I—wanted you to have it with our deepest apologies."

Behind her, Livana could sense Basil's breathing quicken, the vapor puffing from his mouth more vigorously.

Gregor removed his glasses, revealing two large pink scars covering his closed eyelids. They had been surgically shut.

Livana had to fight from recoiling. And she hoped to God the kids did not make a comment. But Dmitri was swinging his shoe, as if kicking an imaginary soccer ball, and Cassandra was turning in circles, using her father's arm as a maypole.

Livana quickly shoved the Mets bag forward, into the doorway.

Alysia took the satchel, her jaw set as she threw a look of disgust at Basil.

Basil looked down at the cement stoop and said, "I'm truly sorry this happened."

"Can we go now?" Cassandra asked, still twirling.

Livana waited for some sort of reaction from Alysia or Gregor. A thank-you? A comment of contrition? An acknowledgment that perhaps both parties were to blame? Or how about an apology for starting this whole mess?

But the woman merely pushed Gregor aside, stepped back, and slammed the door.

"TAKE MY TRUCK," Fedor said, "get your stuff. We can put most of it in the garage. I can park on the street."

"Thank-you," Basil said. "I don't know what we'd do without you."

Fedor set a glass of water down on the kitchen table, and Basil took it and drank thirstily.

Niklaus and Dmitri had run off to play in the yard and Cassandra sat on her mom's lap, using crayons to fill in the drawings in the coloring book, studiously staying in the lines.

When Basil and Livana told the landlord that they no longer had the money for rent, he gave them a thirty day eviction notice. They stayed for a week, but Basil did not feel it was right to live somewhere and not pay his fair share.

They had no family in the United States where they could live temporarily, so they looked for a cheap apartment. There was nothing they could afford on the income from his newspaper route.

Fedor invited them to move in with him and Niklaus until either Basil or Livana could find a job. It was not a big duplex, so it made for cramped quarters. But as Livana reminded her husband, beggars could not be choosers.

And as much as they despised the concept, had it not been for Fedor's offer, Livana and Basil would be utterly destitute.

LIVANA HAD NO MORE luck finding employment than Basil had. Lacking education and formal skills, she was nonetheless good with children and offered her services as a nanny. But no one would certify her, and everyone associated her with Basil. Both seemed to be insurmountable problems. She did some babysitting in the neighborhood, but the jobs were sporadic and the pay was low.

She talked about going to nursing school, but that was a long-term solution, even if she could get into one without a high school diploma. And then there was the cost of tuition.

Basil grew a beard and bought a pair of fake glasses from a second-hand store and offered to mow people's lawns or make repairs to their houses and cars for five dollars an hour. He had some takers on the outskirts of town in the poorer areas, but he had to work a great deal to make very little.

They offered Fedor a little money for rent, but he refused to take it. Livana, while feeling uncomfortable, was profoundly grateful for his hospitality.

They needed a more immediate solution.

Basil slapped the table. "This is not right."

"No," Fedor said. "It's not, my friend. But my papa used to say that problems define us. We can take control of the situation or we can just accept what life deals us. You're gonna be fine. You'll get back on your feet. But sometimes these things take time. Be patient. You and your family will stay with me and Nik. One big happy family, eh?" He gave Basil a pat on the shoulder.

Basil nodded slowly.

Livana knew that her husband's pride had taken a substantial hit; any man would have the same reaction. It may be old-school thinking, but providing for one's family was an ingrained instinct, bred into the male of the species going back to prehistoric times. She understood, but that did not ease Basil's pain.

10

Karen Vail turned to her partner, Leslie Johnson, and gestured at the radio. "Go on, acknowledge. That's our call."
Patrol Officer Johnson lifted the transceiver and did as Vail said. "Show us responding. ETA three minutes."

Vail accelerated as Johnson flipped the switch on the center console and the siren screamed. A sense of self-importance came over you when your car was emitting a shrill alarm and people moved out of your way. It sure made it convenient when you had to navigate midday New York City traffic.

Johnson grabbed the dashboard as Vail swerved around a taxi whose driver must have been deaf because he ignored their noisy approach.

"What do you think, another crackhead beat up his girlfriend?"

"We'll find out when we get there."

"You're no fun today, Karen. What's your problem?"

Vail hit the brakes and avoided striking a pedestrian who, like the cabbie, appeared oblivious to their presence. "Tired. Not feeling right."

"Watch it," Johnson said, throwing her other hand against the dashboard. "The idea is to get there alive. Won't do anyone much good if they're scraping us off the pavement."

"You think you can do better, you're welcome to drive." Vail accelerated around the corner at 59th Street, pulled to a stop, and shoved the gearshift into park. Then she held her mouth, fighting back an urge to vomit.

"You okay?"

She swallowed hard, shook her head at the bitter bile that had risen in her throat, and said, "Let's go."

"Are you pregnant?" Johnson asked as they hoofed it along the pavement toward the apartment building, perspiration glistening off the brown skin of her forehead.

Jesus. Yeah, that would explain the missed period and nausea. But this wouldn't be a good time . . .

They pushed through the front door and were stopped by the locked security entrance. "Well, this is a stupid problem to have. Start hitting buttons, someone's bound to let us in." She thumbed the "transmit" button on her radio. "Central, show us on scene. Waiting to get buzzed into the building."

Johnson had pressed the first dozen doorbells on the wall when the metallic groan of the electronic lock sounded. Vail yanked on the handle and they ran up the stairs toward the apartment from which the 911 call had come.

Before they reached the second-floor landing, however, a man with greasy, stringy black hair started yelling at them. He had a knife at the neck of a woman who did not look well. Her eyes were not focusing and she was swaying like a rag doll, without form or structure, arms hanging and swinging freely.

"Bitch won't give me my stuff," the man said.

"My name's Karen," Vail said, her right hand resting on the handle of her Glock. "What's yours?"

"Don't matter what my name is. Juss want my stuff!"

"I talk to someone, I like to know their name," Vail said, advancing slowly on the man, climbing the last two steps to the landing. She glanced quickly at the woman, who was clearly impaired; she was struggling in a drug-induced way to stay erect.

"Name's Alvin. Now how's that help me?"

Johnson squeezed behind Vail and moved to her right by about three steps, near the door of the apartment where the 911 call emanated from. She was backing away from Alvin and keeping her distance.

To their left, a large metal staircase that spiraled up to the next floor dominated the space. There was only an area of about five feet behind Alvin, so they would not be able to flank him. They would have to talk him down.

"Where is it?" Johnson asked. "Your stuff."

"Now if I knew where my stuff is, I'd just get it myself, right?"

"What kind of stuff are you looking for?" Vail asked.

Alvin's expression hardened—he did not like the question. "You gonna help me get it back, or not?"

Vail spread her arms at her sides. "We're here to make sure you don't hurt that woman. But if you need help finding something, we'll do that. You want us to help you out?"

"Yeah. I mean, no. I just—She needs to tell me where it is, but she's not cooperating. Tell her she gots to tell me."

"Looks to me like she's high on something." Vail took another step closer, now only about six feet away. "Could that be, Alvin?"

"Better not be, because if she was—"

"Who is she? You know her name?"

"'Course I know her name. She's my sister Destiny." Alvin shifted his feet, brought the blade against the woman's throat.

"Stop right there, Alvin." Vail stood straighter. "If you want us to help you, you need to get that knife away from Destiny's neck."

"I'm sick of her usin' my stuff. Not right."

"She's not looking too good, Alvin. We need to get a doctor here to check her out. What'd she use? Acid? Angel dust? H?"

Alvin backed up a few steps, right into the wall. His elbow bumped it and the blade moved, and that's when Vail noticed the blood on the edge. She ran her eyes up and down the woman's body but saw no sign of bleeding, so she looked down at Destiny's feet—and saw drips along the floor, leading into the closed apartment to Johnson's right.

Vail was certain Johnson saw it too. Without turning around, she said, "Uh, Leslie, you want to check that out?"

"Is that Destiny's apartment?" Johnson asked.

Just then, the sound of a crying baby emanated from behind the door to Johnson's right.

Alvin shuffled his feet, again pressing the blade against his sister's neck. "Juss want my stuff back, is all."

"There a baby in there?" Vail asked.

"Now how the hell am I s'posed to know?"

"Your sister's apartment. That's gotta be your niece or nephew. Am I right?"

Alvin's eyes widened, and he stuck the tip of the blade into Destiny's neck. "Leave us alone, okay?"

"But you want your stuff. Take the knife away from her neck and we'll help you search her place."

Alvin's eyes shot back and forth, up and down, and he started breathing rapidly. "I—I juss remembered, my stuff's back home. I'm good. We're good here."

"Then lower the knife," Vail said. "Now." She moved her right hand slowly around the grip of her handgun. "Don't make this worse than it already is. Let us help you out here." The baby's cries now bordered on screams. Vail felt the pressure, the child's pleas grating on her, urging her to take action. *Stay cool, Karen. Shut it out. The kid's fine. Just scared. Focus on the perp.* She did not take her eyes off Alvin's as she said, "Leslie, open the apartment door."

"No!" Alvin pricked Destiny's neck with the tip of the blade, drawing blood. "I said I don't need your help no more. Leave us alone!"

Vail cleared leather and had her Glock pointed at Alvin's face. "Last chance. Drop that knife."

Johnson turned the knob of the door and flung it open. "Oh, shit. Goddamn. We've got us a problem, Karen. Big problem."

Vail wanted to look but was not about to pull her gaze away from Alvin.

"DOA. White male, thirties. Multiple stab wounds."

Dead body. Probably the sister's husband or boyfriend.

"Baby?"

"Next to the DOA."

Vail had to look. Even though she should not have done it, she swung her head right, over her shoulder. The body was about ten feet into the apartment, blood soaking the carpet and castoff from the knife spattered on the nearby wall.

Oh yeah, Alvin's going away for a long time.

"You don't understand," Alvin said, tightening his grip on Destiny.

Vail nodded. "Okay. Put the knife down. Then we can talk. You can help me understand what happened."

Alvin shifted his weight from left to right, conflicted as to what to do.

Keep your voice steady, Karen. This can get out of hand very quickly. And there's a baby fifteen feet away.

"I know what happened here, Alvin. Destiny's boyfriend attacked you. You stabbed him in self-defense, right?"

A noticeable band of sweat broke out across Alvin's forehead.

"I totally get it," Vail said. "It wasn't your fault."

"Karen—"

"Shut up, Leslie." To Alvin: "Put the knife down and let me help you explain this. No one's gonna understand like I do. I had a brother who used to smoke my pot all the time. I kept it in my closet in an old shoebox, but one day he found it. Didn't even ask. Smoked it all, pissed me off big-time. And he never paid me back."

Pure bullshit, but I think I sold it. Maintain eye contact. Make him believe it.

"It's—it's not right."

"No, it's not." Vail lowered her pistol and took a small step forward, slowly extending a hand. "Give me the knife, then we can work this out. I need to explain it to my boss. Then we'll go inside and help you look around. Maybe your sister didn't use all your stuff." Another step forward; the blade was pressed against the soft flesh of Destiny's neck—and she was beginning to come out of it. Her writhing was becoming more pronounced, drawing more blood. One wrong move—

Hurry up, Karen. Do something fast. "What are we looking for? H?"

"And crack."

Vail was now a couple of steps away. "Okay. We'll find it. Together." She wiggled her fingers. Give me the knife, Alvin. C'mon. We're running out of time if you want my help. Once the other officers get here, it won't just be me and you."

The baby had worked himself into a frenzy and started crawling toward Johnson. Vail heard the clippity-clap of hands and feet moving on the wood floor. She desperately wanted to turn to look.

"I'll get him," Johnson said as she stepped toward the apartment.

"Stop," Alvin yelled. "Don't go in there!"

Vail brought the Glock back up. "Leslie. Kid okay?"

"No wounds, just freaked out. Alvin, I need to go get your nephew—"

"Shut up!" he said, his eyes getting wide. "Don't go nowhere!"

"Karen," Johnson said. "I—I've gotta get—"

"No!" Alvin slid the blade across Destiny's neck and opened a gaping wound in the flesh.

He flung the woman at Vail and ran up the steps.

Vail caught Destiny but fell backward and felt herself stumbling down the stairs. *Shit!*

In one motion, she dropped her handgun and grabbed for something— anything—and found the railing with her right hand, Destiny nestled in her left. The momentum flung Vail back, and she slammed her head into the bannister.

Johnson was instantly at her side. She grabbed the woman and slapped her left hand against the neck wound. "Go!" she said.

Vail gathered up her pistol and ascended the steps while pulling her radio from her belt. "Foot pursuit of suspect first name Alvin." She took a breath and ran up another flight. "Armed and dangerous. Send a bus to this location for wounded victim. Knife wound to the neck."

Vail rounded another three staircases and reached the roof door. She burst through without stopping to think that the suspect could be on the other side waiting for her. Luckily, her mistake did not prove costly, as she saw him running across the tar toward the edge, which abutted that of another building.

"Alvin, stop! Don't make me shoot you."

But Alvin kept going, and he leaped onto the raised brick boundary and then jumped to the adjacent roof. Vail followed—and thank God it was not a large drop.

Alvin sprinted across the way, but stopped suddenly at the low wall. He turned and headed for the other side, but Vail already knew the next building over was too far away.

He turned toward her—and that's when she saw the snub-nosed revolver.

Whoa! How'd I miss that?

There was no place for cover; she was out in the open. She lined up her Glock's sights and slipped her finger over the trigger.

Make a move, asshole, and I'm going to drill you.

"Drop it, Alvin. Cops are on the way. There's no way out of this. Just let me take you in. I'm your only friend here. You know that, don't you?"

Alvin kept his gun out in front of him, but he was moving, shifting his weight, working it through.

"Once the other cops get here, I lose my bargaining power. Throw down your piece and everything's gonna be fine."

"That's my son in there," he said.

"The baby? In Destiny's apartment?"

"What's gonna happen to him?"

Only a year on the job, without experience in this type of situation, Vail could only spout sterile procedure: "He'll be turned over to Children's Services." Realizing she needed to soften the blow—he still had a handgun pointed at her—she added, "They'll take good care of him till you get out."

But if things go down the way they should, that's a long way off. If ever.

"Who knows when that's gonna be? I killed one, maybe two people. How many years they give me for that? Life? I won't never see my boy grow up."

"I can't help you with that, Alvin. You screwed up. Don't compound it by making another bad decision."

He brought his other hand onto the pistol and started walking toward her.

"Stop," Vail yelled. "Alvin, I'm warning you. Drop that weapon!"

But he didn't; he started running toward her and Vail fired, twice.

JOHNSON BURST THROUGH the roof door and saw Vail kicking away Alvin's handgun.

"Get EMS up here. He's alive."

"You okay?"

"I'm fine," Vail said. "Hurry."

Johnson grabbed her radio and made the call while Vail pulled handcuffs from her utility belt and ratcheted them down.

As she stood up, a wave of nausea boiled up into her esophagus. She ran to the nearest side of the roof. And then she threw up in the corner.

"PREGNANT?" DEACON STARED at her, his attaché case still in his hand, the front door still open. "I can't believe it."

Neither can I. We just got married and I'm only a year into my new job. I'm not ready for a child.

Deacon dropped his briefcase and took her in his arms. "I'm so happy. I—I'm in shock, I think. But I'm—this is amazing. I mean, we used a condom *and* a dia—"

"Don't remind me."

"What are the odds of that happening?"

Obviously, not good enough.

"Are you happy?"

Am I happy? Yes. No. Vail paused. "Yeah. I mean, I wasn't expecting it. The timing isn't the greatest."

Deacon led her to the couch and they sat down. "I'm not sure there's ever a good time. There's always going to be something. But a kid is—well, it's something we both wanted. It just happened sooner than we planned."

A lot sooner.

Her pager buzzed and then started beeping. She leaned to the side and checked the number. "Shit. I gotta take this. It's Russo."

"But we have to talk about it. What the pregnancy means. When you stop working, how the department handles it—"

"I have to look into it. I've got no idea how any of this works."

She rose from the couch, but before she could take a step, Deacon folded her in his arms. "We'll figure it out. This is a great thing, Karen. Now or later, it doesn't matter. We're gonna have a baby."

Vail closed her eyes. *I should be happy. So what's wrong with me?*

11

>ASTORIA. QUEENS
WEDNESDAY. APRIL 4. 1973

Livana sat at the dinner table. Cassandra was unusually quiet, while Dmitri and Niklaus were trading baseball cards that Fedor had bought them earlier in the day.

Livana made the boys put their stuff away, and they had just started saying grace when Basil and Fedor walked in the front door.

"I thought you two weren't coming home till later," Livana said.

Basil took a deep breath, as if trying to push the disappointment from his mind. "How was school?"

"Okay," Cassandra said.

Niklaus and Dmitri turned to Livana—who shared a concerned look—but none of them said anything.

"What's wrong?" Basil asked, following the silent communication.

After a long pause, Niklaus said, "Some kid pushed Dmitri. Knocked him down. And then he kicked him. Stupid idiot."

"Watch your mouth," Fedor said, giving Niklaus a stern look.

"He was a bully, Dad."

"Are you okay?" Basil asked.

Dmitri nodded.

"Why'd he knock you down?"

Dmitri dropped his gaze to his plate. His face twisted as if he was doing his best not to cry.

"Because he was a douche bag."

"Niklaus!" Fedor's face was red. "Apologize for your foul mouth."

"He was, Dad. I told the kid to stop, and then he pushed *me* and said, 'What are you gonna do about it?'"

Basil's mouth tightened and he turned to Livana, who was busying herself with the food. "Did you tell the teacher?" he asked, swinging back in his chair toward Dmitri.

Dmitri shook his head.

Niklaus looked at Basil, then at Dmitri. When Dmitri did not elaborate, Niklaus sat forward. "I punched him, the kid. He ran away and *he* told the teacher on *me*."

"Nik was sent to the principal's office," Livana said. "You have to go talk with her tomorrow, Fedor. Nik might get suspended. I'm sorry."

"Anything happen to the punk who started it?"

Livana tapped her spatula on the side of the pot. "No one else saw it except for Niklaus and Dmitri, and the principal ignored what they had to say about who started it."

Fedor worked his jaw. "I'll handle it."

"When someone picks on you," Basil said to Dmitri, "you have to stand up to him. He's a bully. Punch him, like Nik did. In the nose. Then he won't bother you again. Understand, son?"

Dmitri nodded but did not look up.

"Thank-you," Basil said to Niklaus, "for sticking up for him."

Livana brought over the plates and set them down.

Basil lifted his utensil but stopped. "This bully picked on Dmitri because of—because of what happened with me."

"You don't know that. These things happen in school."

"Even if you don't want to admit it, I know why it happened. And it's not going to end." Basil stopped, took a breath, and said, "We need to move, start a new life. We can't get jobs here. We need money."

"Move?" Cassandra asked. "Live somewhere else?"

Basil stabbed at the canned string beans on his plate. "Yes."

"Where?" Livana asked.

"Where people don't know us."

Cassandra's eyes welled up but she did not speak. Livana placed a hand on her arm, then drew her close. Lifestyle-altering changes could be scary for children, especially coming on the heels of all the recent upheaval they had endured—from being ostracized to moving out of their house and into their friend's duplex, and the family stress of suddenly becoming financially strapped.

While Cassandra did not fully understand what was going on, Livana knew that a child could pick up on adult emotions and internalize them. With all that had happened, she and Basil had to make sure the trauma did not cause irreparable psychological damage to the children.

In a situation that had been spiraling out of control, it was one thing they had some influence over.

THAT EVENING, LIVANA lay in bed holding Basil's hand, not speaking, staring at the ceiling. Thinking.

She knew that what Basil said at dinner made sense. They had tried to overcome the stigma of being the family that harmed the life of a favorite son of the community; they had given it sufficient time to scab over. But rather than heal, it had festered like a pus-filled sore.

"Okay," she said, turning her head to meet his eyes. "We'll move, go where no one knows us."

They fell silent for a while, Livana trying to remember a time when the weight of this problem was not hanging over their family. She tried to keep it in perspective. They all had their health, so money did not matter. They would find jobs and get back on their feet, start anew.

"The World Trade Center opened today," she said. "I think we should take the kids. *Newsday* said we can ride the elevator all the way up to the observation deck, 110 stories high. It's called the Top of the World. You can see fifty miles away."

"When I get a job, okay? I'm sure it's not free."

"I just think it'd be fun. We need to start doing things as a family again. Fun things. The zoo, the park—a Mets game. Dairylea has coupons on the milk cartons. I've been saving them. When we have enough I'll send them in for free tickets."

A tear ran down Basil's cheek. "Sorry," he whispered. "Sorry for everything. All the pain I've caused."

"Agapi mou," she said in Greek. *My love.* She leaned over and let her fingers trace the outline of his face. "I know you didn't start that fight. It happened. We'll do what needs to be done to make things good again."

Basil took a deep breath and closed his eyes.

"Tomorrow we'll start looking for a new place." Her index finger trailed across his forehead. "As long as we do this together, it won't be so bad. It'll be an adventure. In the end it'll be a good thing."

"Guess it can't be worse than what we've got now."

Livana laughed. "Can't argue with that."

12

>ASTORIA, QUEENS
FRIDAY, APRIL 20, 1973

Upon arriving home after mowing a neighbor's front yard, Basil encountered a man standing on Fedor's porch.

Livana walked out of the house in time to see the individual verify her husband's identity, then hand Basil an envelope.

Basil trudged into the house, kicked off his workboots, and then tore open the letter. He pulled out the cream colored thick bond paper and unfolded it, hands trembling in anger as he read it.

Livana grabbed it away and brought it over to the kitchen table light. Seconds later, she said, "I don't understand. We paid them the money, like Mr. Tazor asked."

Fedor walked in and wiped his hands on the dish towel. "What's the matter?"

"That lawyer," Livana said, "the one working for Gregor Persephone. He's suing us. But we paid them the money. Mr. Tazor said that if we paid Gregor's medical bills, they wouldn't sue us."

Fedor looked over the papers, then sat down at the butcher block table. "You need to talk to this attorney. Maybe he doesn't know that you paid them. Get a copy of your check from the bank."

"We don't use checks. It's easier to spend money that way. When you feel the dollar bills," he said, rubbing his fingers together, "you know what you're spending. A check, it's like fake money."

Fedor nodded slowly. "I think you need to go to the attorney and explain. And hope that he believes you."

"You think Gregor and his wife would lie?"

"Well," Fedor said, "we already know Alysia's a liar, don't we? She's the one who started this whole thing by lying."

Basil stood there, mute, then backed away and leaned against the wall. They looked at one another, sadness dragging Basil's face into a mass of jowls and drooping eyes. "So . . ." he started, then stopped. "So you're saying that all our money's gone and we're still being sued?"

"It's like you never paid him anything."

"But we did! Livana was there."

"And she's your wife. She'd say anything to support you. It's your word against his. Kind of like what happened at the bowling alley." Fedor stopped, as if realizing that was probably not a good thing to bring up at the moment.

"I'm gonna go there," Basil said, walking toward his boots. "To his office, talk to Tazor. It's Friday, I need to get there before he leaves for the weekend."

"You need to calm down," Livana said. "We both do. Going there now will just make things worse. We'll go on Monday."

Basil's shoulders slumped and he sat down heavily at the table. "What's the point in suing us? We've got nothing left. You told them that when we gave them the money."

Livana, silent for a moment with her head bowed, sat up straight. "Either Gregor didn't tell him we paid him, or he thinks we were lying about how much money we had. Or it's not about the money. The lawyer said he's a friend of Gregor's. Maybe he knows he's not going to get anything from us, but he, or Gregor—or both—wants to upset us."

"This isn't right." Basil rose abruptly from the chair and headed for the door. He slipped on his boots and stormed out of the house.

"Basil!" Livana started after him, but Fedor grabbed her arm. "I'll go, see if I can talk some sense into him, get him to calm down."

"No, you stay with the kids. I know my husband, I know that he needs to do this, say his piece, and then he'll be okay." She gave Fedor a one-sided smile and then headed out after Basil.

LIVANA CAUGHT UP to him a half block away from Emil Tazor's building. When she called his name, he slowed his pace but did not stop until he reached the door to the law office.

"Basil, please," she said as she reached him, out of breath. "Don't do this."

He turned, hand on the metal knob, and looked her over. "Where's your coat?"

"I just ran out of the house. I wanted to catch you before you did something bad."

He removed his jacket and pulled it around Livana's shoulders. "I'm not gonna do something stupid. I'll talk to Mr. Tazor, tell him we gave Gregor the money."

She knew Basil to sometimes be stubborn and sometimes naive. In this case, he was being both. "Basil, please come home with me."

He studied her eyes before speaking. "Home? We do not have a home."

She took his rough face in her hands, stroked his beard. "Home is where we live with our children. That old apartment where we used to live was not our *home*. It was just a place, that's all."

"We spent five years there. We had memories."

"And we'll make new memories. This is how life works. This is what matters. Me, you, Cassie, Dmitri. Not money. Not apartments."

She felt him relax—just a bit. As the tension in his neck and face lessened, the sadness eased.

But the door to the law office pushed open, revealing Emil Tazor. He saw Basil—and started to duck back inside.

"Wait," Basil said, grabbing the metal handle. Gregor Persephone was standing there, sunglasses covering his damaged eyeballs, the tail of a scar coursing around his left temple.

Basil swallowed, a visible rising and falling of his Adam's apple. "I don't understand why you're suing us."

Tazor glanced around—as if to say this was not the place to be having such a discussion—then said, "I explained to you what would happen. I gave you the opportunity to make it right."

Livana pulled the door open wider. "You said we could pay Gregor's medical bills. And we did."

"We brought the money over to his house," Basil said. "We gave it to both Alysia and Gregor."

Tazor turned to Gregor. "They brought you the money?"

"The same day you came to our house, Mr. Tazor," Basil said. "I went to the bank, took out everything we had, and brought it over. A little over four thousand, just like we told you. It's all we had."

"Greg—did they pay you?"

"I don't know what they're talking about," Gregor said, his voice even. "I haven't seen them since that night. Wait—what am I saying? I haven't seen *anyone* since that night."

Tazor turned back to Basil. "Look, there's nothing more to be said h—"

"We're telling you the truth," Basil said. "We brought the money over in a Mets bag we got a couple of years ago. I—the bank gave me a receipt. I can show it to you."

"All that means is that you took your money out of the bank," Tazor said. "Maybe you took it so the court couldn't confiscate it."

"No," Basil said. "No, that's not true!"

"First you make me blind," Gregor shouted, "and now you lie?"

"You shut up," Basil said, pointing at him. "Look at what you've done, the problems you and your wife caused. You wanted me to pay your medical bills, I paid them—or as much as I could. I paid what I could. What more do you want? An apology? I'm sorry you're blind. But you started the fight, I didn't want to hurt you."

"You really want to know what I want from you?"

"Greg," Tazor said. "Leave it be."

"Leave it be? No, he needs to know that I want him to suffer. The way I'm suffering."

"I didn't do anything wrong," Basil said, taking a step forward. "You accused me of doing something I didn't do, then you punched me. I just fought back, that's all."

"I'm gonna make sure you feel the pain I feel," Gregor said, pushing Tazor aside and stepping forward, about a foot to Basil's left. "I'm gonna ruin your life just like you ruined mine!"

Basil tensed. "You need to start telling the truth, Gregor. Or I'm gonna tell the truth about your father. And the illegal furs he's been importing from Greece."

Gregor's lips parted and his face blanched.

"That's right," Basil said. "I know all about it. I used to work at the factory in Kastoria before moving to America. I know the fur trade, I know what your father's doing, and I never said anything to anyone because he's a good man. But he fired me because you and your wife are liars. You tell him I want my job back. I get my job back, his secret's safe. And soon as I can, I'll pay you the other thousand dollars I was short. For your medical bills." He pointed at Tazor. "And you stop suing me." He looked back at Gregor, whose face was a deep red. "Everyone wins."

Tazor shook his head, then stepped closer to Basil. "That was not smart. You need to leave. And don't come back or I'll report you to the police for harassment."

Livana pulled Basil back into the chilly evening air. The door closed behind them with a clunk. "What illegal thing is Gus doing at the factory? How bad?"

Basil turned slowly and permitted Livana to lead him away from the office. He stepped heavily, and unevenly, toward the curb. He sat down and buried his face in his hands.

"Bad enough. It could put him out of business. Maybe Gus is smarter than his son and he'll give me my job back."

Livana took a seat next to him, put her arm around his back, and buried her head in his shoulder.

13

>ASTORIA. QUEENS
FRIDAY. APRIL 27. 1973

There was no call from Gus. As the days passed, they both acknowledged that Basil was not going to get his job back.

"Maybe Gregor didn't tell his father what I said."

"Just leave it be," Livana said. "You tried. For whatever reason, it didn't work out."

On Wednesday morning, they took the subway to surrounding areas that offered promising employment opportunities. They walked where the train did not go, and after four days their feet were aching and blistered.

Basil finally found a job at the Fulton Fish Market in Manhattan. Although the supervisor said he had read about his altercation with Gregor from coverage in the *Post*, he had no stake in the matter and joked that he had been in his share of bar fights. Livana, on hearing this story, asked if Basil had corrected the man—it was a bowling alley and alcohol was not a factor.

"He seemed to like the idea it was a bar fight. So if he wanted to think it happened in a bar . . ." He shrugged. "Whatever. He gave me a job. I start tomorrow."

Livana embraced her husband: things had finally turned and she was convinced their run of bad luck had ended.

On Saturday morning, the phone rang. Fedor called for Basil and handed him the handset. "It's Gus."

Livana, in the kitchen making coffee, nearly dumped the sugar on the counter.

"Gus," Basil said. "It's good to hear from you . . . Yes, that's what I told Gregor. I was just trying to smooth things over, find a solution that could make everyone happy . . . No, I understand that Gregor will never see again . . . No, of course he won't be *happy*. That's not what I meant—" Basil looked at Livana, concern creasing his forehead. "I—I got another job, so it's not a problem. No, Gus. I was just angry. I'm not gonna tell anyone, I'd never do anything to hurt you . . . Right, yeah, not counting Gregor. But it wasn't my fault—" He held the phone away from his face, then handed it back to Fedor. "He hung up."

"He wasn't offering your job back, was he?" Livana asked.

"He said that as a father, he couldn't see me every day, knowing that I'd hurt his son, even if I didn't mean for it to happen. I guess I understand."

"Doesn't matter," Fedor said. "You got a new job. A new start."

Basil smiled—perhaps for the first time in weeks—and then gave Livana a big hug.

WITH THE ARRIVAL of Basil's first paycheck, they signed a lease on an apartment in Fresh Meadows, a pleasant community not far from Shea Stadium and Queens College. The neighborhood was middle class and safe, by New York City standards. The schools were on par with those in Astoria, but it would mean some upheaval and adjustment for the kids. Overall, though, it would be a healthier environment for all of them.

They found a garden apartment to rent that was a bit of a stretch, but the hope was that Livana could find work as well, relieving some of the financial pressure. It would be tight, but they would get out of Astoria and into an area where they would not be pariahs.

Fedor walked into the kitchen with a large chocolate cake in his hands. "This is for both of you, a housewarming present."

"I want some," Dmitri said, jumping alongside Fedor as he carried the dish to the table.

Livana took it from him and set it on the table. "I think we owe *you* a chocolate cake. We can't thank you enough for taking us in."

"You're like family. This is what family does for one another, right? It was no trouble at all."

Livana knew it was trouble—*they* were trouble, by association—but Fedor was right: if the situation had been reversed, she and Basil would have done the same for Fedor and Niklaus.

While they ate dessert, Fedor turned on NBC News on his old RCA black-and-white console television so they could watch the special report of the day's big event, NASA's launch of Skylab, America's first space station.

"I want to be an astronaut," Cassandra said.

Fedor laughed. "There are no girl astronauts."

"If my daughter thinks she can be an astronaut," Basil said, "she will be one. The best ever. Right, sweetness?"

Cassandra smiled, then turned back to watch a replay of the launch.

"I'm gonna go to the moon," Niklaus said. "Apollo 25!"

"Twenty-five?" Livana pursed her lips and nodded. "I think it'd be more like Apollo 30, if they go that long. Apollo 17 went up last December."

"Well, okay. Apollo 30, then."

After the dishes were cleared away, talks of moon walks and colonies on Mars continued as they began loading Fedor's Dodge Club Cab pickup truck for a more mundane undertaking: a trek to Basil's and Livana's newly leased Fresh Meadows apartment.

The entire clan pitched in, carrying items outside to Basil, who deftly packed everything with bungee cords and ropes. They did not have expensive possessions, but they still had bedding, towels, clothing, kitchenware, and some pieces of furniture.

As dusk faded to darkness, Livana announced they were nearly done—she estimated they each had one more trip out to the truck—when she heard yelling coming from the street.

Livana and Fedor went outside and, in the dim streetlight, she saw four men with baseball bats striking something on the ground.

Not something. Some*one*.

"Basil!" Livana, frozen in fear, brought both hands to her head as Fedor raced past her. When he brushed by her shoulder, it jolted her back to awareness and she followed, screaming for help.

"Get away from him," Fedor yelled as he ran toward the truck. "Stop!"

The men turned and ran, but Fedor tackled one of them from behind. Though they hit the grass hard, the attacker quickly scrabbled to his feet, inadvertently helping to right Fedor, who had a firm hold on his leather jacket. Fedor maintained his grip as the man twisted and pulled and wriggled out of the coat, then continued on down the street.

"Basil," Livana said, cradling his bloody head in her hands. "Basil—"

Dmitri forced his way to his father's side. "Daddy!"

"I'm gonna get an ambulance," Fedor said as he ran toward the house, still clutching the thug's jacket.

"Nik," Livana said, "get me a blanket. We've gotta keep him warm."

As Niklaus ran off, Cassie leaned in closer. "Mom! Dad's trying to talk."

Livana stroked Basil's blood-smeared face. "What? Honey, say it again."

Basil opened his eyes slowly. "Not . . . my . . . fault." His body went limp. And then he stopped breathing.

"No . . ." Livana's tears rolled off her face and onto Basil's cheek.

"Daddy," Dmitri said, "wake up." He slapped his chest. "Get up."

Basil's head went limp in Livana's hands. "No! Agapi mou, open your eyes, look at me. Stay with me." She swung her body toward the house. "Fedor, hurry!"

Fedor ran out the front door, followed by Niklaus. "They'll be here in a minute. I didn't give them our address 'cause if they knew it's us, they wouldn't come."

Fedor knelt alongside Dmitri and locked eyes with Livana.

"Is he . . . is Daddy dead?" Cassandra asked.

Dmitri looked at his mother, at his sister, at Niklaus, Fedor—none of them answered. Livana leaned over, grabbed Dmitri and Cassandra, and pulled them close.

Off in the distance, the whine of a siren pierced the sudden stillness of the night.

14

>ASTORIA. QUEENS
MONDAY. MAY 14. 1973

Livana stood curbside, a few houses away from the children, who were sitting on the stoop in silence, staring at the patrol car and its colored lights as they flashed at regular intervals.

The police arrived first—Officers Kennedy and Morgan—the same ones who had responded at the bowling alley where the entire fiasco began—followed by the ambulance six minutes later.

The paramedics declared Basil dead.

While the officers cordoned off the area and asked Central to assign a detective to the case, Livana took time to gather herself. Fedor comforted her as best he could, but she knew there was nothing he could say or do that would help her get over the stunning reality that her beloved husband was now dead, brutally murdered, rendering her children fatherless.

He did the only thing a friend could—hold her. She felt a strange sense of solace, knowing that she was not alone, that she did not have to face her loss in a vacuum. But beyond that, she was overwhelmed by a sense of hollowness as large and jagged as a post-earthquake crack fissured in bedrock.

She and Basil had only been married for fifteen years, but they had known each other since they were youths in Kastoria, Greece. They grew up together, explored together, found love together. The thought of life without him was frightening.

She could not turn away from her husband's blanket-draped body lying in the street behind the pickup truck, loaded down with all their belongings but now void of the most precious cargo of all.

Kennedy approached her and asked if he could chat with them for a few moments about what they had seen. She and Fedor provided statements as Morgan took copious notes.

"Just so I got this straight," Kennedy said. "One of the attackers—you grabbed the coat off his back. And this is it." He held up the black leather jacket.

"Yes," Fedor said.

Kennedy began examining the garment, patting it down from top to bottom, when he found something inside the breast pocket. He shifted the heavy jacket and inserted a few fingers. He rooted out a matchbook and maneuvered it so that Morgan could shine his flashlight on it.

As soon as the beam hit it, the two officers looked at one another. Morgan's jaw went slack.

"I saw the guy's face," Fedor said.

Kennedy cleared his throat. "You sure about that?"

"Yeah, I can describe him if you want. You got one of those sketch artists? He can draw a picture, you can find this guy. I'll never forget that bastard's face."

Kennedy shifted his weight as he looked again at the matchbook.

"What?" Livana asked. "You need to find the people who killed my husband. Fedor can help you. Is there a problem?"

"Give us a moment, will ya?"

Kennedy turned around and conferred with Morgan.

"I'm gonna go check on the kids," Fedor said, then jogged off toward the stoop by his duplex where the kids were seated.

A few minutes later, Kennedy turned back to Livana. "We're gonna wait till the detective gets here."

"No, I want to know what the problem is. Something's obviously wrong. Tell me."

"As soon as the detect—"

"My husband was murdered in front of me, goddamn it. Just tell me."
She glanced over at the kids, hoping they hadn't heard her words. Best she
could tell, they were talking with Fedor, unaware of her outburst.

"The matchbook I found in the jacket, ma'am. It's from a members-only
club in the city. A well-known club."

"Okay. So?"

"So I guess there could be another explanation, but really the only way
to get one of those matchbooks is if you're there. And the only people who
are allowed in are members."

"You're talking in circles, officer. What are you trying not to tell me?

Kennedy licked his lips. "The people who are members of that club. The
only people who're members of that club, they're mafioso. The mob. You
know about the Mafia, right?"

Livana nodded tentatively.

"Did you see *The Godfather* last year?"

"We don't—" She stopped herself, suddenly aware that the present tense
no longer applied to them as a couple. "We didn't like violent movies." Livana
shook her head. "You're saying my husband was killed by a mobster?"

"All I'm saying is that we found the matchbook of a club in the pocket
of the guy's jacket. And the people who have access to that club are . . .
made men. Wise guys."

"That doesn't make any sense. Basil had no connection to the Mafia."

Kennedy shrugged. "My partner and I have been talkin'. We're not
detectives or anything, but if we put all this together, you need to go back to
the bowling alley incident. I personally believe your husband was only
defending himself. But the guy he cut, he was well-connected."

"Connected?"

Kennedy shrugged. "He has people who care about him, who look after
him."

"What's that supposed to mean?"

"Your husband hit some bad luck. Wrong place, wrong time type a thing,
you know? I think he had to defend himself, but the guy who started that
fight was not a guy you wanted to have a dispute with. Let alone one you
wanted to stab in the eye with a piece a glass."

Livana pinched the bridge of her nose. As hard as she was trying to absorb this information, it was not getting through. "So what are you saying?"

"It might be better for you to back off filing this report. At least take a
night to think about it."

"What's there to think about? Find the men. Arrest them. Put them in jail." She stomped her foot. "I want justice! My husband was innocent. He didn't deserve this. None of us did."

Kennedy looked at Morgan, who tilted his head in a "suit yourself" gesture, then reluctantly moved over to the police car and lifted the radio from its perch on the dashboard.

Kennedy leaned close to Livana's ear. "Look. All I'm sayin'. The people who did this, they won't be happy your friend is gonna finger them. They'll do whatever they need to do to protect their own."

Livana took a step back. "It sounds like you're afraid of them. You're the *police*."

Kennedy stood there staring at her.

That the officer did not dispute her statement made a cold sweat break out across her forehead. "If we don't do this, if we let them get away with it, what happens? Who's really running this city? Are they? Or are the police?"

Kennedy tightened his jaw. "I'm not sayin' you shouldn't do this. I'm gonna take your statement. And your friend's. I just want you to know what you're getting yourselves into. It's my job to protect all a you. And sometimes you gotta let something go to keep your loved ones safe. That's all I'm saying. Now I said my peace. I did my duty. The rest is up to you."

15

›284 E 32ND STREET
MANHATTAN
MONDAY, NOVEMBER 4, 1996

Vail walked into the brownstone on East 32nd Street. The crime scene technicians had already set up shop and were deep into documenting the scene by the time she arrived.

Vail was wearing dress slacks and a blue blazer—in other words, she was out of uniform—having changed two hours earlier when her shift ended. But she did not think Russo would mind her looking more like a detective than a beat cop. Officers did not get to frequent crime scenes after they turned over their initial write-ups to a case detective. For that matter, Vail was not even the first on scene, so she had no business being there at all.

Except that her boss called her.

Vail held up her badge and "tinned" the cop at the door. She slipped on a pair of booties and found Russo who took a lingering look at her attire and let his expression register his disappointment.

Did he expect me to go back to the precinct to change into my uniform?

"I hope I'm not interrupting your evening."

"Not a problem. What do we got?"

"Male vic, forty-six." He led the way down a wide hallway, past expensive pottery, oil paintings, and built-in walnut cabinetry polished to a high gloss.

Red and yellow tulips in delicate Chinese porcelain vases were showcased with downlights in furniture alcoves along the wall.

"Nice digs," she said as she followed. "They had money. Where's the wife?"

"How'd you know he was married?"

"Just a feel. The place has a woman's touch."

Russo stopped in the hallway and looked her over. "Yeah, it does. Good."

"Good?"

"I like the way you think."

"You've told me that before."

"My opinion hasn't changed." He winked at her, then turned and continued toward the back of the house. "In fact, that's why you're here tonight."

I was wondering about that.

Russo stopped into the living room, where a stout male victim sat in a leather recliner. "Oh—congratulations."

Vail pulled her gaze away from the man. "What?"

"Your shoot. You did good."

"How do you know about it?"

"I'm keeping tabs on you, Karen."

Tabs on me, or my career?

"It's called suicide by cop. In case no one pointed that out."

Vail forced herself to look at the corpse in the recliner, willed herself to focus on the crime scene. Why was Russo bringing this up?

"They teach you that at the academy? Suicide by cop?"

"Can we get to the victim sitting across the room? That's why I'm here, right?"

"Except you didn't cooperate. The perp wanted you to kill him, but you missed your kill shot."

Vail swung her eyes over to Russo. "I didn't miss. I wasn't trying to kill him."

Russo tilted his head back. "An unstable perp was running at you with a loaded .38 and you weren't shooting to kill? I'm sure they taught you to—"

"I made a judgment call. I could disable him without ending his life. I knew I'd hit my target in the thigh. He was going down. Even if he got a shot off, it wouldn't have hit me."

Russo squinted. "Not sure if that was very smart or incredibly stupid. Not to mention naive."

"It all worked out, so let's just say it was very smart."

Russo frowned. "Next time you're faced with a similar situation, I want you to take that bastard down. No aiming at the legs bullshit. You shoot to kill, like you were taught. Can you do that?"

"I can do that."

Russo rocked back on his heels, appraising her, seeming to weigh her response, deciding if he had made his point. Apparently he felt that he had, because he said, "So what do you see here?"

Vail took a deep breath and turned to the dead middle-aged man. She advanced on the body and knelt in front of him. A deep gash coursed from the man's left temple across both eyeballs. A jagged slice of glass was protruding from his neck, in the vicinity of the right carotid.

"I see the same MO as that woman victim, Carole Manos, from a year ago."

"First day on the job," Russo said. "Sticks in the memory, doesn't it?"

"Perp was right-handed. He sliced the man's eyes facing him, from right to left, then brought his hand back and stabbed the neck."

"Maybe," Russo said. "That's one possibility. We'll have CSU check for prints on the glass shard. Even if the perp was wearing gloves, we may be able to determine the position of his fingers."

"The position of his fingers?" Vail asked.

"If he was standing behind the vic when he stabbed the neck, the four fingers would be on the top. If he was standing in front of him, the fingers would be on the bottom of the shard. It'd be a backhanded movement to stab the right side of the vic's neck."

The sound of footsteps drew their attention. A second later, the medical examiner walked into the room.

"Doc." Russo nodded at his friend. Finkelstein returned the greeting and glanced dismissively at Vail.

"Your project," Finkelstein said, turning toward her. "Name again?"

I'm a project? "Karen Vail."

"Right. Officer Vail." Finkelstein pulled out his reading glasses and stuck them on his nose, then unfurled a set of latex gloves. "You're out of uniform, aren't you?"

"This isn't my case."

"Hmm." Finkelstein glanced at Russo. "Your doing?"

Russo did not reply. Instead, he said, "Officer Vail seems to think this is related to that case from a year ago. Manos."

"She does, does she? That was a female vic. This looks like a male."

Vail rolled her eyes. "The method of death appears to be the same. The way he cut the victim, stabbed the neck."

Russo cleared his throat. "Could be a coincidence. Or a copycat. That info was unfortunately released to the papers. Not my doing."

Vail pursed her lips. "I guess it could be a different killer. But it . . . feels like the same one."

Finkelstein made some kind of noise that Vail could not interpret. "*Feels* like the same one. You know what a defense attorney—and a jury—would do to me if I ever said that on the witness stand?"

Russo and Finkelstein shared a laugh.

"We need objective measurements," Finkelstein said. "Something scientific that's reproducible, something that can't be discredited."

"I'm just saying, not everything is a measurement. I think it's helpful to step back and ask yourself, What's going on here? Why is that guy lying dead there? And why does he look like he was killed by the same perp as the woman who was murdered a year ago? I think we should look into their backgrounds, see if there's some common thing. Like, did they know each other? Work together? Did they usually go to the same place to eat dinner? Or maybe they did their dry cleaning at the same store? If we answer those types of questions, we may get a better idea of who could've killed them both."

Finkelstein had stopped what he was doing. He was listening. Finally he turned to Russo. "She's smart. I think she's a keeper. Wasted in patrol, though."

I'm starting to like this guy. "What's the status of the Carole Manos investigation?"

Russo folded his arms. "Not a whole lot to report. Some fits and starts but basically, we got shit."

"No leads at all?" Vail asked.

"Nothing that went anywhere. Nothing even worth mentioning."

Vail sighed in resignation. "And this guy?"

"Dominic Crinelli. Already checked, he's got no obvious connection to the Manos vic. But that was just a preliminary search. A lot more work needs to be done."

There's gotta be a connection. I feel it.

"You'll work it with the case detective," Russo said. "He's en route. It'll be a good learning experience. Unless that's a problem for you."

"Not for me, Vail said. "Unless it's a problem on his end. I'm a beat cop with a little over a year under my belt."

"Let me take care of that."

Finkelstein lifted a brow, then removed a speculum from his kit.

Vail took Russo's comment to mean that he knew what strings to pull, and how to pull them. *Who am I to argue?*

"What about Leslie?"

"Who?"

"Leslie Johnson," Vail said. "My partner."

"She'll get assigned a temporary partner for a while. That's not your concern right now. This vic is. And you should start by knowing that Mr. Crinelli here was a member of the Castiglias."

"The crime family?" Vail asked. "Mafia?"

"Correct. A made man. Started out as a soldier about twenty years ago and eventually became a capo."

"Proved his worth, I guess."

"They're gonna be all over this," Finkelstein said as he headed out of the room. "They're gonna want to know who offed one of their ranking family members."

Russo chuckled. "Then that puts us in the strange position of being on the same side. Or at least having our interests aligned."

"Except," Vail said, "we're looking for the guy to arrest him. *They're* looking for him so they can beat his brains in, then chop up his body and drop it in the Hudson for fish food."

"Or just put a .22 round in his brain."

She studied the wounds on Crinelli's face. "You think the killer knew who he was?"

Russo rubbed his hands together. "Good question."

"Maybe *the* question. Because I'm guessing the answer could key us in on who did this. But it all comes back to what Crinelli and Carole Manos have in common." She examined the victim's hands and face for a moment, then said, "A capo has a good sense of criminality, right?"

Russo walked back to the hallway and started examining the photos. "He knows one when he sees one, if that's what you mean. What's your point?"

"Just that there's no sign of a struggle. Didn't look like a break-in, right?"

"Right."

"So he knew his attacker, or at least he trusted him. Or wasn't afraid of him. He didn't see him as a threat."

"Not sure that helps us." Russo leaned in closer to one of the framed pictures. "A guy like that, there's not much that scares him. So someone who may raise the hairs of an average person, this guy may know he can off him like that." He snapped his fingers. "If he wanted to."

"I guess."

"But keep going. I like the way you're thinking."

Vail considered things a second. "Let's go back to him knowing his killer. Either our perp's a big guy who killed Crinelli near the door and then carried him all the way back to the living room, or Crinelli invited him in. And if he invited him in, he felt comfortable enough not to have his guard up. As far as we know, he hadn't drawn his gun. I assume all mafioso have guns."

"Safe assumption. And true, in this case. CSU found two downstairs. A Beretta .40 and a Tanfoglio 9 millimeter."

"Tanfoglio?"

"Italian made," Russo said. "From what I know, they're used more for protection than assault. But in this case, Crinelli never removed it from his drawer. And the Beretta was still in the desk." He stood there thinking a moment, then said, "Okay, I agree with you. Whoever he let through that door did not present a threat to him."

"Someone he knew then?"

"Someone who didn't present a threat," he said with emphasis. "That's all we can say for now."

"He's in an easy chair. Carole Manos was in her bed. Why the difference? And what do you make of that?" Vail gestured at the victim's right hand. "Curled into a fist. Looks glued into position. Just like Manos."

"Manos's fingers were curled into a ball but her index finger was extended, and bent."

"Still, I think there's some similarity here we can't ignore." She walked around the chair containing Crinelli's body and stopped behind his right ear. "You got a flashlight?"

Russo fished around his pocket and pulled it out.

"Shine it right here."

He pointed it at a location along his hairline, near the base of the neck.

"See that?" Printed in what appeared to be black marker was an X, no more than an inch high. In the top quadrant formed by the crossed letters was a D; the bottom contained an r, and in the left wedge was an E. The right had an I. All were uppercase letters except for the r.

"Well, beat me with a stick. Just like Carole Manos." Russo lifted his chin and yelled, "Hey, doc. Come back in here."

Finkelstein appeared seconds later. "Yeah?"

"Manos. Remember that marking at the base of her skull?"

He thought a moment. "The X. Yeah."

"Take a look." Russo backed away and allowed Finkelstein some room.

He slipped on his reading glasses, bent over, and took the penlight. "Yeah, that's it. Exactly the same. Well, almost. It's a little different." He stood there a moment thinking, then straightened up. "The other one had a d where the r is."

"You sure?"

"I'll check it when I get back to the office," Finkelstein said, "but my memory's still pretty sharp. For an old fart."

Russo tilted his chin back and looked at Vail. "So, Officer Vail. Looks like you're right. This is the same killer." He must've noticed Vail's confusion because he immediately explained his comment. "Those markings were not released to the press. Other than us, only one person knows about that X, and that's Carole Manos's killer."

"Now that we've got that out of the way," Vail said, "the next major question is, What do those letters mean?"

16

>ASTORIA, QUEENS
WEDNESDAY, MAY 16, 1973

Livana felt obligated to relate Officer Kennedy's remarks to Fedor; after all, the decision to provide a description of the killer impacted all of them—if what Kennedy had told her was true. And she had no reason to question his veracity.

The detective assigned to the case, Isidore Proschetta, made no mention of the Mafia connection when he arrived. He reviewed some of the information Kennedy had collected and assured Livana he would give the case his full attention.

Now, as they walked to the police precinct to meet with the sketch artist, Livana gave him one more chance to change his mind.

They stopped in front of a storefront restaurant and Fedor faced her, then placed both hands on her shoulders. "This man killed my best friend, your husband, Cassie's and Dmitri's father. I saw him—" He took a breath and looked up at the gray sky. "I saw him beating Basil, Livana. I can't let that go. I couldn't sleep knowing that man, and his friends, are out there.

Who knows if he wouldn't come after us no matter what I do? If I don't help the police, they'll feel they can just keep doing things like this."

They continued on to the station. Fedor spent forty-five minutes with the sketch artist, who produced a likeness that Fedor felt accurately represented the man he had tackled on the lawn.

Two days later, Detective Proschetta paid a visit to Fedor's duplex. Livana cracked open the front door. "Detective. Fedor's at work."

"Actually, I'm here to see you. Can I come in?"

Livana stepped aside and Proschetta stopped in the entryway, his hat in his hand, his trench coat dripping from the heavy rain falling outside.

Proschetta looked to be about her age, which Livana took to mean that he must have proven himself to have risen to the rank of detective at such a young age. Then again, she did not know how the police department worked, so perhaps she was engaging in wishful thinking.

"I heard back from the medical examiner, so I thought it'd be better to talk to you in person, if you're up to hearing his preliminary findings."

Livana dipped her chin, indicating for him to continue.

"The autopsy didn't show any surprises. Cause of—well, uh, cause of death was blunt force trauma, delivered by several round objects from a multitude of angles. Judging by the force and number of blows, it looks like their intent was to kill, not merely injure. Or they were enjoying themselves and got carried away."

"Enjoying themselves?"

Proschetta shifted his feet a bit. "It's a tough concept for people like you and me, I know." He glanced around at the modest, homey surroundings. "Small wood fibers were extracted from your husband's—uh—his head wound, but the best, and most solid, evidence was the matchbook the officers found in the jacket your friend pulled off one of the attackers. The lack of other useful forensics—and the fact we don't have other eye witnesses, means there's a tremendous amount of weight on the statement that you two gave the police the night of the murder—and, obviously, the sketch that was drawn and circulated to officers across the city. And its boroughs."

Livana absorbed all of this calmly. "Thank-you, Detective Proschetta."

"I've also got some good news. Based on that sketch, we've identified the suspect as Dominic Crinelli, a twenty-three-year-old enforcer for a New York City Mafia crime family. But I want you to have reasonable expectations."

"What do you mean?"

"Just that guys like this, they don't roll on their associates." He stopped, appeared to realize that Livana did not understand his cop slang. "Sometimes you can get a perpetrator to tell you who was working with him, or who ordered him to commit the crime. In exchange, the prosecutor gives him a more lenient sentence for his cooperation. Because of who these people are, that's not likely to happen here. I'll try, but realistically Crinelli's the only one we're gonna be able to put away—with Fedor's help, of course."

"I guess it's better to have one in jail for killing my husband than for all of them to go free."

Proschetta looked down at his brimmed hat and said, "You know, I think your friend's exhibiting tremendous courage taking a stand against the mob."

"He's just trying to do the right thing. For Basil."

"Well, tell him we respect him for that. And let him know we're looking for Crinelli right now. Once we bring him in, we'll need Fedor to come down, pick him out of a lineup."

"I'll tell him. He should be home in an hour or so." She hesitated a second, then asked, "You sure he's doing the right thing?"

Proschetta's serious expression exuded wisdom and experience exceeding his years. "Let me put it this way, ma'am. The mob thinks they run the city. If we don't give 'em a bloody nose once in a while, it starts to look like they really are in charge. We can't let that happen. This is not just how I feel, it's the orders we're getting from our lieutenants, captains, chiefs. The commissioner." He handed her his business card. "You see anything unusual, strangers near the house, cars that don't belong, whatever, you call me. You or the kids feel unsafe, same thing. You call me. I'll drop by from time to time, update you on where we're at. If that's okay with you."

"I'd like that."

"You got any questions before I take off?"

"Yeah." She fiddled with the card, her fingers tracing the edges. "When do you think I'll be able to bury my husband?"

Proschetta cleared his throat. "As soon as the medical examiner has finished his work, and we're sure it's safe to release the body to you. There are legal considerations. The arrest, that kind of thing." He studied her eyes and then said, "I'll do my best to get the ball rolling on that."

PROSCHETTA HAD NOT been gone an hour when Fedor walked in the door, his face glistening with raindrops.

"What's wrong?" she asked as she helped him with his coat.

"Nothing. Why do you think something's wrong?"

"I see it on your face. Tell me."

He waved a hand as he bent over and then began pulling off the rubber galoshes covering his shoes. "It's no big deal. There was just . . . a note in my mailbox at work."

"What'd it say? Who was it from?"

"It wasn't signed."

"And? What'd it say?"

He hesitated. "It just said, 'Forget what you saw. Or you and your son will be sorry.'"

"Forget what you saw. About Basil?"

"About Basil's *murder*." Fedor turned and went into the kitchen, where he took a seat at the table.

"The detective—Proschetta? He came by a little while ago. He said they know who it is: Dominic Crinelli. A kid. He's only twenty-three."

"Sounds about right."

"He told me to tell you that they're out looking for him and that you'll need to pick him out of a lineup."

"A lineup? The only lineup I know is Rusty Staub, Bud Harrelson, Cleon Jones." He grinned. "The Mets."

"Not funny, Fedor."

"No." The smile vanished. "Sorry." He shrugged. "I'll do whatever they need me to do."

She pulled Proschetta's card from her pocket and looked it over, as if it gave her the strength to tell Fedor what she needed to say. "The detective said that Crinelli's with the mob. Same as the officers told us."

"What else did Proschetta say?

Livana set the card down and picked up a napkin from the table. She began rolling its corner. "Just that he thought what you're doing is brave, and they think it's the right thing to do."

"And you? What do you think?"

Livana looked away. "Please don't ask me that. I—I can't make that decision for you."

"Hey. Look at me." He waited for her to meet his eyes. "I'd be lying if I said it didn't scare me. But we can't let them go free, either. I think they're just trying to scare me, intimidate me. But I don't intimidate easily, do I?" He leaned back in his chair. "Did he say when I have to do the lineup?"

"As soon as they find that bastard. They're looking right now."

Fedor scooped up the business card and walked to the phone. "I'm going to call Proschetta, see if they can give us some protection for Nik until all this blows over. That seems reasonable to me."

Several minutes later, he set the handset back in its cradle. "Detective Proschetta's gonna arrange for a patrol car to keep a watch over Nik during his walks to and from school and when he's out in the playground—at least until the trial's over."

"That's great."

Fedor headed back to the entryway and started to pull on his galoshes.

"Where are you going?"

"They just brought him in. Crinelli. I've gotta go do that lineup thing."

"Good luck."

He forced a smile and gave her shoulder a squeeze. "Don't worry. I'm gonna hit it out of the ballpark."

17

>DOMINIC CRINELLI CRIME SCENE
284 E 32ND STREET
MANHATTAN
MONDAY, NOVEMBER 4, 1996

Vail borrowed a pen and pad from Russo and began writing down notes and observations, questions for follow-up and reminders for things she wanted to check in the Manos case file.

As she sat there staring at the page, wondering if she had forgotten anything, she heard a commotion coming from the direction of the front door.

She headed into the hallway, where Russo was shaking hands with a man sporting a well-trimmed salt-and-pepper Afro. At first she pegged him as an undercover. But he was dressed in a dark suit and when he moved his arm, his badge swung into view, affixed to his belt.

"Karen, come over here. I want you to meet Detective Timothy Thorne. Timmy, Karen Vail."

Thorne turned fully and as he locked eyes with Vail, his pupils dilated.

"How you doing?" she said, giving his hand a shake. "Timothy or Timmy?"

But Timothy, or Timmy, was enraptured by the redhead and he did not release his grip. Instead, he placed his free hand over hers and held it there.

"You can let go," Vail said. "Now."

Thorne laughed, a belly laugh, as if she had just made a very funny joke. But Vail was not smiling.

"This yours?" he said, turning toward Russo. "Carmine, you dog. You been holding out."

"'Yours'?" Vail asked, looking to Russo for clarification. *If he thinks what I think he means, I may have to kick him in the balls. Probably not the best move, but he's asking for it.*

"I sense some Irish blood in there," Thorne said, eyeing Vail, making a show of appraising her. "I can smell it."

"Yeah. Some," she said. "But I *smell* something else."

"Karen," Russo said. "Do me a favor and take another look at that marking on the vic's neck, will you?"

Thorne's gaze bounced between Vail and Russo. Russo was communicating nonverbally, urging her to leave the room.

Vail frowned and headed down the hall. Thorne reeked of alcohol—either he had been out partying, not on call and not expecting to be called, or he was an alcoholic. Not unheard of in the police ranks, even though department procedure was explicit that a cop was on call 24/7 and he always had to be of sound mind, especially when handling his firearm. No exceptions. It was a good rule, even though it was not pragmatic. What cop didn't drink when he was off duty, particularly after a stressful shift?

Vail did not walk all the way into the other room, preferring to listen to the interplay between Russo and Thorne. Evidently Thorne was going to be the case detective—and that meant she would need to work with him, closely. Their relationship did not begin auspiciously.

"Are you kidding me? She's on patrol? How many years on the job? Can't be more than five."

Russo mumbled something and Thorne, clearly not getting the concept of keeping the volume of his voice low, said, "She's a looker, Carmine. She should be in my bed, not in my office, sharing a case with me . . . No, that's just bullshit."

Bullshit? Yeah, that's exactly what I was thinking.

She walked back into the hallway, her face flushed and her pulse thumping in her temples.

"I should be in your bed, not in your office? I earned my badge, *Timmy*. You got a problem with that?"

Russo covered his eyes. "Karen, please—"

"Matter of fact, I do. I like my women between my legs, not anywhere near my cases. *You* got a problem with that?"

Vail advanced down the hall, headed toward Thorne. "What did you just say?"

"Karen." Russo stepped in front of her and stared her down. Between clenched teeth, he said, "Go wait in your car."

"I don't need you to fight my battles, Russo."

"This isn't your battle and no one's fighting anything. Now go. That's an order."

Don't let this idiot sabotage your career.

Vail brushed her hair away from her face and said, "Yes sir."

She took a long, hard look at Thorne, then headed down the hall, pushing past him and brushing his arm ever so slightly, sending him a three-pronged message: You're an asshole; I *know* you're an asshole; and I don't let assholes push me around.

TEN MINUTES PASSED. Vail was sitting in her car, as Russo had ordered. She wished she had one of those cell phones to call Deacon and tell him she hoped to be home soon. He probably wouldn't wait up for her because he had to leave early for work. But she wished he would, because for the first time, she was starting to feel excited about having a child.

So much had to be reconciled—like Russo's mentoring of her. He seemingly had taken her under his tutelage, first by calling her out to this crime scene, and then by assigning her to work on the case. How long it lasted—Russo's special treatment and the time she would spend working the case—she had no idea. But it was not the ideal time to take maternity leave. And at some point she would start showing, and that could stop everything as effectively as a deployed parachute on a free-falling skydiver.

Vail did not want to get ahead of things. She decided to take it a day at a time and see how it went. That was probably the prudent course of action. There were so many variables that it was senseless to get wrapped up in potential scenarios.

She looked up and saw Russo heading toward her. He pulled open the passenger door and sat down heavily.

"Look. Timmy's not a bad guy, but he's got some issues. 'Women' are issues one through five. You don't gotta like the guy, just work with him, learn what you can, contribute what you can, and get along best you can. Avoid confrontation. Can you do that?"

There's only one right answer here.

"Of course."

"Okay, then. Just remember, your future's bright and it's not worth letting a guy with problems bring you down. You're better than that. Right?"

"Right."

"Now, that said. Off the record. You were right to stand up for yourself. Don't you let any guy walk over you. You're as good as any of the men doing the job."

"Well, I'm only a year—"

"No, listen to me. This is the time when you just shut up and listen. Because I'm complimenting you. I've been doing this a long time, and I've seen a lot of cops come and go. Some stay in patrol their whole career—and there ain't nothing wrong with that. Some go on to detective, or captain, or chief—whatever. But to do that, to move up the ladder, you gotta have certain qualities. Some keep taking tests and getting the promotion but don't know shit about the street and wouldn't know instinct if it hit 'em in the ass. But you got it all, Karen. And more. I know this."

"This is the part where I agree with you, isn't it?"

"Yes, it is."

"Then I agree."

"Believe in yourself, Karen. Be open to learning, because you know shit right now. You've got good instincts, and they'll carry you till you learn enough to make informed decisions. But at some point you're gonna be able to put it all together, and I'm lookin' forward to that day when you know more than me, when you tell me the way things are. And when that day comes, I'll be proud. Like a dad sending his daughter off to college."

"I agree."

"That wasn't the part where you're supposed to agree."

"Russo, I'm pregnant."

He studied her face, disbelief etched in his expression.

Oh, shit. Why'd I say that?

After a long moment, he turned away. "You wanna be off work for nine months?"

"No, absolutely not."

"Then I didn't hear you say that." He let that ride a minute, then said, "You gonna have the baby?"

"I—I just found out today. Actually, I didn't find out anything. I just have a feeling—"

"Fine. Then you're *not* pregnant. And don't tell me anything until your doc tells you that you have to stop working."

Vail squinted. "Okay."

"Ever watch *Hogan's Heroes?*"

Vail laughed. *Is he serious?* "Yeah, of course. Well, the reruns."

"When Sergeant Shultz says, 'I know nothing! I hear nothing.'" Russo gave a chuckle, then got serious. "That's what I'm saying here. I didn't hear what you said. Now—go home and report to Detective Thorne in the morning at the homicide squad."

"I will."

"Meantime, no cigarettes. No alcohol. And keep me posted on this case. We got us a serial killer here and that's never a good thing. Plus, he's stirred up a hornet's nest with the mob. As if I didn't have enough agita, I've now got a case that's gonna make my life a living hell."

Through the windshield, Vail saw Thorne step out onto the brownstone's porch, shield his hands against the gentle breeze, and light a cigarette.

Russo opened his door. "Timmy used to be a really sharp detective. Let's hope he leaves the booze behind and brings his A game to this case."

Vail reached for the ignition as the passenger door slammed shut. *Amen to that.*

VAIL WALKED INTO their Rosedale house—the same one in which she once rented a basement room—and tiptoed upstairs so as not to wake Deacon.

But when she reached the top of the stairs, she saw a crack of light beneath the wood door.

Vail pushed into the bedroom and saw Deacon sitting up in bed, Robert Ludlum's *The Apocalypse Watch* open in his lap.

"You're still up?"

He set the book aside and tapped the area next to him. "I wanted to see you."

"But you've gotta be up early."

"So I'll be tired. I only saw you for a few minutes and then you were off. How'd it go?"

Vail kicked off her shoes and crawled into bed, cuddled into Deacon's arm and rested her head against his chest. "Good, I think. It's a really interesting case."

"Did Russo explain why he called you?"

"I'm not sure. I think he likes me, and he seems to be mentoring me."

"For what?"

"Well, to become a detective."

"That's—wow, I didn't realize that's how it worked. Then again, I don't know anything about how any of that works. It's a totally foreign world to me."

"It's not how it works. This is, well, I'm not sure what it is. Lucky, I guess. I'm certainly not complaining." After a moment, she said, "I've been doing some thinking. About the baby."

"And?"

"I picked up a pregnancy test at Duane Reade on the way home. If it's positive—"

"If? I thought you were sure."

"It's going to be positive. I'm sure, I can tell. Anyway, assuming it's positive, I want to have the baby. I mean, I really want to have it. I just— earlier, I didn't know what to make of it. It kind of hit me by surprise. And this thing with Russo, how he's taken me under his wing, I was just confused."

"And now you're seeing it more clearly?"

"You were right. There's never a perfect time. So this happened for a reason. It was meant to be. We'll have the baby and it'll change things. It'll change us. It'll probably change my career to some degree. But I'm okay with that."

Deacon kissed her head.

"Now put the book away and kill the light. I'm gonna wash up and get undressed. I'll be back in a few minutes."

Vail walked into the bathroom and as she removed her bra, she looked at herself in the mirror. Here she was, twenty-two years old, and she was going to be a mother in nine months.

Am I ready for this?

If I can carry a gun and chase druggies across building roofs, I can raise a child. How hard can it be?

Vail finished washing up, then slid under the covers. She scooted against Deacon's warm body and draped her arms around him. She felt safe and content, ready to enter a new phase of her life.

18

›MANHATTAN SOUTH HOMICIDE SQUAD
230 EAST 21ST STREET
MANHATTAN
TUESDAY, NOVEMBER 5, 1996

After making her way up to C Deck, Vail walked into the Manhattan South homicide squad and found Timothy Thorne standing on the other side of the large rectangular office space. He looked up, their eyes met, and he did not look pleased. He motioned for her to follow him down the hall.

Vail pushed through a door and found herself in an interrogation room: small, containing a proportionately sized table and two chairs. A few seconds after she entered, Thorne stepped in behind her.

"Sir, about last night."

"I don't want to discuss it."

Vail jutted her chin back. "I just want to say that I'm—"

"We're not discussing it. Unless it pertains to the case."

"It doesn't."

"Look, Officer Vail. First, I'm an alcoholic, okay? I've got a problem. I don't let it affect my job. I'm going to meetings, I keep in regular contact with my sponsor. I'm doing good. That's all I'm ever gonna say on it from this point forward."

"If you're doing so good, why'd you stink of alcohol last night?"

His right eye narrowed. "Let's get something straight. You're a patrol officer. You're here because—I'm not sure why you're here. I'd guess Russo's boning you, but it's probably because he owes you for saving his life."

Vail thought back to the incident in the South Bronx last year. *Is that what this is about? He's paying me back for saving his life?*

Thorne pulled open the door and headed out. Vail followed, trying to hear him as he walked.

"No matter what your deal is with Russo, you're working under me. You're a cop and I'm a detective. You won't treat me as an equal because we're not. Clear?"

"Clear."

He reentered the detective bureau and sat down at his desk. "Sergeant Russo thinks the vic, Crinelli, was offed by the same guy who did this woman, Carole Manos, a year ago. So that means we gotta look for anything that might connect these two people. Crinelli's mobbed up, you know that, I think, right?" Vail indicated he was correct. "Jerkoff was arrested three times the past twenty years. So he's been in the system and we've got a sheet on him. Known hangouts and associates, shit like that."

"Okay."

"And I want you to meet with the detective who handled the Manos case, since there's gonna be some overlap. Maybe we can help each other. Maybe the killer left something, a hair or fiber, that'll help us tie him to this murder with certainty, that type of thing."

"We also can't ignore the mob angle," Vail said.

"What are you talking about? Of course we ain't gonna ignore it."

"No, I mean, maybe we're looking at it ass-backwards. It's possible that Carole Manos has mob ties, and she was killed by one of Crinelli's associates. Or a rival family."

Thorne chuckled. "Yeah. I don't think so."

"Why is that funny?"

"Because the mafia has an MO, and when they want to off someone, they don't cut their vics' eyes with a jagged piece of glass and then stab them in the neck. The hit's done with a .22 to the back of the skull. Quiet, efficient, quick. And clean. So, nice theory, missy, but—no offense—you don't know shit." He laughed as he sorted through files on his desk.

"Name's Karen. Or Vail. I don't answer to 'missy.'"

"Yeah, missy. Whatever."

Vail leaned across the cluttered desk, bringing herself to eye level with Thorne. "Let's get something straight. You're my boss? I get that. But I'm still a cop. No, check that. I'm a human being. And you will treat me with respect as a person. You don't like women, fine. You don't like working with women, fine. I don't care what your hang-ups are. Those are your problems. But if you can't give me some common courtesy, then we're not gonna be able to work together."

He leaned forward, challenging her. "Now you're talking."

"See, here's the thing, though. You've got a boss too. And I bet he cares when you show up at a crime scene reeking of whiskey. Am I right? Because I'd feel compelled to tell him why I'm begging off the assignment of a lifetime when he says, 'Are you crazy?'"

Thorne looked away, his hand balling into a fist. Vail knew she was in uncharted territory here: she was playing hardball in a game where she did not know the rules; in fact, she was clueless. The opposite could be true; maybe his superior did not want to know of Thorne's problem—even worse, he might already be fully versed in Thorne's baggage and not care because he was a buddy of his. In which case not only would Vail's threat be hollow, but it could backfire. She could be blackballed. Her career would be derailed before it even got on track.

I should've thought this through a bit more before running my mouth off. But Russo told me to stand up for myself.

Thorne rose from his chair. "I've got an appointment. Meantime, there's a typewriter." He motioned to the right side of his desk as he gathered up a manila folder. "Write up a sixty-one on the Crinelli crime scene. Form's in here." He shoved the file in her hands. "When you finish, you know what needs to be looked into. Check in with me at two o'clock." He grabbed the suit jacket off the back of his chair and left.

Vail exhaled and wiped her brow of the flop sweat that had broken out across her forehead.

TWO HOURS LATER, having typed the last sentence of her report, she reviewed the Carole Manos case file that Russo had sent over for her and Thorne. Unfortunately, there wasn't much she could use.

She set the folder aside and, with the assistance of a nearby detective, started accumulating information on Dominic Crinelli. One item immediately stood out: two of Crinelli's busts were at the hands of someone she was familiar with—one of her instructors at the academy, the man she suspected of putting her career on the fast track: Isidore Proschetta. Protch.

She phoned him and asked if he could meet her to discuss his experience with Crinelli. Proschetta had a better suggestion: he would take her to lunch at an iconic New York eatery.

But when Vail arrived, it wasn't exactly what she was expecting.

19

>ASTORIA. QUEENS
SATURDAY. MAY 19. 1973

Livana awoke early and made her way down the hall into the kitchen to make a pot of coffee. Fedor, like Basil, liked a jolt of caffeine to get his day started. This being a weekend, however, she did not want to wake anyone. Saturday was their only chance to sleep in.

Cassandra had climbed into bed with her at some point during the night. Her daughter had not done this in years, but the girl was clearly missing her father. Or she had a bad dream and needed comfort and security. Whatever it was, Livana did not object and actually found it consoling.

Livana sat at the table waiting for the percolator to boil when she almost thought Basil would come plodding in, not quite awake yet complaining that she had gotten out of bed without kissing him.

Now she wished she could make good on all the mornings when she did just that—not because she did not want to cuddle with him, but because she did not want to disturb his sleep.

She missed him. She missed their life—the way it was before the fight. It was not an existence filled with excess; they hardly had the things they needed. But theirs was a family, a mother and father who attended church, raised their two children right, and kept to themselves. They did not wish harm on anyone and were content to be left alone.

None of that seemed to matter anymore.

Their family had been ripped apart: Dmitri and Cassandra forced to grow up without a father, Livana without a husband. Basil was not the perfect father or the perfect husband. But he was a good man who wanted only happiness for all of them, and he worked hard to achieve it.

Until that one fateful Sunday night.

And now he was gone.

Livana poured herself a cup of coffee and was taking the first small, tentative sip when Cassandra entered the kitchen.

"Mommy, where's Dmitri?"

"Still asleep, baby. Did I wake you?"

"He's not sleeping. He's not in his room."

Livana set her mug down and smiled. "Of course he is. He's probably wiggled under the covers like he likes to do when he's cold."

"But it's not cold."

Livana pushed up from the chair and took her daughter by the shoulder. "C'mon, let's go find your brother."

They walked into the room that Dmitri and Cassandra shared and she was on her way over to the bed before stopping at the window to draw it closed. A light breeze was ruffling the curtain and billowing the sheer blue linen across Cassandra's bed.

"Did you open the window during the night?"

"No. We keep it closed, like you told us."

"Dmitri, wake up." She patted the comforter, her hands covering the entire mattress before she turned to scan the rest of the room. "Dmitri?"

"He's not here, Mommy."

Livana walked out into the hallway and checked the bathroom, then stopped at Fedor's and Niklaus's room. She put an ear to the door and listened. Did not hear anything.

She gently turned the knob and peeked inside: Fedor was asleep on the bed, Niklaus on a cot against the wall. Dmitri was not there, at least not that she could see.

Fedor stirred, then sat up. "Liv? What's wrong?"

Livana hesitated, then said, "Nothing, go back to sleep." She closed the door and backed down the hall. She pulled a light jacket over her nightgown and walked out front. After making a trip around the building, she saw Fedor standing on the stoop.

"I can't find Dmitri."

Fedor helped her search the house, their movements rousing Niklaus from sleep.

Moments later, they reconvened in the kitchen. No one had heard unusual sounds during the night. No one had seen Dmitri get up after they had gone to bed. No one had any idea as to where he might have gone.

As they were running through scenarios, the telephone rang. Fedor grabbed the receiver off the wall. He listened a minute, then said, "Who is this? No, I'm not—wait! Don't—"

He stood there, the handset still pressed against his ear, as he swallowed deeply.

"What is it?" Livana asked.

Fedor licked his lips, then hung up the phone. "They have Dmitri. They took him. Livana, I'm so sorry."

"What? Who's got Dmitri?"

"I think it's the people who—" he stopped and looked at the kids— "The same people."

Livana's face flushed and tears flooded her eyes. "Is he okay?"

"He's fine. They said he's fine."

He took her by the arm and said to the kids, "We'll be right back. Don't worry, Dmitri's gonna be fine."

Fedor ushered Livana into the bedroom and closed the door. "He'll be returned to us if I go to the police and withdraw my statement. I'm supposed to say I was mistaken when I gave them my description, that I was confused. And under no circumstances am I to tell the police that Dmitri's been taken."

"But *who*—who's taken him?"

"They didn't identify themselves. But I'm sure it's Crinelli's people."

"But—"

Fedor held out a hand. "They're calling back in two minutes. If I agree to do what they're demanding, they'll drop Dmitri off somewhere nearby."

"And if you don't?"

He checked his watch but did not answer. "I've gotta get back into the kitchen. I don't want to miss the call."

As they walked out of the bedroom, Cassandra ran up to Fedor. "Is Dmitri okay?"

"He's fine, little one," Fedor said. "He'll be home soon."

The phone rang. Fedor grabbed it up, listened a second, then said, "Yes, yes, I'll do it. Just don't hurt the boy." He listened, then said, "Okay. But when and where can I get Dmitri?" Another moment later, he hung up.

Fedor stepped briskly toward the front door.

"What did they say?" Livana asked, running after him.

"I'm on my way to the police station. Once they have confirmation that I've retracted my statement, they'll call and tell us where he'll be."

"He's safe, though, right? Did they tell you he's safe?"

Fedor reached for his hat, concern painted across his face. He turned away and said, "I know you want answers. I do too. I'm gonna do my best to make sure he comes back to us happy and healthy."

FEDOR RETURNED NINETY minutes later. He trudged into the house and sat down heavily in the living room easy chair, not bothering to remove his coat.

Hearing the front door open, Livana came running in from the backyard, gardening gloves on her hands, followed by the kids.

"I've been a nervous wreck," she said. "What happened?"

"I looked Detective Proschetta in the eyes and told him a lie. And he knew it was a lie." Fedor closed his eyes. "He kept asking me why I was doing this, what had they threatened me with. And I kept telling him that nothing was wrong, they hadn't threatened me."

"And?" Livana asked.

"And nothing. I told him I was sorry for wasting his time and I left."

"Did he say that they were going to release him? Did they say when—"

"No. I mean, I tried asking. He said that without my statement, and if I wouldn't testify at his trial, they probably couldn't make a case. They'd have to let him go. So I said, 'When would that be?' And he said not to worry myself with that stuff. I think he was angry with me. He wouldn't even look at me."

"But if only—"

"I couldn't press it, Livana. I did the best I could. If I said too much, he would've known for sure something was wrong. And as much I would've wanted the police to help us, they said I couldn't tell them."

"Or what?"

Fedor looked at her, his brow hard. "It wasn't an option. I could *not* tell the police."

"So now what?"

"We wait for the phone to ring. That's all we can do."

AN HOUR AND twenty-three minutes passed. They sat together in the living room, Cassandra on Livana's lap with her favorite doll in her hands. Niklaus thumbed through his box of baseball cards and read the backs until he couldn't remain silent any longer.

"I thought you said they're supposed to call, Dad."

"They are, Nik." Fedor's response was terse, as if all his energy was invested in maintaining his composure.

"My son's all alone and there's nothing I can do to comfort him." Livana started combing her fingers through Cassandra's brown locks, then braiding it. Her daughter, who normally did not like her mother fiddling with her hair, did not object, as if she understood that Livana needed to do this for her emotional well-being.

Minutes later, the ringing phone pierced the quiet. They all seemed to jump in unison.

Livana and Fedor arrived simultaneously. Fedor lifted the handset and angled it so she could hear.

"Where can I find him?" Fedor asked.

The voice was measured, though tense. "The police have not released him yet."

"I can't control what the police do. I did exactly what you told me to—"

"Calm down. We know."

"So where's the boy?"

"We'll be in touch when—"

"No! Where's my baby," Livana screamed. "I want my baby!"

The call disconnected. Fedor moved the phone away from his face.

She brought her hands to her cheeks. "They hung up?"

"What happened?" Cassandra asked, running into the kitchen.

Fedor slowly set the receiver on the hook.

"Is Dmitri okay?" Cassandra's eyes teared over. "Is he coming home?"

"Cassie." Fedor gave her a pat on the rear. "He's going to be fine. Just—just go back and sit on the couch with Niklaus. Please."

She bit her lip and made a show of passive resistance as she walked off.

Fedor rubbed his forehead and lowered his voice. "I think you should let *me* talk to them, Liv."

She grasped the counter to steady herself. "Are they going to call back? Why aren't they calling back?"

"They will. Give them a few minutes. You probably just freaked them out."

Livana had a feeling that these people did not get panicked by a screaming woman. They were teaching her a lesson: treat them with respect or they'll hang up. Or—worse, they'll kill her son.

They're going to call back, she told herself.

A moment later, the phone rang.

Fedor stuck his left hand out, keeping Livana an arm's length away from the phone. He turned his back on her and said, "Sorry about that . . . Yes, I know where that is. Okay, but—" He clenched his jaw and looked like he wanted to slam the receiver onto its cradle but stopped himself and set it gently on the hook.

"Well?"

"They gave me an address. They said Dmitri will be there."

"Let's go."

Fedor hesitated. "They don't want me there. It has to be you. Alone." He grasped both of her arms and looked in her eyes. "You can do this."

She took a deep breath. "I know."

LIVANA DROVE FEDOR'S pickup to the designated location near the entrance to Powdermaker Hall at Queens College. The instructions were that vague, and the building was massive: a good two blocks long.

She stopped at the curb across the road from the expansive, and at first glance full, parking lot, and ran onto the grassy quad. She did not care if campus police wrote her a ticket. She just wanted her son back.

School was not in session and despite the gray weather, the temperature was mild and a few students were out tossing a Frisbee or sitting on the grass reading their textbooks. Livana walked up to the building, her eyes rapidly scanning the vicinity, knowing she would instantly pick up her son.

But she did not see him.

"Dmitri," she called out. Her voice was weak, her tone tentative, tinged with fear and more than a hint of hysteria. More strongly: "Dmitri!"

A few students turned toward her, no doubt wondering what was going on. Livana looked older than most, if not all, of the graduate class on campus, so she was either a professor or a mother. Frazzled and frumpy, she did not look like the former. But her appearance did nothing to explain her presence on the campus screaming someone's name.

"Are you Livana?"

She turned so fast she nearly lost her balance. "Who are you?"

A male in his early twenties wearing elephant bell bottom dungarees took a tentative step back. "I was told to give you a message."

"Are you working for them, you son of a—"

"Hey," he said, holding up his hands. "A guy gave me twenty bucks and told me to wait here, that a woman about your age would be coming by looking for someone named Dmitri."

"You found her. Now what?"

"He said to give you something." He reached into his back pocket and pulled out an envelope.

Livana snatched it like a ravenous tiger pouncing on a wild boar. She tore it open and read the typed message:

```
Woodro Deli
1342 Peninsula Blvd
Hewlett
```

Livana stared at the note, then looked up at the man.

"Everything okay?"

"I don't understand. My son—my son was supposed to be here."

He eyed her cautiously. "You don't look very good. Are you okay? Want me to get campus police?"

"No! No, no. No. I'm—I'm fine."

The man started to back away as Livana turned and ran toward her pickup.

She reached it in a dozen strides, jammed the key into the ignition and screeched the tires as she headed down the road, off the campus and then onto Jewel Avenue. Two minutes later she was careening down the Van Wyck Expressway, weaving in and out of traffic. Her eyes were tearing and she had to repeatedly swipe them on her arm.

"Bastards. What kind of game are they playing? Why are they doing this?"

She pounded the steering wheel several times, then took a deep, uneven breath and let it out. Focused herself. If she drove like a maniac without concentrating on what she was doing, she would end up killing herself—and possibly others.

Livana eased up on the accelerator slightly and realized that she was only vaguely familiar with Hewlett, having visited there once, shortly after moving to the country.

She figured she could stop at Green Acres Mall to ask directions or at least find a phone booth with a Yellow Pages directory. Or a gas station—there were several located along Sunrise Highway. Livana stopped into Esso, the first one she came to, and rolled down the window.

"Regular or high test?" the attendant asked as he wiped his fingers on a grease rag.

Livana handed him the typed page containing the address. She was hyperventilating and looked like she had escaped from the local psych ward.

"Need to get there," she gasped. "Fast."

"You okay, lady?" the man asked.

"Directions."

He eyed her, then looked down again at the document. "Keep heading east, hang a right on Rockaway—"

"Write it. Write it down."

She was flustered and did not trust her ability to remember his instructions once she pulled out of the service station.

He pulled a pen from behind his ear and scrawled the directions onto the page, then handed it back through the window.

Without so much as a thank-you, she screeched out the exit and onto Sunrise Highway, then ran the red light and accelerated. Seven minutes later, she turned off Peninsula Boulevard into the shopping center where the delicatessen was located.

Livana saw a candy store, a bagel shop, a supermarket—and the deli. She stopped at the curb and ran out of the pickup.

She burst through the door into the storefront restaurant and saw a tall, thin man behind the register—a manager? He grabbed a menu and started to walk toward a table. "Just you, or is someone join—"

"I'm here for Dmitri."

He hesitated a second. "We don't have anyone here named Dmitri. Is he a customer?"

"No, my son. I was told—" She looked around the interior and started walking briskly past the deli counter and then among the tables. He was not there.

Behind her, a ringing telephone.

"Lady. Livana!"

Livana turned and saw the man holding up a black handset, his palm covering the mouthpiece. "Call's for you."

She ran to the front, grabbed the phone, and stretched the coiled cord across the counter.

"Where is he?"

"My man hasn't been released yet. Be patient."

"Be patient? You've got me running all over the goddamn place looking for my son. I want him back now! *Now*, you hear me?"

"Lady," the manager said. "Please. Keep it down."

Livana lowered her voice. "Stop playing games. I want my son back. Where is he?"

"You listen to me. I'm the one in charge here, not you. I tell you when you're gonna get your son back. And if I change my mind, you ain't gonna get him back. Ever. So shut your trap or I'm going to hang up and never call back."

Livana felt dizzy—and her knees started to buckle—but she grabbed the cash register and steadied herself.

She told herself to breathe. She needed to calm down before she lost Dmitri forever. The manager handed her a wet napkin and she pressed it against her forehead.

"I—I just want him back," she whispered into the phone. "Please don't hurt him."

"Don't give us a reason to. Something happens to him, it's because you didn't do what we told you to do."

"We've done everything you asked. I don't know what more you want from me."

"You don't need to know. Stay where you are. I'll call you when I'm ready."

"But—"

The line went dead. Livana dropped the phone.

She looked at the manager, her mouth dry as straw. "I can't leave. Is there someplace I can wait?"

He came around the counter and walked her over to a chair. "C'mon over here." He guided her to the nearest unoccupied table. "Al, get her some water and a corned beef on rye."

"I'm not hungry," Livana said, almost mechanically, staring off at the back wall of the restaurant.

"Look, I don't know what's going on with your kid, if it's a fight with your ex or what. And I don't wanna know. But you don't look so good. You need to eat." He rested a hand on her shoulder. "I'm Maury. You need something, let me know."

Livana nodded, then bent forward and rested her head on her forearms.

A minute later, a young man whose workboots were encrusted with salt around the sole set a plate down on the table in front of her. "Can I get you anything else?"

She leaned back, looked at the food, and gathered up the sandwich. After starting to chew, she realized how hungry she was.

NINETY MINUTES LATER, Livana had reached the end of her patience. She borrowed the phone and called Detective Proschetta's line. But his shift ended early on Saturdays so he had gone home. She told the detective who answered that it was vital she speak to him immediately.

Three minutes later, Proschetta called back.

"My partner said it was important."

"It's about my son. They've taken him."

"They—" He caught himself, then apparently realized what she was talking about.

"Tell me everything you know."

She filled him in, then said, "I don't know if they're going to call back, if he's alive or—" her throat caught— "dead."

"I know the deli. I'm on my way. Give me twenty minutes. If they call back before I get there, leave me a note with the location. Address it to 'Protch.'"

"Protch?"

"No one knows that nickname except my college roommate and a few close friends."

Livana dug at her scalp with her fingernails, thinking, not answering right away. "They said no police."

"I'm off duty, I'll be in my personal car. I'll change my appearance somehow. But you'll know it's me."

He hung up and Livana took her seat again, drumming her fingers on the table, wondering if she had done the right thing. All she could think about, however, was the fact that they had not called back.

Why? What did that mean? She exhausted herself trying to consider the possibilities—none good.

THE DELI FILLED with patrons for the dinner hour. Twenty minutes after Livana spoke with Proschetta, the phone rang again. Livana sat erect and swiveled in her chair. But no one was at the front desk. Maury, the man who had helped her earlier, was seating a family in the back of the restaurant.

She made her way to the register and lifted the receiver. "Hello?"

"Who is this?"

"Livan—"

"Drive to the phone booth at this address: 3954 Patchogue Road, Port Jefferson Station. You have seventy-five minutes to get there. Don't be late, and don't bring the police. We'll be watching."

PROSCHETTA HAD NOT arrived yet. But did she still need him now that the bastards had finally gotten back to her? She had thoughts of calling him and telling him not to bother, but she could not trust Crinelli's people.

After the busboy gave her directions, Livana left a note at the counter marked "For Protch" and ran out, not bothering to thank Maury for helping her and not thinking to leave money for the food. Her single-minded fixation was to get to Port Jefferson Station on time.

Although it was Saturday night, traffic was light. She zipped along the Southern State Parkway, keeping to no more than five miles over the speed limit. She did not want to get pulled over and lose valuable time while the trooper went through his procedural gyrations.

The man had told her not to be late. Whatever reason lay behind his remark, she intended to make her appointment.

The sun was well into its descent, but there was no clock in the truck. She had not put on her watch before she hurried out of the house that morning, and in the rush to leave the deli, she had not checked the time when the call came through.

Now that she thought of it, she realized she should have called Fedor from Woodro and told him what had happened. He and the kids were no doubt well beyond worried and wondering why it was taking hours for her to collect Dmitri. They had no way of knowing what the bastards were putting her through.

Livana pulled up to the address and saw a Mobil gas station. She drove in and parked next to the phone booth in the far corner of the lot. It started ringing the moment she got out of the truck, but stopped just as she pushed open the accordion door. She answered it anyway—but no one was there.

Livana looked around, hoping to see a clock somewhere, but there was nothing. She did not want to leave in case they called back, so she inched her way toward the pumps and shouted to the man who was checking the oil on a Chevy van.

"Excuse me, you got the time?"

He leaned back and angled his watch toward the station's fluorescent lights. "Just about straight up, eight o'clock."

But since she did not know what time they had called the deli, she had no point of reference. And a disturbing thought came to her: if that was the man who had hung up before she had answered the call, maybe she had arrived seconds too late.

And he warned her not to be late.

Livana stood there staring at the receiver. She closed her eyes, then kicked the metal bottom of the booth. "C'mon, damn it, ring!"

A minute later, a car pulled up: a shiny, dark-colored two-door Datsun. The driver extinguished the sedan's headlights and got out.

"I'm sorry," she said as the man approached. "I'm waiting for a call."

"Livana, it's Protch." He had a Yankees ball cap pulled low over his ears and a fake scruffy beard and mustache. "Don't say anything. I just wanted you to know I'm here. I assume they're going to call you and tell you to go to another place. I'm gonna drive down the road a bit and watch. Don't look for me. In case they're also parked nearby and watching, I want it to look like you don't know me."

Proschetta threw his arms out to his sides, making it appear as if he was arguing with the woman who wouldn't allow him to use the phone, then waved a hand in disgust, turned, and walked back to his car. He got in and drove off.

Livana rested her head against the cold metal of the booth and watched as the stars began poking through a small clearing in the cloudy, dusky sky. Passing cars were now using their headlights and Livana was once again beginning to doubt they were going to call.

A few minutes later, she felt the vibration in the handset before she heard it ring. She snatched it up—and nearly dropped it—but managed to get it near her face as she shouted, "I'm here!"

"Your son's just down the road. You're very close. He's waiting for you near the Port Jefferson Station Long Island Railroad station."

"Waiting for me? What do you mean? Is he in a car, an office? Is he alone?"

The man snickered. "He's not in a car. Or an office. But he is alone, and he's terrified, so don't keep him waiting. Once you hit the Esso on the left, look sharp. Park and walk to the train station. A little over one-tenth of a mile from the east end of the platform you'll see a pedestrian bridge over the track. Walk to the center of the bridge. You have nine minutes. And if you don't want to see your son end up like your husband, don't be late." He laughed. "Then again, you could bury them together, two for one—"

Livana left the phone dangling and ran toward the pickup. She got in and turned it over, then sped out of the lot.

THE PICKUP'S HEADLIGHTS must have been coated in dirt, because even the brights did a poor job of illuminating the dark landscape.

A good distance behind her, a car was following her along Highland Boulevard. She hoped it was Proschetta's Datsun.

When she saw the sign reading Esso Standard Dealer, Credit Cards Honored, she slowed to a near crawl, looking out into the dusk, trying to see if she could spot the bridge.

"There!" She slammed on the accelerator and sped into the train station's parking lot, her heart pounding.

"Dmitri, baby," she shouted into the humid night air. "I'm coming!"

Seconds later, she was running along the curving platform toward the bridge, which crossed four sets of tracks. At this time of night on a Saturday, there was no one else around. No matter: she was focused on climbing those stairs, on getting to her son.

Was he there?

She struggled to see the center of the span, as the last vestiges of light had left the sky and there was no moon to speak of.

Livana hit the steps in stride, nearly out of breath and almost stumbling as she threw her hands out and grabbed the metal planking in front of her to keep her balance.

She reached the top and walked out to the center of the bridge. But she did not see Dmitri. Panic enveloped her as quickly as elation had overwhelmed her seconds earlier.

"Dmitri!" She spun in all directions. He was clearly not on the span. "Where are you?" She brought her hands to her face. "Where is he? What have you done with my son?" she screamed into the darkness. "Enough. Give my son back to me!"

"Livana."

She turned to see Proschetta approaching on the run, flashlight in hand, from the same direction she had come.

"Dmitri was supposed to be on the bridge. They told me to go to the middle of the bridge. But he's not here."

Proschetta reached the steps and started to ascend them when he stopped. "Oh my god." He moved his light along the ground. "Shit!" Without hesitation, he jumped down off the platform onto the track bed.

"What's wrong?"

"I got him. I see him—look down, about thirty feet in front of you."

Livana grabbed the railing on the east side of the bridge and did as instructed. The breath left her lungs. She got dizzy and had to steady herself to keep from collapsing.

Dmitri was lying face down on the tracks, unmoving.

"Is he—" Her voice caught. She forced it out, but it was weak and she was unsure Proschetta heard her. "Is he alive?"

Proschetta did not reply. He was walking along the center of the tracks, stumbling over the gravel and wood ties, trying to get there quickly while maintaining his balance.

Seconds later he passed under the bridge and was straddling her son.

Proschetta twisted his torso back toward her. "He's alive." He reached over and pulled on the boy's torso but fell forward. He righted himself and jumped across the rail to bring himself alongside Dmitri's body. "He's chained down to the track. I need something to break the links. You got any tools in that pickup?"

Livana was in shock, hearing Proschetta but not listening.

"Livana, Fedor's truck. Any tools in it?"

"I—I don't know. I can go check."

But at that moment, she felt a vibration. It was slight, but it didn't take a genius to understand what was causing it. "Protch, a train's coming."

Proschetta jerked his head up, then started scurrying about, looking for something.

Livana ran down the stairs, then jumped the three feet to the tracks. Her feet slid in the loose rock, but she stumbled her way toward her son. "Dmitri!"

She reached Proschetta and saw the detective slamming a palm-size rock against the track—no, not against the track, against the chain links that were holding Dmitri in place.

The vibration was intensifying, and Livana knew that meant the train was getting closer. Was it on the same track? No, they would not have done that. This is all just to scare her. They wouldn't actually kill a child.

Would they?

She reached down and stroked her son's head, trying to stay out of Proschetta's way. "I'm so sorry, Dmitri. Are you okay?"

He lifted his chin a few inches and nodded.

"That's my boy. Hang in there."

Proschetta slammed the rock down again and stopped—"Yeah! Got it." He scrabbled over to the other side and started working on the chain securing Dmitri's left arm.

Three more to go.

Proschetta glanced up quickly and looked around. He must have felt the rumbling too, because he gave her a look, then quickly turned his attention back to the task and swung the rock again. "You see any kind of emergency lever, something that'll switch tracks?"

She rose and turned slowly. "What am I looking for?"

"No idea. A lever, a box, a brake."

Livana ran in a thirty foot radius but did not see anything that resembled what the detective had described.

One thing she did see, however, were the close-mounted headlights of a train off in the distance. "No . . ." she said under her breath. Then, more robustly: "It's coming!"

She turned and sprinted back to Dmitri. Proschetta had freed both arms and was working on his left leg. Her son was up on his hands, looking back at Proschetta, who had been whaling away at the track for several minutes. Even in the poor lighting, Livana saw the perspiration pimpling the detective's face, the blood on the knuckles of his right hand.

"Hurry," she said, grabbing her hair.

Dmitri swung his head back toward Livana. "Mom . . ."

"It's gonna be fine, honey. We're almost there." She scurried around and found another rock, then tried to hit the chain by Dmitri's right ankle. It was much harder than it looked; she kept missing and slamming the rail—and once hit Dmitri. He flinched but did not cry out or complain.

"I can't do this," she said.

Proschetta slammed the track again—and the chain popped aside. "One more."

But the train was moving closer. The track was rumbling vigorously.

Proschetta cursed. "Harder to hit when the damn thing's moving!" He kept at it, however, and picked up the pace. But his miss rate increased as well.

"Damn it." He cried out, dropped the stone, and shook his hand. It was swollen, the palm a shiny blood red. He grabbed the rock again and started striking the links, groaning with each blow. "Hang on, kid. I'm gonna get you free. Get ready to run. Livana, go—go to the platform."

The clink of stone on metal was drowned out by the loud blast of a train horn.

"Livana," Proschetta yelled above the din. "Go!"

Instead, she stood up in front of her son's body and waved her arms over her head, imploring the driver to brake.

"He might not be able to stop in time. Get out of the way."

"He has to stop, he's coming into the station."

"He's on the inside track. He's just passing through." Proschetta looked up. "He's coming in too fast, definitely not stopping." He resumed his hammering. "Get on the platform, now."

"I'm not leaving my son!"

"Your daughter's at home," he said between strikes. "Her father's gone. She needs you."

Livana started jumping, waving her arms at the same time, doing what appeared to be a crude type of calisthenics.

"I'm gonna get him free, I promise. Now, just go!"

Livana did not stop. Proschetta did not stop either.

And neither did the train, which was now squealing its brakes, sparks flying from both sides of the car.

The headlights were blinding as Livana froze in place, no longer moving her arms, paralyzed by the conflict of not wanting to leave her son and not wanting to leave her daughter.

But as the train barreled down on her, she heard what sounded like three rapid gunshots. Almost immediately after, two hands grabbed her and yanked her to the side.

Her face slammed into the rough gravel as the hulking mustard and black locomotive rumbled by her head. The brakes released, the screeching ceased, and the train gathered speed, moving on down the track.

The intense wind blew her back as she attempted to get to her feet. She covered up and waited for it to pass, then saw Proschetta lying atop her son, who was pushing to get out from under his weight.

"Dmitri!" She rushed to his side and helped him up, and she hugged him, held him close. Nothing—no one—was ever going to take him away from her. Ever again.

IN A MOMENT OF desperation, Proschetta had removed his service revolver and shot the lock, but also hit Dmitri's leg. He carried the boy to his car and, leaving Fedor's truck in the lot, they brought the boy to the nearby St. Charles Hospital.

While the doctors worked to remove the bullet, Livana called Fedor and told him what had happened—and that Dmitri was safe. She promised to update them as soon as the doctors gave her a report.

The round had not damaged an artery and had not struck bone. Given where he was hit, he was fortunate that it went clean through the calf muscle.

He would have some difficulty walking until it healed, but unless he planned to be a professional athlete, it would not cause him any disability.

"I've seen my fair share of gunshot wounds," Proschetta said. "I'd say that's a damn good report."

"I'm just glad he's safe."

"The chains were so tight against his legs, I knew there'd be no way to shoot the lock or the chain without hitting his body—not to mention the danger of a ricochet. As it was, I got off a lucky shot. Coulda been a lot worse. Not like I had a choice." Proschetta chuckled. "Of course, I'm gonna have a hell of a time explaining why my revolver was run over by a train."

"Is that a problem?"

Proschetta thought a moment before answering. "Like you said, the important thing is that your son is safe."

"How's your hand?" It was splinted and wrapped in thick gauze.

"Three broken bones. Guess I smashed my fingers more than the chain. Fortunately, my aim with a gun was better than with a rock."

They both got a chuckle out of that.

A few minutes later, Livana called Fedor and told him Dmitri was going to be fine. But when Fedor said, "We need to talk," her sense of relief turned to unease. "When you get home," he said. "Now's not the time. It can wait."

She did not know what the problem was, but since it was apparently not an urgent matter, she was too mentally exhausted to deal with it at the moment.

When Livana walked into recovery, she saw Dmitri lying on a cot, an IV connected to his forearm. His body was covered with deep abrasions as well as long, pink welts across his back and large bruises on his face, something his surgeon had commented on—and asked about.

"It looks like this child's been abused. That, combined with the gunshot wound, I'm going to have to call—"

"Hang on a second, doc." Proschetta rooted out his badge and told him that it was a sensitive case and that they could not divulge the details of what had happened to him. The doctor reluctantly accepted his explanation.

He made a note in the chart, then clicked his pen closed and faced Livana. "We'll put him on antibiotics to guard against sepsis from the bullet. I'll make sure you get complete instructions."

When the doctor left, Proschetta pulled a chair next to Dmitri's bed. He waited another half hour for the boy to become lucid and the anesthesia to clear his system. After he stirred and opened his eyes, Proschetta moved across the room to give Livana a moment to talk with him.

When he returned to the bed, Livana smiled broadly. "We're grateful for everything you've done. How can I thank you?"

Proschetta sat down. "Just doing my job, Livana."

"I think you went beyond the call of duty."

Proschetta smiled. "Maybe just a bit. I'm glad to be able to help. Thanks for trusting me enough to call. I knew something was up when Fedor came into the station and recanted his statement. But there was nothing I could do. He insisted everything was fine." Proschetta turned to Dmitri, then cleared his throat. "So, bud, you comfortable?"

Dmitri nodded, but turned his gaze toward the ceiling.

"We need to talk about what happened, when those people took you from your home."

"It wasn't my fault," Dmitri said. He pounded his fist on the bed. "Not my fault!"

"No one said it was. I just want to know—"

"Detective," Livana said. "Do you think—"

"Yes. This is important." He looked sternly at Livana, then swung his gaze back to Dmitri. "Did they hurt you, son?"

He turned his head away, then nodded.

"Tell me what happened."

Dmitri closed his eyes. He hesitated for a moment, then said, "I don't wanna talk about it."

"Did they hit you?"

He gave Proschetta a slight movement of his chin. *Yes.*

Proschetta leaned in close. "Did they, you know, hit you with a belt? On your back?"

Another nod.

"Did you get a look at the men? Can you tell me what they looked like?"

Dmitri's mouth became contorted, as if he was trying to keep himself composed. He lifted his head and brought it down into the pillow, repeatedly.

"Hey, it's okay," Proschetta said, rising and placing a reassuring hand on the boy's shoulder. "It's okay, son."

"Honey," Livana said. "Stop that. Stop." She stroked his hair and he slowly relaxed, letting his head rest on the pillow and turning away from Proschetta. "I think he's done answering questions. There's no point. These people are animals. We're not going to press charges. One's enough." She looked hard at him; she could tell he understood that she was talking about losing Basil. "I just want this to go away."

Proschetta stood up straight and took half a step back. "I know. I was—I'm sorry. I didn't mean to upset him. Or you." He pulled the baseball cap from his pocket and stood there for an awkward moment. Finally he said, "I'll go, leave you two alone. Is there anything I can get you?"

Livana massaged her forehead, trying to release the stress. She was mentally and physically spent. "Just my car. It's back at the train station."

"I'll grab an orderly on break and we'll bring it here. And you know how to get in touch with me if—" He gestured for her to follow him to the door. "You need something, you just give me a call. If you hear from the bastards again, if they threaten you—" He stopped, realizing Dmitri was lying within earshot. He lowered his voice. "If they contact you for any reason, please let me know."

Livana smiled and thanked him, but wondered what the police could do to protect them. Her mind flashed on the question she had asked Officer Kennedy the night of Basil's murder. And she felt like she could now answer it herself: the Mob, in fact, ran New York.

20

›137 EAST HOUSTON STREET
The Lower East Side
Manhattan
Tuesday, November 5, 1996

Proschetta took Vail to Yonah Schimmel's Knishery, a New York City icon famous for its potato knishes and all the variants it had developed over the years: mushroom, salmon, jalapeno, cheese. No matter what they chopped up and put inside, however, it all came down to the special Yonah Schimmel recipe that made the stuffed dumpling a delicacy in Jewish American cuisine.

Walking up to the storefront, Vail noticed that the yellow, blue, and red sign claimed that its origins dated back to 1910. She believed it, as the eatery looked to be every day of its eighty-six years. She stepped up into the narrow restaurant and the smell of baking bread and sautéing onions hit her nose. She breathed in deeply and her stomach rumbled.

To her immediate left was a stainless steel and glass display case where dozens of knishes sat, begging to be eaten.

"Karen."

Vail whipped her head right and saw Proschetta seated at one of the wood tables against a wall covered with yellowed newspaper clippings about

Yonah Schimmel and the knishery alongside photos of celebrities, including a large one with Woody Allen taken pretty much where she was standing.

"Protch, good to see you."

"How's the NYPD treating you?"

A broad conspiratorial grin spread across her lips. "Couldn't be better."

Protch slapped the table. "Good. As it should be. You deserve it all, and don't let anyone tell you otherwise. Your reports have been thorough and well-written. And the detectives who've followed up leads based on your reports found them extremely helpful. The command staff took notice. All I did was put you in a position to succeed, and point them in the right direction, to put you on their radar. Everything else you've done yourself."

A busboy set a bowl of pickles on the table.

"Try the half sours," Proschetta said. "They're out of this world. If you like pickles."

"I like pickles." She snatched one off the plate and took a bite, her gaze moving around the small restaurant. In the back, full soda cases of Coke, Dr. Brown's, and Sprite were stacked against the wall. "Interesting place."

"Place? This is a New York City *institution*. Wait till you taste the knishes."

They ordered, made small talk, and then Proschetta lifted his glass of Dr. Brown's. "I'm enjoying this, Karen. Don't get me wrong, but I know you didn't call up your former instructor just to have lunch."

"It's a nice thought, though."

"But not likely. So Dominic Crinelli."

"Can we talk here?"

Proschetta chuckled. "No one's here at the moment. I'll make it fast before anyone comes in. Besides, Jews eat here. Italian mobsters, not so much. Don't worry."

"We found Mr. Crinelli murdered last night in his house."

"You can drop the 'mister.' Guy was a lowlife thug all his life, nothing less. And to make things worse, I couldn't make the charges stick. As to his murder, I heard. All senior ranks got an alert this morning. In case there are repercussions."

"Then you know why I wanted to meet?"

"Not a clue."

The server set their knishes in front of them.

"Mmm." Vail leaned over the food and inhaled deeply.

"You live in New York and you've never had a knish?"

Vail shrugged. "Life's full of exciting experiences." *Though I'm not sure this qualifies as one of them.*

"So Crinelli." Proschetta took his knife and fork and cut into his knish. Steam rose and he leaned away, out of its path. "First time he crossed my path was back in '73. I'd just made detective and I caught this case where some meathead starts a fight with this family guy in a bowling alley. The guy fights back and hurts him real bad. Family guy claims it was self-defense, and I believe him.

"Problem is, the injured asshole's in with the mob somehow. The Castiglia family. His father was their accountant or something, don't remember." He snapped his fingers. "Illegal furs, that's it. The father's company was bringing in furs from overseas, purposely mislabeling them because it was against the law to kill certain animals. Anyone checked, the label showed a legal fur—but it wasn't.

"Anyway, the Castiglias, they kinda owned part of the business. Skimming the profits." He stabbed a fork into the knish and scooped up a piece. "Family guy who was in the fight, he threatens to go to the police about the illegal furs. They dispatched a crew to send a message, work the guy over with bats, break some bones. I don't think they had orders to kill him, but the thugs got carried away and bludgeoned him to death."

"Was Crinelli one of them?"

"Oh—yeah, sorry. Someone saw what was going down, and he chased one of the assholes down—Crinelli—and got a decent look at him. Gave us a good likeness, and we picked him up."

"This story doesn't have a happy ending, does it?"

"Not even close."

"They went after the witness?"

"Indirectly." Proschetta proceeded to recount the details of the child's kidnapping and eventual release.

"Damn."

"Damn *effective* is what it was. They knew that if they killed a kid, all hell woulda broken loose. We woulda declared war. You probably don't remember because you were just a teenager, but about ten years ago a Mexican drug cartel killed an undercover DEA agent, Kiki Camarena. Feds went nuts, shut down the drug trade, made life miserable for the cartels. The mob sure didn't want any part of that happening to them.

"But the Castiglias almost blew it big-time because the kid nearly died. Don't know what they were thinking, chaining him down like that." He held up his right hand, which featured three bulbous knuckles. "Fractured three fingers slamming the rock against the track. Arthritis kills me in the winter and firing my pistol ain't much fun anymore. But I'm not sorry. I'd do it again, no question."

His gaze drifted off for a moment. "Anyway, even if they went about it the wrong way and got lucky because I was there for the kid, they ended up sending the right message. It hit home. Crinelli walked and there was nothing we could do about it because no way in hell would the family testify against them. That family . . . talk about heartache." He shook his head and seemed lost in thought for a few seconds.

"Second time?"

"Different cast of characters. Same story. Nine years ago, after he was made a capo. Someone on his crew got into trouble. We had stuff on the guy and the FBI had been watching him for a while. He rolled on his boss and it looked like we were finally gonna show Crinelli the inside of a prison cell. Somehow they got to the witness, slipped some cyanide in his coffee while he was waiting to testify."

Vail realized her knish was getting cold, so she scooped up a forkful. "Wasn't he in protective custody?"

"Karen." Proschetta frowned. "This wasn't the first time we'd been down that road."

"So how'd they get to him?"

"Inside job."

Vail stopped chewing. "How?"

"The Castiglias had two cops on their payroll. Hard to believe they flew under the radar for twenty years, kept their noses clean for two decades."

"How could we not see that? How could we not make the connection?"

"Cops can't become made men. Against the rules of La Cosa Nostra. So there was no connection to be made. No. The Castiglias were smart, approached the two after they were cops, did a dance, felt them out, tested them. They passed with flying colors and the money started to flow. Not just money —women, fine wine, offshore accounts. Nothing traceable that could raise alarms.

"But I noticed something about one of 'em. Made me think. I told the FBI and Internal Affairs and they thought my theory had merit. They set up a wiretap and within six weeks we overheard a conversation that basically implicated the cop in the murder. He bragged about it, pointed out its importance. Felt he should've been compensated better."

"Good old greed," Vail said as she scooped up another helping. "This knish is really good."

"I used to come here all the time as a kid. Ironically, it was my dad, who was Italian, who brought us here. My mom, who could trace her Jewish ancestry to the Spanish Inquisition—her ancestors were Conversos—she doesn't like knishes. Go figure."

"So you have anything on Crinelli that could help my case?"

"*Your* case?"

Vail flushed. "Well—Thorne, actually Russo—called me out to the crime scene. It had similarities to a murder I'd . . . helped with a year ago."

"Tim Thorne?"

"Know him?"

Proschetta coughed into his hand as he said, "Asshole. Drunk."

Vail smirked. "Apparently I've already experienced both of his personality traits."

Proschetta sat back in his seat. "Russo set you up with him?"

Vail lifted her Dr. Brown's and took a sip. "I guess you could put it that way. But I'm not complaining. I'm working a case."

"Yeah, well . . . be careful. Shit has a way of sticking to your shoe and dragging the stink with you. Then everyone thinks you're the one who caused the stench. I'm not sure that's worth any points you'll score by cutting your teeth on Crinelli's death."

Vail considered that. "I have a feeling this case is going to be much more than the death of a mob capo. I think this is a serial case." Vail walked him through the Manos murder, the same MO that was used on Crinelli, and the unusual manner in which the fingers were glued together.

Proschetta's brow rose. He shoved a piece of potato into his mouth, his fork poised, limp wristed, as he worked it through. "I see your point. I'll amend my advice to you, then. Be careful. Know what you're getting into with Thorne, keep your eyes open and your shoes clean. Promise?"

Vail grinned. "Promise, *Dad*. I'll be careful."

21

>MANHATTAN SOUTH HOMICIDE SQUAD
230 EAST 21ST STREET
TUESDAY, NOVEMBER 5, 1996

Vail returned to the homicide squad in time to see Thorne outside, ready to get into his car.

"You're late," he said. "I told you to be back here at 2:00."

Vail twisted her wrist and consulted her watch. "It's 2:03."

"Like I said. You're late. Now get in the goddamn car."

Protch's admonition was suddenly echoing in her mind: *Be careful.* She pulled open the door and slid into the seat.

"Where were you?"

"None of your business."

"Bullshit. You're on the clock, and I'm a senior officer, so you will answer my question. You're supposed to be working this case. Did you type up that report?"

"I did."

He turned over the engine and pulled away from the curb. "Then where were you?"

"Meeting with Detective Proschetta, out of the—"

"I know who he is. Why were you meeting him?"

"I was working the case."

Thorne laughed. "You're working the case? You're a pissant beat cop. What the hell do you know about working a case?"

Vail squirmed in her seat. "I did a temporary assignment with homicide when I got out of the academy."

"Oh, so you're an expert now."

"Of course not. I'm following my gut instinct, looking at things logically. I'm trying to understand why the killer is doing what he's doing."

"*Understand* him." He glanced over at her. It was not a look of confidence. "Really?"

"Yeah. I figure that if I can get a handle on the victims, understand who the victims were as people, I might be able to get a bead on why he killed each of them. It might even tell us something about who he is." She saw he was not buying her explanation. "Look, I'm just doing what we talked about. Looking for a connection between the two victims."

"I was talking about a hard connection. An acquaintance, a known associate, a forensic common to both crime scenes. Not some touchy-feely bullshit about 'understanding' the vic and killer." He shook his head. "Is this the kind of crap they're teaching at the academy these days?"

She turned away, looked out the window. "I didn't learn that at the academy. It's just something . . . that makes sense to me."

He turned at the next block and glanced over at Vail. "Let me give you some advice. Not that you're asking for it or anything. But stick to procedure and the stuff they teach you. That's the way you're gonna make detective. You talk about some fairy tale new age shit, they're gonna laugh you off the force. Forget about getting your shield."

Vail clenched her jaw.

"Listen to me. The job ain't to think outside the box. The job is to follow established procedure, to do things the way they teach you. That's the only thing the NYPD's organizational structure understands." He turned the corner and accelerated. "I'm serious about that. The department's a bureaucratic mess. They don't want advanced thinkers. They want cops who'll follow protocol." He glanced back at her. "I know you don't like me. You don't have to. But I'm giving you some good advice here. Clear?"

I'll verify that with Russo or Protch, but for now I'll accept it. "Clear."

"You don't have to believe me. But lemme give you an example. Buddy of mine retired a couple of years ago. Had a degree in mathematics, predictive logic. He developed this method where he could apply his mathematical formulas, his methodology, to his cases. He studied every home invasion perp who'd been caught in the city. From that, he developed a predictive model using a dozen points of commonality in those cases. And he solved every one of 'em."

"Very impressive, to say the least."

"It was impressive. But I'm the only person who knew about it, and only then because he got loose with the tongue while we were . . . while we were out drinking one night. Being an alcoholic, I hold my liquor better than some, and he was going on and on about this method he used to solve his cases. And after a while, I thought, man, there's something to what he's saying. Come morning, I guess he realized he might've run his mouth off. I said, 'Yeah, you told me all about it.' He just about begged me to keep my mouth shut. I never told anyone about it till just now. Because he woulda been kicked so far off the force he wouldn't be able to find his way back."

"Sounds backward to me." *And stupid.*

"Just telling you the way it is."

Vail looked at him. "I appreciate that."

"Russo likes you, that much is obvious. You didn't need me to tell you that. Let's just say he'd kill me if I did anything to fuck up your career."

She thought again of Protch's analogy of shit on the shoe.

I hope Thorne's familiar with that concept.

22

Vail and Thorne arrived at the apartment of a man who had called the Manhattan South homicide squad claiming to have information about the Dominic Crinelli murder.

But the witness was not home when they arrived. Thorne left his card and a note asking for a phone call.

From there they paid a visit to the ME, where Finkelstein apologized for lacking groundbreaking information.

"No surprises," he told them. "What you saw at the crime scene was what you get."

They returned to the squad and Thorne reviewed Vail's report. He sat back in his creaky metal chair and nodded. "Nice job. I see why Russo's so high on you."

"Assuming I drop the new age shit."

"Assuming that, yeah." He twisted his wrist and checked his watch. "We'll review that file Russo gave you, then we'll knock off. You gonna be around in case that witness calls about Crinelli?"

"I'm meeting my husband for dinner."

"Hopefully the guy won't call till morning, but I'm never so lucky. Where you going?"

"Landmark Tavern. Know it?"

"Good choice. Nice presentations. Chicken Rollatini's my favorite."

She looked at him.

"What, you don't think I know good food?"

Vail grinned sheepishly. "I didn't think so, no."

"A lot you don't know about me, Vail."

VAIL ARRIVED AT THE Landmark Tavern early. While standing out front waiting for Deacon, she lit a cigarette. *What am I doing? Start thinking like a mother, Karen.* She tossed it to the ground and killed it with her shoe, then used the pay phone on the corner to touch base with Russo.

"Is there any way to check if there were other victims with that kind of writing on their necks?"

"I'll poke around," he said. "See what I can find. You mean in the city?"

"I was thinking nationally. Just because this killer's here in New York right now doesn't mean he didn't kill in Montana, or Georgia, or Arizona."

"I don't think there's anything that c— Wait a minute. There was a memo . . . some kind of database that's going to be made accessible to the department. Vie-something. I'll see what I can find out."

"Hey, another question. Off topic." She repeated what Thorne told her about the bureaucratic approach of the NYPD and how they did not want outside the box thinkers.

"He was being straight with you. But I don't want you to listen to him. Keep thinking creatively, it suits you well. If we always do the same thing, we don't find new approaches and better ways of clearing cases. But the brass don't think that way. They're stuck in policies and procedures. There's some value in that, but it can also hold us back. We don't see important clues. But Timmy's right about it hurting you, so keep that thinking to yourself—or only share it with people you trust."

Vail caught sight of Deacon and motioned to him to wait.

"How are things going with you and Thorne?"

"We're good, actually. We've come to an understanding, I guess. This may sound crazy, but I think he's trying to mentor me. In his own way."

"He's a good cop, Karen. I wouldn't have set you up with him if he wasn't. That said, he's found his share of trouble with the drinking, and it's put a cloud over everything he does."

"Protch said he's an asshole and that I should be careful."

"I can't disagree. But his piss-poor attitude comes from the alcohol and other personal problems. I've known him a really long time, before all that shit hit. He was my first partner. Take what you can from him—but most important, help him solve that case."

VAIL JOINED DEACON inside the three story restaurant, which featured high, decorative ceilings and hand-tiled flooring.

"How'd you find this place?" Vail asked, craning her neck to take in the decor.

"Buddy at work recommended it," Deacon said. "Said they've been around since like 1886."

"That's right," the man behind them said. "Follow me." Menus in hand, he led the way into the main dining area. "We started out as an Irish waterfront saloon on the banks of the Hudson. We're still one of the oldest continually operating establishments in the city."

They were seated in the main dining room opposite the large bar, which featured the most elaborate wood carving on the facing of its counter that Vail had ever seen.

After studying the menu for a few moments, Vail closed it and said, "I was thinking of the Chicken Rollatini, but I'm going with the Long Island duck breast. You?"

"Steak."

The waiter was upon them immediately and introduced himself as Warren. He took their order and said, "Anything to drink with that?"

"What wine would you recommend?"

"A Napa Valley red, probably Charles Krug Cabernet. It's the oldest winery in the region. Are you familiar with Napa?"

"It's in California," Vail said. "That's about all I know."

"You must go someday," Warren said with flair. "They've been making exceptional wine there for over a hundred years, but up until twenty years ago they were considered vastly inferior to French wines."

"What happened twenty years ago?" Vail asked.

"Blind taste test," Deacon said. "Napa Valley wines beat French wines, put them on the map. Beautiful country."

"That's right," Warren said.

Vail cocked her head. "And how do you know this?"

Deacon chuckled. "Right before we met, my company sent me there for a leadership training conference. Lucked out, actually. The guy who was supposed to go got sick and they sent me in his place. We'll have to go someday. Get a bed and breakfast, kick back, do a mud bath—"

Warren cleared his throat. "Would you like the Cab, then, sir?"

"The Cab's fine. Just a glass for me."

"And you, miss?"

"Would love to. But I'm gonna pass."

Warren collected the menus and walked off.

"I've done some thinking about names," Deacon said.

"Really. Male or female?"

"Joseph or Jonathan if it's a boy, Rose or Lily if it's a girl. What do you think?"

Vail lifted her brow. *Giving it a name makes it more real. Am I really going to have a child? Me, a mother?*

"C'mon, just give me your first impression. Don't overthink it. You have a tendency to do that."

"What, me? Overthink things?"

They laughed.

He reached across the table and took her hand. "I can't help but think what my life would be like if I hadn't gone for pizza the night we met."

"Or me. Then again, not a whole lot of places to eat in Rosedale. The odds were kind of stacked in our favor."

Their food arrived a few minutes after Deacon's wine, and they made it through dinner without interruption. But just after Warren brought the dessert menus and made his recommendations, Vail's pager beeped. She checked the display.

"So much for chocolate cake. Gotta go meet that witness." She rose from her seat, tossed her napkin on the chair, and took a few steps toward the front of the restaurant. Out the front window she could see Thorne's car.

Vail scampered back to the table and gave Deacon a kiss. "Jonathan," she said. "Or Lily."

He grinned. "Okay."

"I'll see you back at home. Hopefully not too late."

VAIL CLIMBED INTO the vehicle and pulled the door shut.

"How was dinner?" Thorne asked as he swung out into traffic.

"We'll go back, for sure. You heard from the witness?"

"He called the office half an hour ago. I wanted to give you enough time to eat, so I told him we'd meet him at nine." He turned onto the West Side Highway and accelerated. "I put together a backgrounder on the guy." He lifted a manila folder from between the seats and handed it to Vail.

What'd he do, work through dinner? "Didn't you eat?"

"At my desk. I wanted to make sure we knew who we were dealing with, just in case he called."

Vail admired his dedication. As she opened the file and started to read, a call came over the radio.

"Anonymous caller reporting a panel van possibly containing fertilizer explosive. New York plate 4-0-9-Nancy-Sierra-Tango last seen headed east on 9th at 5-2 Street."

Vail snatched a look at a passing street sign. "That's us."

"Guess a truck bomb takes priority over a murder witness." Thorne hung a right on 52nd and drove along De Witt Clinton Park. The large field lights were on, meaning a game was in progress.

Vail turned on the siren and lights as Thorne swung around slower moving cars, fighting the end-of-rush-hour congestion.

"Seatbelt," Thorne shouted at her.

Shit, how could I forget that? She fastened it around her torso, placing a hand on her pregnant belly. She couldn't feel anything there yet, but she knew a lot was going on under the hood.

Thorne veered around a woman who jumped back onto the sidewalk as he passed. He continued on to Ninth Avenue and hung a right, then navigated around cars and taxis that stood in their way.

"Anything?" he yelled.

"No vans," Vail said, sitting forward in her seat and peering out the windshield. This area of the city had fewer skyscrapers but a larger number of high-rise apartment buildings than midtown.

"Wait, got it!" Vail pointed ahead with her right hand as she reached for the radio with her left.

"Plate?"

"Only got the numbers. But that's definitely it."

"Suspect spotted," Vail told Central over the din of the siren, "headed east on 9th, turning right on 43rd."

Thorne accelerated and swerved onto 43rd, remaining several car lengths back.

"Stop and search?" Vail asked.

"More like just 'stop.' We'll call in EOD, have *them* search. We're not gonna be yanking a door open on a van stuffed with goddamn bombs."

The van sped up as it neared the West Side Highway. It took the turn fast, two tires nearly leaving the pavement.

"If you've got no reason to run, you pull over when a cop car's behind you," Vail said. "Right?"

"Right. Now update our position. On 43rd, in pursuit. Suspect turned east onto West Side Highway."

Vail did as instructed.

"We got the light," Thorne said as he accelerated.

As they swung left onto the wide avenue, tires squealing, a sedan ran the red and broadsided Vail's car, striking the driver's door and forcing them perpendicular to the roadway.

Their vehicle flipped side over side, then came to rest on all four wheels.

Vail was the first to open her eyes. *Did I black out?* She tried to move, forgetting she was still strapped in. Feeling blindly for the release button, she found it and freed herself.

"Thorne," she said weakly. "Tim!"

He did not answer. She climbed across the center console and groped for the seatbelt, then unbuckled him. Got a pulse. *Still alive.* She felt around his torso, checking for blood and broken bones, and hit something hard in his jacket.

Vail patted it down and rooted out a stainless steel flask. As she pulled off the cap, she heard liquid sloshing around inside—and smelled alcohol. *If anyone finds this, they'll automatically assume he was driving drunk.* That would become the story, even if it weren't true. Given his history, he would be disgraced, if not fired.

Vail shoved it into her own pocket, then got out of the car. A man was running toward her.

"You okay?"

Vail was unsteady, nearly falling over as she tried to stand erect on her own, without holding on to the car.

"Call an ambulance," she said.

Another man yelled, "I got it," and sprinted off down the block, no doubt in search of a pay phone.

She went around to the driver's door, but it was too badly damaged to open, so she returned to the passenger's seat and again took a look at Thorne.

"Tim, you there? Answer me." She gently slapped his face, but he was nonresponsive. Two fingers against the carotid, again checking his pulse.

This time, however, it was not present. She grabbed his wrist, felt—same result.

Shit.

She grabbed his shirt and pulled, dragging him across the console and passenger seat, onto the sidewalk.

"Help me get him into your car," she said to the man who was still standing outside the vehicle.

"My car?"

"Now! His heart's stopped. No time to wait for the ambulance." They lifted him by his armpits and legs, and sloppily set him into the backseat of the man's Lexus. It was large and roomy, with soft leather.

As he drove away from the curb, Vail started CPR. While doing compressions, she said, "Closest hospital. You know where it is?"

"Straight shot down 45th. Only a few minutes away."

"Faster the better." As they passed under a streetlight, Vail saw a nasty head wound overlying the left portion of Thorne's face. "C'mon, Tim, stay with me. We're almost there."

A minute later, the man was maneuvering the Lexus into the emergency bay. He came around and pulled open the back door while yelling something at someone nearby. Vail turned to see two medics running toward her wheeling a stretcher between them.

"Broadside MVA," she said as they transferred Thorne to the gurney. "Heart stopped about four or five minutes ago, I started CPR and transported."

A nurse came running out of the hospital with a small briefcase-size device in her hand. She popped it open and pulled out two hand paddles.

"Charging. Clear!"

The other two medics removed their hands and stepped back. "Clear."

The nurse pressed the paddles to Thorne's chest and zapped him. His torso rose.

"Sinus rhythm. Get him inside."

"You a friend?" the medic asked, apparently realizing that since Thorne was black and Vail was Caucasian, she was likely not next of kin.

"Yeah, his—partner. We're cops."

As the man backed into the hospital, he said, "C'mon in, get yourself looked at."

I'm fine. Thorne's the one who needs to be treated.

"I think I'm okay." But as the dark glass doors slid closed, Vail caught her reflection—and saw that her face was covered with blood.

Her hands found her abdomen.

And then she ran into the ER.

VAIL WAS EXAMINED by an obstetrics nurse, who did a urine test to confirm the pregnancy. Not surprisingly, it was positive. After a general exam pertaining to the accident, they cleaned the blood off her face and dressed her two scalp wounds, one requiring six stitches. Next they splinted her sprained right index finger—sustained in the accident or while transferring Thorne to the Lexus—and then the obstetrician entered the treatment suite to give her a pelvic ultrasound.

"This'll determine your gestational age, which will dictate treatment. It'll also give us a look inside to make sure there hasn't been any trauma to the fetus."

A moment later, a noise like a galloping horse emanated from the console.

Vail jerked her head up. "Is that a heartbeat? My baby's heartbeat?"

"It is," the obstetrician said, keeping his eyes on the screen.

Vail watched the monitor, the blacks and whites and grays undulating as the doctor shifted the sound head.

"So," he said, "looks like you're six weeks pregnant." He handed the device to the nurse. "You also have some vaginal spotting, which is consistent with what I saw on the ultrasound. You've got a subchorionic hemorrhage."

"A what? A hemorrhage?" *That can't be good.*

"Yes. But it's very, very minor. And it's not surprising given the accident you had. Good news is that it'll resolve by about twelve weeks and you'll have a normal pregnancy." He lifted his chart and clicked his pen. "We'll draw some blood and monitor you for a bit."

"Is that it?"

The doctor finished his note, then made eye contact for the first time. "There are some risks. An impact like this could have detrimental effects on your fetus. I didn't find signs of blunt force trauma, which is very positive. The fetus looks healthy, from what I can tell. Overall, I think you're going to be fine. No heavy lifting for two months, and no vigorous exercising."

Yeah, like chasing perps across apartment building roofs.

"So you should take it easy, no work for a couple of weeks."

"You're kidding. Take two weeks off?"

The doctor peered over his glasses at her. "Miss Vail, you want to keep this baby?"

Vail gave the man a look.

"Then follow my recommendations. Make an appointment with your OB, have him do another ultrasound. If the bleeding's stopped, that's when you can safely return to work." He made a final note in the chart and then left the room.

Take time off? I just started doing this detective thing. Will Thorne be back to work before me? What do they do in a situation like this? They can't leave no one working the case so soon after the murder.

"You can get dressed," the nurse said.

Vail slid off the exam table. "Any word on Tim Thorne?"

"No idea. Sorry."

Vail had wanted to call Deacon to tell him about the accident, but she knew he would only worry. It would be better for him to see her in the flesh, and know that she was okay when she started describing what had happened. For all he knew, she was still dealing with the witness they were supposed to be interviewing.

Until she received an update on Thorne's condition, however, she would not be going home. She called Russo and told him what happened—but she did not mention the part about having to take time off work. She would save that for when he arrived.

She walked into the waiting room and saw a black woman and teenage girl seated in a corner, holding hands and leaning against each other.

Vail introduced herself, taking them for Thorne's wife and daughter; she was mostly correct, the exception being that the woman was his ex-wife.

They had not heard any news on Thorne's status, other than the fact that he was still in surgery.

Surgery. Well, that's more than I knew before. She did not want to ask what the surgery was for, so she merely nodded and then curled up on the couch in the waiting room lounge and dozed off.

When a doctor entered, she sat up too quickly and had to steady herself from the dizziness.

"Are you Tasha Thorne?"

Thorne's ex-wife nodded.

He lowered his voice but Vail could still hear. "I'm Dr. Lederman. I operated on your husband." He took a breath. "The impact caused a traumatic rupture of his aorta. It's common in automobile accidents and likely due to different rates of deceleration of the heart and the aorta, which is held in place in a fixed position. I'm sorry to have to be the one to tell you this, but he passed away fifteen minutes ago, during surgery."

Vail sat there, no longer listening. She had only met Thorne last night and her first—and second—impressions of the man had been less than stellar. Yet she had come to respect him, even like him.

And now he was dead.

WHEN RUSSO ARRIVED, he saw Tasha Thorne and embraced her, no doubt taking their tear-streaked faces as the bad news he didn't want to hear.

They talked, hugged again, and then he joined Vail when Tasha and her daughter were taken into a room to complete some paperwork.

Russo sat down heavily, visibly stunned.

"I'm sorry," she said.

"What happened?"

"We were in high speed pursuit of that van," she said, assuming Russo had already been briefed on the explosives-laden truck. "Car ran a red, plowed into us. Broadside, driver's door. We had lights and siren, right of way . . ." She closed her eyes as the accident played out in her thoughts. "I liked the guy. I only knew him twenty-four hours, but . . ."

"I'm sorry too." Russo pulled her close. "Just so you know, the department brass is on the way over, including the commissioner. And Mayor Giuliani. They'll be here any minute."

Vail sat up. "What about the van? Did we get it?"

"We did, about half a mile from your accident. Another friggin' 'patriot' movement. Domestic terrorism. Good thing we got 'em, 'cause they were wired for sound. It would've been as bad as Oklahoma City if they'd detonated." He sat there, thinking, then said, "Timmy didn't die for nothing. I guess that's something."

Not much consolation as far as I'm concerned. Dead is dead.

"How 'bout you? You okay?"

"I'm fine. Some stitches in my head and a sprained finger. Oh, and something called a subchorionic hemorrhage."

"Hemorrhage? The baby—"

"It's okay. It's—I heard its heartbeat. It was pretty cool."

"There's life right there in a nutshell, isn't it, now?"

"Come again?"

Russo took a deep breath. "Life and death. A new life inside you . . . balances out Timmy's death." He looked at her, saw her confusion, and said, "Yeah, it's bullshit, isn't it? Dead is dead."

Vail nodded knowingly.

"Something else, Russo." She hesitated. *Do I really want to tell him this?*

"What?" Russo asked when she did not continue.

"The doc said I should be off work for two weeks. I know this is a really bad time, with the murder and now Tim's dead and I'm the only one with continuity on the case—"

"I'll reassign it." Russo stood up and pulled out his phone. "If the department doc gets wind of this hemorrhage, you're gonna have nine months to rest up."

"No. I'll—I've—I've got a sprained index finger on my shooting hand. Can't pull the trigger. The doc'll give me some time off. All I need is a couple of weeks, soon as the bleeding stops. And then I want to be back on the case."

"You take care of yourself." He lowered his voice. "And the baby. There'll be other cases."

But—No, don't take me off this case.

"I have a feeling this asshole's gonna kill again. You'll probably be back on board sooner than you think."

Vail sat forward and buried her face in her hands.

Far as I'm concerned, not soon enough.

23

>ASTORIA. QUEENS
SATURDAY. MAY 19. 1973

Livana arrived home with Dmitri at 10:30 PM. Although she had told Fedor on the phone that Dmitri was going to be fine, she had no way of knowing that her assessment may have been premature. She was speaking emotionally, relieved to have her son back.

But now, seeing his demeanor—withdrawn, refusing to make eye contact, not wanting to talk—she knew something was wrong.

They sat on the front porch, the kids playing cards at the kitchen table. Actually Cassandra and Niklaus were playing. Dmitri was sitting there, not playing, not speaking.

A breeze blew and Livana drew her sweater tight around her body.

"I'm worried about him."

Fedor said they needed to give him some time. "It was a frightening experience that no child should ever live through. He probably didn't know what was going on, why they took him. Or if he'd even see you and Cassie again. Coming so soon after losing his father, he's just in a bad way right now."

Livana wiped away a tear. "He told the detective they hit him, used a belt on his back. They did other stuff, which he wouldn't talk about."

Fedor fisted his right hand. "Bastards. I wish there was something—" He closed his eyes and sighed deeply.

Livana buried her face in her hands. "God knows what else they did to him. I stopped Proschetta from asking him anymore questions. He was really upset and I thought he'd been through enough."

"Whatever they did to Dmitri . . . the details . . . it doesn't matter. All that matters is that he's back and we'll help him feel loved and secure. He'll be okay. Just give him time."

Livana wanted to think that Fedor was right, but she knew deep in her heart that something had been taken from her son today, something he would never get back: his innocence, his sense of security.

He had come face-to-face with evil, and he had the scars to prove it. She and Basil had done everything they could to shield him from the violence that permeated some neighborhoods. Theirs enjoyed relative safety. She never would have thought anything like this could happen.

"I was thinking," Fedor said, "while you were gone. I had a lot of time to think," he said with a wince. "It was all I could do to keep from going crazy. I wanted to take the kids to the park, let them burn off some steam, take our minds off it, but I didn't want to miss your call."

Livana studied his face, and when he did not continue, she said, "You said you were thinking. About what?"

He looked away. "It's not safe here. We're not safe. Then I realized I was being paranoid, worrying for nothing. This thing with Dmitri freaked me out, I was overreacting. But a couple of hours later I got a phone call. I thought it was you."

"Who was it?"

"He didn't give his name." Fedor sat there, staring at the stoop. "Didn't need to. He was obviously with the Castiglias. He said we should move out of the city and not come back. For any reason."

"Move away? What for? We did what they told us to do."

"I think it's to punish us, to make us leave our home, community, my job. He said that just because we're cooperating today doesn't mean we'll keep our mouths shut six months, a year from now. Or two years from now. There's no statute of limitations on murder. And since the kids may've seen Crinelli's face—"

"They didn't!"

"*I* know that. But *they* don't. And they're not about to take my word for it."

"I can't believe this. We have to tell Detective Prosc—"

"No. He said that if they hear anything about us going to the police, they'll . . ." His voice trailed off.

"They'll what?"

"They'll kill all of us, starting with the kids. They'd rather not wipe out a whole family, but they will if we leave them no choice. Can you believe that? That's what he told me. Like they're some kind of good Samaritans by not killing all of us." He turned to face Livana. "He said they'd know if we went to the police. They have cops on their payroll."

Livana shuddered. "My god, what have we gotten ourselves into?" She stood up and started pacing. And then she couldn't help herself: the tears started rolling down her cheeks and she dropped to her knees, sobbing, the stress of the past couple of months reaching a crescendo and boiling over like a pot of water on a high flame.

Fedor knelt beside her and draped an arm around her shoulders. "It's going to be okay. Listen to me, Liv. We're going to be fine."

She sucked in her breath, dragged a sleeve across her eyes. "How can you say that, Fedor?"

"Remember I told you I had a lot of time to think? I came up with a solution. Someone I work with, a few months ago he told me about this guy he knows who moved to Ellis Island."

"Ellis Island. The place where immigrants came over to the US, back in the early 1900s? I didn't know people lived there."

"Nobody's been there for about twenty years. Supposedly there's no one on the island except for a few people who live in the old hospital complex. For the most part, it's abandoned."

"Abandoned? How can we live there?"

"I haven't figured it all out, but we'll make it work."

"Why don't we just move to Connecticut, or Rhode Island, or—"

"My grandparents. I can't be that far away."

Fedor's grandfather was eighty-three and his grandmother eighty-four, having been the first of his family to settle in America from Greece twenty-five years ago. Livana knew he was very close with them and had promised his mother when she was dying of lung cancer that he would look after them.

Fedor picked up a baseball-size rock and played with it in his hands. "I'm going to have to come by and check on them, even if the Castiglias don't like it. The nursing home staff have to see me, so they know I'm watching over their care. It's very important, or they'll be neglected."

"But—"

"I'll be very careful. I mean, really, can they fault me for taking care of my old grandparents?"

"Look what they did to Basil, to Dmitri. These bastards are not reasonable, Fedor."

"This is the way it's going to be. They'll have to accept it." He shrugged. "If you want to take the kids and go somewhere else, I understand. I won't stop you. I can't stop you."

"No," Livana said without hesitation. "They've suffered enough loss. I want them to be around you and Niklaus. You're their family. Now more than ever."

"You could also go back to Greece."

"For what?" Livana shook her head. "We've got nothing there. No friends, no family. No work. No future. Here at least we have each other." She thought a moment, then said, "What will we do for money? Food?"

"I'll get a job in the city, as far away from Astoria as I can get. There are millions of people in Manhattan. Our paths won't cross. I'll keep a low profile. The job doesn't have to be anything fancy, just enough for what we'll need. We'll be living rent free, which is a really big deal."

Livana set her head back against the wrought iron railing, thinking. In her wildest dreams, when she and Basil had left Kastoria, she never thought that in a matter of several years he would be dead and she would be living on an abandoned island, banished from mainstream life by the Mafia.

"What do you think?"

She pulled herself from her fugue and looked at him. "Is it safe? The island?"

"Is it safe." As he pondered the question, Fedor tossed the rock onto the postage stamp-size lawn. "Look at it this way, Liv. It's safer than here. For us, at least."

24

>ELLIS ISLAND
UPPER NEW YORK BAY
JERSEY CITY, NEW JERSEY
40°41'58.4"N 74°2'22.5"W
MONDAY, MAY 21, 1973

The following Monday, while the children were at school and Fedor was at work, Livana went to the Queens library in Long Island City and spent thirty minutes reading the *World Book Encyclopedia*, learning about Ellis Island.

She knew that it served as a major way station for immigrants coming from a variety of countries, but she had not realized that it operated for six decades, beginning in 1892. Millions arrived on boats and gained entry, while some were turned away as being infirm or diseased.

New arrivals were observed as they climbed the stairs from the baggage area to the facility's Great Hall. Those who had difficulty with the steps were more likely to be rejected as lacking the ability to maintain gainful employment in America.

According to the encyclopedia, the people who were too ill to enter the US were placed in the hospital infirmary on Island 2 or in the psychiatric ward on Island 3 of the contiguous three-island compound. After they were well enough to travel, they were permitted to enter the country—or deported. Some never made it out of the hospital.

As someone who had emigrated to the United States in modern times, Livana empathized strongly with the thousands who set sail for America, full of hope. She knew how they felt.

And yet the precariousness of her own dream caused her to wonder: if she had known what was in store for them, would they have ever left Greece?

It was a moot point, she knew. Nothing could turn back the calendar and give her the opportunity to choose over again. Life had thrown her a vicious curve, and she now had to push forward. She and Basil were survivors as youths, so they would find a way, once again, to persevere. Rather, *she* would.

Livana paged further into the article and found information on what appeared to be the place where she, Fedor, and the kids would live: Officially known as US Marine Hospital 43, or the Ellis Island Immigrant Hospital, the complex consisted of over a dozen brick buildings built from 1902 through 1908.

Lacking someone to leave the children with, Fedor and Livana decided they would all travel to the island on the following Saturday to scout it out and make sure it was habitable. Although she had reservations about the move, Fedor felt they had already spent too long in town. Each minute they remained in Astoria they risked retaliation. They used the week to pack and prepare.

According to the friend of Fedor's coworker, Island 3 was a paradise lost. Livana felt that a woman's sensibilities about what was feasible would at worst supplement that assessment, and at best point out gross inadequacies that would make a life there insurmountable.

What's more, taking the word of Fedor's acquaintance about the comments made by someone *he* knew was dubious at best. That said, she did not share her concerns with Fedor. Until she saw the place for herself, there was no point. And other than some wasted time, there was little to lose by packing their belongings and preparing for the best.

"Where is this place?" Cassandra asked.

"Remember that class trip last year to the Statue of Liberty? It's right near there. In fact, it's so close you'll be able to see it from where we're going."

"I don't want to go," Niklaus said. "Why do we have to move?"

Fedor shared a look with Livana. "Sometimes there are things that only adults understand," she said. She turned around to face Niklaus, who was belted into the pickup's jump seat behind Fedor. "This is one of those times." She knew it was a poor answer, but she could not tell him the truth. For that matter, kids were intuitive, and they probably had a decent sense as to what was going on. If not now, eventually—three years, maybe five—they would figure it out.

After renting a motorboat for the day from a merchant near Battery Park, Fedor and Livana loaded up suitcases from the Dodge and set off for the iconic—now abandoned—island retreat.

As they approached, Miss Liberty, which had been a small figure in the distance, grew in size. Although it was still a ten-minute ride away, it looked much closer to its three hundred foot height than when they had pushed off from Manhattan. The day was bright and sunny, and her green skin sparkled against the blue sky.

Fedor brought them around to the south end of the island, closest to the statue, and maneuvered them against the granite block seawall. He tied the boat to one of three vertical steel girders piercing the water's surface. The pillars, which were likely left over from a structure Fedor could not identify, would serve them well as a temporary docking point.

After offloading the luggage and leaving the children to watch over it, Fedor and Livana searched the buildings that covered an area encompassing about a dozen football fields.

While the vegetation was grossly overgrown, the landscaping had a park-like feel. Large trees lined the perimeter of the central quad, brimming with greenery—weeds, vines, and fallen branches.

"Hate to admit it," Livana said, "but this place is really nice. Very pleasant. And no one around."

"I told you, my friend said it was beautiful."

Livana grinned at him. "I had my doubts. But it's winning me over."

While coursing the island, they encountered very few people, as expected. There was one other young family and several rough drifter types that made Livana uneasy. They engaged none of them, figuring that these people were all here for a reason, and it was none of their business. If they left them alone, perhaps they would return the favor. In time, if they struck up a relationship, that was fine.

An unshaven male with long, greasy hair leered at Livana as they passed by him. They stopped and Fedor stared him down. The man turned away and then entered one of the buildings, pulling the door closed behind him.

Livana brought her arms across her chest. "That was creepy."

Fedor clenched his jaw. "He bothers you, you let me know. Remember what Basil told Dmitri after he was bullied? You gotta look these guys in the eyes, stand up to them, make them back down."

After patrolling the grounds, they examined the structures' exteriors and found them in good condition—their tile roofs were sound and they would, with a little work, protect them from the elements. The interiors, however, were in severe disrepair. Windows were broken; doors no longer sat squarely on their hinges. The plumbing ran rusty water and electricity was inoperable because the generators had been shut down, no doubt twenty years ago when the islands were abandoned.

The carpeting had disintegrated, leaving bare wood plank floors that were coated with years of filth. But the architecture was intact, and the design was impressive, with high ceilings and arched window casings.

"This place was beautiful," she said. "Hard to believe it was a hospital."

"This one was a staff house," Fedor said. "There's a fuse box in the hallway listing the rooms of each person who lived here."

The building had a view of New York City, the bay, and Liberty Island. Livana thought the nighttime view of Manhattan's lights would be uplifting. And after being banished to this abandoned hideaway, she welcomed anything that could raise their spirits. With some work, she felt that this could be a very pleasant place to live.

They found the children where they had left them. After lugging their suitcases into the building, Niklaus and Cassandra began fighting over which room they would each take.

Dmitri, not surprisingly, had no preference, so Niklaus assigned him to the one adjacent to his own, while Cassandra claimed the one across the hall that had an attached bathroom. Livana and Fedor took the two bedrooms on the second floor.

Livana had thought of perhaps sharing one with Fedor, but she felt awkward suggesting it. There had never been any attraction between them. Although she knew he was a good soul and she had depended on him since Basil's murder, that was not enough to assume their relationship could blossom.

Livana remained on the island to clean the dust-filled rooms and dirt-covered floors while Fedor returned with Niklaus to Battery Park to load the rest of their belongings and purchase cleaning supplies and food as well as everything they would need to make the house warm during winter and watertight during inclement weather. He also planned to purchase locks for the exterior doors. It seemed silly because there were so few people living there, but at the same time there was no police presence, and thus no deterrent for someone bent on doing harm.

After their last load, Niklaus remained on the island while Fedor returned the boat to its owner. Three hours later, he poked his head into their new house and told Livana he had bought something for them.

They went out to their makeshift dock where a fourteen-foot aluminum powerboat was tied off.

"You bought that?" Niklaus asked. "For us?"

"We need a way to get back and forth. When I was talking with the guy I rented the boat from, I saw this sign a few doors over that said 'Marine Exchange.' I told him I was looking to trade in my pickup truck—"

"You got rid of the truck?" Livana asked.

"I didn't have enough money to buy a boat and keep the truck. When we go to the city, we'll use the subway to get around."

Livana knew it was a more difficult decision than Fedor was letting on. His truck was new, something he had always wanted. Now it was gone.

"So this guy took me over to someone he knew at the exchange," Fedor said. "He was knocking off early, but I told him what I wanted and when he saw the truck, he decided he could stay a little later to get the deal done. He gave me the boat and cash, which I used to buy waterbeds for us."

"What's a waterbed?" Livana asked.

"Some new thing I saw on the cover of a magazine at the marina. You fill it with water and it's a mattress. I have to put together the frames and buy the rest of them tomorrow, but I should be able to get two together tonight." Fedor gestured at the boat. "Some Northern Lakes freshwater fisherman traded it in for a new model. What do you think?"

Niklaus stepped up to the water's edge. "Can I drive it?"

Fedor looked at Livana. "Yeah, of course. Dmitri, you too. Would you like that?"

Dmitri, looking down at the ground, said "I guess," in a low voice.

"Cassie, you're gonna learn too. It's important for all of you to know how to drive it, just in case you ever have to use it in an emergency and I'm not around."

"Can we do it now?" Niklaus asked.

"Not now." As Livana led them back into the house, she said, "We've got other things to get done to get this place ready for tonight. We're all going to pitch in so it goes faster. We've got about two hours of light left, so we need to make sure that once it gets dark, we know where everything is."

"What do you mean?" Cassandra asked.

"There's no electricity." Niklaus flipped the switch on the wall. Nothing happened. "No lights."

Cassandra looked at Livana. "So what are we—"

"We'll use candles," Livana said. "And flashlights. We'll figure it out. There's a lot we have to figure out." She gathered the kids together and put her arms around them. "Look, I know things have been really awful for us these past few months. But we're turning a new page. We're about to start an exciting adventure in our lives. We're living in a gorgeous place. Very few people are as lucky as we are right now."

"I don't feel lucky," Dmitri mumbled.

Livana reached over and ran her fingers through his hair. "From now on, we're going to learn a lot about ourselves. We're going to depend on each other, support each other. That's what families do."

WHILE LIVANA AND Cassandra cleaned the house, Fedor worked with Niklaus for three hours, well past dark, putting new locks on the exterior doors and then assembling the beds.

Dmitri sat in his room reading his paperback, *Stranger in a Strange Land* by Robert Heinlein. Livana wanted him to contribute like Niklaus and Cassandra but did not force the issue.

They finished assembling Cassandra's bed first, then Livana and Niklaus filled it while Fedor took one of the candles and headed upstairs to work on Livana's.

An hour later, as Livana put the finishing touches on Cassandra's room, trying to make it as homey as possible without furniture, her daughter sat on the newly made bed and started to cry.

Livana set aside the clothing she was laying out and sat down beside her. "What's wrong?"

She leaned into her mother, and Livana put an arm around her. After taking a moment to compose herself, she said, "I miss Daddy."

Livana bit her lip, fighting back the urge to let emotion overcome her. At the moment, she needed to be strong for her daughter.

"I know, honey. I miss him too."

"Why'd they kill him? Why'd he get into that fight?"

Livana stroked her hair. "I don't have any good answers for you. I'd like to be able to tell you something that makes sense. But I can't. Your father wished none of this ever happened."

"But why did those people kill him? Why'd they kidnap Dmitri?"

Livana glanced over at her son's room, across the hall. The door was closed and she hoped he could not hear them. In a low voice, she said, "There are bad people in this world, honey. We were very unlucky in how things happened. The men who hurt your father were friends with the man who started the fight, and they were angry with Daddy. Bad people do bad things." Her explanation was accurate but woefully inadequate; she knew the details did not matter. Her daughter was upset, and giving her reasons for why her father was no longer alive would not ease the pain.

"I know you miss him, Cassie. We all do. But you have your memories of him, of going to the park, the playground, the zoo—remember when he was making faces with the chimpanzee?"

Cassandra laughed. "That was so funny. It was like they were talking to each other."

"That's what I want you to think about whenever you miss him. Think of the good times you had with him. No one can ever take those memories away from you."

After a couple of minutes, Cassandra said, "You really think we'll be able to live here? On this island?"

"It's going to work out great. It's an adventure. I bet we'll look back in a few years and realize what a blessing it was, coming here." She examined her daughter's face, wiped away a tear with her thumb. "All right?"

"I guess." She turned and looked over her shoulder. "Is Dmitri going to be okay?"

Livana tried not to let her face betray her thoughts. Truth was, she had no idea if Dmitri was going to recover from that trauma. The doctor who treated him at the hospital said that it could have long-term consequences, and that to expect it to take "possibly years" for him recover.

"We have to give him time, honey. Be patient with him." She rose from the bed. "Now go wash up and brush your teeth."

"But the water's dirty."

"*Rusty*, not dirty. Fedor said it's because the pipes are old and haven't been used in a very long time. Let the water run a bit, it'll clear up."

Livana walked out, stood in front of Dmitri's closed door, then turned and headed upstairs.

25

> ›263-37 147TH AVENUE
ROSEDALE, QUEENS
WEDNESDAY, DECEMBER 24, 1997

Vail walked outside her house with six-month-old Jonathan on her hip, and stopped before she could pull the wood door closed. The snow that had fallen yesterday was augmented during the early morning hours, enough to require her to go back inside and grab a shovel so she could get her car out of the driveway.

She handed Jonathan to Deacon, who was making coffee to take to work in his thermos.

"No, no. I'll do it." He gave his son a peck on the forehead and then handed him back to Vail. After retrieving the shovel from the basement landing, he cleared a path for the cars and they were on their way: Vail to the day care facility and Deacon to his office in Sheepshead Bay.

Deacon had finished his schooling and taken the CPA licensing exam two years ago. He was now working his way up the corporate ladder, impressing executives along the way and earning a spot in the chief financial officer's office.

He had worked from home two days a week while Vail was on bedrest recuperating from her motor vehicle accident—which, coupled with her blue mood from Tim Thorne's death, made her difficult to be around.

She returned to work as soon as her ultrasound was clear of bleeding, two and a half weeks to the day from the accident, but the serial case had been handed off to another detective in the bureau. Vail returned to patrol with Leslie Johnson, but as soon as her standard two-year probationary period ended, she applied to become an undercover cop in narcotics.

Two days later, she got the call. But instead of reporting to narcotics, she was picked up by the Brooklyn South gang division because they needed a female for a case.

It was difficult, at times dangerous work, doing drug and gun buys and "ghosting" confidential informants and other undercovers during operations—activities Deacon repeatedly criticized. Vail maintained it was a short-term placement, something that should fast-track her for obtaining her detective's shield—in department parlance, "the shield."

Deacon's concerns led to an argument two months ago when she was on an undercover stakeout, sitting on a gangbanger's house, her sergeant in the passenger seat catching some shuteye. A call came in on her department BlackBerry, which she had been issued specifically for this case. She had never used a cell phone before, but a quick primer by her chief gave her a working knowledge of the device.

She fished the handset out of her jeans pocket and answered the call.

"Yeah, hi, who's this?" the male voice asked.

"Who's this?" Vail said. "You called me." Jack, her partner, had told her that when someone called and didn't seem to know who answered, her goal was to get them talking so she could ascertain who it was without giving away any information.

"I'm sorry," the man said, "what'd you say?"

"No, what'd *you* say?" *Jesus, this is such a stupid dance. Just give me something.*

"I'm not sure who I called, so I was wondering—"

"Wait, Joey Barnes? That you?" Barnes was in the intel division. "This is Karen Vail, Brooklyn South Gang."

"I didn't know you had a phone. I'm trying to reach Jack. Where are you right now? Where's your sergeant?"

"Frank's in the backseat, sleeping. We're sitting on a house. Jack's out making a buy. Why?"

"Wake him," Barnes said. "We got a problem."

"What kind of problem?"

"You got a CI by the name of Rocky?"

Oh shit. "Don't tell me he's dead."

"Worse, he's been compromised. His cover's blown. He's up in the South Bronx in an apartment at a Latin King meeting, they're beating him and he just gave up your partner—"

"Wait—Jack's cover's blown?"

"Big-time. I tried paging him, but he didn't answer—"

Vail disconnected the call, pulled her Glock, and yelled, "Frank, wake up, I'm going in!" Then she pushed open her door and ran down the block toward the house they were staking out.

Jack was inside and hopefully still alive. The plan was for him to wear a wire but he had decided against it because the gang leader, Dimas Montanez, had grown suspicious in the past few weeks. If his paranoia peaked and he decided to have everyone in the house remove their shirts, Jack did not want to be caught with a device taped to his skin. He would've been interrogated and shot—or injected with a lethal overdose of heroin and dumped somewhere in the South Bronx.

Vail got to the front door, vapor pouring from her mouth. Hyperventilating.

She was prepared to burst in and start shooting. Not the way she had been taught to handle this kind of situation, and not a smart way of going about it. But sometimes you have to throw the book out the window if your partner's life is on the line and seconds and clear-headed thought are the difference between living and dying.

She took a deep breath, cleared her mind.

Do the unexpected. Catch them off guard.

Vail pulled off her sweater and wrapped it around her hand, covering her handgun. She yanked on her blouse and ripped it by the neckline, pulled it half out of her jeans, then spit on her hand and grabbed a handful of dirt from the planter by her feet. She smeared the mud mixture across her face, then swung her head left to right, messing her hair, and gave it an extra few tosses with her free hand. Then she banged on the door.

She wanted to glance out into the darkness in the direction of their car—*where the hell's Frank?*—but seconds were ticking by, and—

"Yeah. Who is it and what the fuck you want?"

Through the door, Vail yelled back, "I need to talk to Jack. Now!"

"Go away, bitch."

"No!" Vail stepped forward and started pounding on the door with her left hand. "Get Jack. Tell him it's Karen and she's goddamn pissed at him!"

More banging. *C'mon, asshole, it's easier to have him answer the door than to deal with me.*

"I want Jack," she whined. She fisted her hand and thumped the thick wood again.

The front door swung open, Jack standing in front of a tall Hispanic dude, a gold tooth glistening in the hallway light.

Holy crap, there he is. Dimas Montanez, in the flesh.

"Karen," Jack said, "what the fuck?"

"I know you said not to bother you, but I need you to come out. It's important. Some guy grabbed me up and beat me. Said he knows you—"

A phone rang and Montanez answered it. He listened a second as Vail tried to signal Jack with her eyes without Montanez noticing—

"What?" the banger said into the handset.

"C'mon out, Jack, I gotta talk with you. Now!"

She was about to grab his collar when she noticed Montanez's eyes widen. He looked at Jack, then leaned away and started to reach behind his back—"

"Jack, get down," Vail shouted as she brought up her handgun and blew a hole in Montanez's chest. She nailed him in the forehead with her second shot, and the large man fell back into the wall.

Jack ran out the front door with Vail, where they nearly collided with Frank, who was headed toward them.

"Go, go, go!" Vail said, pulling the car keys from her pocket. They made it into their vehicle and Vail screeched the tires as she hung a U-turn, gunshots exploding behind them along with the rear windshield.

"Holy shit," Jack said, falling sideways in the rear seat among the shattered glass fragments. "You crazy?"

Frank grabbed the dashboard, trying to steady himself in the fishtailing car. "What the hell is going on?"

"Jack's cover's blown. My CI just ratted him out in Brooklyn. I needed to get you out of there, Jack. That phone call Montanez got when we were standing at the door? That was your death warrant."

Frank turned around and looked at Jack, who had pushed himself up in the seat.

The look on his face was all the thanks Vail needed. A week later, in recognition of her outstanding performance, Russo and her chief presented her with a specialist shield.

Everyone congratulated her with a straight face, but afterward Russo gave her a wink and a smile. Just like a proud father.

26

›MANHATTAN SOUTH HOMICIDE SQUAD
WEDNESDAY, DECEMBER 24, 1997

When Vail walked into the homicide squad at five minutes to six after her team had arrested a gangbanger who murdered a rival member, Russo was already there, waiting for her.

"Don't take your coat off," he said, his voice tight. "Let's go."

Vail followed him out the door and toward the police vehicles parked at the curb. "Gee, Karen," she said mockingly. "How are you? I haven't talked to you in weeks. Oh, and how's Jonathan doing?"

"Yeah," Russo said. "I don't have time for small talk." He moved around to the driver's door and unlocked it.

She got in and buckled. "What's going on? Where are we going? It's Christmas Eve. I was getting ready to go home as soon as we booked—"

"Here." He handed her a thick envelope. "Merry Christmas."

"It's not wrapped."

Russo gave her a look. "Are you kidding me?"

Vail opened it—and her heart skipped a beat. Her throat caught. And then she smiled. It was a detective's shield. *Her* shield. She whipped her head left, caught Russo's gaze.

He glanced up as he maneuvered the car hard on the curve and headed down the street.

"I don't understand. I've still got like nine or ten months before I'm eligible."

"No shit. It's never happened in the history of the department. So you should feel privileged. Honored."

"I do." She looked over at him. "So you're my rabbi?"

"I am, but it took more than that to get this done. The department had a need. You had the skills and a shitload of promise. So congratulations."

She looked down at the shield. It was shiny and gold, with blue lettering. Best of all, it had DETECTIVE stamped into the metal. *It's beautiful.* "Thank-you."

"You earned it. That specialist shield you got for saving Jack Bautista's ass a couple months ago didn't hurt. But believe me, you wouldn't have that gem in your hands if I didn't think you'd do the badge proud."

Vail continued to turn it and view it at various angles, trying to catch the stray glow of a passing streetlight.

"There's a ceremony at One Police Plaza you'll need to attend. We all get together two, three times a year to hand out promotions. Big shindig. Commish is there, all the chiefs, the mayor, the press. You're called up to the stage and the commissioner shakes your hand and gives you a certificate."

"Like a college graduation."

Russo frowned. "Yeah, just like that. Not really." He glanced over at her. "Okay, maybe a little bit."

"I'll be there."

"Bet your ass you will," he said. "Normally you wouldn't get your shield till the ceremony but I thought this was a reasonable exception."

"No argument from me."

"Didn't think so. Now with that out of the way, the real work starts. You notice we're in the car."

Vail, still admiring the shield, looked up. "What? Yeah, we're in the car."

"Our killer's left us another vic."

"Shit."

Well there went the euphoria. Popped like a balloon.

"Yeah, shit. Because the detective I handed the case to when you landed in bed, he just retired."

And that's why my promotion was pushed up. No complaints from me.

"You're smart enough to figure it out yourself, so I'll just come out and say it: because of the circumstances, I made the case to promote you now, rather than later, to let you take over this case. This is the third vic. This is officially a huge goddamn problem, and I wanted you working it. I don't want the news to catch on that we got a serial, or we may get panic. Let's work it quietly. You think you can handle that?"

"Yeah, of course."

"Good. I don't want the killer to know we've keyed in on that. Let him think we're a bunch of idiots. He may get sloppy, make mistakes, because he won't think we're capable of catching him."

"Okay, if you say so."

"I say so."

"What about the gang unit?"

"Transfer's in the works. I took care of it."

Russo pulled the car down 4th Street and stopped in front of the walk-up apartment building. He double-parked and they met the first-on-scene officer, who was standing guard at the entrance. Crime scene tape was stretched across the pavement in a rectangle, securing as much of the area as practical, given that no one knew what was significant to the case.

They ascended the steps to the front door, which was unlocked.

"ME?" Russo asked.

"Delayed," the officer said. "Be here soon as possible. CSU's fifteen out."

Russo stepped inside and flipped the nearby wall switch, but nothing happened. "Yo, what's the deal here? No light."

"Electricity's out," the officer said. "Don't know if it's related. I called Con Ed."

Power company's not gonna be much help at a crime scene.

Vail pulled a small penlight from her pocket. Russo did likewise. "Well, this kind of sucks."

"CSU's got Kliegs and extension cords they can snake out to an adjacent building. We'll get a generator if need be. Won't be an issue. Till then, we do our best." He reached into his pocket and handed her a pair of booties.

"Do we know who lives here?" Vail asked as she stretched the elastic over her shoes.

"Place was leased by a Juli Herod," the officer said, consulting his notepad. "Single, thirty-five. All I know."

They moved into the apartment, Vail struggling to see with her underpowered penlight.

"You go left," Russo said, "I'll go right."

The darkness forced Vail to proceed slowly, spraying the beam across sections of each room as she went, using a grid-like pattern so she did not miss anything.

This is ridiculous. We should just wait for CSU. We're gonna have to redo this anyway once we can see.

They converged on the bedroom, where Juli Herod was seated in bed, looking quite dead.

A glass fragment was protruding from her neck. Her eyes were slashed. On first look, the only difference from the prior crime scenes was that there was more blood. A lot more.

"Okay, that's very interesting."

"Yeah?" Russo asked. "What do you see?"

"Not a whole lot in this shitty light."

"I'm not in the mood, Karen."

Someone got up on the wrong side of the bed this morning. Then again, staring at a violently murdered body can do that to you. "I see the same type of kill we've seen before. But a lot more blood, a lot more mess."

"And that means?"

"No idea. Just an observation."

"Question is, is it meaningful?"

Yes, that'd be a good question. As soon as I find someone who knows the answer, I'll ask.

She thought another moment, then said, "My sense is that it's important. Maybe he stabbed her first, before choking her. Heart's still beating."

"But why?"

Yeah, why? "Maybe he's getting bored doing the same thing all the time."

"Bored."

"Hey, it's just a stab in the dark."

Russo gave her a look.

"Sorry." She thought another moment. "I wonder if there's any significance to the fact that he killed the vic on Christmas Eve."

"I guess there's a 1 in 365 chance of that happening by accident. In the grand scheme of things, those aren't very long odds."

"I think we're going to find that it's meaningful. What it is and when we figure it out, I don't know."

Russo grunted. "I'm going to go look at the windows and doors, see if entry was forced. If the perp approached the kill differently, maybe the whole MO's different. Can't assume anything."

As Russo walked off, Vail moved behind Juli and shined the light on her neck. Her long hair was mussed and should've been covering the area of her skin where the drawing was located. But the strands were parted, providing full access to the design. Like before, there was an X, with an E on the left, an I on the right, a D at the top and, this time, a lowercase f at the bottom.

"No forced entry," Russo said, re-entering the bedroom. "As far as I can tell in the dark."

"So . . . what, you think he cut the power and then posed as a Con Ed worker who's there to fix it?"

"That's a possibility, among others."

"She's got the same drawing on the neck. Come look."

Russo joined her behind the body and leaned in close.

"This has gotta mean something," she said.

He stood up. "You're expecting logic, meaning, and intelligence from this nutcase?"

Vail thought about that a moment. "Yeah, I think the guy's intelligent. And I think there's meaning behind everything he's doing. I can't tell you he doesn't have some distorted view of the world, but I do think he's doing this for a reason."

"Why?"

"Let's put it this way. There's purpose in what he does. He doesn't have to draw the X, but he does. The letters mean something to him. They're almost identical from victim to victim. If we figure out what these letters mean, we may understand why he's doing this. Or we may find a clue as to who he is."

Russo scratched his forehead. "Okay, I'll buy that. For now."

"I'll tell you something else. I think this diagram is important to him."

"Because . . ."

"See that, how the hair's parted?" Vail pointed. "I didn't do that. I'd never disturb the scene before CSU photographs it. Killer used a hair clip."

"So he purposely parted the hair to make sure we couldn't miss it."

"Right."

Russo pursed his lips. "If we only knew what it meant. Why can't he just spell it out?"

"What's the fun in that?"

Russo looked at her. "You think this is a game to him?"

"Maybe. It could also be a way for him to frustrate us. He leaves us these letters, we think it means something significant, and maybe it's just bullshit. Or it means something and we can't figure it out. Either way, he's having fun making us bang our heads against the wall."

"Interesting theory. You making this shit up as you go along?"

"Pretty much." Vail grinned. "What can I say? I'm just reasoning it out in a way that makes sense to me. You know, when I was stuck on bed rest after the accident, I went over to the Rosedale library and did some research and—"

"I thought bed rest means you rest. In bed."

"I got so bored it was driving me crazy. And I couldn't get Tim's death out of my mind. I kept seeing the accident in my head, over and over. I needed a distraction."

"So you went to the library."

"I started poking around, trying to figure out why the killer draws this X on the vic's neck."

"You sure it's an X?"

Vail looked at the design, tilting her head left, then right. "Yeah, I think so. I guess it could just be a design, and he writes these letters in different quadrants of the cross. But I think there's more to it. If it is an X, that has significance in the Greek religion. What if the X comes from the Greek letter Chi?"

"I don't speak Greek, Karen. I've got no idea what you're rambling on about."

"Chi is the first letter of the Greek word Χριστού, which translates as 'Christ' in English."

"I still don't understand what Greek letters, or words, have to do with this killer. Or this case."

"The victims were Greek."

"What?" Russo stepped back a couple of feet as he thought this through. "No. That's not right. Crinelli—"

"Yeah, he doesn't fit. For a lot of reasons. But the two women, they were Greek."

"You sure?"

"No, I'm just guessing, based on their names. Of course I'm sure. I looked into Carole Manos's background. She was Greek. I'm willing to bet Juli Herod is too. She's got a photo of her and a bunch of people who look like family standing near the Acropolis. But even if we just go by their names—which are obviously Greek—maybe that's what the killer's using to identify his vics."

"Can it be that simple?"

"Who knows? But it's a working theory worth pursuing. If he's Greek, or has something against Greeks—"

"He was wronged by one once."

"Sure," Vail said. "Could be that. Or could be other reasons too."

Russo crouched and took a closer look at the symbol. "If you're right— and I'm intrigued but not sold—why this reference to Christ? Does religion play a role in these murders?"

"I don't see any other indications it does. But maybe it means religion plays a role in his *life.*"

"So, he's Greek Orthodox?"

Vail didn't know what to make of that, so she merely shrugged.

"Then what do these other letters mean?" Russo stood up. "Is there a Greek or religious meaning? And why does only one letter change from murder to murder?"

"We've got a lot of work ahead of us on this," Vail said with a sigh of resignation.

"I'm going to add one more thing to your plate. The department offers training courses and seminars to help you develop your investigative skills. There's a three-week deal coming up in mid-January on criminal investigations."

"Three weeks?"

"It's hard to get into, and you need someone to make a call on your behalf. I made that call and got you in."

Jesus. If I now own this case, I need to work it. How can I take three weeks off when I've got a fresh victim? But she understood that this was not the time to decline or even hesitate, not after Russo put his reputation on the line in helping secure her shield—and pulled strings to get her into this class. "I'm there."

"Good," Russo said, clearly pleased with her answer. "So let's roll up our sleeves and see what else we can find here."

27

›263-37 147TH AVENUE
ROSEDALE, QUEENS
WEDNESDAY, DECEMBER 24, 1997

Vail pulled into her driveway at 11:00 PM. She closed her eyes, took a deep breath, and tried to lose the stress and death in her work world, outside the safe zone that was her husband and her child.

She had wanted to stop at a pay phone and tell Deacon she was on her way but did not have any change and figured it would be better to head directly home rather than spend additional time trying to find an open store on Christmas Eve that could break a dollar.

A chill shuddered through her body. Even though she had only been sitting there a few seconds, the warmth inside her Honda dissipated nearly immediately.

She got out and ran up the front porch steps, then jammed her key into the lock and quickly closed the door behind her.

She found Deacon sitting on the couch in the living room, beside the tree, a spreadsheet on his lap.

"Hi," she said, heading straight to him. "Sorry I'm so late. I was ready to leave at six, as soon as I finished the arrest report, but then Russo—"

"So Russo's the one to blame for ruining Christmas Eve?"

Vail pulled her chin back. "Uh, well, there was another murder, that case I was working on when—"

"Yeah, I don't really care, Karen. I mean, who works on Christmas Eve?"

"The world doesn't stop because the date on the calendar reads December 24, Deacon. This is a big case, a serial killer. This is his third victim."

Deacon tossed the spreadsheet aside. "That's why they have detectives, right? I mean, you're a patrol officer on a gang assignment I wish you weren't doing to begin with, working undercover buying guns and drugs from all kinds of dangerous criminals. You've got a baby, for Christ's sake, Karen."

"This is the job, Deacon. You knew I was a cop, and that I wanted to make detective, when you asked me to marry you. I'm doing what I need to do to get that shield."

"No matter what it means to our family. How long are you going to be putting your life on the line with drug dealers?"

Vail removed her jacket and tossed it over a nearby chair. "Funny you should ask. Because tonight, I got my shield. I'm a detective."

Deacon sat forward. "You—what?"

"Where's Jonathan?"

"In his crib. Asleep. It's eleven o'clock. Where'd you think he'd be?"

Vail shook her head, then ran upstairs and gave her baby a kiss on the cheek. She wanted to pick him up and hold him, but she knew better. Instead, she stood there a moment, stroking his face, then headed back downstairs.

Deacon met her at the bottom of the landing. "Have you eaten?"

"Never had time."

"I got you some Chinese, just in case. It's in the fridge."

"Thanks." Vail walked into the kitchen and pulled the pink Frigidaire door open. "Believe me, I would've rather been here with you and Jonathan on Christmas Eve than staring at another murdered woman." She went about dishing out the food.

"Why don't we open presents first?"

Vail stopped, her finger hovering over the microwave's start button, then said, "Sure." She was starving, but she knew Deacon had been waiting hours for her to come home.

They sat down beside one another in front of the tree, exchanged boxes, and tore open the wrapping.

Vail was staring at a diamond drop necklace. Her mouth slipped open. "Deacon, this is—it's gorgeous." *And expensive.* "I love it. Thank-you."

He stopped, about to open the Bloomingdale's box. "I knew you'd like it. Try it on." Then he pulled the lid off, exposing a striped dress shirt. "I love these colors. Oh," he said, lifting the shirt up. "And a tie." He glanced over, must've seen that Vail was hesitating. "What's the matter? Go on. Take it out, put it on."

"Deacon, I . . . I can't. We can't afford this."

"Of course we can. I charged it. We'll just pay it off over time."

"At 20 percent interest? Look, I love it. And I love that you wanted to buy it for me." *Impulsive, actually. And irresponsible. But damn, it's beautiful. Must've cost a thousand dollars, if not more. What was he thinking? He's never done anything like this.*

"Just try it on."

She closed the box. "If I try it on, you won't be able to get it off me. And we can't afford it. I don't want to run up a credit card bill. You're in finance, you know this."

"Like that movie—*Risky Business*? Sometimes you just gotta say, 'What the fuck.'"

"Yeah. But this isn't one of those times." She snapped the box closed, got up, and went into the kitchen to eat.

28

>230 EAST 21st STREET
Manhattan
Monday, January 12, 1998

V ail stepped into the police academy auditorium and stopped. She had not expected to see so many cops here—well over a hundred, she estimated. From the looks of it, just based on the ones she recognized, there were detectives, sergeants, lieutenants, and captains, all taking the course alongside her.

She took a seat and glanced around. The more she thought about it, however, it was not surprising to see the upper ranks here because it was technically possible for a patrol officer to keep testing up to higher grades relatively quickly, before he truly developed and honed the investigative skills possessed by those he would be overseeing. It seemed to her to be an odd and screwy setup, but the NYPD was considered the finest police force in the country, so what did she know? The system obviously worked fine the way it was.

In the middle of the second week, the morning sessions featured two FBI agents from the Bureau's Profiling and Behavioral Analysis Unit, Art Rooney and Mark Safarik.

As Vail settled into her seat, the detective to her left—an older, seasoned investigator, groaned. "If I'd known we were gonna get this hocus-pocus bullshit I woulda brought my pillow. Now I gotta sleep with my head on the desk." He laughed.

The one to her right said, "I woulda brought my Ouija board if *I'd* known." More laughing.

Maybe I could've taken the morning off, tried to get some work done on my case.

But before she could plot a surreptitious route to the exit, Rooney began speaking and Vail leaned back in her seat, resigned to stay put until she had a clear path out.

Rooney spoke about his expertise in arson and bombing, and new and different ways of looking at the criminals who carried out these crimes. While there was a dearth of information on bombers, the profiling unit was beginning to build a general behavioral assessment of who these people were. It was still a ways off from being put into practice with confidence, he explained, but Vail was intrigued by the methods Rooney used to look at the individual psychologically and turn that information into a forensic that could almost be measured, like fingerprints, hair, and fibers.

More broadly, he gave an overview of the personality types of the offenders who commit the types of violent crimes that the unit commonly encounters. "There are several disorders we see. I'll go into each one in detail, but suffice it to say that our personality development is key to determining who we'll become as an adult. If it's disrupted at any point along the way as a child, depending on the age when it happens and the severity with which it occurs, it'll cause various types of perceptual distortions—and psychological disorders.

"These may impact their interpersonal relations or their self-concept development. Interruption of either can have catastrophic effects because these are how we establish our sense of self, how a healthy person learns to identify what he or she likes in others, and how to mimic them. But if they go awry, we end up with an adult who exhibits one or more personality disorders. When there's more than one, I think you can imagine the problems that can arise. In short, we get a really screwed up individual, and if he's inclined toward violence, this is the offender we're tasked with trying to find.

"Now, for our purposes, there are five major personality disorders—inadequate, paranoid, borderline, narcissistic, and psychopathic—and each has its own telltale symptoms and traits. This is important for a number of reasons, for when you do catch the offender, you'll need to interrogate him.

If you use the wrong approach for that type of individual, he'll shut down and you won't get squat. Use the correct strategy, however, and he'll open up to you."

Rooney spent a disproportionate amount of time going through the characteristics of psychopathy, primarily because "it's the most virulent personality disorder known to man. To give you an example, 90 percent of serial killers and 65 percent of molesters and rapists are psychopathic."

Vail had filled several pages of notes by this point and was looking forward to giving her hand a rest when Supervisory Special Agent Mark Safarik took the podium.

Safarik started by recounting his personal story of how he came to his position with the vaunted unit. "I was a detective with the Davis, California, PD, sitting in a training class just like this one, and two profilers came to speak. And what they said opened my eyes to new and different ways of looking at not only an investigation but the offender, as well. Let me give you an example.

"As detectives, when you walk into a crime scene, you're interested in finding the objective evidence that'll identify a specific individual, the perpetrator who committed the violent crime you're investigating. A latent print, some saliva, a handwriting sample. Or even better, a video clip on a surveillance tape. These are all known, proven methods of identifying the criminal you're looking for. But what if you don't have any of that? It can stall your investigation. And even if you find someone you like for the crime, you may have a tough time helping the prosecutor make the case against him.

"When I enter a crime scene, I'm looking for behaviors that the offender left behind. If I can understand who this guy is, it'll help me figure out why the offender chose this victim at this point in time. It'll explain why he lifted her dress up over her face after he killed her, why he defecated at the scene, or cut off a body part.

"I also approach this from the victim's point of view by learning who she was and what led her to cross paths with this offender.

"In essence, I'm looking to identify the *type* of person who committed the crime—by attempting to understand who this person is by evaluating the crime scene behaviorally. You heard the disorders Agent Rooney discussed. This scene will contain clues to the particular disorder the offender suffers from. Why is that? Anyone?"

He looked around the auditorium, but no one offered a guess.

"Reason is because the killer is unknowingly telling us a story. We just have to be receptive to understanding his language, to *learn* his language, so we can recognize what he's telling us."

Holy shit. That's what I've been thinking. Vail sat up in her seat and realized that she had been so riveted by what Safarik was saying that she had stopped taking notes.

At the lunch break, Vail rushed the podium. Rooney was talking with two detectives and a captain, but Safarik was alone, shutting down his Power-Point presentation.

"Agent Safarik," Vail said, bending around the lid of the laptop to make eye contact.

He stood up—all six foot six of him, immaculately dressed in a black suit, white shirt, and intense purple and blood-red tie. "Call me Mark." He extended a hand and she took it.

"Karen Vail. I, uh, I was blown away by your presentation. I mean, I wasn't expecting much—I mean, some of the guys around me were down on profiling and I thought . . ." *Jesus, Karen, get a grip.* "I majored in psychology, so I've been exposed to some of this, but you and Agent Rooney took it to a whole other level. A lot of what you said has been rattling around in my head on my case, and I couldn't figure out what to do with it. What you said about understanding what the killer did and why, that makes so much sense to me."

"It can be pretty powerful, once you step back and allow yourself to see what's there at the crime scene, other than the usual stuff you're taught to look for. It's a totally different way of evaluating your case."

"Speaking of my case, can I—can I ask you about it? I've got one that's really baffling us and there aren't any forensics to speak of. No suspects."

"How many vics over what time period?"

"Three, over a three-year period."

"Tell me about the first one."

Vail gave him a brief rundown of the Carole Manos murder, what she knew of the woman, and an overview of what the scene looked like.

"And you're sure this was the offender's first vic?"

"Uh, no. I'm not sure at all. I'm not sure about much of anything. I was—I was a patrol officer at the time and well, let's just say that I was fortunate to have been at all three fresh crime scenes. I just got my shield and was handed the case."

Safarik nodded slowly. "You must be pretty damn good if they entrusted you with such an important case."

Gee, thanks. No pressure.

He started coiling his power cord. "One of our profilers, one of the founding fathers of the unit, developed a database called VICAP, for Violent Criminal Apprehension Program. Why don't we plug in your three vics and see if we can come up with something?"

"How does that work?"

"Let's say the South Dakota PD finds a body in a house with a severed right index finger. Six months later, the Connecticut PD finds one too. They're both running their own investigations but neither one knows about the other. The offender, or UNSUB—unknown subject—has impunity to kill as he pleases because we're not able to build a complete picture of who he's targeting and how he's finding his victims.

"But what if he made a mistake at the South Dakota crime scene, a crucial error that could help us identify him if we put it together with something he did with the Connecticut victim's body? If we don't know these vics are all from the same killer, we have an incomplete book on him.

"That's why Robert Ressler's VICAP idea was so important. Whenever a law enforcement agency has a murder that meets certain criteria, they fill out a VICAP form and that info gets entered into the database. All unique characteristics of the case are listed—MO, signature aspects, crime scene photos, victim and suspect details, things like that. And we can set certain search-specific parameters to look through all the data. So—give me something from your case."

"The UNSUB draws a diagram in black marker on his vics' necks."

"Perfect. So you could search VICAP for that kind of diagram. Or you could even go broader and look for those cases where the UNSUB has drawn something on the victim. If it pulls up another case in another jurisdiction, and you think they're related, you can then compare or combine the things that detective's discovered with the stuff you've discovered on your case, and now you've both got a more complete picture of that UNSUB—and it could be just enough to help you solve it."

"I need to do this. Like ASAP."

Safarik shoved the laptop into his large leather case. "One caveat. If an investigating agency isn't aware of VICAP, or doesn't take the time to fill out the form and send it to us, that murder won't be in our database. There'll be nothing to find. But identifying that first victim could be key."

"Why?"

"Because it's his first kill. He may not have thought things out as thoroughly the first time around. He's feeling his way, he's inexperienced, he'll probably make a mistake or two, mistakes he learns from as time goes on, as he moves from victim to victim, as he perfects his trade."

"You make it sound like it's a business."

"Not a business per se, but it *is* a career to him. Whether he realizes it or not, he's learning, getting better at what he does—killing people—and honing his skills. That's why it can be so tough to catch these guys. They get better at selecting their vics, at entrapping them, at outwitting *us*. But if you can find his first kill, you might just see something that could implicate him or significantly narrow down your suspect pool."

"Okay."

"That's not to say that they don't make mistakes later. It can happen. They're human—well, that's debatable, but let's just say they're not perfect. Shit happens."

Vail flashed on the car accident and Thorne getting killed. *Shit does indeed happen.*

"You'll get this guy, Karen. Have the liaison at the New York field office send the case over to us. We'll do what we can to help."

"So when you got turned on to behavioral analysis," she said, "how did—I mean, you were with Davis PD. How'd you end up at Quantico?"

Safarik gave a quick glance around, apparently realizing that Vail was asking for herself, and how she could make the same thing happen. "I joined the FBI and hoped my career path would lead me to the profiling unit. That's the only way in."

Another detective who had come up to the podium asked Safarik if he had a moment to discuss his case.

"Thanks," Vail said, backing away.

"Find that first vic," Safarik said.

29

>ELLIS ISLAND
SATURDAY, SEPTEMBER 27, 1975

Niklaus spied the large ferry as it pulled into the inlet formed by the U-shape of the three Ellis Island land masses.

"What do you think that's doing here?" Niklaus asked.

Dmitri, his sweatshirt hood pulled over his head, was whittling a stick with a sharp folding knife.

"Dmitri," Niklaus said. "The boat. Why do you think it's here?"

Dmitri glanced up as he dug out tiny slivers from the wood. "A ferry takes people from place to place."

Niklaus stuck his hands out and parted the tall weeds, exposing a clearer view of the bay. Behind them was the massive hospital building, and behind that were the smaller units of the psychiatric wards, and behind them was the structure serving as their home.

"There aren't any people on it." Niklaus watched the ferry pull to a stop in front of the dilapidated building that once served as Ellis Island's immigrant processing center. "Just two on the top, steering the boat." His gaze wandered beyond the ship. "I think we should explore that one day."

"Explore what?"

"The building. See what's inside."

"My mom said it's where they examined the people who came from other countries."

"Yeah," Niklaus said, "but what's inside? Let's go take a look around."

"She said not to go there."

Fedor and Livana had taken the powerboat to Jersey City to buy food and the supplies Fedor needed to repair the roof. Fourteen-year-old Cassie was placed in charge of watching him and Dmitri. But she had fallen asleep under a tree, enjoying the unseasonable warmth of a sunny day.

"Do we always do what your mother tells us to do?" Niklaus asked.

Dmitri hacked away at the stick, removing a branch nub with one swift swipe. "No."

"I'm going," Niklaus said, releasing the weeds. They shifted back into place and he headed left, toward Island 2, the connecting land mass between the two legs of the U-shaped complex. Twenty feet later, he glanced over his shoulder to see that Dmitri was standing where he had been, running the blade's edge over the thick piece of wood. "Hey! Put that thing away and come with me."

Dmitri frowned, then closed the knife and shoved it in his jeans. The stick went in another pocket.

He trudged on, keeping several feet behind Niklaus—which always drove Niklaus nuts. Why couldn't he just walk beside him like any normal kid?

They hiked along the water's edge, using the wall of weeds as cover, moving behind the immigration building on Island 2, and then continuing onto Island 1.

"Wow, she's a big boat," Niklaus said, eying the ferry.

As they got closer, they moved behind a thick tree trunk and watched as the captain and his mate hopped off the ship and proceeded into the old building.

"Where do you think they're going?" Niklaus asked.

"How should I know?"

Niklaus turned around to see Dmitri hacking away at the stick again. "C'mon," he said, slapping Dmitri's shoulder and moving out of the cover of the tree trunk and onto the broken sidewalk that ran the length of the island, fronting the former immigrant processing center.

He continued to glance over his left shoulder at the large building, watching for movement in case the men returned. He did not know if the authorities were aware that anyone was living on the island, but he doubted it: if they knew, the police would surely have removed them by now.

His father had told them all to keep their home a secret. Under no circumstances were they to tell anyone at their school in Manhattan where they really lived. If they did, they risked losing their house, and they would no longer be able to live in one of the most beautiful areas that existed in all of

New York . . . a place where there was no traffic, no noise, no pollution, no cars. And no rent or taxes.

Although it took a tragedy to bring them there, his father had explained, their life—while by no means easy and often lacking the comforts of modern civilization—was serene and blessed.

Niklaus stole a look at Dmitri, who was easily ten yards behind him, carving away at the stick. "Damn it, Dmitri, c'mon. Hurry!" He quickened his pace and was now jogging toward the ferry. He hopped aboard and moved into an alcove, in case there were others on the boat that he had not seen. Dmitri followed a moment later; when he boarded, Niklaus grabbed him and pulled him aside.

"Put your stupid knife away. If we get caught, we're in real trouble. Let's go."

"Where?" Dmitri shifted his head to the side, inside his hood, so he could see.

"I've never been on a big ship like this. Let's look around."

They walked in, up the flights of stairs, and emerged near the bridge. Niklaus stepped inside and stopped. "Whoa, look at this!"

Large picture windows encircled the room, which featured panels of instruments set into the countertop: levers, dials, lights, and large format maps. A framed yellowing photo with a placard that read, "Capt F. Rudiger" was propped beside the wheel.

"Compass," Dmitri said. He stepped over to the shiny, polished gold handheld device and picked it up. "Wow." He turned it over, catching the light—as well as his reflection—in the mirror-like finish of the rear surface.

"C'mon," Niklaus said, "let's keep looking." He walked out of the bridge onto the exterior walkway and peered out at the immigration building. Rudiger and his mate were returning. "Dmitri, we gotta go, they're coming back!"

Niklaus started for the stairs, then looked back at Dmitri. "Let's go, hurry up."

Niklaus ran down the steps, swung around to the next flight and heard the two men coming. He slipped left, behind a white steel bulkhead. "Dmitri!" he whispered. "Where the hell are you?"

The heavy footfalls of the crew echoed in the metal stairwell, getting louder as the seconds passed. Niklaus peered out, hoping to see Dmitri. Actually, he was hoping he did not see Dmitri, because if he did, the men would too.

Nothing. He probably went down the other set of stairs. As soon as the crew passed, Niklaus would head down, moving as quickly and as quietly as he could.

He had made it to the second flight and was nearing the bottom floor when he heard shouting.

"Hey you, punk! Get back here. Give that back to me!"

Niklaus turned and headed up, but with all the echoes and odd angles of the ship's interior, he could not place the location. He thought Dmitri was above him, but where? It was a big vessel.

But then he heard

struggling
banging
yelling

And then he reached the top floor and saw the captain with his forearm around Dmitri's neck, his stepbrother kicking his legs out and landing a blow against the mate's chin. He went down and skidded backward across the floor. He got up and came at Dmitri and punched him in the face. But his fist also struck Rudiger's arm, softening the blow.

Dmitri buried his shoe in the mate's abdomen and the guy flew back into a counter. Dmitri bit into Rudiger's bicep and the man screamed— then let go. The mate had gotten to his feet and yelled something just as Dmitri grabbed a metal pipe. He brought it back like a bat and was about to swing it at his head when Niklaus stepped in. "No, don't!"

"What the f—" Rudiger turned and reached for Niklaus, but he squirmed away as Dmitri slipped out the side exit and ran for the stairs. They sprinted off the boat and kept running straight into the immigration building.

IT WAS DARK INSIDE and smelled of mildew. They ran through the dilapidated and cavernous, high-ceilinged rooms, peeling paint crunching beneath their sneakers as they moved deeper into the building, their footfalls echoing in the vacant rooms. Weathered wood benches sat askew, a few chairs lying on their sides.

This once-proud structure, with its close proximity to the Statue of Liberty and the gateway to capitalism and democracy—the ultimate symbol of American freedom—now sat abandoned, left to the merciless abuse of the elements.

"Son of a bitch, stop!"

The voice from behind made them run faster into the darkness and then out the back doors into the brightness, and into another colossal brick building.

Rusted iron pillars stared back at them in the sunlight that streamed in through large windows, their broken glass panes having allowed dirt, rain, and humidity to penetrate and degrade the interior.

The brick was crumbling in places, the tiled ceiling only partially intact, its missing sections having fallen across a corresponding area on the cement floor.

They moved into a darker room where the ground was littered more densely with detritus from the falling roof.

"I don't think it's safe in here," Niklaus said, dodging a falling hunk of tile, then craning his neck ceilingward. "As soon as it's clear we've gotta get out of here before something hits us on the head."

"I wanna go now," Dmitri said. He pulled his hood back up and looked down at the ground.

"We can't, not while they're out there."

They moved to the edge of the room, around an alcove, and crouched in front of the wall. There they waited—but Dmitri got spooked when another chunk fell from above and crashed to the floor, shattering on impact and raising a cloud of dust and dirt.

Minutes passed. All remained quiet.

"That man was hurting me," Dmitri said.

Niklaus stood up and took a quick glance around. "I couldn't let you hit him with that pipe. You hurt him, the cops'll come and move us off the island. You want that to happen?"

Rather than answering, Dmitri leaned back against the wall.

"You said that man was hurting you," Niklaus said. "Was it like when those guys kidnapped you?"

"I don't wanna talk about it."

"Just tell me what happened. You've never told anyone—"

"I don't wanna talk about it."

"Fine," Niklaus said. "Whatever."

Fifteen minutes later, when Niklaus was convinced it was safe, they headed back the way they had come, into the main building. Through the windows, they saw the large ferry moving out of the inlet and into Upper New York Bay.

Once it cleared the island's boundary, Niklaus headed toward the front door. "Now we can go."

Moments later, they were walking back across Island 2 and then onto Island 3, where they lived.

"We shouldn't have done that," Dmitri said. He shoved his hand in his pocket and fished around, as if searching for something.

"Would you leave that stick alone? We need to get back before Cassie wakes up."

Dmitri did not answer, but he did pull something from his dungarees. It wasn't the knife, however. It was the shiny gold compass.

THEY STEALTHILY APPROACHED the house, coming up behind the spot where Cassandra had been napping. But the area was vacant, the grass Fedor had planted, where she had been lying, still matted down from her weight.

"She's not here," Dmitri said. "She's not here."

"Where have you two been?"

They turned in unison. Cassandra was standing there, hands on her hips.

"We went exploring," Dmitri said.

"Exploring? Mom and Fedor said we're not supposed—"

"We didn't go far," Niklaus said. "And now we're back. No big deal. You were sleeping, anyway."

"That's not the point. I'm gonna tell Mom—"

"No!" Dmitri said. "Don't tell Mom. Don't tell—"

"Why shouldn't I?"

"Because," Niklaus said, "we'll have to explain how we left without you knowing. And then they'll know that you fell asleep and weren't watching us, like you were supposed to."

Dmitri again shoved his hand deep into his pocket and this time pulled out the knife and stick. "You fell asleep, Cassie." He started carving the wood, then stopped abruptly. He looked up at her.

And smiled.

30

›520 2ND AVENUE
MANHATTAN
MONDAY, FEBRUARY 22, 1999

V ail walked into the apartment on Second Avenue ten minutes early. The crowd for Carmine Russo's promotion party had already gathered, however, and it was a who's who of the New York law enforcement community, from chiefs to captains, detectives, undercovers, and even a few prosecutors and judges.

Sofia Russo, apron still tied around her waist, hurried to the door and introduced herself. She took Vail's hands in both of hers and said, "So you're Karen." She nodded, leaned back a bit, and said, "Now I know why Carmine talks of you all the time. You're a knockout. What I looked like twenty-five years ago." Sofia shook her head at her own comment. "Not really, I was never that good-looking. But in Carmine's eyes . . . " She smiled. "Beauty is in the eye of the beholder, no?"

Whoa, lady, calm down. Did someone shoot you up with caffeine?

"Thanks for the compliment, Mrs. Russo," Vail said. "But I'd like to think your husband talks a lot about me because I'm a good cop."

Sofia smiled, examined Vail's face, and then laughed heartily. "Don't you know, sweetheart? The best way to a man's heart is his stomach or an impressive set of hooters. Or long legs. And not necessarily in that order."

Vail stood there, unsure what to make of that—or Sofia Russo.

"Hey there."

Vail turned—relieved to be rescued from this bizarre exchange—and saw a man a few years older than she, dressed in a suit.

"Ben Dyer. You're Karen?"

Vail squinted. "Yeah. How'd you know?"

"I'm a detective." He grinned disarmingly. "Just bullshitting you. I overheard your conversation with Sofia."

Vail turned and saw that Sofia had moved on to besiege another guest.

"Thanks for the save."

Dyer laughed. "Don't take it personally. She's just a little jealous. He does have a tendency to talk about you."

"Okay," Sofia shouted. "Our stakeout team just informed me that he's in the elevator, on his way up. Everyone into the living room."

The guests shuffled in, squeezing shoulder to shoulder. The lights were turned out, and a moment later the front door opened.

"Surpri-i-ise!" everyone called out in unison.

Russo's mouth dropped open. "What the heck is this?" The lights came on and he smiled broadly.

Dyer held up a beer. "Congratulations, *lieutenant!*"

Russo walked in, giving and getting hugs and handshakes. He worked the room and ended up in the back, where Vail was standing.

"So I'm curious. I've never cooked a meal for you, and I don't have particularly long legs. Is it my boobs?"

Russo tilted his head. "Huh?"

"Sofia—"

"Oh, good lord," Russo said as he craned his neck, trying to locate her. "Has she been drinking?"

"Hey, the way I see it, she threw you a terrific surprise party. You gotta cut her some slack."

Russo, still searching the room for his wife, reached into his pocket and pulled out his BlackBerry. He groaned as he read the display.

A second later, Vail's cell phone rang. She answered it and locked eyes with Russo. "On my way."

"So much for the party," Russo said as he glanced at his watch.

"No way," Vail said. "You earned this shindig. I'm a big girl. I'll give you a full report."

"Maybe I'll stop by after, when things are winding down."

Vail gave him a pat on the shoulder. "Enjoy yourself."

"Yeah, why should I let another murdered woman spoil my party?"

VAIL PULLED UP in front of the apartment building on Fourth Avenue at 7:30 PM. She tinned the cop standing watch over the crime scene and walked up the stairs to 3B. The front door was open and she could see the flicker of flash photography from somewhere inside.

After putting on her booties, she was met in the hallway by one of the Crime Scene Unit detectives.

"Ryan Chandler," Vail repeated as she shook his hand. "I don't think we've worked together before."

"I'm new. Used to be a cop and detective in Sacramento, so I'm not *totally* green."

"I'm not feeling real confident," Vail said.

"Don't worry. I won't screw up your case—or your crime scene."

Whew. Now I feel much better.

"Is that Vail?"

The voice from the other room belonged to the medical examiner, Max Finkelstein.

"It is, Max," she said as she followed the hallway into the bedroom. "We got another?"

But as soon as she stepped over the threshold she knew she could have answered her own question. The body was seated in the bed, a shard of glass protruding from the side of the neck. And plenty of blood soaking the comforter.

"Do we have a name?" she asked.

Chandler glanced at his pad. "We do. Megan Kostas. An interior designer with a big firm here in the city. She was part-owner."

"Kostas. Greek?"

Chandler shrugged. "Probably."

"You start on the body yet, doc?"

Finkelstein slipped on his reading glasses. "Not yet. But I know what you'd like to see."

"Shall we look together?"

"I feel a bit left out," Chandler said. "What is it we're looking for?"

"Writing in black marker on the back of Ms. Kostas' neck, at the hairline. Was she married?"

"Divorced, two years ago."

"Can we move the body?"

Finkelstein shrugged. "Just about to do that myself. Have at it."

"Okay, let's take a look." Vail nodded at Finkelstein, who was wearing a Tyvek suit. She took a pair of gloves from Chandler and began pulling them on as the medical examiner carefully lifted the victim's head and then rotated it to the side. Vail craned her neck, aimed her flashlight, and said, "Oh, yeah. There she is. Ryan, can you get a closeup of this?"

Chandler complied and told Vail he would send a color print to the homicide squad as soon as the film was developed.

"So did the UNSUB do her the same way as the last one, Juli Herod?" Vail asked.

"UNSUB?" Finkelstein asked.

"Unknown subject."

He looked at her over the tops of his glasses. "Where'd you learn that one?"

"FBI."

Finkelstein nodded in approval. "Very good."

"So was Ms. Kostas suffocated, or is cause of death from the laceration of the carotid? I'm guessing the latter based on the amount of arterial spray."

Finkelstein released his hold on the victim's neck and used the back of his hand to push the bifocals back up his nose. "Yes. My preliminary impression is the carotid."

So why did he change his MO with Herod? Why has he stopped suffocating them?

Finkelstein straightened up and gestured to Chandler to help him with the body. "Oh. Mazel tov on making detective."

"Okay everyone, drop everything you're doing because happy days are here again!"

They all turned in unison and faced a trim man of about six foot four, wearing a black suit with a red tie, a collar bar—and cuff links.

"Who the hell are you?" Vail asked.

He walked in and stood in front of Vail, prompting her to crane her neck to look up at him. "Now that's no way to greet the finest homicide detective on the East Coast." He leaned left and saw Finkelstein crouched by the body, behind Vail. "Max! Good to see you. What can you tell me?"

"Hang on a second," Vail said. "I don't think we've been introduced. And 'the finest homicide detective on the East Coast' doesn't quite cut it. How about we start over? I'm Karen Vail."

"Antonio Fonzarella. Homicide squad."

Vail turned to Chandler, and then Finkelstein, who cleared his throat and rose from his crouch. "I forgot to tell you he was coming."

Vail swung her gaze back to Fonzarella. "Let me guess. Your nickname is—"

"Fonzie, yes. But not after the TV character." He obviously noticed her perturbed look, because he added, "Edgardo Alfonzo, on the Mets? Best defensive second baseman in the league. Just like me—best detective on the East Coast. He goes by Fonzie, I go by Fonzie."

Fonzarella. Vail tilted her head in thought. *He should go by Cinderella. Or mozzarella. Wonder if he'd appreciate hearing my opinion.*

"He's a very good detective," Finkelstein said. "Personality notwithstanding."

"Thanks, doc," Fonzarella said. "But I don't need your endorsement."

Make that a "definitely not" for hearing my opinion.

"Why are you here?" Vail asked.

"This is the fourth vic. The chief wanted me to get my ass over here and solve this thing ASAP."

"Good, I'm relieved," Vail said, mocking a wipe of her brow. "Thank God. Because I'm tired of seeing dead bodies, and obviously I don't know what the hell I'm doing."

"You got a nice mouth on you, I'll say that. And—" he cleared his throat— "some pretty good equipment too."

"I've got another piece of equipment in my holster. If you want it to stay there, you'll address me with respect." *Asshole.*

Fonzarella tilted his head, looking her over. He stepped to his right and kept his gaze on her face. "What are you, like twenty?"

"Like, no." *I'm almost twenty-five. Smartass.*

"Yeah, whatever." He spun around, turning his back on Vail. "So, doc, what do we got?"

"Do you know what we're dealing with here?" Vail asked.

Keeping his gaze on Finkelstein, he said, "You mean the sketch he makes on the vics' necks? With the letters? Or the fact that he appears to be targeting Greek women?"

That'd be it.

Not waiting for an answer—or realizing none was required—he said, "So, doc, talk to me."

"Name's Megan—"

"Yeah. Vic four. That's all I gotta know. Greek name?"

"Looks that way."

"What else?"

"We've got that 'sketch,' as you put it, on her neck. More than that, I don't know yet. I got here only a few minutes before you."

"Looks like she got sliced and diced across the eyes, just like the others. So this is the same doer."

That was a pretty damn quick—and superficial—assessment. If this is the best the East Coast has . . .

Fonzarella turned and called across the room to Chandler, who was dusting a chest for latent prints. "And you? Haven't seen you before."

"Ryan Chandler." Apparently realizing that the less he said the better, Chandler kept it simple and short. Then he swung his torso back to the bureau and continued his business.

"That sketch on the neck," Fonzarella said. "Same as before?"

"Almost. All the letters are the same, except the bottom one is a g."

"A g? There was an e on the others—"

"The others," Vail said, "had a capital E on the left, a capital I on the right, a capital D on the top, and different lowercase letters on the bottom. Right, Max?"

"Correct," Finkelstein said.

Fonzarella frowned. "Weren't the others found in a chair?"

"One was," Vail said. "The male."

Fonzarella moved the body to view it from different angles. "And what does it mean to you? Chair versus bed."

"Not sure. I think it's significant, though."

"You're not sure but you think it means something."

"Gut. A woman's intuition."

He laughed. "Well, you got me there. Tits and balls, they think differently."

"And in this instance," Vail said, "thank God for that."

Chandler and Finkelstein chuckled.

Fonzarella's grin vanished. "I don't think it means shit. It's not like we have a large pool of vics to establish much of a pattern. Three he puts in a bed, one he does in a chair."

"He killed one Italian and three Greeks, but you're willing to accept the Greek victim pattern there."

"That's different."

"Why?" Vail asked.

"Because I said it is."

Vail leaned back and placed a hand on her chin. "You know, I think I had you all wrong."

Fonzarella smirked. "Yeah, how's that?"

"Looks like you are just like Fonzie."

"Yeah." Fonzarella grinned. "You know it."

"The TV character, not the baseball player. Narcissistic, putting up a facade to hide your insecurities, all just an act, afraid someone might see what you're really like, who you really are. A figment of your own imagination."

His face stiffened and he pointed an index finger at her. "I got twenty years on you when it comes to solving homicides. And I got a hundred percent solve rate. So I suggest you drop the attitude and try to learn something. That's why I'm here. This is now a high-profile case. So think what you want, but the brass wanted me in charge of this, to make sure you don't fuck it up."

Vail had no response to that. And if this guy really did have the attention of "the brass," she had better dial it back and do her best to get along with him. Even if he was a first-rate asshole in the body of a first-rate detective.

"Those letters are intriguing me," Fonzarella said. "E, D, I, g. The killer's initials?"

Vail lifted her brow. "I hadn't thought of that."

"My point exactly. That's why I'm here."

Vail ignored the comment and instead considered the possibility. "Even if they are, what do we do with it? We don't know which is his first name, last name, middle name . . . I mean, it's interesting and it could potentially help us if we have a bunch of suspects we're looking at. But what does it actually do for us? Here and now?"

"We write it down, file it away, and build a case. Sometimes we don't know—can't know—what all these things mean at the time they come to us."

"Okay. Makes sense." *But why would the killer use his own initials? It's risky. Unless he's signing his handiwork. That's . . . sick.*

Chandler set his kit aside. "I've lifted a number of latents. As soon as I have a chance to run them, I'll let you know what I find. I vacuumed before you got here in case there are fibers worth examining. But I didn't see any tool marks, sign of forced entry. No signs of a struggle."

"And no skin under the nails," Finkelstein said.

"So, like the others," Chandler said, "it's probably someone he knows."

"Or he's good at disarming them," Vail said. "Makes them feel at ease. Someone he trusts, maybe. Security worker. Utility guy. Or someone impersonating a cop."

"That would not be good," Chandler said. "Nothing could stop him from gaining entry or access."

Vail considered that. "Nothing's stopped him so far."

They stayed at the scene until they had gotten everything they could, then Chandler made sure he had their contact information. "I'll get you what I can, as soon as I can."

Vail thanked him and headed out to her car. Fonzarella joined her a few feet from the curb. "You gonna be able to work with me on this?"

What am I missing here? It's my case. "Of course," she said.

"Good. I'll see you bright and early tomorrow morning. We're gonna catch this bastard. Just a matter of time." He winked at her, then turned and walked toward his sedan.

THAT EVENING, WHEN Vail got home, Jonathan was still awake. She played with him, read him a bedtime story, and put him in his crib. Deacon was asleep on the couch when she walked back downstairs.

"Hey, sleepyhead. If you're that tired, why don't you get into bed? You're going to wake up with a backache again."

He pushed himself up and then sat staring at her. His hair was disheveled and he hadn't shaved this morning.

"You feeling okay?"

"Not really."

"What's wrong?"

"I don't know. Just not . . . happy, I guess."

Vail sat down beside him. "With me?"

"No. It's . . . I don't know."

She examined his face. "Did you go to work today?"

"I took a sick day."

"That's the third one you took this month. Aren't you worried they're going to—"

"I don't want to discuss it, okay?" He rose from the couch.

"Keep your voice down. I don't want you waking the baby."

Deacon shook his head, then headed toward the stairs. "Whatever."

Vail started after him. "Maybe you should go see someone, figure out what's bothering you."

"It's just stress. I'll be fine."

Vail watched him climb the steps, shoulders slumped, shuffling heavily up the stairs. "I'm worried about you."

Deacon kept moving. He did not answer, did not stop.

31

›MANHATTAN SOUTH HOMICIDE SQUAD
TUESDAY, FEBRUARY 23, 1999

V ail sat down at her desk and slid her chair toward it. In the center of the blotter was Special Agent Mark Safarik's thick blue business card, crisply embossed with a gold FBI seal over the words "Profiling and Behavioral Analysis Unit." She ran her fingers over the ridges. It felt expensive, prestigious.

She lifted the phone, hesitated, then dialed. As it rang, she wondered what Fonzarella would say about profiling. Almost immediately, she realized that she did not care what he thought.

"Mark Safarik."

"Agent Safarik, this is Karen Vail, with the NYPD. We met at the—"

"Yeah, yeah. I remember. How's your case coming along? Did you find that first victim?"

"Not yet. But I wanted to submit my case to your unit. How do I do that? Do I have to fill out forms, like VICAP?"

"Did you get anything off VICAP?"

"Nothing came up."

"The database is still incomplete, so that doesn't necessarily mean anything. As to submitting a case, it's a pretty informal process. If a law enforcement agency or even the district attorney prosecuting the case wants help, they can call us directly and speak with an agent. If the agent thinks it's something we can help with, he'll prepare a communication explaining the contact and the reason we should assist. He then sets a lead that the case be opened and assigned. Internally, we call it 'O and A'd.'

"The requesting detective can also send a letter directly to the PBAU for help or he can contact the local FBI office. He'd then be put in touch with the NCAVC coordinator—the National Center for the Analysis of Violent Crime—and he or she would make the request."

"Let's keep it simple. Consider this call me contacting you directly."

"Right. So I'll write it up to be O and A'd and give it to my supervisor for approval. He usually approves it. Just send me a written request on letterhead so we have it formalized in the file. A lot of these cases go to court, assuming we catch the offender, and we want to have all the T's crossed. We don't want these guys getting off on a technicality or have the case be subject to challenge."

"I'll get your letter. Let's do this."

"One other little detail. I've got the western region, but the other agent who spoke to your class, Art Rooney, he's got the east. You want me to leave him a message? He's in Germany teaching a section on behavioral analysis at a homicide conference."

"Sure, that'd be great."

"Have you ever been here? To the academy?"

"Always wanted to, but no."

"You're not that far. You have time next week? Come by, I'll take you around."

Vail pulled out her calendar and flipped a few pages. She scheduled Monday around two o'clock, thanked Safarik, then headed over to Fonzarella's desk to check in with him. But she would not mention her trip to the profiling unit. At this point, there was no reason for him to know.

VAIL GOT OFF I-95 at exit 148 and entered the FBI side of Quantico marine base. She followed Agent Safarik's directions and turned left, past a large brown brick wall with metal lettering that read, FBI Academy. It had rusted a bit and bled down onto the stone facing beneath it, but in her eyes it did not diminish its prominence.

She parked in the lot by Jefferson Hall and entered the building, then walked up to an enormous maple veneer administrative desk and faced a prominent red stop sign: "100% ID CHECK. All Visitors Must Sign In."

As Vail presented her identification, she examined the sizable FBI seal etched in a glass pane along the back wall.

"Detective Vail's with me."

She turned and saw Agent Safarik standing there, handing something to the woman behind the counter. After she had her visitor's tag, he led Vail through the glass-enclosed corridors that connected the various buildings on the campus. He took her to the armory, indoor shooting range, cavernous gymnasium, and Olympic-size pool.

"We do a lot of training exercises in there," Safarik said as they stood in the entryway on a level overlooking the water. "New agents have to meet certain basic swimming requirements, but our hostage rescue team has to be proficient in drown-proofing techniques and all kinds of blindfolded recovery exercises. Rigorous stuff."

They ended in the high-ceilinged café, where Vail grabbed a sandwich and a banana and they sat down at a table near a group of new agents, who were sporting red rubber handgun mock-ups in their holsters.

"So tell me about your case," Safarik said as he grabbed a handful of trail mix.

She described the victims and gave their years of death, and then jumped right to the drawings on their necks.

"I haven't been able to figure that out," Vail said. "There's no point to it."

"But there is. First of all, he doesn't have to do it, right? I mean, his goal is to kill the woman—and to enjoy doing it. So if we look at the diagram he draws, it's not to kill her, right?"

"Right."

"The other concern of the UNSUB is to avoid getting caught. Drawing on the body obviously doesn't help him there, either. So if it doesn't serve his two primary purposes of killing her or evading law enforcement, he's doing it for some other reason."

"I sense that you're going to tell me what that reason is."

Safarik chuckled. "I am. It's pretty simple, actually. It's something he enjoys doing. And it's arrogance, to put him in a different category above other killers. He's differentiating himself, drawing attention to himself, taking on more risk. It's like a dog pissing on his territory, or an artist taking credit for his painting by signing his name. And he wants all his vics to be connected in some way so that he gets credit. A guy like this, he would freak out if someone came forward and tried to take credit for one of *his* kills."

Vail stopped chewing. "Wait, so if that's the case, why couldn't we plant a story in the media saying that someone walked into a precinct and confessed to the murders? And that the police are questioning him and that an arrest appears imminent? We'd decline comment because it's an active investigation. Wouldn't that piss him off? He may call in and say, 'No, it wasn't him, it was me!'"

"Oh, it would piss him off all right. I'm not sure it'd make him come forward and confess, but it could make him kill again. If it sets him off, he might kill just to show you that while you have this other guy in custody, another murder's happened."

"Or he could contact me directly, a letter or a phone call, to let me know we have the wrong guy."

"Sure. As long as you understand the risks," Safarik said. He grabbed another handful of nuts. "He'd get over his rage and then enjoy showing you you're wrong. I use the term 'enjoy' loosely because psychopaths don't feel emotions like you and I do."

"How do you know he's a psychopath?"

"I don't. I don't know enough about the case to make an assessment. But a very high percentage of serial killers are psychopaths."

"And crazy," she said with a laugh.

"Not crazy. Not insane. They know what they're doing and they know it's wrong. And they know it's against the law. They just don't care. But they are definitely in their right mind."

"It's just not the 'right mind' for a civilized society."

"Exactly." He checked his outsize watch. "Why don't we head over to the profiling unit? Art Rooney should be back in the office by now. You can hand him your file personally. And I'll put together some research articles to take with you."

VAIL FOLLOWED SAFARIK'S Bureau car—or "G ride," as he called it—down I-95 to the Aquia Commerce Center, about fifteen minutes away.

As they climbed the steps to the second floor, Safarik said, "We used to be holed away in the subbasement of the academy, next to the BSU—the Behavioral Science Unit. No windows, low ceilings, cinderblock walls. It was a bunker. We used to say we worked in a place that was ten times deeper than dead people."

"Kind of fitting, I guess, considering the work."

"They realized we needed more room—and some sunlight—so a couple of years ago they moved us here. But I kind of liked the old place. It put me in the mood. It was grim, spooky. Don't get me wrong—I like my new office—but the subbasement had . . . I don't know, *character*."

They were buzzed in the main door and headed down the corridor. He stopped behind a man in a gray suit with salt-and-pepper hair. "Tom. I want to introduce you to a detective out of New York. Karen Vail. Karen, this is Thomas Gifford, the new ASAC—assistant special in charge—of the PBAU."

Gifford looked her over, then shook her hand. "Detective." He glanced at Safarik. "I thought I assigned this case to Rooney."

"Yeah—I was just showing Karen around the academy."

"Rooney could've done that. I want you to help Phoenix PD get some traction on the poisoner case."

"Just about done with my report. Headed back to my office right now."

Gifford frowned, then gave Vail a nod. "Detective. Good luck with your case."

VAIL MET WITH Rooney, and when she handed over the case file, he invited her into his office. He had a window overlooking a wooded area between the two office buildings on the Aquia complex, the miniblinds tilted down to showcase the greenery.

He settled his lean frame into the high-backed ergonomic chair and motioned her to the guest seat on the opposite side of his desk. His southern accent and crew cut reminded her of the early Apollo astronauts she had studied in school.

"My specialty is arson and bombing, so I'm not too sure why I landed this case. But give me the broad strokes and we'll go from there. And I'll keep Safarik in the loop to make sure I'm tracking the right way."

"That'd be great."

Rooney shrugged. "Mark and I pick each other's brains all the time. Not a problem."

Vail spent the next few minutes outlining the major points of each murder and then got to a question that had been bugging her.

"I can't figure out why the second crime scene was different from the others. Why a male, and why a chair instead of the bed?"

Rooney rocked back a bit as he considered her question. "Variation in a series of crimes could be because of the high degree of impulsivity of the offender. That said, the selection of male versus female could be because the male was special to the offender in some way. He might've had a personal connection, and, obviously, not a positive one."

"He was a Mafia capo. I'm sure a lot of people would've liked to drive a piece of glass through his carotid."

Rooney chuckled. "Then that might not be something that's going to help you solve this case. But differences in victim selection could also just boil down to the killer needing variation. Psychopaths get bored. It's part of who they are, so they'll vary their crimes just to keep it interesting. That's assuming he's a psychopath. Do you have doubts that this vic is from the same offender?"

"No—none at all."

"Okay, I'll keep that in mind as I take a look at the case."

They chatted a bit more, then Vail thanked him. "I've gotta get on the road or the traffic's gonna kill me."

"You headed home or are you staying overnight?"

"Home. Hopefully I'll get to see my baby before he goes down for the night."

And then there's my husband. If only I could figure out what's going on with him.

32

›MANHATTAN SOUTH HOMICIDE SQUAD
Wednesday, February 24, 1999

V ail had an email from Art Rooney waiting in her inbox when she sat down at her desk. She replied, then saw another message from the police commissioner's office outlining the issues facing them with the pending turnover to the year 2000 and what the Y2K issue meant in terms of computer programming and their internal systems. It had been an ongoing effort, since there was no clear opinion among the experts on how widespread or damaging the problem would be when the calendar turned to 2000—or even if there would be a problem at all.

And given the NYPD's spotty record in launching technology initiatives, this is going to be interesting.

As she finished reading the email, Antonio Fonzarella passed her desk.

"Oh," Vail said. "I need a few minutes of your time."

"On our case?" he asked, continuing on, thumbing through a couple of sizable envelopes and not bothering to look at her.

"Yeah. I submitted it to the FBI's Profiling and Behavioral Analysis Unit and wanted to share some of what I learned."

Fonzarella stopped walking and turned, advancing toward her, his face crumpled into an angry scowl. "You did what?"

Vail swiveled around in her chair. "I was intrigued by their presentation and I think we need help. It was assigned to one of the profilers who—"

"That wasn't your call to make."

Vail tilted her head. "What are you talking about? This is my case."

"News flash, rookie. The chief of detectives runs the show. Everything gets run past him and he gives us thumbs up or down."

Jesus, talk about micromanaging.

"You, me, and anyone else who's involved in this case, we're just the soldiers. The case isn't 'yours' to manage anymore. On a minute-by-minute basis, the lead's shared by both of us. We need something, we call the chief. But since you're green behind the ears, the chief's given me the nod to be his liaison. And what all that means, sweetie, is that I'm calling the shots."

Speaking of shots, I've got sixteen rounds in my Glock with your name on them. Asshole.

"Capisce?"

Vail swiveled her chair back toward her desk. "I don't speak Italian."

"Then here's the translation for you: call your buddies at the Bureau and tell 'em thanks but no thanks, that you had no authorization to make the request and that if we need their help, it'll come from me or the chief of detectives."

"I'm not your secretary." Vail grabbed a piece of scrap paper and wrote down the phone number. "But here you go, *Fonzie*. You can call them yourself. I'm telling you, though, I think they can help. They've *already* helped. If you can't see past your ego to realize that we don't know it all, then I've got a lot more on my plate than I thought."

He crumpled the paper and tossed it onto her desk. "Here's one thing I'm sure of. *You* don't know it all. Don't speak for me. Now make that damn call and tell your Fed buddies to stand down. I don't need their help."

33

>ELLIS ISLAND
SUNDAY, NOVEMBER 7, 1976

Niklaus leaned back in the chair in Dmitri's room and tossed an ace of spades onto the bed. The candle burned atop the mantle of the fireplace, which charred its logs low and slow.

Dmitri was looking over his hand, spreading them apart, and then pulled out a queen of clubs and placed it atop the pile. "Do you remember your mom?"

Niklaus froze for a second, then chose another card. "Yeah. Kind of." He paused, then said, "Not really."

"Do you miss her?" Dmitri asked.

"Why are you asking?"

"You never talk about her."

Niklaus tossed down a five of diamonds. "Just play, will you?"

"Do you have any pictures of her?"

"My dad does."

They traded turns a few times before Dmitri said, "How'd she die?"

Niklaus's head snapped up. "What?"

"Your mom. How'd she die?"

"Why do you want to know?"

Dmitri kept his gaze on the cards.

"Dmitri. Look at me." When he did not move, Niklaus leaned forward and angled his face up toward his stepbrother. "Look at me."

He slowly lifted his eyes.

"Why are you asking me about this?"

Dmitri glanced back down at his cards. "I want to know."

Niklaus sat back in his chair and fiddled with his hand. A minute later he said, "Cancer."

Dmitri nodded. "That's when cells grow too much and they take over the body's normal cells, so if it's in your liver, you get useless cancer cells taking the place of real liver cells. And then the liver doesn't work right. And you die."

Niklaus looked at him a long moment. "How do you know all that?"

"It can also be where the tumor grows so big that it crowds out the organ, and eventually crushes it." He set his cards down and clapped his hands together. Hard. "Bam! Like that. It's pretty bad. Cancer is."

Niklaus inched forward in his chair. "How do you know this stuff?"

Dmitri shrugged. "My book."

"What book?"

Dmitri sat for a moment looking down at his cards, then got off his chair and walked over to a spot beside his bed. He felt around, then pulled out his pocket knife, stuck the tip into the floorboard and pried it up.

"What the hell are you doing?" Niklaus asked.

He lifted a foot-long section of the plank and set it aside, then stuck his hand into the abyss.

Niklaus knelt down beside his stepbrother and peered in. "What's down there?"

Dmitri felt around and then pulled out a worn clothbound hardback book.

Niklaus took it and brushed his hand across the cover, dusting off the dirt. "How Humans Die." He thumbed through it, pausing to look at the diagrams showing photos of normal anatomy and diseased organs. "This is sick."

"It's got all kinds of diseases in there. And murder too. Like when you stick a knife in the lungs, it tells you why you die, at a . . . at a microscopic level. The pressure inside the al—alvee—alveoli—"

"Why'd you draw an X on this page?"

"I wanted to show that part to you. There are a lot of really cool things. Like when you have a stroke, the blood supply to the brain is cut—"

"Dimitri, where'd you get this book?"

He looked down at his lap. "A store."

"With what money?"

"I didn't need to pay for it."

"You stole it?"

"No. I just . . . took it."

"What else you got down there?" Niklaus asked, craning his neck to look into the crawl space. He shoved his hand into the hole and felt several more books and magazines.

He pulled out one of them—a worn copy of a December 1970 issue of *Playboy*. "She's a looker," he said, studying the blonde wearing a Santa's hat—and nothing else. He reached down again into the hole and—

"No," Dimitri said. "Leave it alone!"

"I just wanna see what other stuff you've g—"

"I said no!" Dimitri grabbed his arm. "It's mine, Nik. Stop!"

Niklaus extracted his hand—and along with it, another two books: *Killer: A Journal of Murder* and *Confessions of the Boston Strangler*. He turned away, shielding them with his body. "Dmitri, what are you doing with these?"

"Give 'em to me," he said as he tried to reach around Niklaus's shoulder.

Niklaus splayed the first hardcover open and flipped a couple of pages but Dmitri tried to grab it away. He got hold of the edge and the two boys struggled, eventually hitting the floor.

Niklaus regained control and yanked the books away, but they went flying across the room. One struck the door, which opened a second later.

"What the—what's all the noise about?" Livana asked. She bent down and picked up the hardcover at her feet. Her mouth fell open and she looked up. "What is this?"

Niklaus sat up. Dmitri pulled the hood of his sweatshirt over his head. Neither of them spoke.

"Fedor!" Livana called. "Come in here, please."

Niklaus turned to Dmitri, who merely stared at the ground.

"I asked you a question," she said. "What is—I mean, I know what this is. Whose is this?"

Fedor came up behind Livana. She handed him the book.

"Where did this come from?" He looked at Niklaus, who bit his lip and then turned to Dmitri, who did not move.

"A store in the city," Niklaus said, still looking at Dmitri.

"It's yours?" Fedor asked.

"I, uh . . ." He turned to his father, then back to Dmitri. "Yeah."

Dmitri turned to Niklaus, glanced up at him, then canted his eyes down again.

Cassandra poked her head in the doorway, but Livana pushed her away. "Go back to your room."

Fedor bent down and scooped up the Boston Strangler book. He handed it and *A Journal of Murder* to Livana, then took a few steps toward the bed. "What are you hiding there, Nik?"

Niklaus looked down at the other hardback and then handed it over, moving the floorboard over the opening with his shoe as he reached forward.

"*How Humans Die?* This yours too?"

Niklaus swallowed hard. "It's really interesting. You can learn about all kinds of diseases. Like cancer. Now I know why Mom died."

Fedor recoiled. His eyes teared up. He cleared his throat. "I'm taking this with me," he said, holding the hardcover against his chest.

"It's mine," Dmitri said. "The *Playboy* too."

"What *Playboy*?" Livana asked.

"Here." Dmitri pointed at the floor.

Niklaus broke out into a sweat, concerned that she would see the hole in the floor. He looked down to where the issue of *Playboy* was lying face down. He quickly gathered it up and handed it to her.

Livana took it but immediately handed it off to Fedor, as if touching it made her feel dirty.

"I'm very disappointed in you," Livana said. "Both of you, bringing that trash into our home."

"Our *home*?" Niklaus said. He looked around the room. "We live on an *island*. No friends. No electricity. No TV, no radio. Weird people, abandoned buildings—"

"That's enough!" Fedor said. "Go take a walk, clear your head."

"It's pitch-black outside. Where should I go?"

"Out," Fedor said through clenched teeth. "You too, Dmitri. With your brother. Just . . . get out."

Dmitri stood up, repositioned his hood, and trudged out, Niklaus following close behind.

"SO WHO'S TELLING THE TRUTH?" Livana asked. "Whose books are they?"

Fedor, standing in the kitchen leaning against the counter, crossed his arms. "Nik was covering for Dmitri."

"But they both admitted it—"

"I know my son."

Livana felt unsteady. She reached for a chair and sat down heavily. "My god. Why is he so interested in death? Why the book about killers? And the *Playboy* . . ."

"Liv, his father was brutally murdered right in front of him. And he was chained to tracks and nearly run over by a train. Not to mention . . ." He wiped his brow. "I mean, forgive me, but we don't know what those bastards did to him while they were holding him. That would affect any of us. And he was just a kid. Who knows what that whole experience did to him. I mean, we know what we see: he's withdrawn, quiet. He doesn't make eye contact. Whatever happened, it left its mark. It's kind of remarkable he's doing as well as he is, all things considered."

"And the *Playboy*?"

Fedor chuckled. "He's a teenage boy. Do I need to say more?"

Livana set both elbows on the table and rested her head in her hands. "I didn't realize Niklaus was so unhappy here. Has he said anything to you?"

"I think he was just blowing off steam." Fedor was silent for a moment, then said, "He hasn't mentioned anything. This is the first I'm hearing of it. But I know it's tough on the kids. All of them. They're different. Isolated from other kids and what 'normal' teenagers do after school. They get on a boat and get taken back into isolation. I think, for them, it's like a prison."

"Should we start looking at moving?"

Fedor turned away. "I don't know. I'm not sure it's safe."

Livana stood up. "How long can this go on, Fedor? I mean, we can't live in fear the rest of our lives. The kids—they're growing up. At some point they're going to want to live a normal life. We can't keep them here forever. Nor should we. When your—at some point, when your grandparents pass, we should move. To California. Or Texas. Okay?"

Fedor nodded. "Okay."

34

>ELLIS ISLAND
SUNDAY, NOVEMBER 7, 1976

iklaus and Dmitri trudged down the dirt path, flashlights in hand.

"They're really pissed," Niklaus said.

"Not my fault," Dmitri said. "Not my fault."

"Well, it wasn't *my* fault," Niklaus said. "If you hadn't acted like an idiot, she wouldn't have come in."

"I wanna go back." He shivered. "I'm cold. I need my jacket."

"We'll go back when they cool down. They need some time." They walked in silence a moment. "Bummer about the books. If you didn't freak out, they wouldn't have known they were yours. Both of us didn't need to get in trouble. I wouldn't have told on you."

"Maybe they'll give them back."

"They're not gonna give them back."

"Maybe we can find where they put them, take 'em back. They belong to me."

"I'll help you look. But it's gotta be when they go into the city on a weekend, where they can't walk in on us while we're looking. Or you can just buy another copy."

They walked a few more feet. "Doesn't matter, I've got more."

"More books?"

"Yeah."

"More books on killers?"

"I like them. One guy, he built a three-story castle, which was really like a hotel. And people came to stay there and they never left because he killed them."

"No one missed them?"

"This was a long time ago, 1893. In Chicago. The killer's name was Herman Mudgett but he used the name Holmes. Like Sherlock. When the police searched his castle they found hidden stairs, trapdoors, fake walls. The rooms where the people slept were airtight so that Mudgett could kill them by pumping poison gas through pipes that were controlled by valves in his own bedroom."

"No kidding?"

"And he dissected them in his basement, stripped off their flesh and then sold their organs to a local medical school. Some of the bodies he cremated after he was done with them."

"'Done?' With what?"

"He also had torture machines down there. Like a rack to stretch their arms and legs, to pull the limbs off the bodies."

"How many people did he kill?"

"He confessed to twenty-seven, but some think it was two hundred."

"Two hundred? Holy shit."

They reached the island's edge and stared out at the rough, cold waters. Directly ahead of them was the Statue of Liberty, in profile, lit from below. The aura from her torch—barely visible from this angle—put out an orange glow, muted by the thick, foggy air.

"Are you interested in this stuff," Niklaus asked, "because of what happened to you? When those guys took you?"

Dmitri stared out into the darkness but did not answer.

"What happened when you were there?"

"I don't want to talk about it."

"Just tell me what they did to you."

Dmitri clapped both hands over his ears. "Wasn't my fault, wasn't my fault, wasn't my fault!"

"Calm down," Niklaus said. "I didn't say it was."

They stood there, looking out at the statue.

Dmitri wrapped his arms around himself to ward off the chill. "I like her, Liberty."

Niklaus faced his stepbrother. "What?"

"We should go live *there*," Dmitri said. "She's really big. Nobody's gonna bother *her*."

35

> ## >ONE POLICE PLAZA
FOURTEENTH FLOOR
MANHATTAN
THURSDAY, APRIL 1, 1999

Vail sat across from Antonio Fonzarella, chief of detectives Aidan Kearney, and police commissioner Brendan Carrig. Deputy commissioner Sandy Gelber, the commanding officer of the homicide squad, Orlando Mendoza, and borough commander Wallace Yarles rounded out the conference table. Russo occupied the chair directly to her left.

She had never met the commissioner before, and she had a feeling that this would not be an occurrence she would want to write home about, let alone remember.

They had made little progress on the case and the media had started to notice the pattern of murders because of a leaked detail revealing that almost all of the victims were Greek women. And in New York City, when journalists sunk their teeth into something, they were like dogs clamping down on a piece of meat: they did not let go, and it was impossible to distract them or dislodge their prey.

And with attention from the press came press*ure* from the brass. Hence the meeting, called by the commissioner, who sat at the head of the conference room table.

Carrig, a large man with a crew cut and thick features, tossed a copy of the *New York Post* onto the polished wood surface. The bold headline screamed from the paper:

HADES SLASHER SERIAL KILLER
MURDERS FOUR
NYPD hides it from public

Vail closed her eyes. *Great, they've even got a name for him.*

"Hades was the Greek god of the underworld and the dead," Carrig said. "So the *Post* obviously did their homework in choosing his nickname." He removed his reading glasses. "I don't have to tell you that the stakes are now higher—in terms of publicity. Our jobs are now harder. We've had sufficient time to solve this case and what have we got? Very little to show for our efforts." He nodded at Chief Kearney.

Kearney, whose head was narrower at the top and got wider near the shoulders, looked like a former football player whose neck was compressed from too many helmet-first tackles of 350-pound linemen. In a thick New York accent he said, "Let's do a thorough review of what we got in the file. I wanna start with vic one."

"That'd be Carole Manos," Vail said. "But we're not—"

"No," Kearney said. "Detective Fonzarella. Please."

Mozzarella wasn't even there. I was. This is bullshit.

Fonzarella cleared his throat. "Right. Vic one was found in a bed, a shard of glass shoved into the side of her neck." He proceeded to recount the details of the case—until Vail interrupted him.

"Commissioner," she said, "we can't be completely sure Ms. Manos was the first victim."

"What do you mean, we can't be sure? She either was or she wasn't. Was there another victim exhibiting the same MO who was killed before her?"

"No. I mean, we don't know. As far as we know, there wasn't any in New York."

Carrig spread his thick hands. "Then what on earth are you talking about?"

"I spoke with the FBI about this case, their Profiling and Behavioral Analysis Unit, and they feel that—"

"Wait. What?" He turned to Mendoza. "What the hell are you doing?"

Mendoza, his Hispanic complexion darkening in anger, gave Vail a stare that could kill if so empowered. "I didn't know anything about this."

"If I may," Fonzarella said. "Detective Vail took it upon herself to contact them. I put a stop to it as soon as I found out about it."

"And I disagreed," Vail said. "I think they have a unique approach to serial crimes, and we could use the help."

"Maybe we could use the help because we've had the wrong detectives working this case." Kearney's gaze was directed at Vail, not Fonzarella.

Russo inched his chair closer. "If I may, commissioner." Carrig gave him a wave, so he continued. "I've been keeping tabs on this at regular intervals. Detective Vail has done nothing wrong in her management of the case. Nor has Detective Fonzarella. I think their approach has been sound."

"Yet we're nowhere."

"Despite our best efforts, we've failed to generate a lead. I don't have to tell you that sometimes it happens. This killer hasn't left any forensics to speak of. He's smart. And very good."

Kearney laughed. "I like to think we're smart too. And very good."

According to Detective Mozzarella, we've got the best detective on the East Coast working the case.

"Then—for now—we'll keep at it, with the current team intact. Detective," he said, gesturing at Fonzarella. "Continue. Vic two."

"Right. This one was a little different. Different because it was a male vic, the Castiglia capo, Dominic Crinelli."

"Hang on a second," Kearney said. "There was something back a couple of years ago, when Tim Thorne was killed in that car accident. A witness. You two were on your way to meet him." He looked at Vail. "Did you ever follow up with him?"

"I tried. The guy was gone, like he was never there. I brought in a forensic crew. The apartment was clean—like it had been wiped down."

Kearney shared a look with Carrig and then asked, "What about the name of this witness?"

"Bogus," Vail said. "I looked into it. We don't have a way of recording incoming calls, so we've got no voice print, no nothing. We don't even have caller ID. Only thing we could do was trace the calls to a pay phone."

"So what the hell does it mean?"

"I've been over this with Lieutenant Russo. We can't figure out what the deal was with that. There are a number of possibilities, but none make a whole lot of sense. The best one we came up with is that our 'witness' was the killer trying to lure us to his apartment. But he changed his mind and left when we didn't show because of the accident."

"Really? That's the best you've got?" Kearney frowned, then made some notes on his yellow pad.

Vail felt like the principal had just suspended her for a week.

"Crinelli was a capo," said Gelber, the deputy commissioner. "Anyone think of looking at this as a retribution kill?"

"We did," Russo said. "We went all the way back to his early days as an enforcer. This goombah broke heads in all five boroughs. But we checked everyone, cleared everyone."

"Vic three," Mendoza said, without looking up. "Fonzie."

"Right." Fonzarella turned the page in his folder.

Vail buried her nose in her copy of the file and tried to look busy. She was paging through the DD-5 reports from the Manos murder when something caught her eye. The DD-5 was a standard NYPD form that the detective completed after each contact she had with the case: a phone call with a witness, a message she left for a detective in another state, contact with the crime lab . . . anything that happened relative to the case required her to complete, and sign, a DD-5. They now had eighty-nine DD-5s in the Hades file.

But it wasn't the DD-5 that was the problem: it was her signature on the facing page, the sixty-one—also known as the complaint report. It did not look right. She leaned toward Russo and whispered in his ear.

The commissioner cleared his throat. "Sorry if we're boring you, Detective Vail."

"Oh—you're not—I mean, I need to look into something important pertaining to the case." She rose from her chair and gathered up the file. "I'll be back as soon as I can. I'm sure Detective Fonzarella will do a bang-up job until I get back."

Vail walked out and headed to Manhattan South homicide, lights and siren. She found a parking spot down the block and went directly to the aide on duty in the crime analysis office.

"I need the scratch sixty-ones on my case."

Every sixty-one started off with a handwritten "scratch" version that was then transcribed by the police administrative aide, or PAA, who manually typed the data into the Omniform computer system. The original was always retained in case incomplete or erroneous information was created during transcription.

"All the sixty-ones are in that box on the second shelf, arranged by month and year."

Vail started digging through documents, looking for the form she had concerns about. But the report she wanted to see was missing.

As she stood there paging through the documents one more time—to be certain it was not there—her BlackBerry rang.

"Vail."

"Karen, what the hell are you doing?"

It was Russo—and he did not sound pleased.

"Like I started to tell you, something's not right in the file. I'm in crime analysis looking for the scratch—"

"Get your ass back here ASAP. We got a problem."

"What kind of problem?"

"Come and you'll find out." And then he hung up.

VAIL HIGHTAILED IT back to One Police Plaza and arrived ten minutes later—remarkable time, in fact.

But it was too late. When she walked in, the meeting had already adjourned, and she got a cold stare from the commissioner as he was walking back into his office. Kearney did not even bother looking at her.

Only Fonzarella gave her the "courtesy" of a comment. He shook his head and snorted. "You sure know how to make an impression. A *bad* impression."

As he pushed past her, Russo emerged, arguing with the deputy commissioner and chief of detectives. Whatever they were discussing, Russo was losing the battle. Both men walked off and left him standing there, shoulders slumped. He saw Vail down the hall and headed in her direction.

"What's going on?"

Russo checked over his shoulder, then ushered her toward the steps. They pushed through the metal fire door and stood in the stairwell.

"You shouldn't have left."

"But I told—"

"I don't care how important it was, Karen, you don't walk out on a meeting with the police commissioner, his deputy, and the chief of detectives."

"It's not like they were listening to anything I had to say. It's clear they wanted Fonzarella running the show."

"Be that as it may, you have to show them respect."

Vail leaned back. "I wasn't disrespecting them. I noticed something in the file, a forged sixty-one, and I thought time was of the essence—"

"Karen, listen to me. You don't have to convince me of anything. I know that if you left there was a good reason. I know you. They don't. They know *of* you, through me, because of your . . . recognitions of valor. But this Hades case is bad, it's a goddamn demerit on your resume, you hear me?"

"Because we haven't caught the killer?"

"Yeah, there's that. And—oh, yeah—he's killed four people. And now he's on the press's radar. This is an A-list high-profile case now, and they don't think you're up to the task."

This is leading somewhere. Do I want to know where? Vail shifted her weight. "Meaning what?"

Russo set his hand on the gray metal handrail. "I've been around the block so I know what's happening here: they're handing this case to Fonzarella. You're still on board, but you're gonna be marginalized. You'll be given grunt work, bullshit stuff. Nothing even remotely important."

She looked at the door and started to reach for the knob. Russo clamped his hand over hers.

"No. You're not supposed to know what's going on. I've seen it before, and if the brass doesn't want you in the thick of things, you're not gonna be in the thick of things. Way it is. And don't be gettin' on anyone's case about it. Because they'll know it came from me, and I'm already takin' some heat over this."

She didn't need to ask why. Russo had pushed for her promotion to detective and he had pressed for her to take over the Hades case.

Vail dropped her hand from the knob. "Okay." She took a deep breath. "So what do I do?"

"My advice is to keep a low profile. Do your thing, work the case, don't stir up any trouble. Be the perfect little detective. And don't let on to anyone that you know they're trying to fuck you over. Got it?"

"Yeah."

"But don't be surprised when they keep things from you."

"I'll keep my eyes and ears open."

"Stay focused on the main idea: we're trying to catch this killer. You're not doing it for the department, or for Carrig or Kearney or Mendoza or Fonzarella. You're doing it for the innocent people this asshole's targeting next. You work for the victims."

"Okay."

"Let's get back to the house." They started descending the stairs. "So what'd you find? A forged sixty-one? And you went back to get the scratch?"

"Right. Checked with crime analysis. But it's not there."

Russo stopped midstairs. "Shit."

"All's not lost." Vail grinned. "I keep copies of all my reports. I've got 'em back home."

"Then I suggest we take a ride to Rosedale."

IT WAS NEARLY two o'clock when Vail and Russo pulled into her driveway. Deacon's car was parked at the curb in front of the house, where he had left it the night before.

When they walked in, Vail stopped three steps down the hall—for directly to her left, lying on the living room couch, was Deacon. His hair was a mess and he was on his stomach, left arm draped over the side and resting on the floor.

"Deacon," Vail said, walking over to the sofa. "Deacon." She shook his shoulder and he lifted his head, focused on her face, then dropped back to the cushion.

"What are you doing here? Why aren't you at work?"

She knelt down in front of him and immediately drew back. "Oh, Jesus. You've been drinking." As if she needed proof, to his left on the side of the couch was a garbage pail filled with spent beer cans.

Russo cleared his throat. "I'll wait outside. Come get me when you— when you've got this straightened out."

The storm door swung closed. Deacon pushed himself erect and he leaned back, his head falling from side to side until he righted it. "What are you doing here? What time is it? Who's that guy? You having an af—an affffair?"

Vail stood up. "What the hell's going on, Deacon? Answer my question. Why aren't you at work?"

He rubbed his eyes. "Called in sick."

"Again?"

"Guess so." He tried to stand, thought better of it, and sat back down.

Terrific.

Vail left Deacon and ran upstairs to the third bedroom, where she kept the fireproof box that contained photocopies of her case files. She retrieved the Hades folder and clomped back down the steps. Deacon was still on the couch, his head between his knees, vomiting into the garbage pail.

He wiped his mouth with the sleeve of his sweatshirt, then looked up and realized that Vail had returned. He gazed down at the floor, seemingly embarrassed, some degree of lucidity returning.

Vail stood there, unsure of what to do, what to say—but knowing that Russo was waiting for her and she had to get back to work. "I'll pick up Jonathan tonight." He did not respond. "Deacon, look at me. Look at me." He craned his head up, slowly. "Don't you dare get behind the wheel."

Can I trust him? Is he thinking clearly? Can I trust him with my son?

"I'm taking your car keys. And I'm calling the school and telling them not to release him to you."

His head wandered left, then right, then left again.

"When I get home tonight we're gonna have a long talk."

"When's that? Midnight? Nevvvvver see you anymore!"

Vail grabbed Deacon's keys and headed outside, where Russo was waiting for her. "He's drunk."

"I noticed."

"I'm sorry you had to see that."

Russo got into the car, then started the engine. "This happen before?"

Vail closed her eyes. *This is embarrassing. But if I can't tell Russo, who can I tell?"*

"He said he hasn't been feeling good. Said he hasn't been happy, but he doesn't know what's wrong."

"You were a psych major, weren't you?"

"Psych and art history. Double major."

"And what does your schooling tell you?"

She thought a moment. "He's depressed."

Russo pulled away from the curb. "Get him some help, Karen. Before it gets out of hand."

I think we're past that point.

36

>BELT PARKWAY
Springfield Gardens, Queens
Thursday, April 1, 1999

V ail paged through the copy of her file, comparing it to the one they had been using in the meeting—also a duplicate, since Fonzarella insisted on having the original in his possession.

"Anything?" Russo asked as he changed lanes on the Belt Parkway.

"The scratch actually looks okay—just the usual flubs the police administrative aide makes from time to time. Nothing major." *And the forged signature—oh, crap. That's when I sprained my finger. That's why the signature didn't look right. Shit, that's just great. I left the commissioner's meeting for nothing?*

"So what does that mean? It's okay? All this for nothing?"

"No, hang on. Give me a minute." *Think of a bullshit excuse. No. I can't do that to Russo.* She turned the pages, looking for something—anything—and that's when she saw it.

"Wait a minute." Vail flipped the document, went back, and then rifled through the remaining pages. "It's missing."

"What's missing? I thought you said the sixty-one was—"

"No, this is a DD-5. After Manos was murdered, the detective handling the case—Berger—he went down with a hip, right?"

"Yeah, had the thing replaced, never made it back on the job. Surgeon botched it, was wheelchair-bound for a couple years and then had an embolism. He bit the dust last year."

"Okay, so remember when you brought me into the case my first day on the job? Berger let me make a copy of the file to look over, so I could get a feel for how an investigation was run. A day or so after CSU finished up, Carole Manos's mother found a book kicked under the couch that she swore was not her daughter's. She brought it by the precinct and left it with the PAA, who put it in Berger's mailbox. When he got in the next morning, he vouchered the book as investigative in case he needed it at a later date, he wrote up his DD-5, and that was that."

"Right, I kinda sorta remember something like that."

"Well, now DD-5 number 14 is missing from the file."

"Misfiled?"

"No, it's just not there." Vail stared at the copied report. *Doesn't make sense. It was there when I made the copies of the file and now it's not?* "Do me a favor. Let's stop by Property and get a look at this book mentioned in the DD-5."

"Why?"

"Just being thorough."

"What kind of book is it?"

"Something titled . . . " She scanned the report. "Here it is. *How Humans Die.* An old, worn copy."

"*How Humans Die.* What the hell kind of book is that? Fiction? Nonfiction?"

"I'll have to look it up when we get back to the house."

"You do that," Russo said. "Not sure it's something I'd want to read. I've seen enough humans die. That's all I need to know on the subject."

THEY ARRIVED AT headquarters, officially known as One Police Plaza, and entered at street level through the employee entrance. A cop sat behind a duty desk that was lined with gadgets, levers, switches, and LED lights.

"What the hell does all that high-tech shit do?" Vail asked.

"No idea," Russo said as they placed their NYPD ID cards against the electronic reader. He lowered his voice and leaned closer to her. "And I'm sure that cop has no clue, either."

Vail placed her right index finger on the scanner, and after they both got the green light, they entered and headed left, to the Property clerk's office.

They walked through the large, oversize doors and up to the desk, which was secured by a partition with a window and a speaker.

"Hey, Charlie."

"Loo, how's it going?"

"Same old shit, you know how it is."

Charlie reached under the desk and a buzzer sounded. Russo thanked him and they proceeded in.

They told the PAA what case they needed evidence for, and they were directed back to utilitarian storage racks containing labeled boxes.

They located the correct container and rummaged through the items obtained during the Manos murder investigation. But the book was not there.

"This is not good," Vail said. "First the DD-5's missing and now the actual evidence is missing. If it was just the form, maybe you could argue it was accidentally dumped. But the book? In Property? That doesn't just disappear unless someone wants it gone."

"It's in the voucher log," Russo said. "Right?"

"Has to be. I'll check when we get back." She pulled out the DD-5 copy and handed it to Russo. "DD-5's got the voucher number, the voucher officer. It's definitely in the log book."

Russo asked the aide for a list of everyone who had accessed the case materials. Five minutes later she handed it over.

"Everyone's accounted for—Berger, me, you, Fonzarella—except, who's Victor Danzig?"

"Danzig?" Russo shrugged.

"He was a PAA in your office," the aide said. "Had some problems, got canned."

"Oh shit," Russo said. "I remember that jerkoff. Danzig was an addict, heroin and crack and anything else he could get his hands on. Once we realized what was going on, we fired his ass."

"But why would he care about a DD-5 and this *How Humans Die* book?"

Russo thought a moment then locked gazes with Vail. "Unless he's the killer. And he was trying to remove something that could implicate him."

Vail nodded. "Right. For whatever reason, he brought that book with him to the crime scene and dropped it, lost it under the couch, forgot it. Which means maybe there's something about it, or written in it, that could point us in his direction."

"But without the book, we don't have any way of knowing what it was that could be a problem for the killer."

As they started toward Russo's car, Vail said, "If Berger didn't find anything obvious, it may be that whatever it is that the killer's afraid of is subtle—or we'd need to have the bigger picture to make sense of it. But whatever it was, he didn't want to risk it."

"Berger might not have gone through it too closely. I probably wouldn't have, not when it wasn't clear it was evidence." Russo skirted a puddle in the pothole-filled parking lot and got into the car. "Find another copy of that book somewhere. Call used bookstores, see if there are any book dealers or clearinghouses that might carry it or at least know something about it. And if you can find out the publisher, maybe they've got a copy hanging around in their office or a warehouse somewhere. If our clue's in the text of the book, it won't matter if we have the original or a copy."

"But if there were handwritten notes, it won't do us a whole lot of good."

"Gotta start somewhere." Russo hit a particularly deep pothole and the suspension bottomed out. "Goddamn roads."

"How about we start with Victor Danzig?"

"Good point. Let's get moving on that right now."

"We should bring Fonzarella into this," Vail said. "And Mendoza. Right?"

Russo turned to Vail, a devious look in his eyes. "Mendoza first," he said, holding up an index finger. "If this turns into something, I wanna make sure the chief knows you were the one who came up with it, not his star asshole Fonzarella."

"I call him Mozzarella."

"That fits." Russo laughed. "Man, that really fits."

37

›MANHATTAN SOUTH HOMICIDE SQUAD
Thursday, April 1, 1999

V ail got off the phone after laying out the discovery to Mendoza, who was going to inform Fonzarella himself while they located possible locations for Danzig. He was also going to place ESU on alert in case they were able to track him down with reasonable certainty.

He told Vail that she and Russo were to report back to the squad immediately.

As they hit midtown, Vail thought about the implications. Could this be Hades? Could they be so lucky, after all this time, to suddenly catch a break? Could *Vail* be so lucky to revive her career after suffering a serious stall only hours earlier?

They parked and ran into the precinct, where they found Fonzarella, Kearney, and Mendoza in the briefing room, huddled over a large format map. A computer terminal operated by a PAA displayed potential locations.

"What do we got?" Russo asked.

"Danzig's had two run-ins with us since his termination," Mendoza said. "One possession rap, which he beat on a procedural fuckup in chain of evidence, and another firearms arrest when he was threatening his girlfriend. She decided not to press charges so he was released."

"And we have indications he lied on his department app," Fonzarella said. "Danzig may be an alias. We're looking into it, but it's slow going. The records aren't computerized, so we've got a couple guys going through the docs at One PP."

"Anything to indicate he could be Hades?" Russo asked.

"Nothing yet," Mendoza said. "But I'll tell you what. We ain't goin' in there without ESU taking the lead." He reached over and signed a form the PAA shoved in front of him. "Danzig's an addict. He's unstable, probably armed, and unpredictable. If he is our doer, he's now in the news. He knows he's got our attention and we could be comin' after him."

"I doubt he's going to be thinking we're on to him," Vail said. "He did a good job of purging both the evidence and the DD-5. If I wasn't so . . . "

"Anal?" Russo said.

I was thinking "thorough." "If I wasn't so 'anal' about my files, I wouldn't have had a copy of it. But I always keep copies of all my files just in—"

"Yeah," Mendoza said. "Give yourself a pat on the back but spare me the narrative. You got lucky, nothing more."

Lucky?

"Point is," said Kearney, who came up behind Mendoza, "we're gonna assume the worst."

THREE HOURS LATER, they had verified Danzig's whereabouts using Con Ed bills, test phone calls to his home posing as a telemarketer, and a stakeout with two detectives outfitted with binoculars.

A block away from the apartment, Vail, Russo, Fonzarella, and Mendoza sat in the back of a mobile command vehicle alongside several technicians with TARU, the Technical Assistance Response Unit. The ESU truck was parked directly in front of them.

Russo radioed the surveillance team on the point-to-point channel. "Do we have eyes-on?"

"Affirm," came the response. "Male subject, matching the description of the suspect. One subject arrived at 5:57 and left at 6:03. We ID'd him as Felix Rivera. Small-time drug dealer. Danzig may be his supplier. We took no action and he left without incident. No other parties visible in the apartment during the past forty-five minutes."

The ESU lieutenant stepped into the mobile command center and huddled with Mendoza and Russo.

"We've made phone calls to the surrounding apartments and quietly evacuated as many residents as we could," Mendoza said. "Standard bullshit—told them there's a gas leak, yada yada."

"So we're as ready as we can be," Russo said.

"Affirm. You people still want to join us? Because I wouldn't recommend—"

"Our case," Fonzarella said. "You take the lead, but we're going with you." He paused, glanced at Vail. "*I'm* going, don't know about her."

Vail fought the urge to roll her eyes. *Like I'm going to let him go without me.*

"This is the most high risk entry we do," the lieutenant said. "Close quarters and no way of knowing what's on the opposite side of the door. And because we've got apartments on both sides, above and below, we have to control our shots. Even though we tried to evacuate as many as we could, an errant round can be a bad friggin' nightmare."

"Understood," Fonzarella said. "You guys are running the show."

"Fine." The lieutenant looked at Vail, then Russo, then Mendoza. "Whoever's going, suit up, meet us outside in five."

THEY MOVED QUICKLY and quietly in the shadows wearing vests and helmets, 5.11 Tactical TDU pants, Vertex radios, MP-5 semiautomatic submachine guns, and Glock sidearms—except for Vail and Fonzarella, who had only service pistols and raid vests. They took up their positions in the front and rear of the brick apartment house.

Mature large-trunked trees, which had shed their leaves months earlier, provided cover from the streetlights and casual gawkers in adjacent buildings.

The ESU officers did their thing, using hand signals to position themselves and observe the suspect's residence. Vail and Fonzarella brought up the rear, staying close to the breaching team going in the front.

Five minutes later, they had climbed the four flights of the tight stairwell and stacked up along the railing opposite the door to the apartment.

Two officers took a position on either side of the entrance, the one on the left bearing the heavy roll-shaped battering ram in both hands. There was a wide-angle lens in the door, which they covered with a piece of blue tape.

"On my mark," the lieutenant said.

Vail brought up her Glock and trained it on the door, as the other officers had done with their MP-5s. But as she awaited the breach order, she noticed what looked like a series of security cameras hidden in the ceiling of the hall-way.

"Uh, loo, we got cameras!"

His response came over her earpiece for all to hear. "Fuck."

Cameras . . . is Danzig monitoring us, aware that we're lined up in the hallway, about to breach his front door—

As that thought rattled around her mind, a barrage of automatic gunfire blasted through the walls, spewing lead projectiles, wood chips, and plaster chunks at them.

Vail and Fonzarella were driven backward into the railing as several bullets struck their vests.

She hit the wrought iron hard, getting the wind knocked out of her. She managed to hold onto her Glock and twisted toward the doorway, watching for the suspect to emerge.

But some of the rounds must've taken out the hallway lightbulbs because the area suddenly went dark. The echoing noise in the small space was deafening.

A second later, there was yelling in her ear and all firing ceased. A dense haze filled the small rectangular space, which was now lit by the head-lamps the officers had switched on. The beams danced up and down, left and right, as the men swiveled their heads and advanced on the blown-out door.

"Officers down!" someone shouted in Vail's earpiece.

Vail swiveled and used her flashlight to survey the carnage. Two men were on the ground, one bleeding from the thigh and the other sprawled face up, unmoving.

As the others entered the apartment in search of Danzig, she called in a 10-13—officer needs assistance—for the injured man, then ripped a strip of cloth from her pants and tied it around his leg above the wound.

Next she scrabbled toward the other officer, negotiating the debris piled atop the worn tile.

Vail angled her light onto him to check his pulse, and found a nasty neck wound with a lot of blood pooling under his head. *Shit.* A round had struck him in the carotid, resulting in a rapid arterial bleed-out. To her right, a bright red spray pattern was spattered across the floor and nearby wall.

Realizing she had not seen or heard from Fonzarella, she swung her torso around and scanned the area. Aside from the two downed officers, she was the only person in the hallway. Had he gone in with the tac team?

Vail heard noise at the bottom of the staircase and brought her Glock up. "Police, don't move!" She swung over the top of the railing and looked down. It was a little brighter at the bottom, since the lower stairwell lights were still burning. But what she saw made her stomach contract.

Fonzarella lay dead at the bottom, his limbs—and head—twisted in an unnatural position.

AN HOUR PASSED and Vail was still numb. She had removed her tactical gear to be examined by a paramedic, unaware of much of what she had been asked during her debrief—or what her answers had been.

At some point, while she was seated at the curb, Russo came over and sat down next to her.

"I heard you've got some bruised ribs. You doin' okay?"

Not really. "I'm fine." She sat there a long moment, Russo giving her time. She brushed her red hair back off her face. "Wasn't a secret that I didn't like Fonzarella. But I feel a genuine sense of loss. He was a member of the team, he wanted what we all do—to catch the bastard. He didn't deserve to die like that. I just feel like crying." Another pause, then she managed a chuckle. "I guess that's a good thing because up until a few minutes ago, I wasn't feeling much of anything." She pulled her gaze over to his face. "How'd he fall?"

"Best we can tell, he was hit in the chest and fell backward, over the railing. Because he was so tall, he tipped right over. We'll know more later, but Finkelstein's pretty sure he broke his neck on impact."

"The other officers?"

"One's dead, I think you knew that. The other's gonna be okay. GSW to the thigh. He'll make a full recovery, thanks to you. Good work with the tourniquet."

Vail closed her eyes. "And Danzig? I heard they still hadn't located him."

"Looks like he slipped out. He apparently had his escape planned. Best guess is he survived our barrage using a ballistic shield, like the riot shield we use in crowd control. They found it in the living room.

"Loo thinks he went up to the roof because he couldn't go down. We had officers there, and he probably knew that. He spent years around a precinct. He picked up a lot of stuff about procedure, techniques. And I'm guessing he had his getaway route planned because of his drug dealing business. If things went south, he had a preplanned way out. And he saw us coming on the cameras. Plenty of time to get things ready."

"Anything in the apartment suggesting he's Hades?"

"I think that's gonna take awhile. I called Ryan Chandler personally and asked him to get down here. He was off duty, but he's here now. He and his team just started processing the scene."

"Can I go up, take a look?"

Russo grinned. "I think you've earned your pay for the night. Go home. Your son."

"He's at my mom's. I called her when I realized I wasn't going to be able to pick him up from day care."

And I sure as hell wasn't going to trust Deacon with that.

"So go get your son. Help your husband. He needs you."

Vail pushed herself up. She was exhausted, as if someone had put an IV in her arm and siphoned away all her energy. "Okay. You're right."

"I usually am." He laughed. "We both know that ain't true."

"Glad *you* said it."

"If Sofia were here, she woulda beat me to it." He glanced around at the CSU techs milling about. "You know, you're gonna get a rep."

Vail turned to him. "For what?"

"Bad shit happens to people you partner with." He chuckled again.

Forgive me if I don't think that's so funny. She let it pass. She had other concerns. "Seriously—you think I got a problem here?"

Russo faced her and shoved both hands in his jacket pockets. She was sure he knew what she was asking: because she had been the one to bring them the Danzig lead, which resulted in the death of both Fonzarella and the ESU officer, she would be blamed. Not officially, but within her precinct, if not in the broader close-knit department.

His face turned serious. "You really want to discuss this now?"

I don't think I want to discuss it at all. Ever. "Give it to me straight."

"I'm not gonna lie to you, Karen. Yeah, it's a problem. I'm not saying I think it's right—I'm just as much to blame, if *either* of us is to blame for anything. That remains to be seen. But sometimes the facts don't matter, you know what I mean?"

Vail took a deep breath. "I do."

"Go home, get a good night's sleep, and we'll see just how bad things are in the morning once the dust settles. I'll know as soon as I walk in tomorrow. Just . . ." He paused, shrugged. "Look, my time on the job tells me to expect the worst. Anything better than that'll be a pleasant surprise. Okay?"

"Yeah." Vail forced a smile, then said, "Thanks."

She turned and walked away, not sure of what she was thanking him for: pushing her promotion to detective? Standing by her when things got difficult? Mentoring her? Being a friend? Maybe all of that.

But she saw where things were headed, and it was likely to get worse before it got better. *If* it got better. Even with rabbis like Russo and Protch solidly behind her, she did not think the opinions of an entire department could be changed. She was on the verge of becoming a pariah. Damaged goods.

And she had a feeling that asking Russo and Protch to remain her ally would tarnish their reputations as well. As Protch had told her regarding Thorne, things had a way of sticking to you by association. And it was hard to get the muck off. She could not do that to them.

And then there was Jonathan. After seeing Fonzarella's twisted body on the ground floor of the apartment stairwell, she started to doubt the wisdom of working the front lines, being in the thick of violent crime on the streets of New York City. If something happened to her, her son would be in Deacon's care. And right now, her husband was not a fit parent. Until he got his act together, she could not be comfortable with the prospect of Deacon raising her boy. Regardless of how office politics played out, Jonathan was her primary concern.

When she sat down in her car, she switched on the dome light and pulled Special Agent Mark Safarik's business card from her wallet. On the back was his cell number. It was nine o'clock and she was sure he had left the office hours ago. But she called him anyway.

He answered on the second ring—and she hesitated for a second as she asked herself if she really wanted to do this. *Yes. I want to. I have to.*

"Agent Safarik, it's Karen Vail. I'm sorry to bother you so late, but I was wondering if you could walk me through the process of applying to the FBI."

VAIL STOPPED IN TOWN to pick up a pizza for a very late dinner. As she stood outside dragging on a cigarette and waiting for the pie to come out of the oven, she glanced in at the counter where she had been sitting when Deacon walked into her life. He was so happy then, with a career full of possibilities. Now? She was not sure what the future held for him.

First on the agenda would be getting him some counseling. Perhaps that could help him recapture the promise he was poised to achieve not that long ago.

She was sure Deacon had not eaten dinner—or if he had, it would've been a peanut butter sandwich. Not that pizza was anymore nutritious, but it seemed like a more substantial dinner. Besides, given everything that had happened, she was craving salty, fatty, as-unnutritious-as-you-can-get comfort food.

She pulled up in front of her house and sat in the vehicle for a few moments, then gathered up the box and kicked the door closed with a foot.

When she walked in, Deacon was at the kitchen table—a bottle of Jif open with a knife sticking out of it.

So much for a sandwich. Too much work.

Third Eye Blind's "How's It Going to Be" was blasting from the radio. Vail reached over and switched it off.

Deacon was asleep, his head resting on his forearms, which were crossed atop the butcher block table. Once Vail set the pizza down, Deacon lifted his head, flared his nostrils, and licked his lips.

"Karen. You're home."

"A late dinner. I hope you're hungry."

He sat up and shielded his face from the bright incandescent lights. An empty bottle of Merlot was on the counter, a glass by his elbow showing a residual drop of red liquid at the bottom.

His eyes were bloodshot. No surprise. "You been drinking again?"

"A little bit."

Bullshit. You drank the whole bottle. It was sealed when I left this morning.

"My mom's gonna be by in a bit with Jonathan. She's gonna spend the night so she doesn't have to drive back to Westbury. You might want to be upstairs in the bedroom when she comes." *I don't want her to see you like this.*

"Oh." He looked around, as if he was trying to remember something. "Someone came by, dropped something off for you."

"Yeah?" She pulled open the cabinet door and removed a couple of plates. "What was it?"

"I put it somewhere so you'd see it if I was asleep." He lifted some papers on the table, then got up—and after steadying himself against the counter, made it across the room where he found a white envelope next to the toaster.

Vail pulled open the cardboard box and served the slices on plates. "Who brought it by?"

"Don't know. Some guy."

She unfurled the typewritten note:

```
Detective Vail

Sorry to hear about your troubles. And to
think I'm responsible. No fears. We'll meet
again. I promise.
```

Yours VERY truly
The Hades Slasher (I kind of like that name!)

Oh my God. "Get me a paper towel!"

"There are napkins—"

"Now, goddamn it. Just—give me something clean."

Deacon handed it to her and Vail placed the letter atop it. Next she found a large Ziploc and, using a pair of rubber dish gloves, inserted the document and sealed the bag.

The odds of getting prints from paper were not good, and what's more, this killer was not careless. He was not one to leave latents on a note he gave to a detective. Still, she followed procedure.

"What is it?" he asked, his words running together slightly.

"What time did this guy come by?"

Deacon squinted. "Well shit, I don't know. I didn't look at the clock. Not long before you got here."

Vail rose from her chair. *Holy shit. Was he there when I was sitting out front in the car?*

She walked to the living room and peered out the miniblinds. Nothing. *Is he watching our house?*

"What'd he look like?" she called into the kitchen.

Deacon took a moment to answer. "I—don't know. I wasn't really of sound mind. If you know what I mean."

"You were shitfaced. Of course I know what you mean. Can you tell me anything about him? Short, tall, fat, thin, black, white?"

"Average height—well, maybe he was tall. Medium build, I think. White." His eyes narrowed in thought. "He had a beard. And he was wearing an Islanders hat, dark glasses."

"At night?"

Deacon shrugged. "I wasn't exactly 'with it.' But they were at least tinted, I'm pretty sure."

"What exactly did he say? Did he ask for me?"

"He seemed to know you weren't home."

My car wasn't in the driveway. So he knows what kind of car I drive, and that I drive to work each day. Has he been watching me?

She went back into the kitchen and dialed Russo, told him what had happened.

"I'll be by in about forty-five minutes. We'll pick up the letter and get it over to the lab. And I'll have a patrol car sit on your house tonight. I'll see what I can do about a longer-term basis, until we catch this bastard."

"If he wanted to hurt me, he could have."

"I'm not putting my trust in a serial killer. You got a problem with that?"

"Of course not. It's the right thing to do." She massaged the bridge of her nose. "Russo, I also . . . I've got some news."

"Yeah, what? Tell me."

"I'll wait till you get here."

"Karen, I'm sitting in a car, driving. I've got time to waste. Tell me now."

Vail hesitated. This was something she preferred to discuss with him face-to-face. But did it really matter? "I'm leaving the department. I'm going to apply to the FBI."

Deacon threw his head back and looked at Vail through glazed eyes.

After a long pause, Russo said, "I understand. Smart move. You know you've got my full support. Use me as a reference."

"Of course."

"See you ASAP."

Vail hung up and sat back down in her seat, staring at the plastic-wrapped letter. Worrying about Jonathan.

He didn't hurt me. Would he hurt my son?

"You're quitting your job?" Deacon asked.

"Looks that way."

"Why?"

Vail closed her eyes. "I've had a really long day. A shitty day. I lost a colleague. My partner on this case." She took a deep breath and looked at Deacon. "Can we discuss this tomorrow?"

"Be better anyway. Maybe I'll be sober." He chuckled, as if that was somehow funny.

Vail turned her attention back to the letter.

He knows about my problems at the precinct today. How can that be? And he left it at my house. He's sending me a message. Well, bring it on, asshole. You've found me. Now I'm gonna find you.

38

>ELLIS ISLAND
SATURDAY, APRIL 22, 1978

Livana was on a ladder using Windex and a rag to clean the dirty windows. The rain and wind made the task an ongoing job. But the view was so rewarding it was a shame to look out of muddy, streaked glass.

She climbed down off her ladder and had started toward the kitchen to get a towel when something caught her eye several paces off to her right: an animal of some kind lying on its back atop a downed tree trunk.

As Livana approached, she could see that it was a squirrel, its belly sliced open and its organs removed. Bugs were crawling across it and—

She cupped her mouth as bile threatened to explode from her stomach, then turned and ran into the house.

"Fedor! Fedor, where are you?"

"In here. Fixing the fireplace in your bedroom."

She headed up the steps and locked eyes with him as she walked into the hallway.

He tossed his screwdriver down and ran toward her. "What's wrong?"

Livana found it difficult to form words. "An animal. Outside. It's—some-one cut it open, cut out its organs, there's blood all over the tree, bugs are all over the place. Right outside the kitchen window."

"Someone cut it open? You mean another animal attacked—"

"No, not an animal. Someone . . . took a knife and sliced it open." She shuddered. "Surgically."

"Show me."

Livana took him downstairs, around the house to the fallen tree.

Fedor examined the corpse with detached curiosity. He backed away and joined Livana, who was doing her best to avoid seeing it.

"Why would anyone want to do that?" he asked.

"There are only a few people on the island. The other family keeps to themselves. They never come over this way. And those weird guys that live in the big hospital building, we hardly see them, and when we do it's only when we go by the dock."

"So then who?"

Livana thought of the books she had found in her son's bedroom. "Dmitri?" She said it at a near whisper, but Fedor heard her—or he had reached the same conclusion.

"Dmitri!" Fedor yelled. "Niklaus! Come around back."

A moment later, the boys ambled over, followed by Cassandra.

"Cassie," Livana said, "go back in the house."

"But—"

"Please, just listen to me. I'll be there in a minute."

Cassandra frowned, then turned and huffed off.

"Boys," Fedor said, "Either of you know anything about this?"

Dimitri pulled his hood back and looked at the ground. Niklaus, his gaze fixed on Dimitri, waited a moment before turning to Fedor.

"Well? Who did this?"

Niklaus looked at his father, then turned toward Dimitri.

"Did you both do it?" Livana asked.

"Nik did it," Dimitri said, keeping his head down.

"What?" Nicklaus stepped back.

"Niklaus!" Fedor said.

"Dad, that's not true." He turned to Dimitri. "What are you doing?"

Dimitri did not respond.

"Dmitri, look my dad in the eyes and tell him to his face that I did it."

"Not my fault," Dmitri murmured. "Not my fault."

Fedor glanced at Livana. "Dmitri, go wait in the kitchen for me."

He trudged away, swiping his sneaker at a rock as he walked. It skipped along the ground and struck a tree trunk.

Fedor turned to Niklaus. "Tell me what happened."

"I don't know. I didn't do it."

"Did Dmitri do it?"

"I have no idea."

"Are you telling me the truth or are you covering for him again?"

Niklaus looked away, then glanced up, then found his father's face. "I don't want to get him in trouble."

"He's already in trouble," Fedor said. "Now answer the question, son, before you join him."

Niklaus frowned. "He told me he saw this squirrel out back and he threw a rock at it and missed, so he picked up a stick and cornered it by the stoop. It started to go up the wall but he swung and hit it in the head."

"You didn't see this?"

"That's what he told me. No, I didn't see it."

"And then? The damn thing's cut open."

Niklaus licked his lips, lowered his voice. "He said he wanted to see what was inside. When I saw it, he'd already . . . well, he'd done it."

Livana recoiled. "That's gross. How could he do such a thing to a little animal?" She glanced at the bloody squirrel. "I have to go talk to him."

"I'll do it," Fedor said. "Probably should come from me."

Livana knew what was left unstated: this kind of talk needed to come from a father. Dimitri's father was gone, so Fedor filled that role.

"I'll get this mess cleaned up. Nik, go fetch a bucket of water and some bleach. You'll help me."

"But it's gross. Do I have to?"

"You have to. Now."

"Be stern with him," Livana said after Niklaus walked off. "He needs to know this is . . . it's just an awful thing to do." She shot a glance at the squirrel. "I'm concerned about him, Fedor. I mean, what kind of child kills defenseless animals and cuts them open?"

Fedor chewed on his lip a moment. "The kind of child who's fascinated by how people die, by killers and other kinds of deviants. The kind who's been kidnapped and beaten and . . ." He looked away. "A child who has problems, Liv."

She put a hand over her mouth to stifle a wail. Tears filled her eyes. "How did this happen to us?" she said. "We didn't deserve this."

"No. But in life, we don't always get what we deserve. Or want. Or need."

Livana looked up at the sky and took a long, deep breath. "You'd better go talk to him."

Fedor rubbed his forehead. "Yeah."

"You sure you want to do it?"

"How many times have we talked about this?"

They had indeed been over it multiple times. Realizing they both had to fill voids in their children's lives and knowing the importance of having mother and father figures, they operated as a family unit, even if it was not something official or legal.

Fedor gently cupped the side of her head. "I'll take care of it."

39

>ELLIS ISLAND
WEDNESDAY, JULY 4, 1979

Livana was readying their makeshift barbecue on the interior of the island in a spot that would not be visible from the mainland or Liberty Island. Using other buildings, tree cover, and angles as a shield was a precaution they had been taking since they moved there, something they had discussed with their cohabitants shortly after arriving.

Fedor felt strongly that they should take steps during daylight hours to prevent people from seeing them. Although it was no secret that drifters were living on Ellis Island, he thought that if they kept to themselves, stayed out of sight most of the time, and did not cause any trouble, the authorities would probably leave them alone.

The same went for nighttime fires, which would be visible for a distance, possibly all the way to Manhattan. Any possibility of a blaze would send the FDNY scrambling to control it before it scorched the entire area. It was easy enough to choose specific locations where line of sight to the mainland was difficult, if not impossible. It was common sense, Fedor explained. No one objected.

Despite their precautions, however, a couple of months after Niklaus and Dmitri had snuck aboard the ferry, Fedor saw men wearing construction hats arrive on Island 1. He had watched them enter the main immigration building at 8:00 AM, but how long they remained and what they did were a mystery, because the crew was gone when the family returned from the city later that evening. The workers, however, returned every weekday morning for a month.

Three weeks later, Niklaus was home ill from school. Using a pair of binoculars he had purchased at a thrift shop near Dmitri's used bookstore, he spied a ferry arriving with several dozen people aboard.

The glasses weren't powerful but they were good enough for him to see larger objects such as approaching ships. Dmitri liked to borrow them in the summer and watch the bikini-clad women on speedboats, especially when the vessels hit a wave and bounced.

Despite a fever, Niklaus left the house and hid in the brush by the main hospital building, watching as the ferry pulled into the inlet and docked. It soon became apparent the people aboard were tourists.

In the ensuing weeks, Livana determined that these ferries launched from Battery Park and followed a twice weekly schedule. The signage at the pier spoke of guided tours of a new National Park Service museum commemorating the time when Ellis Island was a portal for prospective US residents.

Fedor sat at the kitchen table chewing his sandwich. "These ferries aren't going to be stopping anytime soon."

"And what does this mean for us?" Livana asked.

He took a moment to answer. "For now, it doesn't affect us. They come on weekdays when we're gone. If we draw the shades before we go to work and don't leave anything scattered around outside, I think we'll be okay."

"What if they want to do tours of our—*this* island?"

Fedor chuckled. "Of the old hospital? There's nothing to see here."

Livana wondered if the park service would want to tear down these abandoned buildings to build something new. She did not bother asking Fedor about it because if that happened, they would have to leave their home. There was no point in worrying about it.

But she did worry. However, as the months—and then the years—passed, Livana began to feel secure, confident that their island home was not in jeopardy.

Until yesterday. They had both gotten off early from work for the Fourth of July holiday. When they arrived home, they noticed that construction workers had returned. Like a few years ago, the men wore hard hats and looked official.

Fedor walked into his bedroom and came up alongside his son, who had the task of using binoculars to observe the workers from his father's second story window. "What do you see?"

Niklaus sat back from the edge of the shade he had been using for cover and detailed what he had observed: the men were carrying tripods, tape measures, and other types of equipment in long toolboxes and caddies. They walked the length of Island 1, doing a lot of pointing as they surveyed the grounds around the main building. Before leaving, they gathered in front, conferring with one another in small groups.

"Sounds like they were checking the place out this time, not just cleaning it out and fixing things up."

Niklaus turned back to the drawn shade. "I think they're planning to build something. Or tear something down."

Fedor rubbed his temples. "I hope you're wrong."

"But if I'm right, and they're building *there*, we may be next."

Fedor chewed on that a moment. "Don't say anything to your brother and sister. It'll only worry them and there's nothing we can do about it. Just let me know if you see them come back."

"I don't think it's a matter of *if* they come back. It's *when*."

THE FOLLOWING DAY, as they stood around the barbecue, Fedor took the metal poker from Livana and shifted the coals around to cultivate the flame. "We've got pretty clear weather. We should be able to see the fireworks tonight."

"That would be a real treat. Last year it was so overcast I felt like it wasn't really the Fourth because we couldn't see anything." She fell silent for a moment. "I miss barbecues in the old neighborhood. Going to movies, block parties. Going to church."

Fedor's response was matter-of-fact: "That hasn't been our life for a long time."

Livana knew this to be true. But that did not make it any easier to accept.

She reached over and slapped a mosquito that landed on her forearm. "I'm gonna run in and get some bug spray or we'll get eaten alive. You need anything?"

"Bring the hamburgers I bought this morning. They should be defrosted now. I think we need about ten more minutes and the fire'll be ready to go."

Livana walked into the house and removed the meat from the cooler and set it on a plate, but couldn't find the repellant. She had given it to Cassandra to use yesterday and that girl, bless her . . . she never put things back where she took them from.

As Livana neared the door, she heard the shower going. She stepped into the bedroom—and saw Dmitri standing outside the partially opened bathroom door, his pants down, and his penis in his hand—"

Livana let out a scream and dropped the plate in the same instant.

Dmitri quickly pulled up his pants but had difficulty tucking away his erection. A second later, Fedor and Niklaus came running in—as did Cassandra, wrapped in a towel, her hair dripping wet.

"What's wrong?" Fedor asked.

Livana was crying, her right hand clamped over her mouth. She turned and pushed past Fedor, then ran up the stairs.

A moment later, Fedor was knocking on her door. But he did not wait for an answer to enter. He sat down on the edge of the bed. "Tell me what happened."

Livana related what she had seen.

Fedor closed his eyes and sighed. "He's thirteen. He doesn't see many girls outside of school, and I'm sure he doesn't see them showering." He swallowed. "Naked."

"You think that's all it is? Cassie's his *sister*. I don't think—I don't think that's . . . normal. There, I said it. Oh my god. I finally said it. My son's not normal, Fedor, and I . . . " She buried her face in his chest and began sobbing. A moment later, she got control of herself. "I don't know what to do to help him. I don't know what to do for him."

"Tomorrow," Fedor said, "we'll see if we can find a doctor in the city. Maybe he can tell us how to handle this."

40

>103RD STREET
HARLEM
MONDAY, AUGUST 6, 2001

Karen Vail turned to Special Agent Mike Hartman and showed him the *New York Times* headline as he negotiated the turn onto 103rd Street. "Ralph Nader drew 7,000 to a rally he held at the Rose Garden."

"That guy is single-handedly responsible for putting Bush in the White House. How one man can alter world events is beyond my comprehension."

"Oh come on, Mike. There are lots of examples throughout history. George Washington. Abraham Lincoln. Thomas Jefferson."

"Positive impacts. All those people made our society a better place. You think we're gonna say the same thing about George W. Bush twenty years from now?"

"Miracles have been known to happen."

Vail and Hartman laughed.

"So where we meeting your CI?"

"Marcus Garvey Park."

"You got your paperwork this time?"

"I've got it. And she'll sign it, no problem."

"Just making sure we're clear on this. She wants to change the rules of engagement, you gotta have the paperwork filed."

The Bureau's procedure regarding confidential informants was strict and clear: your agreement with the CI was contractual. You agreed to pay a certain amount, and they had to countersign so that there were no misunderstandings—between you and your informant and between you and the Bureau.

They found a spot along Madison Avenue. Hartman waited in the car while Vail entered the park and walked along the adobe- and gray-colored brick pathway. She sat down on one of the benches and pulled out her copy of the *Times*.

After paging through the main section, she folded it in quarters as someone sat down beside her.

"Eugenia," Vail said. "How are things?"

"You know, I had better days. My kid's hangin' out with the wrong crowd and I can't seem to get him to listen to me. You gots the money?"

"I do." She handed her the folded front section of the newspaper. "First sign the new agreement. Page nine."

Eugenia took the pen that was clipped inside, signed the paperwork, and handed the *Times* back to Vail. Vail then handed over the sports pages, likewise doubled over into quarters. "It's inside. Stick it in your pocket, count it later. You know the drill." She glanced around and looked at Eugenia. Her face had more creases than the last time they had met. Worry wrinkles.

"I got you more money. That means you have to deliver more."

"I knows it. And I gots something for you. A shipment of illegal guns about to be sold on the street. Comin' in from Russia. Also a few dozen assault rifles. Some sniper rifles. Guy by the name of Sergei, goin' down at a warehouse three blocks from here."

Vail thought a moment. "Yeah, I know the place. When?"

"I heard midnight but I'm not sure if it's the ninth or the nineteenth. S'posed to be shipped out the next day."

"Where to?"

Eugenia shrugged. "Don't know."

"You hear anything else, ring me up." Vail faced her and studied her eyes. "How's your dad?"

"You know. Not so good."

"He seeing a doctor?"

"No money for a doctor."

"Take him. He needs to go." Vail pulled out a pad and wrote down a name and number. "This doc won't charge you. Just make sure you tell him I sent you."

In truth, Vail would be paying the tab—but Eugenia didn't need to know that or she might not go.

Eugenia took the paper. "Okay."

Vail got up from the bench. "Talk to you soon. Be careful out there." She gave her a wink, then turned and headed back to the car.

EUGENIA'S TIP PROVED fruitful. The buy, which took place on the nineteenth, allowed the FBI and Bureau of Alcohol, Tobacco, and Firearms to get a lead on the supplier; they let the sale go through but maintained a vigilant watch on where the guns ended up. Three weeks later, they moved in and busted the operation in New Jersey.

Vail felt vindicated that Eugenia had come through; she had faced resistance from her boss, the assistant special agent in charge, about increasing the amount they paid the CI. But she insisted the informant was solid and worth taking a chance on. In this instance, Eugenia proved her worth.

Three weeks later, with the weather beginning to feel more like fall and the leaves starting to change, Vail blew on her hands as she unlocked the front door to her house with Jonathan in tow.

She stepped inside and found the place freezing—as well as Deacon asleep on the couch, a bottle of Ketel One vodka lying on its side.

"Oh Jesus."

"Mommy, I'm hungry." Jonathan grabbed onto Vail's pant leg and swung back and forth. "I'm hungry."

Deacon, what the hell? I thought we had this under control.

He had seen a psychiatrist and went for counseling, and was diagnosed with bipolar disorder. Once they found medication that worked for him and determined the correct dosage, the challenge—as predicted by the psychiatrist—would be ensuring that Deacon continued taking the pills. Many bipolar patients liked to feel a bit high, or hypomanic. Being "of normal mood" made them feel slow and inadequate. As a result, many stopped taking their medication. Deacon, however, promised her, and the doctor, that he would be compliant. *So much for that.*

"Mommy, now."

"Okay, baby. I'll get you something." She left Deacon on the couch and took Jonathan into the kitchen. "I'll make dinner in a few minutes, sweetie." As she unpeeled a banana, Jonathan's face brightened. He took it and shoved a big bite into his mouth.

Vail unwrapped their new copy of *Dinosaurs* and put it in the DVD player in the small dining room. As the Disney logo filled the TV screen, she rejoined Deacon.

She sat down on the coffee table opposite the couch and looked at her husband, who was lying on his side, asleep. She reached over and gave his shoulder a shake. He opened his eyes slowly but his face showed no reaction. But that's when she noticed the half-smoked marijuana joint in a dish on the floor, near Deacon's head.

Shit. "Deacon, what the— What are you doing?"

His eyes studied her face but he said nothing.

"Have you been taking your meds?"

"I'm hungry. Can you get me something to eat?"

"Answer my question. Have you been taking your meds?"

He looked at the ceiling. "I don't like the way they make me feel."

"We've been through this. You don't have a choice. If you want to have a normal family life, if you want to keep your job, you have to take them."

Deacon laughed, more of a pathetic moan. "That's no longer a problem. They fired me this morning."

Vail sat there, her mouth agape. She had warned him that he had better do everything possible to make his employer happy because keeping a job was a lot easier than finding another. Now that was a moot point.

"What happened?"

Deacon leaned back against the couch. "Accounting irregularities."

"What does that mean? Sounds like a catchall bullshit term."

"Things didn't add up. The company had to restate earnings. CFO took the heat. I took the blame. So . . ." he sang, "Bye-bye Deacon."

"Did you do anything wrong? Was it your fault?"

"Only thing I did wrong was being a CPA in the CFO's office. And being the new guy on the block."

"We should contact an attorney." And then she realized that a lawsuit would expose Deacon's bipolar condition and they would end up spending a lot of money on a case that might become so muddled that even if they ended up winning, the stress and time invested would make them losers in the end. And there was no way Deacon would get his job back.

"I'll talk to some people at work who know about corporate politics and job hunting. I'll see what they recommend about applying for a new job, what you should and shouldn't say in an interview about getting fired."

"Can I get something to eat?"

"I'm sure you can." *But you're gonna have to get it.* "I'm going to find your meds—and make sure you take them."

Vail walked into the kitchen and checked on Jonathan, who was watching with fascination as the large egg made its journey from one dinosaur to another. She found Deacon's pills on the counter, grabbed a cup of water, and found him asleep on the couch, curled into a ball.

"Mommy," Jonathan called from the other room. "I'm still hungry!"

"Coming, sweetie."

Vail gave Deacon a shove to wake him, then handed him the medication. As she watched him swallow it, she thought of something her mother had once told her: sometimes things have to get worse before they get better.

THE BLACKBERRY BUZZED as Vail stepped into the elevator for her morning appointment. She pulled it from its holster and recognized the number.

"Russo, you old dog. How's it going?"

"I'm gonna ignore the 'old' reference because I'm such a nice guy. Do you want the bad news or the not-so-good news?"

"What's the bad news?"

"We got another vic. Hades."

"And the not-so-good news?"

"You ain't here to work the case."

"Yeah, well, I think the NYPD may consider that *good* news."

"Any chance you can stop by before you start your work day?"

"Already started. Came in early today for an interview with a banker who was snagged in an insider trading sweep. He's agreed to talk to us assuming I can win him over. I'll drop by the crime scene after. Maybe a couple of hours? Three at the outside."

"No good," Russo said. "Max is on his way. He'll be done with the body well before then. Probably be tagged and bagged, if not shipped out."

Fresh body. Fresh crime scene. And I really want this bastard.

"On my way to the scene right now," Russo said. "Tribeca, on Duane near Church."

"Well, shit," Vail said as the floor numbers on the elevator readout continued climbing. "That's not far from here."

"Can you postpone your meeting for an hour or two?"

Vail pushed the next floor button and got off. "Email me the address. I'll see what I can do." She hung up and called the witness and asked if she could reschedule their interview. He sounded relieved—and when she offered to take him to lunch instead, he was all too happy to make the change.

Vail got back into the elevator headed down. When she reached the ground floor, Russo's email hit her inbox.

She walked into the apartment on the fifty-first floor of the high-rise building at 8:35, fifteen minutes after Russo's call—not bad for the one mile rush hour commute in New York City's financial district.

She badged the cop at the door to the apartment and stepped inside.

"What a view," she said as she took in the large picture windows on the far side of the great room.

"Ain't gonna do the woman of the house much good anymore."

Vail turned to see Russo standing there, a pair of latex gloves on his thick hands. Vail spread her arms and he joined her at the door, then gave her a hug.

"You got a pair of booties?"

"Of course," he said as he dug into his pocket. "See what happens? You no longer work important cases so you've got no need to carry 'em around anymore."

"Nah, the FBI doesn't get any important cases. Just busy work. All procedure and reports. Boring shit."

"Yeah, like I believe *that*." He gestured with a tilt of his head. "C'mon, she's in the bedroom. But you already knew that, didn't you?"

I've got a feeling I know what this crime scene looks like without even seeing it.

She walked in and—although the victim was sitting on the bed, the large picture window drew her attention yet again. "Stunning."

"We already went through that, didn't we?"

"Sorry. I don't have anything like this in Rosedale." It was a spectacularly clear day and visibility was distant. Skyscrapers rose in all directions like a manmade mountain range. Most prominent was the view of the World Trade Center, the two towers pristine in their uniformity—and enormity. "That's where my meeting was," she said. "I made it up to the 88th floor when I got off and came here. I told the witness I was going to take him to lunch. But now I'm thinking I sold myself short. I'm sure his office has a view of the city that might just put this one to shame."

"Windows on the World. Hundred seventh floor. Take him there for lunch. On the Bureau's dime, of course."

"Now you're talking. See, you can still dish out some wisdom in your old age. Oh—sorry about the 'old' reference."

"*Again.* You mean you're sorry, *again.*"

"Yeah," she said, preoccupied. She took one more look out the window, trying to avoid the matter at hand. Another mutilated victim. "Can you imagine waking up to a view like this every morning?"

"Yeah, well, our vic ain't gonna be doin' that no more."

"Right." Vail dropped her gaze to the adjacent queen bed, which sat parallel to the window. She moved to the foot of the mattress and studied the victim. "What's her name?"

"Doris Vassos."

"Vassos," Vail said. She looked at Doris, trying to picture the woman's face without the blood and protruding glass shard, then walked over to the side of the bed facing the window. "Greek?"

"That'd be my guess. I looked around a bit before you got here but didn't find a whole lot. Pretty sure she's single. I'm waiting for a call with some background on her. Found some letters in the desk, checking account and brokerage statements."

"Do we know what she did? Professionally?"

"She had a position with the ad agency J. Thomas Walker. We'll know more once I get that backgrounder. Whatever she did, she earned a very solid salary. To live here."

"What about that drawing on the neck?"

"Figured I'd wait till CSU got here. I didn't want to move the body till we got some shots. I asked for Chandler."

Vail leaned in for a closer look at the wounds. "Who's got the case now?"

"Since I've been involved from the beginning, Kearney asked me to work with Joe Slater, bring him up to speed. He's on the way."

She looked at the ceiling, searching her memory. "Joe Slater. Don't think I know him. He good?"

"He was promoted in to replace Fonzarella after—well, after that Danzig debacle."

Vail straightened up. "Speak of the devil—anything on Danzig? Any reason why he'd want to kill Greek women and an Italian mob capo?"

"Still in the wind. And no, we couldn't find any connection."

In the next instant, Vail saw, over Russo's left shoulder, a commercial jet whiz by, way too low and—

"Holy shit!"

The north tower of the World Trade Center swallowed the large airplane. As Russo spun around, Vail felt a vibration shake the window, followed immediately by the sound of an explosive impact—

"What the hell did I just see?" Vail said. "It looked like—it was—Jesus Christ, a plane flew right into the building. How the hell . . . ?

Russo grabbed his two-way radio as Vail pulled out her phone and started dialing.

"Manhattan South homicide lieutenant to Central." He proceeded to report what Vail had seen as her phone call connected.

"Agent Vail for the ASAC . . . No, get him on the phone right now—it's an emergency."

He was on the line less than five seconds later.

Vail related what she had seen.

"Are you sure? A passenger jet?"

"That's what it looked like. It happened so fast, it was flying real low and then—"

"You have eyes on the tower?"

"I do, sir. I'm—I don't know, three-quarters of a mile away."

"Stay there. Monitor the situation. I'll call you for updates. We'll get in touch with the FAA, see what the hell's going on. Navigational malfunction, whatever—wait, hang on."

Navigational error? It flew right into the damn building.

Muffled voices, then her ASAC: "Just got word American Flight 11's been hijacked." To someone else: "Is that eleven? Did eleven hit the towers? . . . Yes or no? . . . What do you mean they don't know?" She heard him yell something to someone, then the line disconnected.

Vail could not tear her eyes from the orange flames and dense gray smoke billowing from the tower, the fire and blackness spreading to the floors above and below the jumbo jet's point of entry.

Russo lowered his radio. "Sanchez," he called into the hallway. "Get over to the Twin Towers. A plane hit the building, they're gonna need help evacuating."

He started to back out of the room. "I'm going over there, see what I can do to help. You'll be able to wait here with the body till CSU gets here?"

"At the moment, my orders are to stay put. My ASAC wants me to be their eyes till they get up to speed on what's going on."

Russo looked back at Doris Vassos's body. "Try to give her everything you've got. She deserves no less."

"Of course."

Russo left and Vail tried to keep her gaze from moving back to the window, but she couldn't help herself. The steady flow of smoke was building into a dense, relentless plume that was blowing out across the Hudson.

The drone of sirens rose and fell as emergency response vehicles whizzed by. Off to her left and looking like children's toys, FDNY engines raced down Broadway, followed by two ambulances.

Focus, Karen. There's nothing you can do about the fire. But you can help Doris Vassos. And other women who are being targeted by this UNSUB.

Vail turned away from the window and tried to clear her thoughts. If she was ever going to get her mind off what was happening outside, she needed to look around the apartment and create some form of record for Detective Slater when he arrived.

She slipped on Russo's gloves and searched the place, finding a PDA, unopened mail, a half-read paperback novel by John Lescroart—and a Canon EOS SLR camera. She looked it over, turned it on, and checked to see how many shots she had left on the roll: nineteen. Not exactly procedure—using the victim's camera to shoot crime scene photos—but she would not be destroying any evidence, so it would do.

She first spent a couple of minutes looking through the PDA, lingering on Vassos's calendar. Nothing jumped out at her. Then again, before she knew more of who the woman was, important entries could look like innocuous notes, devoid of meaning.

Returning to the bedroom, she began snapping photos of the body and the room from wide-angle perspective shots to closeups of the wounds, using the remaining photos with care. After capturing the scene as best she could, she pulled a pen from her pocket and gently parted Vassos's strands of hair along the posterior aspect of her skull.

And there it is.

As she revealed the design drawn in marker, any doubt as to whether or not Vassos was murdered by the same killer vanished. She shot a few pictures of it, then set the camera on the floor and examined the illustration. The UNSUB had sketched the familiar X, along with the capital letters E, I, D, and a lowercase h.

Vail stood there staring at the letters. She tried, once again, to understand the pattern. D could stand for Danzig—if he was in fact the killer. But what were the other letters? His first name was Victor, yet there was no V. And Danzig was an alias. Did they ever find out what his birth name was? There was no way she would bother calling now to find out.

As she mused on the lettering scheme, a thought occurred to her: the last victim, Megan Kostas, had a g. This is an h, the one prior—Herod—was an f.

Is it possible that he's numbering his victims? Why letters instead of numbers? And why did the first victim have a d instead of an a? Unless the d was meant to be an a, but was poorly written—or misinterpreted. She would have to ask Russo or Slater to check that against the Manos crime scene photos. But it still would not explain Crinelli and the r.

And even if he was numbering his kills, it did not add up. They had five confirmed victims, but h was the eighth letter of the alphabet. Agent Safarik's admonishment about finding the killer's first victim rattled around her thoughts. Finding that first victim could be key, he had told her.

Manos may not have been the first—Vail had considered that many times—but could she have been the fourth?

The increasing clamor of sirens pulled her attention back to the fire. She glanced at her watch. It was nine o'clock and the black smoke continued to course skyward. She could see the clear delineation of the entry point of the plane in the tower's skin, a diagonal rip covering several floors.

Despite the continuing waft of smoke, Vail no longer saw flames. Per-haps the building's sprinkler systems were keeping things under control until the fire department could hook up their hoses. But how did that even work in a skyscraper, let alone one that was 110 stories? She had never pondered that.

However they fought a fire in a building of this size, she hoped they got it under control fast. The smoke was so thick that there was no way anyone trapped on those floors could breathe. She imagined people were already evacuating the tower—but what about those in the offices where the plane entered? Dead, extinguished on point of impact.

Vail played the image back in her mind. She still found it difficult to be-lieve: the jet flew directly into the side of the building and was literally swal-lowed up inside the huge structure. She shook her head in disbelief.

What could explain that? Navigational or instrumentation error? Two dead or incapacitated pilots? Or was it purposeful, some sort of suicide at-tack—"

As that thought formed, she saw what looked like another plane ap-proaching the towers from the opposite side. It disappeared from view and then—"Oh my god. What the hell?"

An enormous mass of fire and flame exploded from the outer edge of the south tower, gathering and then pluming upward like a mushroom.

We're being attacked. This is a goddamn terrorist attack.

Vail instinctively reached for her Glock—and then realized it would do her no good. Her jaw slack, she watched helplessly as the cloud rose, ex-panded, and consumed.

I can't stay here. I've gotta go—I've gotta go.

Vail ran to the hallway, stopped and went back into the kitchen, found cellophane tape—as good as she could do under the circumstances—then pulled off her crime scene booties and gloves. She started to close the front door behind her, but hesitated before the latch engaged. She didn't know if she should lock it or leave it open to permit her return.

Lock it. Worry about getting back in later. Secure the scene best you can.

After pulling it shut, Vail unrolled the tape and sealed the joint, covering both the jamb and the door's edge. There would be little chance that someone could open it without tearing it—and leaving sign that the crime scene had been disturbed. She pulled a pen from her pocket and scribbled her initials at various points along the strip, then headed for the elevator.

Outside, she hit the ground running, checking over her shoulder for taxis, but finding them full or moving swiftly in the opposite direction. She jogged on, turned onto Church Street, and headed toward the Twin Towers.

VAIL STOPPED SEVERAL police officers who were en route to the trade center complex. They directed her to assist with the evacuation effort, where they were attempting to channel people to areas where they could get away from the immediate vicinity or seek medical attention if they had been injured or suffered smoke inhalation. With thousands of people still in the building, the job was enormous—and things were still in disarray as law enforcement got its bearings and established a coordinated response.

As she neared the towers, she had to step around debris that had been thrown off when the jets impacted the buildings. The gray and black smoke continued pluming up and out, but also downward, soot-thick and obscuring in its intensity.

Firefighters stood ready beside their vehicles, jackets on and equipment in their hands.

"I'm FBI," Vail said. "What's the plan?"

The man's nametag read, "Brennan." He brought a hand up to the bill of his helmet to get a view against the smoky glare. "We got several companies in there, they're going up as far as they can to bring people out."

"Both towers?"

"Both," Brennan said. "Pretty fuckin' dangerous in there, shit's falling all over. Even the lobby—the windows are blown out, I heard over the radio that jet fuel shot down the elevator shaft, caught fire, and exploded."

"But the people at the top—"

"Everyone above the impact zones is trapped. Twenty-something floors of people in tower one, fifty floors in tower two, and we can't get 'em down. Elevators are out and the stairs are useless. Staircases were built with sheetrock, not concrete, so anything above the fires, they're just toast."

"You know the place pretty well."

Brennan kept his gaze on the buildings, watching the conflagration. "I'm with Ladder 1, seven blocks from here. We're out at the towers every week, sometimes five times in a shift. I know those buildings like nobody else. And I can tell you this: way these buildings are built, those people up there, they ain't got no way to get out."

Vail's throat constricted from the soot and debris floating down in a continuous stream. She swatted away as much of it as she could. "Roof evacuation?"

"With all that smoke, I doubt they can land. A day like this, roof landing's out anyway, because of the antennas and all the other crap they got up there. Just can't see. Chopper goes down . . . definitely don't need that shit on top of all that other shit."

People continued moving past her as two more FDNY engines maneuvered into place.

"We're just trying to get the fires out, get as many people down as we can."

"How are you going after the fire?"

Brennan looked at her for the first time. "Only thing we can do. Elevators are out, we have to walk it. With all that gear—maybe seventy pounds of it—we gotta haul up eighty flights in tower one alone."

Walk up eighty flights? That's gotta take an hour, if not more. "What can I do?"

"Nothing, right now. We're awaiting orders to go in. Idea's to get people out and away from the buildings. So wanna make yourself useful, make sure people move along. We don't want them stopping to watch."

Brennan got a call over his radio. He listened for a moment, then turned to his men. "Okay, that's us. Let's go!"

Vail thanked Brennan, wished him luck, and watched as the men huffed it forward, toward the awninged entrance to 1 World Trade Center. She ventured closer, directing onlookers to clear the area for arriving emergency vehicles.

As she moved to within half a block, she craned her head up toward the impact zones—and something whacked her on the arm, knocking her back onto her ass.

"What the—"

A body struck the pavement at her feet, pancaking upon impact and spattering blood and tissue across her clothing. *Oh my god—*

She scrabbled backward, away from the remains, just needing to get away, to somehow wipe that image from her mind. She had viewed several corpses during her time in law enforcement, but this was different. This was something she could never forget.

She rolled onto her hands and knees and got up, expecting more bodies to rain down on her. She sprinted toward the nearest building's edge, ten feet away, and looked up again.

Several people were hurtling down from the upper stories, dark forms bicycling through the air, free-falling, plunging toward the pavement a hundred stories below.

In a momentary clearing of smoke, she could see dozens more perched on the edge of the structure, above the gaping holes torn by the jets, and she realized they were pondering their fate: burning alive in an oven-like fire or leaping, ending it all in a matter of seconds. Frightening, but painless.

How could this be happening?

Vail ran forward, into the rubble-strewn plaza, skirting chunks of concrete, strips of metal, paper, glass, and body parts—and engaged a throng of people, moving them along, onto the street, channeling them away from the complex.

As they stumbled past her, she heard people saying what she had been thinking: this can't be happening.

Twenty-five minutes later, she heard a chest-pounding rumble that sounded like an avalanche. She looked up to see an expansive cloud of dust and debris moving down from above. On a nearby police radio Vail heard, "She's going! Tower one's coming down—evacuate, evacuate!"

Vail could not move. *It's falling? How—*

Someone grabbed her arm and pulled her away—a uniformed cop. "C'mon, you gotta get outta here!"

She turned and ran beside the officer, but in seconds they were engulfed in a thick white dust cloud. He pulled her into a Burger King and slammed the door closed behind them.

They watched as the dense haze filled the street, high and wide. In the back of her mind she was aware of the smell of french fries. It seemed oddly out of place with what she was seeing. But before she could process that thought, the door swung open and more officers poured in, including a sergeant.

"We're setting up a command post in here," the sergeant announced. "Clear everything out. We need room!"

"Karen Vail," she said to the officer who had pulled her into the Burger King. "FBI." She looked at his gold name tag: Prisco. "Thanks for yanking me out of my funk. I just . . . I couldn't believe what I was seeing. I was born and raised here."

Prisco cleared away stacks of boxes filled with paper goods. "Started as such a nice day. Sunny, seventy degrees. And then it all went to hell. People were jumping from eighty, ninety stories. Never seen anything like it."

Vail helped Prisco move a couple of long trays off the backroom counter, clearing the area for the sergeant, who was plugging in a couple of radios.

"I saw the first plane hit. I was in a high-rise at a homicide scene."

"Homicide?" Prisco stopped and faced her. "I thought you're FBI."

"A case of mine from way back when. My old loo asked me to take a look before they moved the body."

The restaurant had filled with two dozen officers and detectives, and a handful of sergeants and lieutenants.

Outside, the gray-white particulate cloud of pulverized cement, soot, and gypsum continued to move up the avenue.

The door opened and three more cops entered—including Russo. They were covered in a film of white powder from head to foot. They immediately began brushing the stuff off their faces.

One of the cops bent over and yelled, "Water! I need water! I got shit in my eyes. They're—they're burning."

Vail filled a cup and brought it over to the officer and helped him flush the dirt out, then moistened a rag and handed it to Russo.

"What the hell are you doing here?" he asked as he dragged the cloth across his face. "There's no way CSU showed up."

"I—no, no one showed. I saw the second plane hit and I had to help."

"We got thousands of uniformed personnel onsite for security, crowd control, and evacuation. ESU and FDNY are doing their thing to clear the area. These people are a whole lot better equipped and trained to handle this than you. And we got no one at that apartment securing the crime scene. Now, I can't order you because you don't work for me anymore, but I'm asking you, as a favor—"

"All right everyone," a lieutenant said, his back to the storefront windows. "Listen up. We're setting up a command center. Anyone who's not NYPD, you need to get outta here right now."

Russo turned to Vail, who frowned.

"Fine. I'm going." She turned to look at the room of assembled NYPD personnel. She realized she was no longer part of the team. As much as she wanted to remain and assist, she knew Russo was right. She placed a hand on his chest. "Be careful. And be safe."

Vail hoofed it back to the Vassos crime scene. But when she was a block from the apartment building, she heard another rumble, followed by a loud moan as masses of people turned to gape at the lone remaining tower as it too collapsed.

She stopped and watched the dust and debris drop from the sky, moving down inexorably as the weight of the concrete carried it to the street.

Vail closed her eyes, then headed up the block and into Doris Vassos's building.

ONCE UPSTAIRS, VAIL knocked on the apartments adjacent to the crime scene. She would have to kick in the door to get into Vassos's place, but she could not enter wearing filthy clothing.

Fortunately, one of the neighbors down the hall was home, live news accounts of the trade center collapse blaring from her TV and audible through the door. Vail showed the woman her FBI creds, explained that she had been at the towers, and asked if she could shower and change because she had a crime scene to secure.

Oh, and by the way, as if this day wasn't shitty enough, your neighbor's been murdered.

Vail left that part out, but the older woman—after a brief hesitation—must have taken pity on her visitor's haggard appearance. She invited Vail in and showed her to the bathroom.

Vail wanted to stay under the hot water and cleanse herself of the tragedy she had just witnessed. But she knew that was not possible. The memories, the pain, the images of the planes disappearing into the buildings, of the dismembered arms and legs, the falling bodies, the one that pancaked beside her on the pavement . . . these would remain indelibly burned into her mind, her being, forever.

As she mused on that, however, she realized that it was not so bad a fate compared to those people standing on the 95th floor, pondering how best to die . . . some burned alive, others jumping to their deaths from a thousand feet above the ground.

Those last seconds of life, what were they thinking? Of loved ones? Of their parents or siblings? Of intolerable fear or sorrow? Or if only they had called in sick that morning?

Called in sick. Had Russo not phoned her and asked her to come to see Hades's latest victim, she would've been one of those people perched on that ledge of death.

Vail collapsed to the floor of the shower, the water pounding against her neck, and wept.

41

Livana finished her day at the Italian Ices shop on the Lower East Side and took the subway to the Meatpacking District, where Fedor worked. As they had been doing for the past three years since the children had gotten older, when his shift ended at five o'clock they would collect the kids at a central meeting place, the mouth of the Bowling Green subway station, and then walk together to the dock, where they would retrieve their boat for the ride home to Ellis Island.

Cassandra, a senior in high school and the more responsible of the three of them, was in charge of making sure they were all heading to Bowling Green at the appointed time. After a long day at work, Livana and Fedor did not want to stand around and wait for the kids, not knowing where they were or when they were going to show.

Dmitri, in particular, had a tendency to wander off when school got out, and show up late. Cassandra had gotten on his case of late and finally told her mother that she needed to talk with him, because he no longer listened to her—and when he did, he did so reluctantly.

Livana checked the clock. It was eleven minutes after five, which was very unusual. Fedor was always punctual. He would clock out, remove his blood-spattered apron, wash up, and be in the admin area, where Livana waited for him, by five after five.

As he descended the steps, his face exhibited anguish, concern, and fear.

"Fedor," Livana said as he walked right past her. "What's wrong?"

He pushed through the door and stepped outside, took a deep breath of cold air.

"Fedor. Tell me."

"The police just called me. We have to go. Right now."

"Go? Go where?"

"The school."

"Did Dmitri get in trouble again?"

Fedor continued walking to the subway, not bothering to reply.

THE SUBWAY DOORS parted at the Rector Street subway station and Fedor stepped off.

"Will you tell me what's going on?"

"The police called. About Cassandra." He ascended the steps, Livana following closely, dodging rush hour commuters who were pushing down the stairs as they were moving up—in essence, they were swimming against the tide.

After they fought their way to street level, Livana grabbed Fedor's arm and pulled him to a stop. "Now. Tell me."

He looked in her eyes but could not hold her gaze. "The police found my work number in Cassandra's purse."

She waited for more, then said, "I don't understand. She lost her purse? What's the big—"

"No, Livana." His voice was taut. "They found a body. A young woman's body." He stopped, fought back tears. "They think it's Cassandra."

Livana stood there, looking at Fedor, trying to make it register. "My baby is—my baby is—no. They're wrong."

"That's what I'm hoping. They want us to identify—to see if it's her."

Livana stood up straight, then reached out and took Fedor's hand. They were not lovers and had never touched in any intimate manner. But right now she needed the assurance of his presence, of his strength, as they approached the school.

A blue Plymouth police cruiser sat idling at the curb, its lights rotating rhythmically.

They came upon a uniformed officer at the perimeter of crime scene tape.

"We were told to see Detective Jenkins," Fedor said. "We're here to—" he closed his eyes—"identify the body."

The officer turned toward the playground and keyed his radio. "I've got the parents." He swung around and lifted the yellow tape. "Go on in. The detective's the black guy over there in the gray suit."

As they headed toward Jenkins, Livana felt her legs moving, but not much else. Everything had lost color. The city was suddenly devoid of honking cars and the chatter and heel clicks of pedestrians. She was sleepwalking, eyes open but seeing only a sheet-covered body lying across the steps of a side entrance near the back of the building.

Livana stopped abruptly, yanking Fedor backward.

"You want me to look?" he asked.

Livana bit her lip, afraid to know yet *needing* to know. She shook her head and moved along, toward the steps.

Jenkins crouched beside the drape and lifted the top, giving them a view of the girl's face.

The air left Livana's lungs. She fell back against the brick building and clawed at her throat, her vision going gray, consciousness fading to black.

LIVANA OPENED HER eyes and saw Fedor crouching in front of her. Her brain registered time and place—and she began crying. Fedor took her in his arms, holding her head against his shoulder as he said, "I'm so sorry, I wish I could just turn it into a bad dream."

Livana did not want to move, did not want to face the truth of what lay five feet to her left. Finally she pushed away from Fedor and faced Jenkins.

"Who . . . who would do such a thing?"

"That's what I was going to ask you, ma'am."

"Where's Detective Proschetta?" She got to her feet and turned her head away from the body. "I want to talk to him."

"No idea. But your daughter's case is mine, and the homicide detective who's on his way, and I'm going to do ev—"

"I'll only talk with Detective Proschetta. Please, just call him."

Jenkins frowned, stared her down for a moment, then grabbed his radio. He walked a few paces into the darkness, talked with someone at length, and then returned.

"Proschetta's on his way. Probably take him fifteen-twenty to get here. Anything you want to tell me in the meantime?"

"Anything I have to say I'll say to Detective Proschetta."

"Where were you and your husband this afternoon?"

"He's not my husband." Livana wiped away a tear. "We were both at work. We were supposed to meet—" She turned to Fedor. "The boys, they're waiting—"

"Are you okay here?" Fedor asked. "I can go get them."

"Don't bring them in here. Just have them wait on the corner."

Moments later, a sedan pulled up to the curb across the way, lights and siren announcing its arrival. A few seconds later, Isidore Proschetta got out and jogged toward them. As he approached, Livana thought he looked a little thicker, older, and more mature than the last time she had seen him.

"Livana," Proschetta said, leaning forward and giving her a hug. "I'm so sorry. Detective Jenkins told me what happened, I got here as soon as I could."

"Thanks for coming. I know you didn't have to."

"Not a problem. How can I help?"

She glanced at Jenkins, then said, "Can we talk alone?"

"No," Jenkins said, "Anything you got to say, you can say in front of me. This is my case. Proschetta ain't even in this precinct."

Proschetta took Jenkins by the shoulder, turned him, and walked with him as they talked. A moment later, Proschetta rejoined Livana, leaving Jenkins a couple dozen feet away.

"How did she—how did she—" Livana grasped her forehead.

"My experience? The parents don't really want to know. I mean they *do*, but they don't. I can tell you she didn't suffer." Proschetta waited a beat, then said, "How old are your boys now?"

Livana sniffled, tried to compose herself. "Fifteen and seventeen."

"How's Dmitri doing?"

Livana knew what he was tactfully asking. She shrugged. "It affected him badly. He won't make eye contact—not much, anyway. He doesn't talk to me a whole lot, unless it's something he's really interested in. He's kind of a loner."

She thought of the books and *Playboy* magazine she had found in his room, the dissected squirrel, his masturbating to Cassandra while she showered. But how could she possibly tell him that? The police would instantly consider him the killer, and they'd arrest him, put him behind bars. The poor boy had been traumatized enough in his life, between losing his father—seeing him murdered in front of his own eyes—and then getting kidnapped and beaten . . .

But what if he did this? What if he killed his sister? My daughter.

"Livana," Proschetta said, "you okay? You spaced out on me there."

"No, I'm . . . I'm fine. Dmitri is doing okay in school. He doesn't have many friends, and he's got some issues from the kidnapping. He hasn't really been the same since. But I can't blame him, can you?"

Proschetta adjusted his hat. "No, of course not. But at the—"

"I'm sorry, I just can't . . . " She leaned back against the wall again. "I can't deal with this right now."

"I get it. I—I'll follow up with Detective Jenkins. But he's right. It's his precinct, his case." The sound of a car door slamming drew their attention. A man in a rumpled suit shuffled around the front of the sedan and headed in their direction.

"That's the homicide detective," Proschetta said. He turned back to Livana. "I'll help out any way I can, okay?"

She nodded but did not look at him.

He cleared his throat. "I know you don't want to talk about this, but they need some stuff to go on. Can you answer a few questions?"

Livana took a deep breath. "Yes. Yeah, okay."

Proschetta watched as the approaching man spoke with Jenkins. Proschetta took Livana by the arm and led her about thirty feet away, as if protecting her from them. "Did Cassandra have problems with anyone at school? Any boys harassing her, any—"

"Some boy about six months ago," she said. "But I don't think it has anything to do with . . . with this. It wasn't serious, just, you know, he wanted to go out with her and she didn't like him, that kind of thing." Livana hesitated, looked over at Jenkins, then lowered her voice. "Do you think the Castiglias are behind this?

Proschetta tilted his head. "Why? Have you had any contact with them since . . . well, since that day?"

"That night, when we got home, Fedor said he'd gotten a call. Someone—it was obvious they were with the mob—they told him we were to move away and not come back or they'd kill our whole family. But Fedor's grandparents aren't well and they live in a nursing home in Queens, so . . ." She wiped a tear that had coursed down her cheek. "We work in the city and never go near Astoria—never go into Queens. Except when he visits them. But he's very careful and keeps to himself."

"You think they had a hand in this?"

"Who else would want to—to kill my sweet girl?" Livana fought back tears and said, "If anyone can figure it out, if those bastards are involved, you can. You know what happened, you can look into it without making a big deal about it. Because if they didn't do this, I don't want to, you know, wake the sleeping giant. We've had enough problems. I don't want them coming after us again."

"Did you tell Detective Jenkins?"

"I don't know him. I don't trust him. The Castiglias had people in the department who were on their payroll."

"That's been cleaned up, far as I know. But I get you. I'll do it under the radar, real quiet. Okay?"

Livana nodded.

Proschetta rubbed his cheek and shifted his feet. "You know, I gotta be honest with you. First thing we look at in a case like this are the people close to the victim."

Dmitri's behavior flashed through her mind again.

"Particularly the father. Have you remarried?"

"Uh, no. I live, we live kind of a sheltered life. We merged our families. You remember Fedor?"

Proschetta chuckled, a "How could I forget?" laugh. "How's Fedor been with Cassandra?"

"Fedor?" Livana shook her head. "He's been a godsend for us. He's a kind man, a good father figure. He couldn't have done this."

Proschetta looked out into the darkness a moment. "I gotta ask again. How's Dmitri? Could he have done this? Did he have any problems with Cassandra? Or Niklaus?"

"Nik's been fine with her. Dmitri . . ." She wiped her eyes. "Protch . . . you mind if I call you that?"

He gave her a half smile. "Of course."

"Dmitri's been through enough. Terrible things no one should ever have to go through. You know that. I don't want to put him through more trauma. The stress of being interrogated."

"I gotta talk to him. Because if I don't, Jenkins and the homicide detective are going to. And I'd prefer it be me. So would Dmitri, don't you think?"

"I want to be there."

"Of course. And I'll make it look like I'm talking with everyone, so he doesn't realize I'm singling him out."

"He's a block away, waiting with Fedor."

"I gotta clear this with the detectives. They ain't gonna be happy, but I'll use my charm." He gave her a wink.

As Proschetta spoke with the two men, it was clear they did not look pleased at this break in protocol—and the perceived hijacking of their case. But a couple of minutes later, Jenkins threw up his hands and the other detective uttered what looked like a few choice words.

Proschetta joined Livana and said, "That went about as well as I expected."

They walked together to meet with Dmitri and he greeted Fedor with a firm handshake. Dmitri seemed to recoil when he laid eyes on Proschetta—no doubt dredging up bad memories. Livana had not thought of that, but given the alternative, this was the lesser of the two evils. Proschetta was a good man, and she trusted him to keep his word.

"Hey pal, how you doin'?" Proschetta asked Dmitri. The youth glanced up at him, then looked down and pulled his sweatshirt hood over his head.

"I want to tell you all how sorry I am about this. There's nothing I can say to make you feel any better. This is gonna hurt for a long time. The only thing we can do is catch the guy who's responsible. It's not gonna bring Cassandra back, but it's something." He paused, and none of them reacted.

"So tell me what you guys know. Fedor, you were at work, right? Did you leave the building at all during the day? Did Cassandra call you today? Anything unusual about the day?"

"Did my regular shift. Same old stuff, you know? I cut meat, I'm on my feet all day. I don't leave—I mean, a bunch of us get lunch from the truck that comes by at noon. Weather's nice, we eat out front. If not, we go to the break room." He shrugged. "I didn't go anywhere today. Didn't hear from Cassie. It was just a normal shift."

"Do you work by yourself, or alongside other guys?"

"Next to a bunch of other guys in a big room."

"Any idea who might wanna hurt Cassandra?"

Fedor's eyes flicked over to Livana, then back to Proschetta. "Other than the Castiglias?"

"Other than them."

"No. She was a sweet girl, never hurt anyone. There was a boy who asked her out, but I can't believe Cassie rejecting him would make him do something like this."

Proschetta handed over his spiral notepad and a pen. "Jot down the names of the guys you had lunch with today, and the ones you worked with in the afternoon, okay?" Without waiting for an answer, he turned to the boys. "Why don't you guys tell me about school. Anything unusual today? Niklaus?"

Niklaus shrugged. "Same as most days. We sometimes meet after school and hang out, do homework while we wait for my dad and Livana. Sometimes we hang with our friends. Then we meet up and go home together."

"You don't go home right after school?"

"Why would we do that? We're teenagers."

"Right," Proschetta said.

Livana was glad Niklaus did not mention where they lived, or why they *really* waited around. Still, there was truth in what he said. Even if they lived in the city like a normal family, the kids would likely get together with their friends before heading home. Home was not cool, but going places in Manhattan with your buddies—without your parents—definitely was.

As Proschetta took the spiral pad back from Fedor, he said, "Dmitri—anything seem strange to you today?"

He shook his head but did not answer verbally. He began playing with a discarded soda can with his right shoe. Livana wanted to tell him to stop and pay attention to Protch, but she held her tongue.

"When was the last time you saw your sister?"

"About 2:30. When we got out of class."

"And?"

"And what?" Dmitri asked, still playing with the can.

"Hey buddy, can you look at me for a sec?"

Dmitri glanced up, then back down.

Proschetta licked his lips. "Did you see her again, or did you notice anything strange about her, like was she upset about anything?"

"Nope. Nothing was wrong. Didn't see her again."

"Niklaus, where'd you go after you got out of school?"

"There's a playground on Second. I play basketball."

"Dmitri, how about you?"

"Not my fault. Not my fault. Not—"

"Whoa," Proschetta said, holding out his hands to calm the boy. "What's not your fault?"

Dmitri rolled the can with his foot.

"Hey, buddy. Would you mind giving that to me?"

Dmitri hesitated, then bent over and picked up the can. He handed it to Proschetta, who took it by the lip and casually held it away from his body.

"So are you talking about Cassandra? That her death is not your fault?"

Dmitri nodded.

"That's okay. I'm asking everyone the same questions here. My boss makes me write up a stupid report and then he checks it over. I don't ask the right things, he sends me back to meet with all a you and do it all over again. So just tell me where you were."

Dmitri did not answer.

"He was with me," Niklaus said. "Playing ball. The guys there, they needed an extra player for three on three."

Proschetta frowned. Livana figured that Protch was thinking what she was: why didn't Dmitri just say that? Was it true?

"Is that right, Dmitri?"

He nodded, kicking the toe of his sneaker into the sidewalk repeatedly.

Proschetta sucked on his front teeth. "Hey Niklaus." He held out the pad and pen. "Write down the names of the guys you were playing with for me. Boss is gonna ask."

"Don't know their names. We just go there to play. It's a pickup game."

"And you've never seen them before?"

"Mighta seen a couple, like a few weeks ago. Don't know their last names."

"First names? You talked to 'em on the court. You didn't say, 'Hey, you, pass me the ball.' What'd you call 'em?"

"Joe, Juan, and Billy."

"Joe, Juan, and Billy." Proschetta forced a chuckle. "That narrows it down to about half a million guys in the city." He frowned at Niklaus, then turned to Livana. "Again, I'm sorry for your loss. I know you need time as a family to deal with this. You think of anything else, you give me a call, okay?" He handed Livana his business card. "What's your address these days? The detectives are gonna need it for their report in case any of them have questions."

They both supplied their work addresses, which Proschetta noted on his pad. "And home?"

Livana and Fedor shared a look.

"Protch, can I have a word with you alone?"

"Liv," Fedor said.

She gave him a reassuring smile. "It's okay."

Proschetta and Livana walked a dozen feet away. "When the Castiglias told us to get out of town and not be seen around here again, we moved away. To Ellis Island."

"Ellis Island. But that's abandoned. No one—"

"We do. In one of the old hospital complex buildings. But please don't tell anyone."

"You've been living there? For . . ." He thought a moment, did the calculation. "Seven years?"

Livana looked away. "We fixed it up, made it a real home. All the other buildings were falling apart. This one, well, we took pride in it. Painted and decorated it. Fedor repaired things." She glanced at Proschetta. "We don't make a lot of money, Protch. It seemed like the safest place we could go, near enough to Fedor's grandparents, where the Castiglias wouldn't bother us." She sucked in some air, then started crying. "I guess we were wrong."

He motioned her closer and took her in his arms. "I know it's been difficult. And for what it's worth, I don't think the Castiglias are involved."

She pushed away and wiped at her tears. "Why not?"

"It's not how they operate. Cassandra was—" He stopped himself. "She was strangled. As a rule, they don't do that. And they've got bigger problems right now than your daughter who's minding her own business and staying out of theirs. She *was* staying out of their business, right? She wasn't going after them or anything? Actually, were any of you?"

Livana sniffled. "We've got no desire to dredge all that up, Protch. I'll ask, just in case there's something I don't know about. But we don't want any trouble. We don't even talk of them—of that."

"Just the same, Dmitri appears to be hiding something. I don't know why or what, but Niklaus is covering for him. I don't buy that Joe, Juan, and Billy story. He knows the names of the guys they play with. But my money says Dmitri was somewhere else. And if he gives me their real names and I question them, they'll confirm that Dmitri wasn't there. Maybe you can gently ask him about it. Let me know if you find out anything." He looked away. "I know that places you in an impossible position. But if Dmitri did have something to do with it, better that we know so we find out why. And get him help."

"My son's got his issues, Protch. His doctor said his behavior's not surprising given what happened to him. So him being different from other boys, don't take it to mean that he killed his sister."

Proschetta stepped squarely in front of her and bent forward, down to her level, and peered into her eyes. "Livana, do you trust me?"

Livana held his gaze. "I trusted you with my son's life, didn't I? And I've just told you things I've never told anyone else." Still, there's a limit. I can't tell him about those books on murder and death, or the squirrel, or him watching Cassandra— She could not implicate her son, even if he was guilty. But if he did do this—

"Then trust my instincts. Dmitri isn't telling the truth. Doesn't mean he's a killer. But he's hiding something."

"I'll see if I can find out. He doesn't always talk to me. If anything, he might tell Nik."

"Then see if Nik will help us out."

She nodded tightly. "Okay."

"I'll do what I can, but remember, this is Detective Jenkins's case. Him and that homicide detective. I'll talk to them and my lieutenant, see if I can be a part of the investigation, but I gotta be honest with you. They don't need me on the case, so there ain't much chance of it. But I'll poke around a bit, see if there's anything goin' on with the Castiglias."

"What—what am I supposed to do now? With Cassie, with her—" Livana cleared her throat. "Her body."

"She's probably gonna be taken to the morgue very soon. In cases like this, they're going to do a thorough check to make sure they've got the cause of . . . death right. Then she'll be released to you so you can plan the funeral."

Livana teared up again.

"I'd like to be there, to pay my respects, if that's okay with you."

"I would like that. Thank-you, Protch. For everything. I owe you a lot."

"Nonsense. I'm happy to be here for you. My job, I don't always deal with nice people, with good people. You deserve better, and I'm gonna do my best to see that you and your family get it. Go home, grieve together, be there for one another." He gave her a hug and then headed back toward his car.

WHEN LIVANA REJOINED Fedor and the boys, she told them they were free to go home.

Niklaus looked from his father to Livana. "That's it? Just go home?"

Livana had to swallow down the urge to cry. She knew what Niklaus was intimating: how could they just leave Cassie behind? Going home seemed so inadequate, so shallow and . . . hollow. To Livana, it felt like she was abandoning her daughter.

She related what Proschetta told her, then said to Niklaus—though it also served as a reminder to herself: "There's nothing more for us to do here."

They headed over to the marina and sat quietly as they motored toward Ellis Island. About halfway across, in the light of a full moon, Livana told Fedor to stop the boat.

"What are we doing?" Fedor asked.

"Dmitri," Livana said. "I know you weren't playing basketball with Nik. Look at me." He met her eyes. "Were you with Cassie?"

Dmitri swung his gaze toward the dark waters. "No."

"Why won't you look at me?"

He turned to her.

"Tell me where you really were."

He glanced off again, this time toward Manhattan. "I don't want to say."

"Livana," Fedor said.

"Not now. I need to know. I need to know if my—if my son had anything to do with . . . I just need to know." She moved in front of Dmitri, the boat swaying as she shifted her weight. "Tell me."

"I went to a bookstore."

"Which one?"

"A used one where they have the books I like."

"And where are the books that you bought? In your backpack?"

"I didn't buy any."

"Did anyone see you there?"

He shrugged. "Don't think so."

Livana clenched her jaw. She did not know what to believe. First he lied, then he told her a story that would be hard to verify. "What's the name of this store?"

"I don't remember. It's on Second Street."

"Tomorrow you're going to take me there."

"It's my place, I don't want you there!"

"Dmitri," Fedor said. "It's just a bookstore. Anyone can go there. If your mother wants to go, you don't have anything to say about it."

"He's saying that it's his," Niklaus said. "His special place, where his parents don't go."

Livana thought a moment, then reseated herself. "Take us home, Fedor."

As they set off toward the island, Livana saw a new addition to their neighborhood: some sort of flat-topped barge with the words "Anderson Salvage" lettered in white on the side.

She and Fedor shared a concerned look, then headed to their mooring in the rear of the complex. The event that she had anticipated, and feared, for the past year or so had arrived: the government was going to renovate the dilapidated buildings. The place would soon be crawling with workers, surveyors, supervisors, and inspectors.

Their days on the island were numbered.

42

›UPPER NEW YORK BAY
NEW YORK/NEW JERSEY TERRITORIAL WATERS
SATURDAY, JANUARY 7, 2006

The ferry was moving through Upper New York Bay, and the weather was unseasonably pleasant: mid-forties with a cloudless sky.

With Manhattan island receding as they moved away from it, Vail could not help feeling a sense of loss. She still had not gotten used to seeing the New York skyline without the Twin Towers. Their absence was like a weeping wound that refused to heal.

Vail swiveled in the bench seat, which ran the length of the ferry beneath a wall of windows, and pointed. "Jonathan, see that? It's called Ellis Island. Remember I told you your grandfather came over from Ireland? That's where his boat docked."

"What does 'docked' mean?"

"It's like parking a car, but instead it's a boat. They tie the boat to the big wood walkway, so it's safe for the people to get off. You'll see one in a few minutes when the ferry gets to the Statue of Liberty."

A moment later, Jonathan squirmed in his seat.

"Look, Mommy, there it is!"

No matter how many times Vail saw the copper green skin of Lady Liberty, from near or far, the grandeur of the iconic symbol of freedom moved her, filled her with a sense of pride. "Isn't she beautiful?"

"C'mon, let's go!" Jonathan jumped off the bench, took her hand, and pulled her off her seat.

She laughed as she let him lead her toward the exit. "We have to wait till the boat stops, okay?"

Five minutes later, the ferry had tied off and the passengers were disembarking, heading toward the base of the statue. "It's so big, isn't it?"

Jonathan craned his neck skyward and shielded his eyes against the glary sky. "I wanna go inside. C'mon."

They made their way to the back of the island and went through the security screening procedure, then walked the fifteen feet toward the base's entrance, which was protected by large granite bricks stacked on either side of black metal doors with vertical copper handles.

Entering the statue's pedestal, Vail and her son were met by a man in a park ranger's muted clay-colored uniform.

"Welcome to the statue," he said. He must have noticed Jonathan's fascination with the copper colored two-story structure behind him, because he knelt down and followed the boy's gaze. "That, young man, was the original torch."

"Cool," Jonathan said, as he started to climb under the metal bar that kept tourists a safe distance away.

"Jonathan, sweetie, stay over here. You can't go under there." She smiled and said, "I'm Karen Vail. We're supposed to meet Ranger Harris."

The man chuckled. "He's the resident expert on Liberty Island. A bit eccentric, but he can tell you anything and everything you want to know. And I mean *everything*."

"That's what I was told. He's going to be giving us a tour of the crown."

"Crown's been closed since 9/11," the ranger said. "Nobody goes up."

"I realize that's the official Park Service line, but we both know exceptions are made if you're the right person with the right connections." She winked. "Can you just locate Ranger Harris for me?"

The man frowned, then mumbled, "Give me a minute," and headed off to the left, out of sight.

"Can we go up to the crown now?" Jonathan asked.

"Just a minute, sweetie. Ranger Harris is the only one who can take us up."

A middle-aged man with a receding hairline approached and said, "Agent Vail?"

"Ranger Harris, good to meet you."

"I've been told to take you to the crown." He checked his watch. "I only have thirty minutes. Should be enough time."

"My son's been talking about this for a week."

"Is the crown as cool as the torch?" Jonathan asked.

"Did anyone tell you about the old torch?" Harris asked. "This is the one built in 1884. The torch you saw out there when you were on the ferry, it was put there twenty years ago in 1986. It's got a copper flame covered in 24 karat gold, just like this one. Other than the light, the new one's an exact reproduction of the original."

"Can we go into the torch too?"

Harris leaned back. "Sorry, son. Only way to get to the torch is through Lady Liberty's arm, and it's really narrow, barely the width of my shoulders. And the arm sways from side to side as you climb the ladder. Pretty dark and scary in there. The only person who's allowed in is the maintenance ranger, to change the lightbulbs. Same ranger's been doing it the past nineteen and a half years. Twenty in June."

"You ever been up there?"

"I have." He looked around. "But don't tell anyone."

"Can we go to the crown now?"

"We sure can. Are you ready for the climb, young man? It's 168 steps to the top."

"A hundred and sixty eight? Is that a lot?"

"I would say so." Harris scratched his head. "It's the equivalent of walking up a twenty-two-story building. Are you ready?"

"Yeah!"

As they started walking past the torch, Vail's BlackBerry rang. She looked at the display and cursed under her breath. *My boss? On a Saturday?*

"Go on ahead," she said. "I'll catch up."

"You can't come up unescorted," Harris said. "Gotta be with me. And if I wait for you, we may not be able to make it up and down in time."

Vail answered the call. "Sir, one second please." To Harris: "Can you take him up without me?"

"I sure can."

"Jonathan, go with Ranger Harris, okay? I'll meet you right here when you're done."

Jonathan, unfazed, turned and walked alongside Harris as the ranger spouted more facts and information.

Vail brought her phone to her face as she headed back out the same doors they had entered moments ago.

"Karen," the assistant special agent in charge said. "Sorry to bother you on your day off, but we've got movement on that bank robbery case and I wanted to keep you in the loop."

"Appreciate that, sir."

"So we think the four suspects you identified yesterday are our guys. Great work with that. Looks like there's a pattern to their drug buys and the robberies, just like you thought there'd be."

"Do we know when they're gonna strike next? And where?"

"Working on it. You want to be part of the discussions this afternoon? I've called a meeting for 1:00."

Yeah, I would.

"I'm on Liberty Island with my son and my husband isn't available today." *Actually, I just checked him into rehab.* "Thanks for the heads-up, though. You want me to come in tomorrow?"

"I think we'll be okay till Monday. Enjoy the day with your son."

Vail hung up and headed back into the pedestal, then walked through the museum. She had vague memories of taking a trip to the island with her fourth or fifth grade class. In truth, for some reason, she had more vivid memories of the ferry ride than the time they spent in the statue.

As she stood there staring at the true-to-life mockup of Liberty's face, her thoughts turned to the bank robbers her ASAC had called about.

IT WAS MONDAY, and Vail sat through the morning briefing with her team as they reviewed surveillance reports prepared by the agents who had been watching four men suspected in a rash of violent "take over" bank robberies the past three months. Their modus operandi involved taking a female hostage and holding a gun to her head while the others collected the money. They had murdered a woman during their last heist and decided to lay low to let the heat and media coverage subside.

After going dormant for eight weeks—their longest stretch without a job—Vail noted a pattern in their behavior based on information her CI, Eugenia Zachary, had given her: the robbers were drug dealers who had not gone longer than sixteen days between jobs.

But Vail found a pattern to their heists, and it involved their heroin buys. With info from Eugenia, she was able to track their purchases to the first of every month. When their supply sold out, they knocked off another bank to subsidize their habit. Vail surmised that the robberies also served another purpose: it gave them the thrill of the chase, a high-adrenaline rush that trafficking in illicit drugs could not provide.

Today was day fifteen, and Eugenia had tipped Vail about talk that some fresh heroin and cocaine were going to be hitting the streets in three days. Vail surmised another heist was on the horizon, and the surveillance crew confirmed activity consistent with a change in their demeanor and daily routines.

Vail's team had gotten an early start, as the suspects, who normally slept until noon, were on the move by 9:00 AM.

They were tasked with following the perps until they were ready to enter the bank—and then take them down.

Vail and her four colleagues took turns tailing the men, who were in two cars, through the Bronx, Queens, and Manhattan. At 11:33 AM, they drove into a secluded neighborhood just outside Coney Island, whipped out their paraphernalia, and shot up.

"This is not good," Vail said into her lapel microphone as she drove by. Agent Rick Chi was a block away. "Coming up behind you. I'll pick them up."

Five minutes later, Chi's voice blurted over the radio. "Holy shit, he shot the guy behind the desk."

"What desk?' Vail asked.

"A bodega. One of 'em pulled out a suppressed handgun, but the owner didn't want to hand over the cash. He shot him and emptied the register. He's a cold-blooded SOB. Sorinson, he's the shooter."

"Status?" Vail asked.

"Owner's down, took a head shot, gotta be dead. Sorinson fled back to his buddy in the car."

"That'd be Bodene," Vail said, "the driver. Call an ambulance but do not engage the perps. We need to be able to connect them to the bank robberies. If I'm right, they're on their way to another job. That's when we take them."

"Affirmative," Chi said. The two other team members acknowledged as well.

They followed the two sedans, each carrying two men, for an hour. Both vehicles pulled into the empty parking lot of a defunct big box electronics store.

"Anyone got eyes on?" Vail asked. "What are they doing?"

"McKay and Demarco are getting into Sorinson's car," said Agent Tiriko, the third team member. "And they're shooting up again."

They're using the drugs to build up the courage to knock off the bank. "I think this is it." Vail grabbed her two-way and requested aerial support.

"Negative," came the response. "It's tasked with mob surveillance on the island. A million dollar transfer's going down. They're a day late."

And apparently I'm a dollar short. "Ten-four." Vail moved her sedan a block away so she would be in position to follow the moment the suspects made their move. When they were done using, Sorinson and Bodene stumbled to their car and a couple of minutes later the two vehicles left the parking lot, driving erratically.

Trying to follow them when they're all over the road is gonna be tough without getting made.

But Vail was able to maintain a discreet distance without giving away her presence. Three miles down, however, Tiriko broke radio silence. "Uh, we got a problem. McKay got out of Demarco's car and he got into his own that was parked in the South Bronx. I'm staying on McKay. Who can pick up Demarco?"

"I got it," Tiriko said.

"I'm still with Sorinson and Bodene," Vail said. "We're approaching Queens Boulevard. They're stopping in front of a newsstand. Two guys getting in. Male Caucasians, medium build. Average height."

"That's a huge help, Karen," Chi said. "Aren't many men fitting *that* description. No wonder you couldn't cut it with NYPD."

Had Chi been within reach, she'd have kicked him in the balls. She would have to remember that comment the next time she needed to visualize a target on the shooting range.

Knowing that her transmissions could be monitored or recorded, she kept her response professional: "Just reporting what I see."

"Don't do us any favors."

Vail keyed her radio. "Suspects turning onto Queens Boulevard."

Chi's voice: "Ah, shit. My car just died." Over the open mic, Vail heard his car engine cranking but not turning over. "Are you kidding me?"

She resisted the urge to laugh—or give him a dig.

"All right, here we go." Vail stopped half a block away and watched as three of the men—Sorinson, Bodene, and one of the newer guys—got out of the car and headed into the bank, wearing black ski masks.

Vail pulled up to the storefront and opened her door, then, using it as a shield, stepped out and reached for her radio. "Dispatch, this is Agent Vail. I'm in position, thirty feet from the bank's entrance. I've got a visual on three well-armed men dressed in black clothing, wearing masks. ETA on backup? I'm solo here. Over."

"Copy. Stand by."

Stand by. Easy for you to say. My ass is flapping in the breeze outside a bank with a group of heavily armed mercenaries inside, and you tell me to stand by. Sure, I'll just sit here and wait.

Vail was informed that SWAT was en route, but before they arrived, Mike Hartman, her former partner, radioed that he was responding, along with an NYPD cruiser.

As Hartman pulled up, the three masked men emerged from the bank with money bags—and MAC-10 machine pistols—in hand. They let loose a barrage of rounds, two of which struck Vail in the left thigh.

The deep burn of a gunshot wound was instantly upon her, and a bloody circle spread through the nylon fibers of her tan pants. She grabbed the back of her leg and felt two tears in the fabric, indicating the rounds had gone right through. Assuming they didn't hit a major artery, she'd be okay for a bit—but it sure hurt like hell. She hit the ground and returned fire.

As lead projectiles flew in both directions, two of the perps went down—along with the cops, Hartman, and his partner. The remaining robber—by body type it looked like Bodene—bent over and lifted the large canvas bag from his dead comrade's hand and turned to hightail it down the street.

Well, this isn't good. Mike and his partner down, a couple cops dead, and the shithead's about to make it away with the cash? Not on my watch.

Vail rolled left, got prone against the ground, and brought her Glock to the front of her body. This would be an insane shot—below the cars and above the curb—but what did she have to lose? With all the shooting, there were no innocents around. She squeezed off several rounds, the weapon bucking violently. Bodene stumbled, then limped—he was hit.

Vail grabbed the edge of Hartman's car door and pulled herself up as best she could, her thigh burning like a red-hot poker, her muscles quivering as she groaned and pushed with her right leg to get herself upright.

As Bodene limped away, Vail pulled herself erect using the side view mirror as leverage. "Federal agent," she yelled. "Freeze!"

Did that ever work? Nah. Usually not. But Bodene wasn't too smart, because he turned toward her, his MAC-10 still in his grasp, and that was all she needed.

Vail fired again and flattened him against the pavement. And then she let go of the mirror and joined him in a heap on the asphalt as she heard the uneven scream of approaching sirens.

FOUR DAYS AFTER Vail was released from the hospital—with a dose of antibiotics, a few stitches in her thigh, and a bruised ego—the Office of Professional Responsibility initiated its review of the bank shooting.

That afternoon, Vail requested papers for a promotion to the Behavioral Analysis Unit, as the profiling group had been renamed.

Her ASAC laughed, then told her it was not that easy. She knew that, of course, from her conversation with Agent Safarik. But she felt she needed to do something. Aside from her goal of joining the BAU, hooking on with the FBI put her in a safer environment; the number of agents killed in the line of duty was far fewer compared with their NYPD counterparts.

Her boss assured her he would do everything in his power to help her get the promotion. Vail took that to mean the odds were no better with his help than without. But she appreciated his assistance nonetheless.

He told her that in two days she would start assisting a couple of local police departments with cold case files they needed an extra set of eyes to review. It had the benefit of taking her out of the field while OPR conducted its assessment, and he felt she could use a break from handling active cases. Translation: he would keep her behind a desk where she would not have to fire a weapon, or be fired *at*.

A numbingly cold day in mid-January with the threat of snow was not an ideal time to drive to the FBI's Behavioral Analysis Unit, but she was still limping around, so she used it as an excuse to take a personal day and head to Virginia.

She arrived at the Aquia Commerce Center and made her way up to the second floor entrance, where she was buzzed in.

"I've got an appointment with Agent Safarik," Vail said. While she waited for Safarik, the ASAC she had met six—no, seven—years before, Thomas Gifford, exited his office. He stopped and looked at her, but it wasn't a "glad to see you look." In fact, it seemed to be the opposite.

"Agent Vail," Gifford said as he approached.

Oh shit. He remembers my name. How can that be? Is that good or bad?

"Agent Gifford. Good to see you again."

"Why's that?"

"Because I hope to have a desk here one day and it's good to know the people you'll be working for."

"Your ASAC already contacted me. I told him we don't have any openings and the near future isn't looking so good, either. Sorry."

Sorry? I've wanted to be a profiler for years, I've shaped my career around it. Sorry?

"Well, life's funny sometimes," she said. "You never know what's gonna happen, right?"

Gifford gave her a look of confusion, then a dismissive nod and walked on. "Good luck with that," he said as he headed down the hall.

A moment later, Mark Safarik came up the same corridor and smiled when he saw Vail.

"Everything okay?" he asked as he approached. "You look a little tense."

"Am I being profiled?"

"Just a simple observation of your body language. Your hands are curled into fists."

"Oh," Vail said with a laugh. "That."

"C'mon back to my office."

Vail sat down in the chair opposite Safarik's desk. A blue California license plate that read "DETECTIV" sat atop a bookshelf packed with three-inch ring binders bearing spines with provocative labels: Sexual Homicide, Psychopathy, Criminal Investigative Analysis, Autoerotica, Sexual Homicide of Elderly Females, Violent Crime Seminar/SFPD—among others.

"You have an interesting assortment of reading materials."

He laughed. "Yeah. I'd like to say I've got eclectic interests, but it's probably more accurate to call it—"

"Violent?"

"I was thinking 'professional.'"

"I'll accept that."

"So this case you wanted to discuss. This is the one you told me about back in . . . '99, right? Or 2000?"

"Ninety-nine. And I'm still not sure if I've got the first vic."

"That'd be helpful, but it doesn't mean we can't do some good work without it."

"You're not gonna get in trouble for discussing this with me?"

"We like our rules and procedures, so if you want the unit to officially work the case, we've got to do it right. But on an informal basis, just you and me talking about it, we can certainly do that."

"I saw Gifford in the hall. He knows I asked my ASAC about a promotion to the unit."

Safarik's eyebrows rose. "Really."

"Means nothing. Gifford didn't seem to want me anywhere near the BAU. Not sure why." *Maybe my record at the NYPD made its way to his desk. Unless it wasn't by accident. Did he check me out? Shit, did he talk with Kearney? Carrig? Mendoza? I'd be totally screwed.*

"What'd he say?"

"No openings. Nothing in the near future."

Safarik gestured for her to close the door. When it clicked shut, he held up a folder. "My retirement papers. I'm done here in six months."

"No shit."

"I'm gonna be doing the same thing with Robert Ressler for a private company. Twenty years with the Bureau, I've been fortunate. I've had a very rewarding career. Time to shake things up. Point is, there'll be an opening here around July."

Vail couldn't help but smile.

"Okay," Safarik said, leaning back in his chair, "so I made your day. No more clenched fists. Now let's talk about your case."

Vail recounted the details of each victim. Safarik listened intently, asking occasional questions.

"So what I'm hearing is that the offender is making the Greek women into the posers he thinks they are."

"What do you mean?"

"Let's say that there's something in his childhood where a woman did something to him. Abused him or caused him to suffer some kind of hardship as a result of something she did. Maybe a prostitute or maybe his father had an affair with a Greek woman. Maybe he sees them as women who encouraged the flirting and then claimed innocence. It's his goal to expose the fraud by showing everyone what kind of sluts they really are. He does this by posing them not just in sexual positions but in provocative positions."

Vail nodded. "The hand, the fingers."

"You said he used superglue to hold the digits in a specific position." Safarik rifled through the file and pulled out a close-up of Carole Manos's hand. "He positioned it to suggest the woman is curling her index finger as if to say, 'Come here.' He used superglue to get the finger to hold that curl."

"That's why he sits them up in bed and spreads their legs with their dress pulled up slightly, their arm raised as if gesturing, 'come here.'"

"Exactly."

"I like it," Vail said. "So we're looking for someone who's got a beef with Greek women, someone who was wronged by them."

"Maybe—keep in mind that it's the offender's *perception* of being wronged. To you and me, it may not seem that way. But it could be. I'm just saying keep an open mind. Don't dismiss something because you don't think it's traumatic enough. It doesn't have to be much because it's in the offender's mind. He creates this grudge and builds a ritualized behavior around how he's going to play it out."

"And what do you make of this Crinelli murder? He's the only male."

"That's a little more difficult. First impression—and they can be wrong—is that this is a personal murder. Not too different from the others, really. Those are revenge killings. Maybe it's the same thing with Crinelli. He was a mafioso, he's got a lot of enemies. Maybe he wronged your offender, and this is how he disposed of him, his favorite way to kill."

Vail considered this. "Okay. But how did this UNSUB get the drop on a mob capo? He was killed without any defensive wounds."

"A ruse, perhaps. Somebody he knows and trusts. He lets him get close—too close."

"There are finger marks on the back of the shard of glass that indicate he was killed from behind."

"Right, so there's little movement, little resistance. Or in this case, no resistance. No defensive injury. Any print detail?"

"None."

"DNA testing wasn't standard back then, but you may want to run it now. You might find some touch DNA on that shard."

"Looks like he wore a thin latex glove, which is consistent with the other crime scenes. No latents at all. What do you make of what he does to the eyes?"

"Postmortem," Safarik said. "They're symbolic. Like posing the body. Emotionally, he's got a deep-seated need to do it."

"You sure?"

"Let's keep this in perspective. I'm looking at this case and giving you an off-the-cuff impression. So, no, I'm not sure. But that'd make sense."

Safarik looked through the file again. "I don't see anything about Taser marks on the body. Talk with the ME. Check the photos again, get 'em blown up. That'd be an ideal way to incapacitate a guy like a capo who wouldn't hesitate to kill you—and who can probably do it with his hands if he doesn't have a weapon nearby."

"I'll see what we can find."

"One last thing: I'm pretty sure Manos isn't his first vic. Crime scene's too neat. Just looking at these photos, at the vic, it was all very well thought out. He's what we call an organized killer—bright, everything's planned. Not a whole lot of blood, few defensive wounds because he knows how to avoid a confrontation or how to incapacitate them without a struggle. It's possible he just put a lot of thought and study into it before killing Manos. But I still think there's a first kill out there, not as complete as this, not as careful. He was still experimenting, learning to kill. This guy is very advanced." Safarik closed the file. "That's all I've got right now."

"That's a lot. Really good stuff. Thanks."

He handed her the folder. "See if your ASAC can get you a position as an NCAVC coordinator in New York," he said, referring to the National Center for the Analysis of Violent Crime. "You'll interface with the unit and be one step closer to this chair."

Vail thanked him and walked out determined to make the BAU the next rung on her career ladder. If Thomas Gifford had other plans, tough.

43

›MANHATTAN SOUTH HOMICIDE SQUAD
MONDAY, JANUARY 16, 2006

T he sky was unusually dark and gloomy at 8:00 AM when
Vail walked into the old precinct house where the homicide squad was located. She commiserated for a moment
with a bunch of patrol officers and a handful of detectives
she had known back in her NYPD days. They talked about grabbing a beer
at the Pig and Whistle, a favorite Fed watering hole, when she caught sight
of Russo across the room.

"You just stopping by for a visit?" Russo asked as he stepped into his office. "Shoulda told me you were coming."

Vail followed him in and glanced around. Things were largely the same
—department memos stuck to the wall, alongside a new framed photo of
Sofia and one of Russo with Commissioner Carrig at a formal event. There
was a bit more dust and a few extra stacks of papers on the desk, but
otherwise it felt as if she had never left.

"Here on business. I need to talk with the detectives handling Hades.
Slater?"

Russo grabbed his overcoat off the rack in the corner. "Good memory.
He's still got the case. But believe me, he wishes he didn't. He used to have
a hundred percent solve rate."

"No one's perfect."

"I'll let you tell him that. But you'll have to wait for another time. He was called out fifteen minutes ago. Another vic."

"Hades? He's been dormant for years."

"Far as we know. Also could've been in another state. Or prison."

"You didn't call me?"

"Karen, he got the call fifteen minutes ago. And it's not your case anymore." He held up a hand. "Sorry, I didn't really mean that. But it's true, you know that."

"You still used to call me—"

"I'll make sure you're notified in the future. But hopefully we'll catch this asshole and there won't be any more vics."

I don't think I'll hold my breath.

"Are we going to the scene?"

Russo, slipping on his coat, couldn't help but smile. "We are."

THEY PULLED UP in front of the building once known informally in police, and community, circles as Fort Apache. Vail knew it only because of its location and its relevance to her career.

"Welcome back to the South Bronx."

"The place that launched me as a cop."

"And almost got me killed. If it wasn't for you."

"You know," Vail said, facing Russo with a playful tilt of her head, "Sofia never thanked me."

"She probably doesn't think you did her any favors." He chortled as he nosed the vehicle in at an angle, its front end a few feet up onto the sidewalk, consistent with the other police sedans parked on either side of theirs.

"Your old stomping grounds," Vail said, taking in the recently refurbished three-story structure, tan stone siding with large brick archways above each of the ground floor windows and doorways. "Why are we here?"

"This, Karen, is our crime scene." He shoved the gearshift into park, sat back, and looked at her.

"Our what?"

"This here building, a landmark which used to house the 41st Precinct, which is now home to the Bronx Homicide Task Force, Night Watch, and the Special Victims Division, is where our new vic is located." He winked, then popped open his car door.

"Hang on," Vail said, following him under the yellow police tape and through the large wood doors. They stepped into a grand marble-tiled lobby that led up to a massive oak registration desk and wood-paneled wall that more closely resembled a judge's perch than a duty officer's work station. "How can a police station be our crime scene?"

Russo stepped up to the desk and spoke with the woman, who rose to greet him.

Vail glanced at the high-tech electronics, including a state-of-the-art surveillance system with four monitors set into an opening below the oak counter.

"Here you go," Russo said as he handed Vail a pair of blue booties. "Follow me."

She struggled to slip them over her shoes and ascended the well-maintained ivory, gray-veined marble steps to keep stride with Russo. *Good thing I loaded up on the Motrin this morning.* As she hobbled up the stairs, she pulled out her FBI shield and clipped it to her belt.

They emerged on the third floor and entered the homicide task force, a long rectangular room that spanned the length of the building. Detectives' desks sat along the row of large picture windows.

Mounted on the far wall was a banner:

NYC DETECTIVES
the GREATEST DETECTIVES in the WORLD
Serving the People 24 hours a Day

"I certainly felt that way," she said, indicating the sign. "Now if we can just clear this case."

"We?"

"You."

Russo eyed her. "You happy with the Bureau?"

"Very." She said it without hesitation. But did she answer too fast? She *was* happy. And until a week ago, safer. Or was it just an illusion?

"You're limping."

"You noticed," she said.

"I'm one of 'the greatest detectives in the world.' Of course I noticed."

They both chuckled, a throwback to old times.

"Shooting. Bank robbery. Took a couple in the leg." She waved a hand dismissively. "I'm fine."

"Of course you are." He led the way past the metal desks. Above them hung a poster of the New York City skyline, prominently featuring the former Twin Towers, an oversize American flag superimposed behind it. A quote was lettered beside the flag: "Our unity is a kinship of grief and a steadfast resolve to prevail over our enemies."

Amen to that.

"Sounds exciting," Russo said.

His voice pulled her away from a quick flashback to 9/11. "Huh?"

"Your case, the bank robbery shootout. Exciting."

"A little more excitement than I'd prefer. Three LEOs dead," she said, slang for law enforcement officers.

They stopped midway into the room and turned right, through a door and into a corridor. An orange sticker on a filing cabinet reminded the detectives that:

PROPER TACTICS
SAVE LIVES
Cover ✦ Isolate ✦ Contain

"Where's our vic?"

"You're not gonna believe it," he said. "*I* didn't when the call came in." They entered another section, walked past the room where lineups were conducted, and into the area containing the holding cells. Attached to the black iron diamond grating were traditional vertical metal bars. There were two entrances, one on either end, with a plain, varnished wood bench along the left cream-colored cinderblock wall.

This particular holding cell had something else inside: a dead female body.

A CSU detective was doing his thing, partially blocking Vail's view. She moved aside to assess the victim. "Positioned like the others. Finger glued in place, legs spread like a slut."

"Why the hell's a Fibbie here?"

A man on the other side of the cell, just outside the bars, wearing a blue shirt and dark blue suit, peered across the way at Vail.

"This is Karen Vail," Russo said. "Karen, Joe Slater."

"So you're Slater."

"So you're Vail."

Slater was probably mid-fifties with a severely receding hairline. He was beer-belly heavy but carried his weight well.

"Heard a lot about you and your hundred percent solve rate," Vail said.

"*Was* a hundred. This fuckin' case is screwin' it up. Thanks a lot for bailing on it."

"Guess I knew when to jump ship."

Russo looked uncomfortable with her last comment—perhaps sensing that the conversation could get out of hand fast. He cleared his throat and said, "Dyer here yet?"

"Downstairs," Slater said. "Reviewing the surveillance tapes."

"Ben Dyer?" Vail asked. She noticed Russo's quizzical look. "Met him at your surprise party a few years ago."

"Right. You'd like him. Shoulda introduced you two a long time ago. My mistake."

"Well, looky here."

They turned to see Max Finkelstein and, just behind him, Ryan Chandler.

"Max," Vail said. "If you weren't old enough to be my grandfather, I'd give you a big kiss." She sidestepped him and embraced Chandler.

"What are you doing here?" Finkelstein said.

"This case is like a piece of gum on the bottom of my shoe. Can't get rid of it. And with this vic, the offender's definitely taking his game to another level."

As Chandler set down his kit and Finkelstein gloved up, Vail stepped around one of the men and entered the jail cell, taking care to avoid the pooling blood, and knelt in front of the wood bench. "Pretty ballsy for him to come into a police station. Not to mention he had to be lugging the body somehow. This guy's smart and careful. He knows what he's doing. He'd assume there are cameras. We get any usable images?"

"Nothing yet," Slater said. "Wore a ski mask, bulky coat."

"And the body?"

"In a trash bag, far as I saw. But I only watched a couple minutes. I can tell you he took the elevator."

"Still," Russo said. "Very risky that someone would see him."

"It was Sunday night. Place is dead, almost no one here except the Night Watch detectives. They went out on calls. And yeah, I checked. Both were bogus."

"So he lured away the biggest risks," Vail said. "He knows his way around the place. A cop? A PAA?"

Russo locked eyes with her. "You thinking Danzig?"

"If Danzig was our guy." Vail turned to Slater. "You familiar with Dan—"

"Our one and only suspect? You kiddin' me?"

"Chandler," Vail said, "can you guys do a match of the body type and build of the perp on the video to Danzig's vitals?"

He splayed open his kit. "Consider it done."

Vail examined the woman's fingers: glued in place. Her legs were spread and the dress was pulled up high on her thighs. The eyes were gouged and a glass shard was protruding from the neck. "Injuries the same as the others." Vail stood up and stepped back out of the way. "Looks like COD is more like the recent ones—she wasn't strangled. I'm guessing she was killed here, given the volume of pooling blood. You agree?" she asked, turning to Finkelstein.

"If you let me get in there, I'll let you know."

She stepped out of the holding cell and let Finkelstein pass. "Assuming I'm right about that, we have a radical shift in his MO. He brought the vic here alive—so he must've drugged her or incapacitated her somehow, killed her onsite, and then did his ritual with the body."

"Ritual?" Russo asked.

"It's a behavioral thing. I've been reading some papers a profiler at the Behavioral Analysis Unit gave me."

"I thought Fonzarella killed that profiling shit," Slater said. "Back in '99. It was noted in the file."

"He did," Vail said. "But Fonzarella's dead, and this is no longer his case."

Slater crossed his arms. "It's not yours, either."

"I'm here for continuity. To help. You got a problem with that?"

"No," Russo said firmly, addressing his comment to Slater. "We don't."

"Good, because I came away from the profiling unit with some insight into the offender. He kills the woman because it's something he has to do to carry out his ritualized behaviors, which feed his emotional needs. But the stuff he does to her body afterward, that's got nothing to do with the murder: gouging the eyes, stabbing the neck. He doesn't *have* to do those things because she's already dead. Follow?"

"Okay," Slater said. "So what?"

"He does it because he wants to, because it's comforting, it fulfills a need. It has deep meaning to him. The eyes are symbolic for something. Just like the way he poses the body."

"What do you mean?"

Vail stood there, lost in thought. "I think he's humiliating these women in death by positioning them—legs spread, dress hiked up—as if they're sluts."

"And how does this help us?" Slater said.

Vail sighed. "I don't know enough to say. But I think it gives us an under-stand—"

"Understanding why this jerkwad did this shit don't help us," Slater said. "Does it now?"

I wish I knew enough to say, to put this guy in his place. It does help us, it has to.

Chandler glanced at Vail. She got the feeling he wanted to jump in to defend her but thought better of it.

"One thing that's very upsetting," Vail said, sidestepping Slater's question, "is what's gotten under his skin? What's suddenly set him off? Why is he getting bolder, why is he taking on a lot more risk? Seems to me that he's turning up the pressure on the department. Killing this vic in a police station— and a famous one at that—is putting it right in our face. It's like he's extending his middle finger at us."

"You didn't see it?" Chandler asked.

"See what?"

Russo walked a few paces and picked up a newspaper off a nearby desk. "This." He headed back, then handed her the *Daily News*.

The headline consumed nearly the entire front page:

NYPD: HADES SLASHER
TURNS SELF IN, CONFESSES
Commish declines comment:
"Active investigation"

Vail looked up from the paper. "We discussed this years ago and decided not to do it."

"That was then," Slater said. "And we were nowhere, so we decided to stir the soup."

"We?" She looked at Russo.

"Me and Dyer," Slater said. "Chief signed off on it. We leaked to the press that the killer's come forward and confessed. Our hope was that he'd contact us."

"We didn't do it back then because of the risk. This risk," Vail said, gesturing at the body laid out before them. "It could incentivize him to kill again. And that's exactly what happened: he wanted to make a very bold statement. He's saying, It's not *him*, dumbshits, it's *me*. These are *my* kills."

"Interesting theory."

"It's not a theory. Those Xs he draws on their necks. He's marking his victims."

"What?"

"Chandler." Vail moved in closer and nodded at the woman's head. "Does she have that logo on her neck?"

Chandler got in behind the victim with tweezers and a flashlight. "She does. Capital E, I, D, and a lowercase i."

"An i," Vail said. "At least we know we haven't missed any."

"Makes me feel so much better," Russo said. "But what'd you mean about marking his victims?"

"When he draws that X, he's telling us, 'This is one of mine.' And that's why he got so pissed when someone supposedly came forward and took credit for his work. That X is like a signature. An artist signing his painting."

"This guy is seriously disturbed," Slater said.

"I think she's right," Finkelstein said, pushing up the glasses on his nose with the back of a gloved hand. "I remember when you were a pup your first day on the job." He shook his head and turned to Russo. "Time flies and the kids grow up so fast, eh?"

Russo could not stifle his chuckle.

"Anyway," Finkelstein said, "Your scenario looks right, *Agent* Vail."

"Do we have an ID?"

"I've taken a set of prints to confirm," Chandler said, "assuming she's in the system.

"I found a driver's license wedged under her left thigh." Slater held up a card in front of his face and squinted to read the text. "Teri Callas."

"Callas," Vail repeated. "Is that a Greek name?"

"Yeah." Russo wiped his brow. "Greek. And I'm really getting pissed off at this goddamn perp."

"Welcome to the club." She turned to Slater. "Let's get back to Danzig. I assume you've checked into him since the shootout."

"I know him as well as the inside of my underwear."

"That's not a good image," Vail said. "All I want to know is if he had any known contact with any of the vics."

Slater walked through the adjacent holding cell and emerged on Vail's side, then took a seat at the nearest desk. "Danzig's an alias, you knew that. The real Victor Danzig died in a car accident a year before our guy took the job with the department. But we found a link to the Castiglias. We think they're the ones who set him up with the alias and helped him get the job with the NYPD. Back then the family had people on the inside."

"What kind of connection?"

"He'd do things for them, get information, pull stuff from case files. He worked off the books with a law firm that's got known mob ties. Santangelo & Rici. He was feeding them info they'd need to get their clients off—or a leaner sentence."

Vail nodded. "That would make sense, how he got the DD-5 from the file. What *doesn't* make sense is killing Crinelli. Why would he kill his meal ticket? I'm sure they were compensating him well for the info. Not to mention that it's crazy to declare war on an enemy who could wipe you out with one phone call."

Russo looked over at Teri Callas. "If the family doesn't know he killed Crinelli, they wouldn't come after him. And the law firm would keep paying him for the info he got them."

Vail thought about that a moment. *This is not adding up.* "What about the other vics? Any connection to that law firm or the Castiglias?"

Slater began rocking in his chair. "Haven't been able to find anything. But that don't mean Danzig didn't pick them randomly, or meet them in a market or a bar."

"Yeah, but why only go after Greek women?" Vail asked. "Gotta be a reason. Any beefs with the Greek community?"

Russo scratched his forehead. "None we could find. But it doesn't need to be the community, just a single person who wronged him. Bottom line is, we're no further along with Danzig than we were before. And he's still at large. I was him, I'd be in Mexico or Canada."

"I don't know about that." Vail gestured toward Callas. "If he is our guy, he's obviously in New York. And he was standing right here in this very spot a few hours ago."

44

>ELLIS ISLAND
SUNDAY. MAY 17. 1981

Livana sat down on the edge of Niklaus's bed and fanned her neck with a piece of cardboard against the unusually warm weather and humidity.

"Niklaus, wake up."

Niklaus stirred, then fluttered his eyes open and gathered his pillow into a ball beneath his neck. "What time is it?"

"It's noon."

"So?"

"So it's time to get up. We've got a lot of things to do and you've slept long enough."

He groaned and pulled the covers over his head. "Where's Dmitri?"

"Out. Walking the island." She waited a moment, then said, "What would you like me to make you for breakfast? Tomorrow's your birthday."

Fedor knocked on the half open door and walked in. "Morning. Or should I say afternoon?"

Nick groaned. "It'd be 'good afternoon' if you didn't wake me up."

"Your father and I figured we'd celebrate your birthday today because tomorrow's a school day."

Niklaus peeled back the covers. "I'm a senior. I can take tomorrow off."

"I thought it'd be nice to spend it together. Maybe go fishing. And we have work tomorrow."

"Still skipping school tomorrow."

Fedor approached the bed. "Any particular reason?"

"Because I can."

"You have three weeks left before school ends. Then you'll have plenty of days off."

"I'm moving out when I graduate. Off this island. I'm gonna get a job and an apartment."

Livana and Fedor shared a look. "Since when?" she asked.

"I've had enough of living in a prison. How many times have I told you I was unhappy here?"

"We've done the best we could," Fedor said. "And this may not feel like a great place to live, but it's had a lot of advantages."

"Guess we'll have to disagree on that." He threw the covers back and got out of bed. "I'm not gonna live my life in fear. I'm going to go back home, to Astoria."

Fedor rubbed at his forehead. "Nik, we need to talk about this. It's dangerous."

"Yeah, I've heard the speech." He pulled out a shirt and slipped it over his head. "But when you don't stand up to bullies they push you around. You shoulda stood up to them when they kidnapped Dmitri. Soon as we got him back, you shoulda gone right back to the police."

Fedor stifled a chuckle laced with frustration. "Look, you're eighteen, so you think you know everything about life. But you don't. We did what we thought was best. And we still think it was the right thing to do."

"That turned out great, didn't it? Cassie's dead."

That comment silenced them all. Livana felt it internally, like an ice pick to the gut.

"And you two think you know stuff, but there's a lot you don't know."

Livana gathered her thoughts and looked up at Niklaus. "What are you talking about? Like what?"

Niklaus frowned at her. "Like it wasn't Basil who cut that guy's eyes in the bowling alley. It was Dmitri."

"What?" Fedor said.

Livana and Fedor looked at each other a long moment, trying to work it through, reason it out.

"He was just a kid," Fedor said. "Why would he do that?"

Niklaus turned away. "I shouldn't have said anything. Just forget it."

"Forget it?" Livana asked. "Niklaus, you can't make a statement like that and tell us to forget it like we never heard it."

"Basil hit the guy with the Coke bottle and it shattered. The guy fell and hit his head, didn't move. Guess he was out cold. Dmitri ran over, grabbed one of the pieces of glass and sliced it across the guy's eyes. Basil pulled the glass out of his hand and pushed him away. That's when you came in."

Livana remembered seeing Dmitri a few feet away when she walked in. "Why didn't you say anything?"

"You seriously asking that question?" He waited but neither his dad nor Livana had a response. "Same reason Basil didn't say anything. He woulda gotten in trouble. A lot of trouble. Look at what happened to Basil. Dmitri was only eight or nine, who knows what they woulda done to him."

Livana got up off the bed and began pacing. "I knew Basil was keeping something from me. I didn't know what it was. Did he say anything to you, Fedor?"

"No. He never told me this."

Livana shook her head. "Basil kept saying it wasn't his fault. I thought he was talking about that slut. Gregor's wife. And because he didn't start the fight. I didn't realize what he really meant—that it wasn't his fault because he didn't cut Gregor. I wish he'd just told me."

"*None* of it was his fault, Liv."

Niklaus gathered up a pair of jeans on the floor. "Can you guys get out so I can shower and get dressed?"

Livana pulled herself up from the bed then started toward the door.

But Fedor did not budge. "We still need to talk about your plans, Niklaus. You want to do that later, fine. But we need to make sure you've thought this through. Where you're going to work, how you're going to pay for an apartment—"

"Fine. Yeah, okay. Later."

FEDOR AND LIVANA stood in the kitchen. They were silent, each knowing what the other was thinking: How did our lives get so screwed up?

As they stood there, they heard the backdoor open and close. Dmitri walked in, head down, and opened the pantry.

"Where'd you go?"

"Out."

"Out where?" Livana asked.

"Immigration building. I wanted to see what they're doing."

The past several months they had done well avoiding the authorities and the construction workers, leaving before the men arrived each day and coming home after dark, when their shifts had ended. Others came to the island on the weekend, but Sundays were usually off days for everyone.

"No one saw you?"

"They were busy with their own shit."

"Watch your mouth, please."

"Dmitri," Fedor said. "We need to ask you about something, back when we lived in Astoria. At the bowling alley, when your dad got into that fight."

Dmitri glanced up at them. "What about it?"

"When your dad was trying to defend himself, he hit Gregor—Mr. Persephone—with the Coke bottle. He fell and lost consciousness. What happened after that?"

"Mom came in and she started screaming."

"I wasn't screaming," Livana said.

"Liv." Fedor shook his head. "Go on, Dmitri. Right before your mom came in."

"Don't know. I was hiding under the table."

"You didn't pick up a piece of broken glass?" Fedor asked.

"Why would I do that?"

"Do you know who cut Mr. Persephone's eyes?"

Dmitri looked down. "Why are you asking? Why are you asking?" He started tapping his foot on the floor.

"It's nothing to get upset about," Livana said. "We're just asking you a question."

"No." He started pacing the kitchen. "Not my fault. Not my fault, not my fault!"

Livana started toward Dmitri, to calm him. But there was a knock at the door. She stopped and turned. They all looked at one another, fear falling across Livana's face like a translucent mask.

"Dmitri," Fedor whispered. "You sure no one followed you here?"

Dmitri put his hands over his ears and started pacing again.

Livana walked to the door and pulled it open. There were two uniformed men standing there, large sidearms holstered on their belts.

"Ma'am, we're with the United States Park Police. May I ask what you—" he looked around her body—"and your family are doing here, on the island?"

Livana felt dizzy, as if the blood was rushing from her brain, draining toward her feet. She grabbed for the doorjamb but that was the last thing she remembered as everything faded from view.

WHEN SHE AWOKE Fedor was at her side, a bottle of bleach in his hand. The smell burned her nose and she shook her head, instinctively pushing it away from her face.

"You fainted," Fedor said. "I think you scared them off. They started talking real fast, told us we need to get off the island by tomorrow or face imprisonment for trespassing on federal land."

"Who were they?"

"Police. They must've seen Dmitri and followed him here."

"Where is he?"

"In his room. I heard his door slam."

Livana rolled onto her side and got to her feet. "I need to go check on him."

"While you're in there, tell him to start packing. I'm gonna head into the city before it gets too late, see if I can get us a motel room until we can find a place to live. And tell Niklaus to get his stuff together. He's getting his wish."

45

>DEAD EYES TASK FORCE
FAIRFAX, VIRGINIA
WEDNESDAY, FEBRUARY 2, 2011

K aren Vail sat at the rectangular utilitarian folding table across
from Spotsylvania County homicide detective Mandisa
Manette.

Vail tossed her pen down. "You're saying we're done here."

"Kari, I know you don't wanna hear this, but life can suck the big one.
And from your perspective, this is a mouthful."

Vail rolled her eyes. "This isn't about me, Mandisa. I'm telling you, Angelina Sarducci is a Dead Eyes vic. There are some discrepancies in the crime
scene between the first two vics and Ms. Sarducci, but this is the same guy."

"But we've got no way to support that claim," Manette said. "You know I
don't get your psychobabble bullshit, but even if I admitted that you made a
good case for it, it's subjective. It's just an opinion."

"I have to agree," said Fairfax City detective Bubba Sinclair. "If we take
away Sarducci, the Dead Eyes killer doesn't look so impressive with only
two vics under his belt. If the brass wants to disband us, what can we say?"

Vail spread her hands. "We can say that Angelina Sarducci is one of his
vics, so he's got three kills and that's enough to keep us working."

Vienna detective Roberto Enrique Umberto "Robby" Hernandez leaned forward in his seat. "I'm with Karen. What happens when we fold up the tent and a few months from now another woman ends up eviscerated?"

Paul Bledsoe, the detective in charge of the Dead Eyes task force, pushed his chair back from the table and unfolded his short, stocky body. "Look, I understand we've got a difference of opinion here. Karen's convinced that, behaviorally, this is the same guy. But it's tough to support based on the facts. And honestly, the brass makes the decision. We can sit here and debate—and I wanted to give you all the opportunity to discuss it. But fact is, the chief said we're done here. I'm sorry." He tossed a file onto the table. "And I hope to God, Hernandez, another mutilated woman doesn't turn up a few months from now."

Vail's BlackBerry buzzed.

"All right, let's take fifteen minutes to clear our heads."

Vail knew the number on her display: Carmine Russo. She hadn't heard from him in a few years. They had grown apart, not on purpose, but because of the business of life. Her career as a profiler had moved along at a breakneck pace. Although her marriage had not experienced the same good fortune, she had a sense that the case that had dogged her for sixteen years—unsolved—was about to get more interesting.

"Russo, you old dog."

"Karen, you've gotta stop calling me that."

Vail laughed. "Yeah, but as the years pass, it gets closer to the truth." She nodded at Robby, who was hanging around doing his best to look busy. "How've you been?"

"Took the captain's exam last month."

"No shit. Did you pass?"

"Woke up with a migraine, called in and asked if I could postpone it. Guess what the answer was."

"Tough shit?"

"Pretty much. I'll take it again, no biggie. Anyway, same old shit here. You know how it is. And you?"

"Doing the profiling thing. It's fascinating. I love it, best career move I ever made. Jonathan's a petulant teen, but I wouldn't trade him for anything."

"And how are things with Deacon? Or do I not want to ask?"

Vail glanced around. Robby was within earshot, as was Bledsoe—but no matter. "Slow downward spiral. Talk about same old shit. Every once in a while he decides to stop taking his meds and he falls apart, loses his job, and we start all over again. Hasn't been fun. Last month he punched me—"

"He what?"

"First time. And last time. After I gave him an iron skillet to the head, I hit him with divorce papers."

"Karen, I'm sorry."

"You know what, Russo? It's okay. In a way, I'm relieved. I gave it everything I had, tried to help him turn his life around. But the bipolar thing, if you don't take your meds, it's just bad all around. Forget about me, it's not healthy for Jonathan. So what can I say? I've got a colleague here who likes to say that sometimes life sucks the big one. I guess that's my life right now." She looked up and Manette had walked into the room. The detective threw her dreadlocks back over her shoulder and gave Vail a wink. "So is this just a social call?"

Russo gave her a tense laugh. "Wish I could lie and say yes. We've both been bad about staying in touch. But we got something here, and I thought you'd want to know."

"Don't tell me. Another Hades vic?"

"Yes and no. A vic who got away. Escaped."

"Holy shit." Vail's heart was racing. If she still smoked, she would have lit up. Instead, she headed out the backdoor into the yard of the soon-to-be former Dead Eyes task force command center to get some fresh air. "Is she Greek?"

"Yeah."

"Did she see the offender?"

"No, but she gave us some interesting info on him. I thought you might want to talk with her. Maybe—I don't know. Maybe you could get more than we did."

"Not sure there's anything I can do that you can't, but I'd sure love to talk with her." Vail took a deep breath of the moist, cold air. "Assuming my ASAC and unit chief will sign off, I'll come up."

"Don't worry about a hotel. You can stay with me and Sofia."

Uh, no thanks. Sofia the space cadet? I'd have to kill her.

"Thanks for the offer. We'll see. I may make it a longer trip and stop by Westbury, see my mom and aunt." She told him she would get right on it and text him the flight info.

"Everything okay?" Robby asked.

Vail slipped the phone back into its holder on her belt. "Old case. Very old, actually. Goes back to my first day on the job. We may finally have a break."

"Congrats." He stepped out and handed Vail her jacket. "Thought you might need this. It's a little chilly out here."

She watched the vapor trail away from her mouth. "A little?" She slipped it on and thanked him. "You always seem to know what I'm thinking."

"Yeah, well, in this case I didn't need any kind of ESP. It's winter, it's cold, and you didn't have your jacket."

She zipped it up and rubbed her arms to create some warmth. "You think I'm right about Dead Eyes? About Angelina Sarducci?"

Robby, at six foot seven, had a tendency to block the light when he stood with his back to the sun. There was no sun today, but his presence still dominated the space. "Look, I think you're right. Yeah. But I've got no way to back you up. It's more of a feeling."

"I know." She blew on her hands. "But there are gonna be other vics. Because I have a feeling too. And when it comes to stuff like this, my feelings tend to be right. Not always, but this is one of those cases where I'd like to be wrong. You know?"

"If there's anything good to come from this—and maybe this is a stretch—it's that we got a chance to meet. You've got some very special talents. Working with you has been eye-opening."

Vail was lost in thought, but she pulled herself back. "Dead Eyes is gonna kill again, Robby. This group'll be back together soon enough. Six months, maybe nine. You won't even have time to miss me."

46

›MANHATTAN SOUTH HOMICIDE SQUAD
THURSDAY, FEBRUARY 3, 2011

Karen Vail walked into the homicide squad at 9:56 PM, having endured two plane delays due to weather. She met Russo near his office. He was a little thicker around the waist—Sofia's pasta, no doubt—but otherwise looked good. He gave her a long embrace and then leaned her back to give her a once over.

"The FBI agrees with you."

"Yeah, not so much. We've had plenty of arguments, mostly over procedure."

Russo laughed heartily. "I see you haven't lost your sense of humor."

"Actually, I regained it when I lost my deadbeat husband. Funny how that works."

Russo lifted a case file off his desk and handed it to her. "When your flight was delayed I rescheduled our meeting with the vic for tomorrow. Have you eaten?"

"I was gonna grab something when I got off the plane, but then I thought, all the great restaurants in the city and I'm going for airport food?"

"Then let's go. I've got an open invite at a new favorite place of mine." As they walked to his car, he tapped out a text message. "I'm having Ben meet us there. Ben Dyer, you remember him, right? You met when we had that vic in the Fort Apache holding cell."

"How could I forget? Still blows my mind. No offense, but that fake news story that the killer confessed was a pretty reckless stunt."

"Offense taken. I was on board with that."

"Hopefully this vic will give us the break we need."

THEY PULLED INTO a parking spot on Third Avenue and headed toward the brick-faced corner bar and restaurant with its trademark scripted "P.J. Clarke's" sign lettered on the building's second story.

The eatery, in existence since 1884, was known for its award-winning burgers and the two human leg bones embedded in the ceiling above its entrance. Not to mention the beloved dog that was hit by a car fifty years ago, then stuffed and mounted over the bar. In short, P.J. Clarke's was a classic Manhattan institution.

Russo said his regards to a couple of staff members, then met Ben Dyer as they made their way to the table.

"Good to see you," Dyer told Vail. "Hey loo, wish I could stay, but I'm just gonna grab a beer and go. Got something goin' on tonight with Amy."

"I think I'm craving a burger," Vail said, sneaking a peek at the meal on a neighboring table. "Russo said I have to get the smothered onions and sautéed mushrooms."

"He should know, he comes here all the time. If you like smothered onions and mushrooms, it's good. I don't eat that shit."

Before they could take their seats, Russo's and Dyer's phones vibrated.

Russo read his display. "Shit on rye."

"Definitely not as appetizing as the mushroom burger," Vail said.

"You gotta be kidding." Dyer threw his head back. "Amy's gonna kill me."

Russo pushed his chair back under the table, then leaned in close to Vail's ear and said, "Another Hades vic."

THEY ARRIVED AT Bryant Park in a matter of minutes. The first on-scene patrol officer greeted them at the periphery, where he was starting to string out the crime scene tape.

The park, first designated a public space way back in 1686, was a ten acre square of greenery amid the skyscrapers and modest buildings of mid-town Manhattan. It sported a public game area—with the French bocce-relative Pétanque and Chinese chess—an open-air library for literary events, a carousel, food kiosks, and a Great Lawn for concert events. Movable metal tables and chairs enabled visitors to sit where, and with whom, they desired.

On a summer day, several thousand typically enjoyed the park's formal French garden design and its airy, tree-covered shade. But now, late night on a winter evening, there were only a scattered few walking along the field-stone paths.

It was dark, the park lit only by a number of dual-armed light posts. But as four police cruisers pulled up to help cordon off the crime scene, their red, white, and blue lights threw an eerie strobe of color across the dark green and brown landscape.

Russo handed out booties, and after they slipped them on Vail led the way up the steps near the corner of 42nd Street and Sixth Avenue. She hung a left, following the officer's directions to the body.

It was not difficult to find.

As they walked along the path, past the ivy-filled planters and umbrella-covered tables, they came to a bronze statue of a bearded man in a long coat, his right elbow resting on a Greek-style column, standing on a granite base.

Dyer turned on a flashlight and shone it across the gold letters engraved into the stone. "William Early Dodge."

"Dodge," Vail said. "Is that supposed to be significant to the vic? Or the offender? Or is it a taunt, that he's been able to dodge us for so many years?"

Dyer lowered his beam. Directly in front of the planter at the base of the monument, seated on one of the park's green metal chairs with her legs spread and fingers glued into the familiar curl, was a woman with her eyes gouged and a glass shard protruding from her neck.

"Where have I seen this before?" Russo said.

Vail took a step forward, carefully maintaining her distance so as not to compromise the crime scene. "Too many places."

"No arterial spray," Russo said. "Killed somewhere else."

"So," Dyer said, "is there significance to the fact that the asshole had a vic escape a couple days ago so he has to kill a new one?"

Vail nodded. "Actually, Ben, yeah. I think there is. He kills to satisfy a need, a hunger. It builds over time and when it hits that threshold, he strikes. If he doesn't make the kill—and complete his activity with the body, these behaviors we see here with the eyes, the broken glass—he hasn't satisfied that hunger."

"So Nyssa Bari's escape doomed this woman to death?" Russo asked.

"Strange way of looking at it," Vail said, "but yeah. What did Ms. Bari say? About the offender."

"A guy dressed like a patrol officer came to her door. She opened it but it was dark so she couldn't really see his face."

"Why was it so dark? Where was she?"

"She was in her apartment," Dyer said. "But Slater and I went over there, took a look around, and the bulbs had been unscrewed from the light fixtures in the hall."

"Interesting," Vail said. "Makes sense."

"Makes sense?" Russo asked. "We haven't seen that at any of the other crime scenes."

"That we know of," Vail said. "Who the hell would look for that kind of thing? I sure didn't."

"I'll give you that."

Vail curled a lock of hair behind her ear. "Even if he hadn't done it before, it doesn't mean anything. It's all about being successful. MO changes over time for a lot of reasons, but the main idea is that they adjust the MO to make their crimes less detectable and themselves more successful. If he'd never done that before with the lightbulbs, for some reason he figured it was necessary in this case.

"The fact that MO changes is the primary reason profilers put so much emphasis on differentiating between MO and need-driven behavior—what we call ritual. They're things the offender does to the victim, or at the crime scene, after he kills her. He's aware he's doing those things to the body—gouging the eyes, posing the hands—but he probably doesn't understand why he's doing them, or why he *needs* to do them.

"Point is, since they have nothing to do with his success in killing the victim or getting away with the crime, there's no need to change these ritual behaviors."

A couple of car doors slammed to their left, along 42nd Street. They looked over in unison and saw Ryan Chandler and Joe Slater walking toward them.

"I also called Finkelstein on the way over," Dyer said. "Figured it'd be good to have continuity. He's been with this case since the beginning. Felt bad, it was his day off."

"It's okay," Russo said. "Max doesn't have a life."

"And you do?" Vail asked.

"You got a point. But watch your mouth, young lady. I could be your father. Show some respect."

Vail subdued her grin.

"Hey Karen," Chandler said as he approached. "Long time no see." But then his gaze found the body and he slowed his pace. "Ah, shit."

"I'd give you a hug, Ryan, but doesn't seem like the time. Or the place."

"No kidding."

Vail blew on her hands as Slater came up behind Chandler. "Joe."

"Karen," Slater said with all the enthusiasm of a dead fish. "You're back."

"Good to see you too."

"Yeah. Whatever. Another fuckin' body."

"Another *victim*," Vail said. "She's a person."

"No, she's more goddamn work. And she ain't a person no more."

Vail gave him a cold stare.

"Yeah, awright, I know, it's a dead woman. Blah blah blah."

Russo and Vail exchanged a look.

"Wife left me this afternoon," Slater said. "Forgive me if I'm in a bad fuckin' mood."

She may be on to something.

Finkelstein trailed Slater, lugging his silver box and clipboard, dressed in a pair of Levis, bootie-covered workboots, and a pea coat. "Joy." He set down his kit and unlatched it. "Ryan, let's hang a few sheets to block the view and get some lights set up."

"Let us know when you're done processing the body," Vail said. "And we need an ID and time of death."

Finkelstein stopped what he was doing and gave her a "Really?" look. "Been doin' this job twenty-eight years, Karen. Good thing you told me what to look for, 'cause I wasn't quite sure."

"Guess I deserved that." She led Russo, Dyer, and Slater several feet away to give Finkelstein and Chandler room to work.

"So we're standing outside, in the middle of New York City," Vail said. "In a public park. And the UNSUB somehow gets the victim here, carries the dead body in, positions her on the chair, jabs the glass into her neck, and leaves."

"And no one sees nothin'," Slater said.

Vail tipped her chin back and found herself staring at a light post. "Maybe not 'no one,'" she said, gesturing toward a large NYPD surveillance array on the pole.

Slater turned and looked at the gray box with the blue and gold NYPD logo mounted above the words, "SECURITY CAMERA."

"Here we go again," Dyer said. "This guy's too good. Remember the Fort Apache holding cell? Asshole got into a police station, rode the elevator, and put the body inside the cell. And the whole time he wore a hat, loose-fitting black clothing, and he made sure to keep his back to the cameras. I don't think he's gonna make a mistake and get caught on film."

Slater pulled out his phone. "Let's be sure. Guessing's not gonna get us anywhere." As he started putting in his request, he turned and began walking out of the park, presumably toward the cameras to provide an identifying number.

"You started to tell me about the vic who got away," Vail said. "Nyssa Bari."

Russo blew on his hands. "Yeah, so Bari said the perp looked like a cop. He claimed he needed her to look at a piece of evidence they found in the hallway of her apartment. She didn't know what he was talking about, so she opened the door, and he stepped inside. As soon as he kicked the door closed behind him, she knew she was in trouble, so she grabbed a paper-weight she has on her shelf.

"You'll appreciate this—paperweight's actually a hunk of brass the FBI commissioned decades ago for the Hoover Building, some kind of fitting for their plumbing system. But the contractor screwed up and measured wrong, so they were useless. They stamped "FBI" on them and gave 'em out to friends and family to use as paperweights. Bari's grandfather was a Fibbie, so she got it when her father passed on."

"And it saved her life," Vail said. "I assume she hit him with it?"

"Hit him twice and ran. Got out, flew down the stairs, and kept running till she found a fire station. That's where she called it in. By the time a uni got to her apartment, bastard was gone. CSU combed the place, didn't find any blood. Or any other usable forensics. Story of our life on this case."

"So dressed as a cop," Vail said. "How good was the costume? Assuming it was a costume."

"Good enough. She thought it looked legit. Hat, badge, blue uniform."

"How tall?"

"'Taller.' She's 5 foot 2." He held up a hand. "I know, just about any guy's taller than she is. All she could tell us is he was 'probably a few to several inches taller' than she was. She was barefoot, so she couldn't judge. 'Taller.'"

"Taller. Great." Vail started flexing her calves, doing toe stands in place to get the blood circulating. "Distinguishing marks?"

"Glasses. Mustache and beard."

"Let's assume for a second he's a real cop. What's department policy on facial hair?"

"Mustache only with sideburns above the earlobe," Russo said. "No beards."

"Then it was a disguise."

"Not necessarily. There are some exceptions. Undercover assignments, medical issues that prevent you from shaving, religious requirements that don't allow you to shave."

"Transit police don't have any restrictions," Dyer said. "Beard, mustache are both fine."

"Rebels without a cause," Vail said. "So this doesn't help us a whole lot. Even if he really is a cop."

"Which would be pretty stupid if he is. Anyone sees him there around the time she's killed—"

"But we already know," Vail said, "that the offender's smart. How old was the guy? Wait, let me guess. It was too dark and it 'happened so fast.'"

Russo chuckled. "Pretty much. He wasn't as old as me, but older than Dyer."

"She wasn't a real helpful witness," Dyer said. "She did say he was white."

Already figured that. There aren't that many nonwhite serial killers.

"So a white middle-aged male, between thirty and sixty," Vail said. "I knew that from the profile I drew up. Oh, and taller than 5 foot 2."

Russo said, "Danzig would be in that age and height range. And he worked in a police station. We already knew he was a scumbag. Maybe he swiped a standard issue hat and a shirt before his ass got fired. And you can pick up metal knockoff cop badges made overseas for fifty bucks. Can't tell 'em from the real thing."

"All it means," Dyer said, "is that we still can't rule Danzig out. Can't find him, either."

Vail looked over her shoulder and peeked at Finkelstein, who had already moved the body. Chandler was helping him remove her clothing. "Did you show Bari an age-enhanced photo of Danzig?"

Dyer twisted his lips. "Oops. First thing in the morning."

"It's a long shot," Vail said. "Not only was it dark, but she was scared, and we all know that witnesses don't remember shit when they're freaked. Especially when they're fighting for their life."

"Have anything to add?" Russo asked, pulling up the collar of his jacket. "That behavior stuff you've been doing at the Bureau. You said you drew up a profile?"

Vail slapped her gloved hands together to get the circulation going. "It was more of an exercise after I was promoted to the BAU. I was playing around, seeing if I could come up with something cogent."

"And?"

"And to be honest, I haven't touched the thing in a few years. But we're looking at a male Caucasian who's between thirty-five and fifty, bright and well-educated, though not necessarily book smart. He's streetwise and knows his way around a police precinct. There's a chance he spent time in law enforcement, the security industry, or the military."

"The military?"

"Maybe. He's very organized in his methodology. I mean, look at the way he approaches the victim. Disabling the lightbulb in the hallway to increase the chances of success of gaining access to the vic's apartment indicates forethought, planning, and intelligence. One of the places where he could obtain strategic thinking is the military. But law enforcement is another. It's also possible he has an engineering background because of the structured nature in which he kills. I'm less certain about that, but it's possible. There've been virtually no forensics left at the scene. And he knows how to avoid security cameras, so he's thought it through, scoped it out, identified where the cameras are."

She stopped to blow on her hands, shuffled her feet.

"Keep going."

"He's a psychopath, which is a pretty safe bet. You didn't need me to tell you that."

"Actually," Dyer said, "*I* did."

"And there's likely an element of revenge to his murders. His victims are Greek women, so it's probable he holds a grudge against a Greek woman for something traumatic that happened to him. Maybe he was molested, but I don't think so. There's a sexual component to the way he poses the bodies, but he doesn't penetrate them, so it's not a sexually based action. It could be more subtle, like he blames them for something one of them did to make his life miserable. An overbearing mother, or—wait, I just remembered—"

"Got something," Chandler yelled to them.

Vail turned and started toward him, but Russo grabbed her arm.

"Hang on, what'd you remember?"

"Something a former profiler told me. He said that the way the UNSUB superglues the fingers into place—as if the woman's saying 'Come here'—and the way he spreads their legs, with the dress drawn up, might be his way of recreating something he saw a woman do when he was younger. Maybe his father had an affair with a Greek woman and the offender saw her as the instigator, the one who encouraged the flirting and then denied it. He's posing his vics in provocative positions to show everyone what kind of sluts they 're-ally' are."

"How can that help us?" asked Slater, who had rejoined them a moment ago.

"When we have a pool of suspects to choose from, or when you've got a guy in custody, we'll have an understanding of who we're dealing with and why he's doing it. That'll help direct the questioning toward a confession. Unless, of course, you've got him dead to rights."

"I'd rather just have him dead," Russo said. "For all the agita he's caused me in my career. Sixteen years I've been after this joker."

"Then there's Crinelli," Dyer said. "Which doesn't fit."

Vail glanced back at Chandler. "Be there in a minute." She turned back to Dyer. "Maybe it does. If these are revenge murders, and Crinelli is killed the same way the women are, maybe the offender's getting back at Crinelli for something he did to him. And he disposes of him the best way he knows how. The way that brings him comfort and enjoyment."

"So Crinelli may be of no help at all in solving this," Slater said.

"Not necessarily," Russo said. "There could be some commonality to whatever the Greek woman, or women, did to this perp and Dominic Crinelli. Find that connection—"

"And we may have our offender." Vail turned and trudged back to Chandler and Finkelstein.

They had the body laid out on a gurney, which stood on the flagstone path, about a dozen feet from where she had been found.

"Your victim is Monica Glavan."

Russo tilted his head. "Glavan."

"I did a quick search," Chandler said, adjusting the wide camera strap on his shoulder. "It's Greek. And—I know your next question will be about that thingy he draws on the vics' necks. Yes, Ms. Glavan has one. And the lowercase letter is the only variable here, right? This one's a j."

"That's . . ." Slater stuck out his gloved hand and began counting off fingers. "The tenth victim. Shit, this guy's prolific. And we're so incompetent that we've let him get this far."

"We're doing our best," Russo said. "Ain't nothin' any of us coulda done differently that woulda made a difference."

"But the more important point here is that we've got seven bodies and ten letters," Vail said. "Assuming this numbering scheme is right. Even if we accept that there's a first victim that's unaccounted for, we're still coming up short. If we can find that first victim, she may hold clues to who this guy is. Not just what type of person he is, but it could lead us to *who* he is. His name."

"How do you figure?"

"First vics are more spontaneous. The killer's raw, untested—well, maybe he's experimented on animals, but in terms of planning his kill in a way that he can get in and get out successfully, without getting caught, he's never done it. He's a rookie, and rookies make mistakes—in business, in sports, in murder. Just like all of us during our first days on the job, right? If we find that vic, we may see something he left behind that gives us what we need. Or maybe she holds a key piece of evidence that links Crinelli with this Greek woman he seems to be killing over and over again."

"And how do you suggest we find this first vic?" Slater asked.

Vail had no answer—but neither did anyone else.

Vail snapped her fingers. "Remember I said they looked like revenge murders, because of the way they're posed? The r on Crinelli's X. Maybe it stands for 'revenge.'"

"A mobster killed by someone who wants revenge." Russo laughed. "Back in '96, when I asked Lou Castiglia for a list of people who'd want to kill Dominic Crinelli, he cracked up. Once he picked himself up off the floor, he said there were too many to count. We got nowhere."

"While you ponder that," Chandler said, "Ms. Glavan is a fashion designer at J.D. Furriers on Seventh Avenue. Twenty-nine years old. Lives in Chelsea."

"Killed elsewhere?" Vail asked.

"Yes," Finkelstein said, turning away from the body to face them. "And I did a liver stick. I'd place time of death at between 9:30 and 10:00 PM tonight. She was dead when he pierced the orbits and stabbed the carotid with the hunk of glass. Also—I found two marks that are consistent with Taser probes."

"Because Nyssa Bari was able to get the drop on him," Vail said. "The offender adapted. I hate to compare him to us, but if we do something that doesn't have a good outcome, we're gonna try something different. Same thing with offenders. Bari clobbered him and got away, so he found a way to make sure that wasn't gonna happen again. He Tasered her, incapacitated her. Then he choked her before he did his thing with the eyes and carotid."

"We've also got smudges on the glass," Chandler said. "Looks like he was gloved, like before. No useful latents."

"Okay," Russo said. He gestured at Slater. "Anything off that camera?"

"We got him all right. We can kind of see him in the park, over by the Dodge statue, at 10:21. He was blocking our view, and it was dark and a bit grainy, but it looks like he was doing his thing with the eyes and neck, then he stepped back to admire his work. And—just like at Fort Apache, he took a photo and then left."

"He took a photo?" Vail asked. "You didn't tell me that."

"I thought I did, when I reviewed the tape—"

"Okay, okay," Russo said. "Anyway, he took a picture of the vic. He's a sick motherfucker, so what?"

"It fits," Vail said. "His way of reliving the kill. He's probably got photos of all, or most of, his vics. A trophy. And I'll tell you something else. He's not killing as often, but when he does, it's in our face. Outdoors, letting us know that he's still here. He's probably 'embarrassed' by letting Bari escape." She turned to Russo. "Let's check the cameras of the immediate area in case he's somewhere nearby, watching."

Russo pulled out his BlackBerry to make the call.

"And see if they can extrapolate his height and weight from the footage. There's gotta be a way because he's standing near the statue."

"I'll have them get on it." He hit send and walked away as he talked.

"Not exactly what I had planned for tonight," Dyer mumbled.

"Oh yeah?" Vail said. "Sorry to keep you up past your bedtime."

Dyer laughed. "I was going to propose tonight. Had reservations for a midnight cruise on the Hudson. You spend a couple hours cruising around Manhattan while you dance the night away. Thought it'd be romantic, with the city all lit up and shit. I figured I'd ask Amy if she'd marry me as we were passing the Statue of Liberty."

"Ben, it's in the thirties. Didn't you think you two would be cold?"

"It's mostly indoors. My buddy said they got big windows. Amy woulda loved it. Instead, I got a DOA in Bryant Park, a reminder that this asshole's still thumbing his nose at us. And there ain't shit we can do."

"There's always tomorrow."

"Which means I gotta get my nerve up again. It was enough pressure just waiting to do it tonight."

Vail winked at him. "Patience is a virtue."

"Guess I'm not very virtuous."

VAIL MET UP with Russo at the edge of the park, near the steps that spilled onto 42nd Street. "I think we should get the BAU involved in this case. Officially, so I can devote real time to it, and so we'd have complete access and don't have to do things behind people's backs. My ASAC doesn't like it when I do stuff like that."

Russo chirped his car remote and pulled open the door. "I'm never gonna convince Kearney to make the request. But he's talking about retiring and I've heard rumors of who's gonna get the nod. That happens, I think you'll get what you need. So you gotta be patient."

"Tell that to the next victim."

47

›MARINE TWO CRASH SITE
VIRGINIA COUNTRYSIDE
NOVEMBER 7, 2012 12:03AM

Vail left FBI Supervisory Special Agent Aaron "Uzi" Uziel and Department of Defense operative Hector DeSantos at the site of Marine Two's helicopter crash. She walked among the wreckage, surveying the carnage, all the while starting to formulate a profile of the bomber. The Behavioral Analysis Unit had amassed as much information as there was available on these types of offenders, but the sample size was smaller than they would like.

Small sample sizes invited error. If you drew erroneous conclusions because the data was flawed—or inaccurate—it could send law enforcement investigators off in the wrong direction.

That someone would target the president-elect—and nearly pull off the mission—said a lot about the perpetrators. It spoke to an offender who was intelligent and had access to key actors, places, materials, and secure facilities.

Vail made a mental note of all of this. She would regurgitate all of it back to Uzi when they sat down to review her findings.

Her phone buzzed. She stepped over a smoldering hunk of metal, which was covered in A Triple F, a chemical designed to smother fire, and checked the display: Robby, her boyfriend, had just gotten home and wanted to know where she was. She texted back:

> wont be home for a few hours. del monaco stuck
> in traffic on way back from new york so gifford
> sent me. marine two case. cia nsa marines fbi virg
> state police ntsb all here. lucky me

She was reholstering her BlackBerry when it rang. The number surprised her.

"Russo. Long time no speak."

"My interrupting?"

"Not at all. I'm standing in a field of helicopter ruins with fire and smoke and lots of brass from every intelligence agency we've got."

"You're working the assassination attempt?"

"I thought that's what I just said. Can it wait?"

"Yeah, no problem. I just wanted to let you know we found Victor Danzig."

A man bumped her as he passed by in a rush. The phone flew from her hands, but she scrambled and pulled it from the loose dirt.

"Hang on," she said as she blew the stuff off her handset. "Sorry, I dropped you. Is Danzig talking?"

"Not to us. Found him upstate, near the Canadian border. Looks like he was living outside Toronto. May've been coming back to the US for another kill. But the troopers screwed up big-time and he got away. In the wind again. We've got resources deployed—air units, ground units, thermal equipment—the works. But . . ."

"But it's upstate and there's a lot of land to cover."

"I just about hit the roof when they told me. We had him. We *had* the bastard. We had Hades."

"You're assuming he's Hades."

"Who the hell knows."

"Hopefully *we* will in a few hours. You going over his place, looking for trophies, anything connecting him to the vics?"

"Haven't found his residence yet. We're looking, but he's a careful SOB. I'm on my way to the airport right now. This is gonna be a long night."

Vail sighed. "Me too. Look, you find out anything worthwhile, let me know. Either way."

"You got it."

"Hey," Uzi said, coming up behind her.

She turned as she was slipping the phone into its case on her belt. "Anything?"

"Unofficial opinion. This isn't looking like an accident. Looks deliberate."

Already figured that.

"Thanks for the heads-up."

"You get anything useful?"

"Yeah. Looks deliberate."

Uzi looked at her. "I said useful."

"Confirmation of an opinion is useful."

"Don't disappoint me, Karen. I need you to get inside the mind of the killer."

"As soon as I feel some psychic energy, you'll be the first to know."

Uzi winked. "Knew I could count on you."

As he moved off into the darkness, Vail knelt in front of a foam-covered mound of pulverized helicopter skin. *Danzig's still at large. Is he Hades? If they catch him, is it case closed?*

She stood up and looked out over the crash site. It was coordinated, organized bedlam. Emergency responders were still combing the ruins, investigators were taking measurements, making notes.

The United States was attacked tonight. I can't have my mind stuck on a seventeen-year-old case.

Vail took a deep breath and turned her body—and her attention—back to the crime scene.

Hades will have to wait.

48

>ALCATRAZ
SAN FRANCISCO BAY
ALCATRAZ, CALIFORNIA
AUGUST 3, 2013

V ail was standing with her friend and colleague, Napa County sheriff's detective Roxxann Dixon. They were in the middle of San Francisco Bay on a fog-socked Alcatraz near midnight, having just concluded a manhunt on the island for a missing person.

The whipping wind blew Dixon's blonde hair across her face. "Oh my god, it's freezing."

"You have too much lean muscle mass, Roxx. You need some body fat to keep you warm."

"No thanks."

"Just sayin'."

Another gust tossed her hair into her eyes. As she sorted it out, Vail started dialing her BlackBerry.

"Who are you calling now?" Dixon asked.

"I forgot something."

"Karen, trust me. You turned the toaster off at home."

"That's not funny."

"We've gotta get that CSI over here to document—"

"Burden's on his way, I'm sure he's bringing Price with him. Just give me a minute." Vail hit send and the call connected. Three rings later, a groggy Carmine Russo answered.

"Russo, it's Karen."

"Karen?"

He sounded distant, like he was trying to place the voice.

"What time—are you crazy? It's the middle of the night."

"I know. I wouldn't have called if it wasn't real important."

A fog horn blasted in the background.

"Where the hell are you?"

"Near Broadway and Times Square."

Dixon gave Vail a look of confusion—but Vail's comment seemed to have the desired effect, because it woke Russo up.

"You're in town?" he asked. "Why? What's going down?"

"Actually, I'm in San Francisco, on Alcatraz, just outside the cell house, and the blocks are named Broadway, Times Square—anyway, I need your help on a case."

"Karen, you there? Hello?"

"I'm here, I'm here." Vail walked a few feet toward the water, which was crashing against the rocks below. "Listen, the reception on the island is spotty. I've got a serial killer case out here and I need your help. Remember I told you about that informant I had, Eugenia Zachary?"

"The one you paid for information even though you shouldn't have?"

That's not exactly how things went down, but close enough.

"Did you tell anyone about how I paid her, about what happened?"

"Who the hell would I tell?"

"C'mon, Russo. It's a good way to poke fun at the Feds. A good story to tell over a few beers at Walkers or Tribeca Tavern. Especially to guys who didn't like me."

"First of all, I'd never do that to you, you know that."

"Anyone? I know it was a long time ago, but think about it for a minute. Is it possible you mentioned it to someone? Even a close friend. Protch, maybe? Sofia? This is really important."

"I'm telling you, Karen. I didn't tell anyone. Why? What's so important about the way you paid your CI?"

"Nothing I want to go into right now. But trust me, it's critical. If I can cross this off my list, it'll help a lot."

"Cross it off. I didn't say nothing about it to no one."

That'd be a double negative, meaning you did actually tell someone. Stop obsessing, Karen. How many times does he have to say the same thing?

"She's dead, by the way. Eugenia. Just found out."

"Sorry to hear that," Russo said. "I know she meant something to you."

"Yeah, it wasn't the typical confidential informant–cop relationship. Guess I got too close." *A bit of an understatement.* "Anything new on Hades?"

"Everything's been quiet. I know that doesn't help. We still don't know about Danzig. Haven't found him."

"His place?"

"Haven't found that, either. We're working with the Canadian authorities. And trying to keep the media away. Not an easy task."

"So either way, the offender's still at large. And until we know otherwise, Hades is still an unknown subject."

"For now, yeah. Look, I'm goin' back to sleep, you mind?"

"Hey. Thanks, Russo. Sorry for waking you up. Call you soon."

"During the day."

Vail grinned. "Right." She shoved her phone into its holster and stood there looking at the dead body in front of her.

"Who was that?" Dixon asked.

Vail saw Inspector Lance Burden approaching in the near darkness as she considered Dixon's question. *How do I describe Russo?* "My rabbi."

Dixon warded off a chill. "Say what?"

Despite the revolting appearance of the body in front of her, she chuckled. "My mentor in New York. A father figure. The cop who broke me in my first day on the job. The guy who pushed the brass to get me my detective's shield, the guy who's always had my back."

"And you repaid him for all that good stuff by waking him in the middle of the night?"

"Just wait, someday I'll do the same to you."

"Don't try to be funny. I'm still mad at you."

Vail rolled up her jacket collar. "I'll add your name to the list."

49

>DULLES INTERNATIONAL AIRPORT
1 SAARINEN CIRCLE
DULLES, VIRGINIA
PRESENT DAY: WEDNESDAY, JULY 16

Robby Hernandez plugged his iPad into the charging port and sat back in his seat at the gate of the American Airlines terminal.

"You need to charge anything?"

Vail checked her watch, took a deep breath, and pulled out her Surface tablet. "Did it last night." She rested her head against Robby's shoulder and fell silent for a minute. "Must be me."

"Huh?"

"I was just thinking about when we met, the Dead Eyes case. The eyes were important. And in this Hades case, the eyes seem to be a focal point."

"Think there's something to it?"

"Absolutely nothing. It's kind of like me and banks. Haven't you ever wondered why I avoid them?"

"I guess I figured you don't like banks. You probably blame them for the woes of the working man, like everyone else in this country. They've been demonized. 'Bank' is just another four-letter word."

"Very funny. No, I don't like banks because for a while there, every time I walked into one it seemed like it was being robbed. One of the last times I went into a bank to actually do something is when the perp took a hostage. After I shot him, I got a text from Bledsoe. Dead Eyes was back in business, and so was the task force." She fell silent again, rechecked her watch, and then said, "That case changed my life, you know?"

"You mean because of who the killer was?"

"You're being diplomatic. I appreciate that. No, I mean because that's where we met. This is kind of a sick way of looking at it, but without that *killer*, without that case, we probably would never have met."

"Hey, I almost didn't catch that case. Another detective was supposed to get the call, but he—well, he couldn't go."

Vail leaned back and looked at him. "What does that mean?"

"Nothing."

"Tell me."

"He had diarrhea."

Vail play-slapped him. "Are you saying we met because your partner had the shits?"

"I did *not* say that. But . . . it does happen to be true."

Vail sat up straight and faced him, crossed her legs and set the Surface in her lap. She looked at him a long moment, trying to formulate her thoughts. "I'm not sure who's benefited most—me or Jonathan. You've meant so much to him. Deacon, he was a total train wreck, I don't have to tell you that. You, though, you've been that positive father figure Jonathan never really had."

"Despite what he went through with Deacon, he came out okay. He's a great kid. We have good times together."

Vail sat there another few moments, then checked her watch.

"You okay? You look tense. Not 'serial killer tense.' Something else."

"I didn't realize I had a 'serial killer look.'"

"You do. This is different." He leaned back and looked her over. "You're nervous."

"No, I'm not."

He squinted at her. "Yes, you are. What's wrong?"

"It's—I'm not sure—" She stopped, thought a second, then said, "Are you sure that black dress looked good?"

Robby grinned. "I told you at home. You looked stunning. Alluring."

"But not too alluring, right?"

"You're asking your significant other if the dress you brought to a formal party makes you look too sexy? I'm not sure I can be objective."

"The heels weren't too high?"

"They're pumps."

"I don't usually wear heels, so they seem high."

"Okay," Robby said. "I give up. What's really going on?"

Vail turned on her Surface and swiped up, then entered her password. "I just want to make a good impression. These people have never seen me in a dress, let alone heels and jewelry."

"I've hardly seen you in a dress, heels, and jewelry."

"Maybe I should've worn the blue one. Or the white top."

"You made the right choice. You're stressing over nothing."

"I'm telling you how I feel."

"Right. And I'm telling you they may die of a heart attack because they've got some serious eye candy coming their way."

Vail looked up from the tablet. "Is that what I am to you? A shapely lollipop?"

Robby laughed. "You know what my mind can do with that image?"

Vail glanced around at the people behind and beside them, then leaned closer to Robby. "I'm more interested in what you can do with something *else* of yours, involving a certain something *else* of mine."

Robby held up his right arm, which bore a cast down to his hand. "Good thing it wasn't a broken leg. That wouldn't have been so good."

"You think that would've stopped me?"

THEY ARRIVED AT the Waldorf Astoria Hotel and walked into the spacious, richly appointed lobby. Enormous square marbled columns stretched from the hand-woven wall-to-wall rug to the elaborately patterned twenty-foot ceiling.

"Stunning," Vail said. "I'm glad you talked me into this over the Motel 6."

"There aren't any Motel 6s in Manhattan, Karen."

"Well, if there were, this would definitely be better." She got in line at the registration desk. "You know, as architecturally striking as the Hyatt was in San Francisco, this is, well, more grand. Elegant."

"Didn't see the Hyatt in San Francisco."

"That's right. I shared the room—and the bed—with Roxxann."

Robby held up a hand. "I don't think I want to know." He thought a moment. "Then again, maybe I do."

"I'll ignore that." She gave another sweeping look at the lobby, the wood paneling on the walls, the ornate clock in the center, which reminded her of the one in Grand Central Station. "I'm glad you're going to get a chance to meet Russo and Protch. They're so much a part of who I am as a cop, Russo especially. Just—if they start telling stories about me, don't believe them. Unless they're flattering. Then believe them."

"You're making more of this than it needs to be. It's a retirement party and a promotion party, rolled into one. Why are you so nervous about it?"

"I told you. They've never seen me like this. And, well, I'm bringing home the boyfriend. You know?"

Robby tilted his head. "You afraid they won't approve?"

"You know family. Sometimes you never know how they're going to react."

"I'm a good catch, Karen. They're going to love me."

While Robby checked in, Vail pulled out her phone to call Russo to confirm their meeting for the next morning. She saw her visit to New York as the perfect opportunity to get the brain trust together for a comprehensive review of the Hades case file, to see if there was something they had been missing. They had gathered in recent years at crime scenes, when they were in crisis mode trying to process a new victim. It prevented them from stepping back and looking at things anew.

In the intervening time, Vail had also gained some distance from the specifics of the case, something a detective rarely has the luxury of doing. She had learned that sometimes things poked up out of nowhere, things that were right in front of you but you did not have the perspective to see.

"We're all set," Russo said. "It'll be me, you, and Protch to start, then Slater will join us around nine, nine-thirty. Joe's gotta go before a judge first thing in the morning."

"And Dyer?"

Russo cleared his throat. "Yeah, that. He's not coming. He's . . . out of commission."

"What, did he hurt his back or something?"

Russo hesitated. "He's having medical issues, needed time off. Nothing I want to get into right now."

Sounds fishy. Did he have a breakdown? "Next time you talk to him, tell him I missed him."

"I'll do that."

She hung up and joined Robby at the elevators. Since they had only two rolling suitcases, he had declined the concierge. Vail did not care. She was still soaking in the opulence. *Decadence?*

Once inside, Robby reached over, swiped his card, and pressed the floor button. "You okay in here?"

Vail took a deep breath. "You mean am I going to have a claustrophobic anxiety attack?"

"I wasn't going to phrase it that way, but . . . yeah."

"Just keep talking to me."

Robby rocked back on his heels. "I got us a room upgrade."

"Cool. Any particular reason?"

"The woman behind the desk found me irresistibly sexy."

Vail looked at him. "Are you serious?"

"About the upgrade or finding me irresistibly sexy?"

"Both."

The elevator chimed and the doors slid open.

"Whoa, this is really quite nice," Vail said, rolling her suitcase out. "I guess you were serious."

"Thought you'd like it. They walked up to the room, which had a sign that read, "The Cole Porter Suite."

"Suite?" Vail asked.

Robby was already sliding his card through the lock. He pushed open the door and Vail's jaw dropped. "Are you shitting me? This is 'a room upgrade'?"

"I told you," he said. "She thought I was irresistibly sexy. Why do you find that so hard to believe?"

She stepped in and turned slowly, doing a three-sixty. The walls were ba-by blue with gold leaf surrounding inlaid frames on the walls. Thick floor-to-ceiling drapes hung across the large windows. And a baby grand piano sat in the corner. "I'm speechless."

"For you, that's impressive."

"This room is impressive. It's not a room, it's . . . like a lavishly decorated apartment. Like, I don't know . . . what Frank Sinatra's apartment would be like."

"He stayed here once."

Vail turned to face him. "You're kidding, right?"

"Nope." He gestured behind her. "Look, there's even a bottle of champagne."

He walked over and handed her the sealed envelope. She turned toward the light and tore it open, then pulled out the card. It read:

Karen Vail, will you marry me?

This is a joke. It's a joke. So why aren't I laughing?

She turned around, and Robby was on a knee, a small black velvet box in his hand. "I want you to spend the rest of your life with me. That's assuming, of course, you don't get eaten alive by a serial killer who's—"

He did not finish his sentence, as Vail planted a kiss on his lips, and did not let go.

50

>JUNIOR'S RESTAURANT
1102 8TH AVENUE
BROOKLYN, NEW YORK
PRESENT DAY: WEDNESDAY, JULY 16

Junior's was founded in 1950 and claimed to serve New York's best cheesecake, the choice of actors, singers, prominent politicians, professional athletes, and authors. It also served a pretty good breakfast, and Russo had suggested it as a meeting place where he, Protch, and Vail could spread out in the back and grind through the details of the Hades case, point by point.

Junior's served lunch too—a good thing, because not only did Russo think they'd be there all day, but because he couldn't order a piece of cheesecake for breakfast without getting an argument from Vail . . . though she claimed she might "allow" him to have some later in the day.

The waiter sat them down and handed out menus. Vail dumped their cardboard filing box on the chair to her left and then leaned back to study the framed photos on the wall, most with a Brooklyn Bridge theme: black-and-white photos, art deco drawings, and pen-and-ink architectural sketches of the structure, along with an authentic yellow reflectorized street sign commemorating its centennial:

BROOKLYN BR
CLOSED
ALL DAY
MAY 24 1983

"Always good to get together with you two," Proschetta said, "but other than having a whole lot of free time now, I'm not sure what I can do to help you out."

Vail wanted to tell them about her engagement, but they had a job to do and she did not want to take time out of their important session, and divert their energies, from the task at hand. If they had time later, or if they took a break, she would pass on the news.

"You're not sure what you can do to help?" She pushed aside the breakfast menu. "You had forty-three years on the job. That experience counts for something."

Russo looked at Vail over the top of his menu. "I think it counts for a lot."

"I was kidding." Vail turned to Proschetta. "First off, our case involves an obsession with Greek women. And you know the Greek community. You spent time in Astoria, right?"

"About fifteen years, yeah. At the 114th. I told you about that case I had with Dominic Crinelli and that family back in 1973—"

"Wait a minute." She looked at Russo and her mind flooded with such a rush of excitement she could not form the thoughts, or the words, fast enough. "Crinelli. The Greeks. The women— Your case with Crinelli, the kid."

Proschetta chuckled. "Karen, you're not making much sense. But yeah, like I was saying, I told you about that case twenty years ago. At Yonah Shimmels."

"Yeah, yeah. When Crinelli beat the rap. And the kid they kidnapped, chained to the railroad tracks—"

"Hang on a second," Russo said, setting his menu down and turning to Proschetta. "I remember that, when you broke your knuckles with the rock trying to bust the chain."

"Right. This Greek family had all sorts of trouble, then the kid was taken—"

"They were Greek?" Vail asked. "The family, that kid?"

"Yeah, Astoria had—has—a strong Greek population."

Vail reached across the table and grabbed Russo's forearm. "This is the connection. This is it, I know it."

"Well, *I* don't know it," Proschetta said. "I don't know what the hell you're talking about. Talk in complete sentences, okay?"

"Okay, fine," Vail said. "Let's back up." She recapped the time line of the Hades case for Proschetta. When they finished, Vail sat back. "We're definitely onto something here."

"Go on," Russo said.

Proschetta inched forward in his chair. "Yeah, so this guy had a fight in a bowling alley. The one who started it—something with a G. George or Greg. Gregory. No, Gregor. He got injured pretty bad, ended up blind and disabled. The community ostracized the other guy—pretty sure his name was spelled like a spice."

"Herb?" Russo asked.

Proschetta frowned.

"What? That was a good guess. I was gonna say rosemary, but—"

Proschetta snapped his fingers. "Basil. Basil worked as a furrier in a factory owned by Gregor's dad. After the fight, his father fired Basil and no one in the area would hire him. Can't remember exactly what happened, but Basil tried to patch things up with Gregor. That didn't go too good, so Basil got desperate and told Gregor to tell his father that he wanted his job back or he'd tell the police his dad was importing illegal furs from Greece. Next thing, Basil's beaten to death by four thugs. Dominic Crinelli's the one who got fingered."

Vail stood up and began pacing. "So we've got a Greek family whose lives are destroyed by a fight this guy Basil had with this other guy Gregor—who I'm guessing was mobbed up?"

"Right again," Proschetta said. "The family Crinelli worked for, the Castiglias, had their hands in that fur business. They were skimming the profits. When Basil threatened to rat out the furrier, the Castiglias protected their investment."

Vail spun around and faced Russo. "Hang on a minute. You said this Gregor was blinded in the fight, right? Our UNSUB slashes, *destroys* the eyes." Vail sat back down. "Protch, tell me about the fight."

Proschetta laughed. "You're kidding, right? That was forty years ago. I've done pretty damn good remembering this much."

"We need that info. This is the Hades case, right here."

Proschetta pulled out his phone. "Let me make a call, see if they can pull the sixty-one from the file." He dialed and wandered off.

Russo and Vail sat and stared at each other. "We got everything but the link to the women." She looked up to find Proschetta standing next to her.

"Just remembered something. After that episode when the kid was kidnapped, the family moved." Proschetta stopped, twisted the phone handset back in front of his lips. "Yeah, pull the file. I'll be right over."

He ended the call and continued: "They moved to Ellis Island. They felt threatened—or they were threatened, I can't remember—by the Castiglias. Yeah, they told them to get out of town and not come back. But one of 'em had elderly grandparents in a home or something, so they moved, but not so far that they couldn't visit them."

"Ellis Island?" Vail asked. "Wasn't it abandoned?"

"Yeah," Russo said. "Park service turned the main immigration building on Island 1 into a museum in the late '70s, I think, then did a major renovation in the 80s. But the hospital complex, Island 3, they've never done anything with those buildings. Too expensive."

"They lived there for several years," Proschetta said. "Like maybe '73 to '80 or '81. Until their daughter was murdered."

"Wait, what?" Vail stood up from her chair. "Their daughter was murdered?" *The first vic?*

"Probably '80 or '81. The mother—Laura, or something like that—she had me called out to the crime scene, a high school in the city, near Battery Park. She refused to talk to the detectives. Would only talk to me. She was worried the Castiglias were involved, and back then, in the '70s, the Castiglias had people in the department on their payroll. She didn't trust anyone but me."

Vail's mind was awash with questions. "We need the autopsy photos from that case. We need the whole case file." She pointed at Russo. "Can you call? Get it?"

Russo started dialing.

"Did the vic have a design on the back of her neck? The daughter?"

Proschetta canted his eyes up toward the ceiling as he thought. "Not that I can remember."

"An X," Vail said. "With letters in the quadrants formed by the X?"

"Wait, an X. Yeah, there was an X drawn on the base of the skull."

Russo raised a hand and wiggled his fingers in front of Proschetta. "Deputy Inspector Proschetta will tell you exactly what we need." Russo handed him the phone and rose from his chair. "I can't fuckin' believe this,

Karen. The answers to this case have been in front of our noses the entire time. I feel so stupid. And incredibly happy."

"We need to go to Ellis Island."

"Ellis Island? You heard Protch. They left there thirty-some odd years ago."

"Some serials have a place, a sanctuary, where they either do their killing or bring their trophies. They store the trophies there to relive the kills. We have to search the hospital buildings. The whole island."

"We'd need an army of officers."

Proschetta hung up. "An army? For what?"

"Do you know where they lived on the island?"

"The old hospital buildings on Island 3, that's all I know. A few days into the investigation, I was taken off the case. Not surprisingly, because it wasn't my case to begin with."

Vail pushed her chair in. "Let's go. Harbor can take us over. I'll call them on the way. We'll start looking until you can get us a more specific location."

"*If* I can get you a more specific location," Proschetta said. "I'll see if I can locate the mother. Laura. Or Lana. Or—"

"We're taking the car," Russo said. "I'll have a uni pick you up."

"Oh," Vail said. "Whatever happened with the daughter's case?"

"I called for an update at some point. It was—" He looked down at the table. "Oh, come on . . ." His head snapped up. "Jenkins. Horace Jenkins had the case. He said it went cold. They were looking at the girl's brother, but they couldn't make a case and, well, the kid had been through enough. He's the one who was kidnapped by the Castiglias."

"Oh, shit. Okay, I see where this is going."

"I'm sure Jenkins worked the case up. The kid was a little strange. There was something off about him after the kidnapping. 'Course, back then, no one knew about post-traumatic stress disorder."

"How was she killed?"

"Uh, suffocated. And they found a sponge soaked with chloroform at the scene."

"Chloroform. To incapacitate her, quietly. Probably from behind. Cuts to the eyes?"

Proschetta shook his head. "Not that I remember."

"Get in touch with Jenkins," Vail said. "And try to locate the kid. Call us with anything. I have a feeling we're gonna be there awhile." She gave Proschetta a pat on the shoulder. "And you thought retirement was going to be boring?"

51

>BATTERY PARK
LOWER MANHATTAN
PRESENT DAY: WEDNESDAY, JULY 16

They arrived at Harbor Patrol and found their ride waiting. The SAFE rigid inflatable boat had a rim of NYPD blue and a small light gray cabin, and was large enough to carry a handful of passengers.

Vail and Russo boarded and were greeted by the officer, who was decked out in cargo pants and a fleece jacket.

Vail followed him into the cabin and stood to the man's right, at the control panel. After his radio chirped the all clear by the dock worker, he gunned the dual Yamaha outboard engines and they set off for Ellis Island.

He glanced over at Vail a couple of times, then asked, "Have we met before?" He apparently found his own comment humorous, because he laughed and quickly added, "No, that's not a pickup line. I mean it. You look familiar."

She quickly scanned his face. "You too. I was with the department back in the '90s."

"I've been at Harbor most of my career."

She noticed his name badge—Prisco—and immediately placed it. "Nine-eleven," Vail said. "You pulled me into that Burger King when the first tower fell."

"That's right."

"If you don't mind," Russo said, "I'd rather change the subject."

That makes two of us. Probably three.

Russo grabbed the knob of the rear cabin door and swung it open. "Gonna grab some air."

"Hang on out there, loo. Don't want to have to fish you outta the drink."

"That would really screw up our day," Vail said.

"You're not kidding," Prisco said with a chuckle. "Trust me, it's happened. Not fun for the guy who takes the plunge." He twisted around and checked on Russo, then said, "So, you left the department and went over to the dark side. The FBI."

"Yeah, it seemed like a good idea at the time." She laughed, then steadied herself against the rock of a wave.

"Going over to the island on a case?"

The boat lurched a bit more violently on a larger wave. "Sorry about that. Water's a little choppy today." He turned around and yelled, over the engine noise, "Lieutenant, hang on, please!" He swung back and moved a lever. "Let me get out of the ferry's wake."

Vail tightened her grip, and as she reached for the bar with her other hand, saw a shimmering of silver on the floor. Maintaining her hold, she bent over and picked it up.

"Whatcha got there?" Prisco asked.

"An earring. A nice one."

He glanced over. "Pretty. But it's not mine. Honest." He laughed. "Probably belongs to Maria. She's got the night shift. You should bring it by the Harbor Patrol office when you get back, tell 'em it's Officer Lopez's."

"Mind doing it when you get back there? I've got a full plate."

"Yeah, no worries," Prisco said. "I'll take care of it."

Vail handed it over and he slipped it into his pocket.

"And there she is," Prisco said, gesturing with his chin toward the large immigration building as it became visible in the distance. "The place took a big hit from Sandy. Lotsa damage. They had to take some exhibits off the island because the windows and doors were trashed. Place was closed for months."

"As a native New Yorker, I hate to admit it. But I've never been here."

Prisco cut back on the engines and the boat slowed. "You know how many friends I got who've never been to the Empire State Building? Or the Statue of Liberty? It's a thing with New Yorkers, I guess."

A few minutes later, the main building passed before them. Vail imagined her ancestors coming over from Ireland, walking through those very doors, lugging all their possessions in one or two suitcases. She would have to try to find a moment when her mother's mind was lucid enough to get some family history from her.

The water was calm around the inlet, which was a welcome development since Vail's stomach was starting to get queasy from all the up and down motion.

"Where would you like me to drop you? Front of the building here, or around back?"

"We're going to the old hospital complex."

"That'd be Island 3. Let's make it easy on you. There's a small dock around back, north side. I'll let you off and you can just hike southwest along Island 2 then hang a left, south, onto Island 3. It's all connected."

A couple of minutes later, they were disembarking onto the small pier.

"Want me to stick around, wait for you?" Prisco asked.

"No idea how long we're gonna be. We'll ring you up when we're ready. At least one other detective's gonna need to come over. Joe Slater."

"Got it. If anyone's coming over, I'll be their ferry."

Vail and Russo started walking along the path behind the buildings, past the Ellis Island bridge that led to New Jersey, en route to the hospital complex.

Russo's phone vibrated as they made it to a narrow path along the island's edge that followed the exterior of a long, enclosed brick hallway.

"I don't see a way into that corridor," Vail said.

Russo answered his phone while Vail pulled out her BlackBerry and called up Google Earth. She zoomed into the satellite imagery and waited a second for it to load. Although she struggled to make out details on her small screen, it looked like they could access most of the buildings from the periphery.

Russo hung up. "That was Protch. He's still working on locating the file, but it's been archived. They're trying to dig it out right now."

Vail knew the department didn't computerize key aspects of its records system until—unbelievably—2007.

"Protch remembered that Livana, the mother, told him that they'd fixed up the building they were living in. So if we can find one that's in better condition than the others, that's probably it."

Two-thirds of the way along the brick corridor, they came across a break in the building about twenty feet wide. Part of the roof was still intact, leading Vail to conclude that something had destroyed this missing section. They cut through and saw a couple of workers behind a dump truck.

"Hey, can we ask you something?" Vail held up her FBI badge as they approached the men. "We're looking for one of the hospital buildings that's in better condition than the others. Know which one that might be?"

"We're just here rebuilding the seawall." The men looked at each other. "Whaddya think," one said to the other. "That corner building John pointed out on the walk-through."

His colleague shrugged. "Probably."

"How 'bout you take us over there?" Russo asked.

The man glanced at the badge clipped to Russo's belt, then sighed. "Yeah, I can do that."

He led the way along an old aggregate concrete sidewalk and past large brick buildings that must have been grand when new. The foliage was overgrown with weeds, wild grasses, and large trees.

"You should see pictures of this place when Ellis Island was fulla immigrants," he said as he trudged along, his low-slung leather equipment belt clicking and clacking as the tools slapped against his thighs. "Buildings are kinda trashed inside, but it was once real nice."

"Looks like it," Vail said. The sound of crickets and what she thought were cicadas chirped loudly as they made their way past the buildings.

"Still," the worker said, "it was a hospital, you know? If you were here, chances are good you were in a bad way, bad enough they didn't want you bringin' over that shit to the US and infecting people. And then there was the whacko psych ward."

Whacko. Got it.

He led them to a building at the southern tip of the island, on the corner, and up a set of aging concrete stairs.

"This is it. Hope it's what you're lookin' for." He turned and headed back the way they came.

"Thanks," Vail said.

The man raised a hand, not bothering to turn around.

Russo grabbed the rusted knob and pushed the door open. The wood slat floors were bare, the varnish long since eroded and worn through. The walls were peeling chunks of plaster down to the brick substructure, and the metal fixtures were rusting.

Vail continued walking into another section of the building and stopped in the doorway. "Bingo." This area was like a different world. The rooms were well cared for. Although the paint had faded and some of it had been absorbed into the dry, thirsty walls, the place had a lived-in feeling.

"This was a home," Vail said.

"Not bad, if they were living here for free."

Vail walked into a fairly sizable room with four windows. Old-style radiators sat by each window and what appeared to be a framed mattress of some sort was pushed up against a far wall. She moved closer and crouched in front of it, poked at the material. "This was a waterbed."

"Were waterbeds around in the mid-'70s?"

"If they weren't, this wasn't their place."

"Look it up."

As Russo scouted the hallways and other rooms, Vail pulled out her BlackBerry and discovered that the beds were, in fact, being sold at that time. "That's a yes," she said. "So this was probably their house. Russo?"

"In here. Found something."

Vail followed his voice and pushed open a partially closed door. Flowery drawings covered the yellow walls. "A girl's room."

A poster was hanging from an area over the bed. Half of it had fallen and only the back was visible. Vail walked over and lifted it up, exposing the front image: Lee Majors as the Six Million Dollar Man.

"Definitely a girl's room," Russo said. "The murdered teen."

Aside from a few pieces of furniture, which were empty, there was not much there. Vail paused at one of the windows. "Hell of a view of the Statue of Liberty. It's so close."

"C'mon. Let's get on with this."

They moved across the hall.

"Boy's room," Vail said, looking around at the blue walls. "And a fireplace."

She walked closer to the area where the waterbed was located and noticed markings on the wall. "Look at this." She leaned in close and—"Holy shit. Is that what I think it is?"

Perfectly drawn Xs were lined up in rows and columns, each no larger than an inch.

Russo cleared his throat. "I got that feeling. You know what feeling I'm talking about?"

"The rush of excitement in your chest? That you've scored something big and you've taken a major step toward finding your suspect?"

"That'd be it."

She knelt down low to examine the Xs more closely—and a floorboard shifted beneath her weight. *Ow.* She moved to ease the pain on her kneecap and noticed that the wood panels had been cut transversely.

"Russo, help me with this."

"What'd you find?"

"I think a trapdoor to something." Vail tried to pry the slat up with her fingernail, but Russo produced a pocket knife. She unfolded it and jammed the tip underneath the edge, lifted the section up and— "There are books in here." She pulled out her BlackBerry and shined the light into the space. Seeing no rodents or booby-traps, she stuck her hand into the hole and pulled out multiple hardcovers and paperbacks, one or two at a time. They were covered in dust.

"You got gloves?"

Russo checked his pockets and rooted out a flattened mass of polyvinyl. He knelt beside her as Vail separated them, then stretched them over her hands and read off the titles of the books.

"*The Cannibal: A Study of Prolific Killer Albert Fish,* by Mel Heimer; *Confessions of the Boston Strangler,* by George Rae; *Bloodletters and Badmen,* by Jay Robert Nash; *Urge to Kill,* by Ward Damio; *The Co-ed Killer,* by Margaret Cheney; *The Torture Doctor,* by David Franke; *Chloroform in the Murder of William Marsh Rice,* by Shoshana Ellis; *The Killers Among Us,* by Douglas Underwood." She looked at Russo.

"Holy fuck. We've got him, Karen."

"Yeah, but who is he?"

"Dmitri," Russo said. He gestured toward the edge of one of the books, which bore the name, written in pen across the yellowed pages.

"D," she said. "And where are we? Ellis Island—an E and an I. The X logo he leaves on his vics. An E, an I, a D—and then a lowercase letter, seemingly in sequence, corresponding to each one of his kills."

"So the kid had a fascination with killing. Anything else down there?"

She reached in and found another hardcover—*How Humans Die*—and a collection of *Playboy* magazines. She carefully thumbed through a few of the books, and noted some markings on the inside of the chip board covers.

"So what do you make of this?"

Vail thought a moment. "Assuming he was a young kid when he moved here, he found something that piqued his interest. Judging by the prices written in pencil on the inside of the covers, these were used books. I'm guessing he saw them at a store in the city and bought them, then squirreled them away under the floorboards so no one else would find them. He obsessed over killing and death. Maybe it met his curiosity, fed his dreams, fantasies, until it was no longer sufficient and he decided to experiment, to find the thing that would satisfy that building need.

"Common thing is for the offender to kill a small animal, sometimes cut it open to explore, see what's inside. He does that, it excites him. Eventually, when it no longer satisfies him, he goes full bore, on a human. His sister may've been the first. She'd be easiest because she was here. He knew her, knew her habits. If he's a psychopath, he has no problem with killing a member of his family. He's got no bond, no connection."

"Isn't that more risky?"

"Absolutely, but psychopaths live for risk: the riskier the situation, the more thrilling it is, the more fun it is. But until we have the complete picture, we don't know his reasoning. Even if we catch him, we still may never know. That said, maybe all the scrutiny after his sister's death taught him to choose vics that have no direct connection to him."

"That could be the rookie mistake we were looking for."

"Right." But she was preoccupied with the stack of books. "Wait a minute. *How Humans Die*—I think that was the one taken from Detective Berger's mailbox, the book Carole Manos's family found under the couch after CSU left. They brought it to the squad, it was put in Berger's mailbox, and he vouchered it."

"The missing DD-5."

"And the missing book."

"The killer brought his book back to his lair."

"Assuming it's not a different copy." *The one on the DD-5 was described as "worn." This isn't new, but it's not worn. How subjective is "worn"?*

Vail bent down, turned her phone light on again, and swept the hole. "One more thing down here." She reached her arm fully into the space and fished out what looked like a photo album.

She set it atop the pile of books and sat down beside it, then opened it.

"What the hell?"

"A scrapbook of his kills. Newspaper clippings." She continued turning the pages and found a photo of herself. *Okay, that's creepy.* "Wonder if that's when he sent me that note."

"That doesn't make me feel so good. He's been watching you?"

"If he wanted to kill me, he would've—could've—done it years ago. I don't think my life's in jeopardy."

"Still . . . " Russo crouched beside her.

Vail flipped another page and stopped, sat up straight. "Oh."

Pictures of each victim, meticulously laid out on the pages.

"Those aren't crime scene photos," Russo said.

"No, they were taken right after death. By the killer."

They both sat in silence as Vail paged through the pictures, three for each one: the face and neck, the logo he drew, and a long shot, straight on, between the legs.

Russo cleared his throat. "If there was any doubt that this Dmitri is our killer, I'd say they're all gone now."

Vail went back to the beginning and turned the pages more slowly, taking in the precisely cut newspaper articles, small and large, from New York's major tabloids, covering the murders Vail and Russo had been fretting over the past nineteen years.

Russo's phone rang, pulling them out of their fugue. He said, "Talk to me, Protch," then placed the call on speaker.

"I remember the kid's name. Dmitri—"

"Yeah," Russo said, "we got that. We found a shitload of stuff here, books on killers and death, and a scrapbook of keepsake articles on all his murders."

"Shit. I was really hoping it wasn't gonna be the kid."

"Protch," Vail said, "no offense, but we've been chasing this asshole for almost twenty years. Russo and I are—"

"Ecstatic."

"I care about the family is all," Proschetta said. "They went through a lot of crap."

"Can't make it *your* crap," Russo said. "We've talked about this."

"Since when do we take each other's advice?"

Vail set the scrapbook down and stood up. "Any progress finding the mother—or even better, Dmitri?"

"Spoke with Jenkins, the detective who caught the girl's murder back in '81—Cassandra—and he said they looked at him, hard, but there were no forensics tying him to the crime scene. No witnesses who could place him there. And the mother wasn't very cooperative."

"You had a good relationship with her," Vail said.

"Livana. Don't know why I thought it was Laura, or whatever I called her. Nice lady, she trusted me. But it wasn't my case, so I had to turn everything over to Jenkins and the homicide detective. I did take a look at the Castiglias, just to make sure they didn't have a hand in it. Found nothing. So I did as ordered. I dropped it. Haven't talked to Livana since. But I got some calls out to locate her. And the file should be here any minute."

"Call us back as soon as you get it," Vail said. "Actually—wait a minute. That guy, Gregor? Whatever happened to him? And his wife. See if Jenkins knows."

Russo disconnected the call and they searched the remainder of the building, including a storage area underneath the staircase that led to the second floor.

"They really did a nice job fixing this place up. Even mothballed for thirty-plus years, it's in pretty decent shape." Vail stopped at the circuit breaker box, its door severely rusted. She pulled it open and chuckled. "So according to this, this building was the 'staff house.' And H. Z. Altberg, Incorporated, was the electrical contractor who did the wiring. The phone number starts 'Circle 7.' That tells you how old this place is."

As they ascended the stairs, Russo said, "I remember when phone numbers were like that. Mine was Fieldstone 1, which got shortened to 'Fi-1' before they dropped the letters altogether and went with numbers only." He shook his head. "Guess I'm showing my age."

They finished the search upstairs, found nothing of note, and walked into the kitchen when Russo's phone rang.

"You're on speaker, Protch. Go."

"Right, so I spoke with Livana, but I also got a hit on the kid. Get this—Dmitri Harris is a ranger with the National Park Service, stationed at Liberty Island for the past twenty-four years."

Ranger Harris? Holy shit, I remember that guy. The resident expert on the statue. He took Jonathan up to the crown when I got called away. Vail felt dizzy. She steadied herself against the cabinet. *I left my son with a serial killer?*

Russo moved to the window and peered out. "I'm looking at the place right now."

"Are you telling us," Vail said, "that the killer we've been chasing for nineteen years is just a few hundred yards away?"

"That's what I'm telling you. And he's on duty today. Wait, hang on a second. It's Livana, his mother. Call you back."

THEY TOOK THE hardcovers, paperbacks, and scrapbook in tow. Bringing them along was not ideal, but there was no better alternative. They couldn't leave them unattended.

"I saw the ferry pulling in when we were upstairs," Vail said. "Gotta still be loading. If we hurry, we can get on it, have them take us over."

They ran out and headed toward the inlet, hoping to flag down the ferry captain and signal him to wait. As they approached, they got the attention of a ranger on the pier and conveyed the message. They sprinted along the water's edge, Russo getting winded and falling back as they made it within fifty yards of the dock.

"Get us over to Liberty ASAP," Vail said to the deckhand between gasps, her throat raspy and painfully dry. She held up her creds, bent at the knees to catch her breath, and said, "Stop loading. Take us to Liberty." She stood up and looked the man in the eyes. "Now!"

That got him moving, and as Russo huffed his way on board, the ferry started to back away.

Russo sat hard on the bench seat against the windows.

"Makes sense," Vail said. "Working on Liberty. He can keep close to his sanctuary. No one's gonna question a ranger making occasional trips to Ellis Island. Perfect setup."

Russo grunted, still out of breath, just as his BlackBerry rang. "Shit." He pulled it off his belt and handed it to Vail. As she took the phone, she grabbed a water bottle from the concession and handed it to Russo. In this heat and humidity, she didn't want him to suffer heat stroke. She brought the phone to her mouth. "Protch, it's Karen. Russo's winded. We just ran to catch the ferry to Liberty. What do you got?"

"Livana gave me the lowdown on Dmitri. He—"

"You didn't tell her what we found—"

"Karen, give me a little credit, huh? I wouldn't give her a chance to tip her son off. Just asked her how she's doing, where she ended up, and then I asked about how Dmitri was doing. She said he really grew up and matured, went to Queens College and majored in history. He overcame some learning problems and hooked on with the Park Service after graduating—which we already knew.

"But she said he's still kind of different and doesn't have many friends. He mostly keeps to himself, but they go to church together and have dinner every Sunday. She seemed sad that he wasn't well-integrated into society—those are my words, my interpretation. I was tactful about it, but she said he doesn't have a girlfriend or anyone he's close with, other than her. Even at that, he seems distant. Her words, not mine."

"Anything on that guy—"

"Oh, yeah. Gregor and Alysia Persephone. They were found murdered in their home in '85—"

"Murdered? How?"

"Execution style. I called the loo at my old precinct. He's having the file pulled, but he remembered they were lookin' into the father for mob ties. Father's the furrier Basil was gonna rat out—"

"Right, got that."

"Anyway, they never made an arrest, but they were pretty sure it was the Castiglias. Word was that the family wanted more of the profit, but the fur business was tanking because of all the bad publicity about animal rights and shit. Gus Persephone, the owner, supposedly said no, and about three weeks later, they found his son and daughter-in-law shot behind the ear with a .22."

I'm not so sure it was the Castiglias. I bet it was Hades taking out the primary cause of his problems. Maybe his first in a long line of revenge killings. If the MO was too much like Cassandra's death or the subsequent ones, they might look at Dmitri instead of the Castiglias. He couldn't risk that.

Vail leaned down and glanced out the window. The ferry was nearing Liberty Island, the copper green profile of the statue looming large. "Okay, good stuff, Protch. Do me a favor and call the Park Police, let 'em know we're coming. But don't tell them what the deal is. I don't want them freaking him out. It may be an island, but I'd rather not spend the rest of the day combing the place for a fugitive serial killer." She thanked Proschetta, then handed Russo back his phone. After giving him a quick recap, she said, "You feeling better?"

"I haven't run like that since my forties. I'm too old for that shit."

"Well, captain-to-be, you shouldn't have to. That's why old guys like you got young'uns like me." As she finished relaying the information Proschetta had gotten from Dmitri's mother, the ferry slowed and started moving laterally toward the dock. Vail paid for the water she had given Russo, then grabbed a large plastic tote bag and slipped Dmitri's books into it. It was not an ideal way to preserve evidence, but it was better than lugging them around without any protection.

They headed toward the gangplank, picking their way through the crowd, much to the consternation of the waiting patrons who were lining up for their closeup glimpse of Lady Liberty.

Moments later, they made land and hung a right along the newly laid brick path and lush green lawn that fronted the statue's granite-block base, headed toward the center of the island. Vail grabbed the first ranger they saw and told her they were looking for Dmitri Harris.

"He's right there," the woman said with a head gesture over her left shoulder as she fielded a question from an Italian tourist.

That's him. Slow down, take a breath.

"Son of a bitch," Russo said.

Vail could tell by his heaving chest that Russo was as amped up as she was.

Dmitri was in front of a low brick wall chatting with a woman and her son, who looked to be about eight. Behind them stood bronze statues of people significant to the statue's creation. If Vail recalled, they depicted the sculptor, the architect—who had also designed the Eiffel Tower—and the woman who wrote the sonnet with the famous line: "Give me your tired, your poor, your huddled masses."

"Should we call in the troops?" Vail asked. "Park Police. Surround him."

"Lots of loaded guns in a public place packed with women and children? Not to mention an unstable violent offender." Russo shook his head. "If we had time to prepare, we could do this right. But we don't have time. And I'm not letting him out of my sight. Which means at some point he's gonna realize I'm following him."

"Then how do you want to play this?"

"Easy. I walk up to him and put a fist in his nose. Then I cuff him and haul his ass outta here. Short, sweet, effective."

"I got a better idea." Vail nonchalantly glanced at Dmitri. Still with the mother and her son. "First, we should breathe." She grinned at him. "Do what I'm doing. Wipe the stress, the urgency, from your mind—and your face. Relax your fists and let your shoulders drop. We're just gonna go up to him and start talking. Totally disarming, right?"

"He knows what you look like. That letter he left at your place. The photo he took of you—"

"Even if he knows who I am, he doesn't know that we know he's the killer. That's why we go in quietly, smiling and friendly. He'd never expect that. He'd expect a full frontal assault. And a punch in the nose." She studied his face. "Okay?"

Russo clenched his jaw. "I've been chasing this fucker for two decades, Karen. He's killed—" He lowered his voice. "Lots of people."

"Then maybe you'd better let me handle this."

"You outta your mind? My biggest collar in a dozen years, you think I'm gonna sit it out?"

"Fine, then smile. Or I'm going to tickle you."

Russo took a deep breath. "Okay."

"Okay. Follow my lead." Vail walked toward Dmitri, who had bent over to shake the boy's hand.

"Ranger Harris," Vail said as they approached. "Karen Vail, remember me?"

Dmitri tilted his head.

She smiled broadly. "You gave me and my son a tour of the crown about eight years ago. Actually, you took my son. I got a phone call and couldn't go up."

He shook his head. "Sorry, don't remember. I do lots of tours. I've *done* a lot of tours. This is my twenty-third year on the island."

"This is a friend of mine, Carmine Russo."

They were standing in front of Dmitri, a gleaming brass name badge pinned to his well-pressed, perfectly tucked in clay-colored ranger shirt, a pair of dark sunglasses resting on his nose. He seemed at ease. But it was unnerving not to be able to see his eyes. The eyes were said to be the windows to the soul—for a psychopath, however, they were even more than that. Theirs had a penetrating snake eyes look that seemed to bore right through you. *I want to see your eyes, goddamn it.*

"Good to meet you," Dmitri said with a nod at Russo. "Do you have a question about the statue?" he asked, looking first at Russo, then at Vail.

"Not exactly," Russo said. "My question's a little more generic. Like, are you armed?"

Dmitri jutted his chin back. "I'm a park ranger, not Park Police. Rangers who are GS4s don't carry sidearms. Article 5 of the Federal Office of Personnel—"

"That's okay, Dmitri," Russo said. "I just needed to know if you had a weapon."

You're freaking him out, Russo. Go easy.

Dmitri looked at Vail, then back to Russo, but he was clearly focused on Russo, and he was beginning to sweat. Then again, it could have been the heat and humidity.

"That's an odd question," Dmitri said. "About being armed. Usually people want to know how many steps it takes to climb—"

"We're not most people," Russo said. "I'm a lieutenant with the NYPD. And one of the things I do is investigate homicide. Murder. And Karen here is with the FBI. She helps us catch serial killers. You have an interest in serial killers. Don't you, Dmitri?"

Dmitri backed up a step. "I don't—I don't understand. What do you want?"

"Maybe we should talk about your sister."

Dmitri pushed his glasses back up on his nose as he swallowed deeply. "I—I—that was a long time ago. She was killed."

"We know. We also know about your books." Russo reached into the plastic bag, pulled out the photo album, and splayed it opened to a picture of his sister. "Look!"

Dmitri's face contorted—but that was the last thing they saw because he raised his right hand and sprayed their eyes with liquid from a small leather canister.

52

>LIBERTY ISLAND
New York Harbor
40°41′21″N 74°2′40″W Present
Day: Wednesday, July 16

atch it!" Vail said as she instinctively threw up a hand and simultaneously swung her head to the right.

"Ah shit, it burns, it burns," Russo said, bending over at the waist.

"Pepper spray," Vail said, blinking rapidly. "You okay?"

"Can't see, feels like it's boiling right through my skin." He started coughing violently.

"I blocked some of it," she said, knowing she had to resist the urge to touch the liquid. "Got my cheeks, some in the eyes. I'm going after him."

"Gonna find a restroom and wash it out. Goddamn it."

Vail ran forward, coughing, hoping to find a Park Police officer.

Her vision was blurry; her eyes stung and they felt swollen and irritated. *Son of a bitch.*

Vail stumbled into the security tent and grabbed her badge off her belt. "FBI, out of my way!" She pushed through the line and got to the mouth of the screening room, where airport-type X-ray and metal scanners were located. If there was going to be a law enforcement presence, this is where she would likely find it.

"Whoa, hang on. Where do you think you're going?"

Vail tried to make out who was talking to her, but all she could tell was that he was a ranger. "I need Park Police." Cough. "Hurry!"

"Carl, over here," he called. Then to Vail, "Who are you?"

She pulled out her creds and held them up. "Karen Vail, FBI. I've—"

"Officer Kraut," he said. "What's going on?"

It was another man's voice, and he seemed to be in front of her. "I've got a suspect on the run," Vail said. "Lock the place down, no ferries are to load or offload. Hurry."

She heard him key his two-way, then repeat the order.

"We already had an alert to secure the island. Is that what this is about?"

"You have a ranger, Dmitri Harris. Put out a BOLO. My partner, NYPD Lieutenant Russo, was questioning Harris about a murder when he shot us with pepper spray and ran." Cough.

"Ranger Harris? Are you serious? He's a strange bird, a loner. But he's never late and never misses a day of work. He wouldn't hurt anyone."

"I'm sure you're basing that statement on information you obtained using sound law enforcement investigative techniques. But for now, just do what I say. We can debate your opinion later. Have you seen him?"

"He came through here a couple of minutes ago."

Interesting choice. He knew he wouldn't be able to get off the island, so he came in here. Does he know a place to hide?

"You want me to call SWAT?" Kraut asked.

"No time." Cough. "I need some help—you. Be my eyes until this shit clears up."

Vail kept blinking, squinting, and tilting her head, trying to clear her visual field. It was improving, but not fast enough.

"SWAT's right here on the island."

"Then hell yes, call them, tell 'em to search for Dmitri Harris. He's armed with pepper spray and assumed dangerous. If we're right, he's killed ten people."

Kraut conveyed that information by radio.

After hearing the affirmative, Vail said, "You know this place? As good as Harris?"

"No one knows it as good as Harris. But I've worked here eight years."

"Then I need you to think like him. Take me to where you think he'd go, where he can hide."

Kraut stood there, silent.

Vail tried to focus on him—and finally was able to get a sense of who she was talking with: a pasty white guy with thinning hair.

"Kraut, now would be a good time."

"Right, follow me."

They passed through security, the officer telling the screeners that it was cool to let her bypass the X-ray machine, which did not go over well because it bucked procedure, but all Vail cared about was that she got through without losing time.

He led her into what Kraut described as Fort Wood, the original structure that existed on the island before the pedestal was built for the statue.

As they walked past the old torch that she remembered seeing when she was here with Jonathan, Vail said, "So if you want to hide inside the statue, where would you go?"

"Tough question. There are a few different closed areas, but we've got a state-of-the-art security system with high-resolution cameras, fitted with motion sensors and infrared. The detail is so good you can practically read the time off my watch. If he's in there, we'll know."

"Who's monitoring those cameras?"

"Our Park Police station offsite. But it's real-time. Anyone goes into a closed area, even staff, we'll catch it."

Somehow that doesn't seem comforting.

They stopped on the other side of the torch. And that's when the power went out.

53

"Oh, shit." Kraut said it matter-of-factly, without panic.

Vail removed her BlackBerry and turned on the flashlight. "So these closed areas. If you had to choose, which ones offer the best chance for escape?"

"Depends on how you define 'escape.' There's the basement, which is really the old Fort Wood. It's basically a long tunnel with a couple of branch-like passageways. The walls are the same granite blocks you see on the exterior, but the ceilings are arched and made of red brick. Pipes run along the ceiling and there are lights—"

"Access?"

"Interior and exterior doors. But it's got multiple levels of security—meaning there are multiple beat keys required to get in. Each key's on a different ring."

Cross talk chirped through his radio's speaker. It was apparently not directed at Kraut, who occasionally stopped for a second to listen but felt no need to join the conversation.

"Who's got these keys?"

"The buildings and utilities part of the Park Service. They've got a maintenance division. Maintenance rangers have the most access of the regular ranger staff. Then there's all of us—Park Police, which includes SWAT, sergeant and above, unless they're doing their rounds. Most of the rangers on the island have never seen the basement, the arm, or the torch because they don't have access."

Vail cleared her throat to head off the tickle of a cough. "So what would stop a perp—an insider—from making copies of these beat keys, like a wax mold of some sort?"

"Nothing, if he really wanted to and knew what he was doing."

"How about someone obsessed with the statue, who's worked here all his life, who wants the ability to access places no one else can get to?"

"The security cameras."

"Right. But these cameras weren't always there."

"After 9/11."

"And maybe it's not about doing it so much as being able to do it. Was Harris ever a maintenance ranger?"

"Years ago he was the guy who changed the bulbs on the torch when the ranger who'd been doing it for a gazillion years retired. Park Service finally got around to filling the post, so Harris only did it for a while."

"Tell me about the torch," Vail said.

"Only way to the torch is through the arm. That's the other closed area."

And if he had the keys before 9/11, before security and terrorism became a way of life in America . . . before things were tracked as closely as they are now . . .

"Take me there."

Kraut led her up the stairs, which featured some kind of bright yellow glow in the dark coating that illuminated the blue rubberized steps. Vail coughed the entire way, jogging up to Level 6P, the top of the pedestal, and then climbed up a narrow staircase.

As they ascended, she realized she could see again—but not clearly. It would have to do.

"This is the way to the crown," Kraut said, starting up the helical stainless steel staircase. "The arm's this way too, but we'll get off well before we reach the top."

Just then, a klaxon started sounding. Emergency floodlights kicked on, glary, harsh, and uneven—but it was significantly better than her phone's anemic glow.

Vail could now see that they were standing inside the body of the statue. A steel skeleton of thin "bones" was bolted to the interior and conformed to her curves, keeping her upright.

As they arrived at the portal that led to the arm, Kraut cursed under his breath.

"What?"

"Someone's in there. The door, it's open. You need several keys—just like the basement—to gain access. But once you go up, there's no way to close and lock it from the inside."

"What's it like in there?"

"Todd—the maintenance ranger—told me there's a forty-two-foot ladder inside the arm that leads to the top. Ladder's not actually attached to the copper skin. There's a metal framework that holds the ladder up. That's why it's so tight in there. Very little room."

That's just terrific. London all over again, the climb from the underground's rail car to the surface. There I had Hector to talk me through it. Now I've got . . . a serial killer armed with pepper spray. No biggie, Karen. You can do this.

"There's a 45 degree angle when you first get in," Kraut continued, "and like I said, it's real narrow."

"Tight and narrow with very little room. Got that part. What else?"

"The thing sways a lot. It's copper, remember? Even with its skeleton, the arm sways about eighteen inches from side to side. The copper was meant to breathe and sway with the wind."

"Sounds . . . exciting." *Frightening.*

"Worse when you're up on the torch. Then it *really* sways."

"Sounds like you've been up there."

"Once. Todd needed help with a bulb. But it wasn't an official visit."

Official? Whatever the hell that means.

"The torch you saw downstairs, the new one's an exact copy of the original, right down to the access hatch. Except for the flame. New one's 24 karat gold plated."

"So it's just a straight shot up the arm?"

"When you get to the elbow, the ladder turns and twists a bit. It narrows down even more—like shoulder width—as you get close to the wrist. And there are other doors you need to get through—"

"Same thing, though, right? If Harris keyed them open, he's got no way to close them behind him."

"I think so. But there's that hatch when you get to the top of the arm, at the torch. He might be able to lock that one once he's out. I have no idea. I do know it's easy to hit your head going through," he said, absently rubbing his scalp.

If the killer doesn't hit me on the head first.

"Okay, thanks." Vail drew her Glock.

"Whoa, whaddya think you're doin' with that? You fire that thing, you'll poke holes in her copper skin. It's only the thickness of two pennies."

"Thanks for the tip. Meantime, I'm going up."

"No, you're not. This area has extremely limited access. Senators have been denied access. No way *you're* going up."

"Listen here, dumbshit, there's a guy in that arm who could be the Hades slasher. We've been chasing him for almost twenty years. I don't know what his endgame is, but if *he's* up there, *I'm* going up there."

Kraut keyed his radio. "Lieutenant, this is Carl. Over."

Vail did not wait for permission—or denial. She grabbed hold of the stairs and started up toward the access door.

"Hey, stop!"

But Karen Vail did not stop. She plunged into the dark armpit of Lady Liberty.

54

As promised, it was dark. And tight as hell.

This is not a good idea, Karen. He's got pepper spray. Maybe —he got off two long bursts at me and Russo, which might've emptied his canister.

Vail climbed one rung at a time, but after several feet she realized that holding her Glock in her right hand was not only slowing her down but would not do her much good in a close-quarters fight. She could actually lose it if she was struck unexpectedly.

She stopped and reholstered it, then continued her ascent, fighting the anxiety of being in a long vertical tunnel with the edges of the tube scraping her shoulders on both sides.

My chest feels like it's got a goddamn weight on it. And the gnawing tickle in the back of my throat from being burned . . . Fun times. I should do this more often.

She fought to push aside the intense feeling that the tunnel was closing down on her, as well as the urge to lash out with her arms and break through the copper walls. She had to focus on the killer—who was somewhere above her.

Vail had climbed a dozen rungs when she stopped and listened. She heard nothing but felt the intense lateral sway of the arm. It sure seemed like more than eighteen inches. The queasiness in her stomach, coupled with the perspiration that was trickling down her torso, led her to think she might be the first person ever to vomit inside Lady Liberty's arm. It would be a story to tell her grandchildren one day.

Then again, maybe not.

She kept moving skyward. *How high did he say it was? Forty-two feet? Am I insane?*

Hector, where are you when I need you?

Vail stopped and listened. Footsteps above. And the space was getting tighter against her shoulders. She took a deep breath and tried to slow her racing heart. Was it racing because she was so close to getting clobbered by the killer? Or because there was barely room to move, let alone breathe?

Tough question. Not one she wanted to ponder at the moment.

Her hand struck the top—and she felt around and found the access door to the outside.

Now was the time to draw the Glock. She slowly removed it, taking care not to drop it. That would totally suck if it clanged its way down the narrow, four-story tube.

With an anxiety-slick hand, Vail grabbed the knob on the torch access panel and gave it an authoritative push.

55

The hatch swung open, the three copper hinges creaking and the bright sky forcing her to close her eyes. *Brilliant—the killer may be ready to smash me in the face and I can't even see him. Wasn't the pepper spray bad enough?*

Vail willed her eyes open. A whipping wind struck her in the face and took her breath away, as did the view of the New York and New Jersey skylines. She felt like she was in the middle of the bay, thirty stories up.

Only because I am.

Look later. Find Harris.

But there was no sign of him. Had the unlocked, open door to the arm been a ruse?

That'd just about make my day, climbing forty feet in a tight metal tube while the killer slipped away through some other hidden tunnel Kraut didn't know about.

The visible portion of the platform, a nine-foot circular structure with a thin railing and a low, airy decorative wall, was clear.

With the Glock tight against her chest and both hands wrapped around the handgun, she stepped out—and struck the top of her head, as she had been warned.

Vail rose from her crouch and swung around quickly, sweeping the torch's platform—and immediately felt the thing sway toward her, her weight no doubt bending the flexible copper skin as if it were a noodle. An overwhelming sense of queasiness grabbed her.

Don't throw up, Karen. Please, not now.

She took her left hand off the Glock and steadied herself on the thin railing. But it didn't help, as the arm continued swaying back and forth, whipsawing one way, then the other. She knew the steel ladder would prevent the appendage from breaking away from the body, but it was still unnerving.

Vail sidestepped the floor-mounted spotlights that were aimed at the 24 karat gold flame directly above her and moved laterally, peripherally, around the platform—while watching the other side in case he lunged at her from the opposite end of the torch.

One more step and she saw a workboot sticking out from behind the flame's base.

Vail thrust the Glock out in front of her, two fists gripping the weapon, and said, "Show me your hands. Now!"

Dmitri Harris did not move. But Vail did, stepping slowly around to the front of the torch, angling to the side to get a view of her suspect's face.

And then her BlackBerry started buzzing.

Her thoughts flashed back to an operational drill she was required to participate in at Quantico's Hogan's Alley following a bank shooting. That time it was training, and she answered the phone. This, however, was not an exercise.

As she inched closer, the handset continued vibrating. *I'm kinda busy. Leave a message.*

When Dmitri Harris came into full view, he was sitting on the copper floor of the platform, fingers interwoven with his hair, palms covering his eyes.

"Get up," Vail said. "Slowly." She was too close to him, but there was nothing she could do. There was no room to move back without tipping over the edge of the thin railing.

"It's not my fault."

"We've seen your books, we've seen your photo album, the Xs on the wall in your room. You killed your sister and ten people are—"

"Not my fault!" He grabbed his hair with both hands. "Not my fault. Not my fault!"

"Whose fault is it, Dmitri? You killed your own sister!"

He leaped toward her—Vail fired and missed—and he delivered a body slam, driving her right arm up and pinning her lower back to the railing.

Shit, he's trying to push me over.

Vail grabbed his hair with her left fist and tried to pull his head back. But he was enraged and clearly not feeling the pain.

She tightened her abdomen, trying to keep herself from bending backward over the thin metal bar, trying to lower her Glock, trying to gain some kind of advantage.

Vail hooked her left foot around his right boot and headbutted him. In that instant of shock when Dmitri's arms went limp, she pushed him off her and he tripped backward over her leg.

He landed on his back and struck his head on the spotlight mounted on the platform—and lost consciousness.

Vail handcuffed him to the torch wall, then checked his pulse. He would probably regain consciousness any minute.

Now what? How the hell do I get him down from here?

As she removed her BlackBerry, it started ringing again.

"Vail."

"Who the fuck do you think you are, going into a restricted area without authorization?"

She held the phone away from her face and looked at the display:

Superintendent
Nat'l Park Service

She disconnected the call, then dialed Russo.

"Karen," he said. "Thank god. You okay?"

"I've got the suspect in custody. Can you come get him?"

"Jesus—of course. Be right there. Where are you?"

"You're not gonna believe me."

"Try me."

"About three hundred feet above the water, standing on top of Miss Liberty's torch."

There was a long silence. "What?"

Even Vail had to laugh. "Like I said."

56

Shortly after Dmitri regained consciousness, Vail had placed him under arrest—in case the Park Police wanted to take possession of the prisoner. Because the island was under federal jurisdiction, the NYPD had no ability to take any action. And she knew Russo wanted the bust very badly.

Vail had removed the handcuffs and followed Dmitri down the arm, keeping a significant distance above him and the Glock firmly seated in her hand. When they reached the bottom of the ladder, three SWAT officers were waiting to assist.

Using the Park Police's so-called moose boat, a SWAT sergeant and a couple of his men helped Vail and Russo escort Dmitri to Battery Park, where—under Vail's orders—a waiting BuCar from the FBI's New York field office transported them to the Manhattan South homicide squad for questioning.

As they watched Dmitri through the two-way glass, Joe Slater to Vail's left, Horace Jenkins stepped in and closed the door quietly.

"Is Ben coming," Vail asked, or is he still indisposed?"

Russo kept his eyes on Dmitri. "He won't be coming."

"I wish Thorne and Fonzarella could be here," Vail said with a sigh of resignation.

Slater snorted. "Amen to that."

The door to the room opened and Commissioner Brendan Carrig, homicide squad chief Mendoza, and Manhattan borough commander Yarles walked in. And then Mayor de Blasio followed.

Slater turned to Russo and gestured at the glass. "So this is the asshole who's run us ragged for twenty years?"

Vail glanced at Russo. "That's what we're going to find out."

"It's him," Russo said.

"Good," Carrig said. "Good work, all of you."

De Blasio moved closer to the glass and shook his head. "What kind of monster kills ten innocent people?"

"Nine innocent people," Vail said. "Dominic Crinelli was a lot of things, but innocent wasn't one of them."

De Blasio looked around the room and his gaze settled on Carrig. He kinked his neck toward Vail. "Who's this?"

"*This*," Vail said, folding her arms, "is Karen Vail. FBI. I'm the one who made the arrest on the torch of the Statue of Liberty."

Carrig frowned, as if that was a fact he did not want to acknowledge—or publicize. "She's a former NYPD detective, Mr. Mayor."

De Blasio nodded, then said, "Again. Thank-you, all." He turned and left the room.

Vail and Russo shared a look.

"Well, time to get this thing started."

Carrig consulted his watch. "The mayor and I have a press conference on the arrest in forty-five minutes. Excuse me."

When the door clicked shut, Russo said, "Joe, with me. Karen—"

"No problem, Russo. I only made the arrest because that's the way it had to go down to get him in this room. This is your baby."

He nodded a silent thanks. Vail faced the glass and watched as the two men entered the interrogation room.

The door swung open again and Proschetta walked in. He gave Vail a bear hug and whispered, "Congratulations" in her ear.

"Your info was crucial," Vail said, "and impeccably timed. Thanks."

He leaned back and looked her over. "What happened to your face?"

"Asshole got us with pepper spray." She leaned both hands on the ledge in front of the glass. "Wait till you see Russo's face. I didn't get it so bad."

"Shit."

"Yeah, well, it's okay. We caught him. All's good."

"I called Livana on the way over here," Proschetta said. "I wanted to tell her before she heard it on the news. She's a good woman. After losing her daughter, I knew this would kill her. No pun intended."

"And what did she say?"

"After losing it, she composed herself and admitted that she had concerns. They found a squirrel on the island a couple of years before they moved. It was dissected."

"You're kidding."

"No. She also found him masturbating once while watching his sister shower."

"I'm going to text Slater, tell him about this." Vail pulled her phone and tapped out the message. Seconds later, Slater read the display and shared it with Russo, who nodded.

Russo smiled—the confidence of a cop knowing he had a suspect by the balls. He started off by reminding Dmitri of his rights, but their suspect declined representation, saying he had nothing to hide.

"See," Russo said, "it's interesting that you put it that way, being that we found those books in your lair. In the secret compartment *hidden* beneath the floor of your bedroom."

Dmitri looked at the wall, then the ceiling—but did not reply.

"Mr. Harris, are you familiar with someone named Dominic Crinelli?"

"He killed my father."

"I take it you didn't like him."

"He killed my father."

"Right, and it's understandable that you didn't like him. I mean, if a guy like that had killed my dad, I'd have to even the score."

"What score?"

Russo cleared his throat. "You killed Crinelli to get back at him for killing your dad. I understand that. No one here would have a problem with that. Just tell me how you did it."

"How I evened the score."

"Yeah, like how you got him to let you into his house. That must've been tough. He was a real careful guy. A dangerous guy."

"I don't know where his house is."

"Right," Russo said. "But when you walked up to his front door, what was it like? Were you excited? Angry? Or did you not feel anything?"

"I don't know."

Russo squirmed slightly in his seat. "When he came to the door, what did you say to him? What did you say to make him let you in?"

Dmitri grabbed his left arm. "Not my fault. Not my fault. Not my fault."

Russo nudged Slater, then gestured at something with his chin. Slater lifted a briefcase onto the table, then unsnapped the locks. Russo removed the photo album then slid the attaché to Slater's left.

He flipped some pages and found the one showing the photo the killer had taken of Cassandra.

Vail turned up the volume on the speaker. On a nearby monitor, she had a good view of Dmitri and a wide shot of Russo and Slater.

"Your sister," Russo said. "Recognize her?"

Dmitri started rubbing his arm.

"This is yours, Dmitri. I know it is."

"What's with the arm rubbing?" Proschetta asked Vail.

She shrugged. "He's nervous." *But that doesn't fit with a psychopath.*

"It's not mine," Dmitri said. The rubbing quickened.

"See, it was in your bedroom. Hidden in your bedroom. I told you that a couple of minutes ago, dumbshit. And when the lab does its thing, I bet we're gonna find your fingerprints all over it."

"It's not mine."

"And how about these?" Slater bent down and removed the hardcovers, paperbacks, and *Playboy* magazines. He set them on the table.

"I'm allowed to have books."

"Not just books," Russo said. "Books on killing and murder. Not just murder, serial killers."

"They weren't called serial killers. That term wasn't invented until Robert Ressler—"

"Don't be a smartass, Dmitri. You know what I'm asking. Why did you have books on killing? To teach you how to do it? Because you got off on reading about how other killers murdered people?"

"I'm allowed to have books."

"And what about the magazines? These are from 1970, 1971. Did your mother approve of you having them? Did she know?"

"Yes."

"Really? I think you're lying. Should I call her right now, ask—"

"No!" He stood quickly, the chains tightening on his shackles and pulling him back into his seat.

Russo, however, instinctively drew back and nearly tipped his chair over. He slammed his hands on the table and leaned forward. "You asshole. You murdered ten people! Admit it."

Dmitri started moving his right hand up and down, left and right. Crossing himself.

"Jesus can't help you, Dmitri. But maybe he'll forgive you if you tell us the truth about all the people you've killed. Are you willing to tell the truth?"

"Okay. Yes."

"Are these books yours?"

"Yes."

Russo sat back. Vail could hear his sigh of relief through the speaker. He waited a minute, then said, "Tell me about the squirrel your mother found on Ellis Island, the one you dissected."

"I didn't dissect a squirrel."

"How'd it make you feel?"

"I didn't dissect a squirrel."

"Son of a bitch!" Russo slapped the table again. "You said you were gonna tell the truth."

Dmitri recoiled and began rubbing his arm harder.

This was not tracking the way Vail thought it should. In certain respects Dmitri was not behaving like a typical psychopath. But she was also seeing signs of something else—and it had nothing to do with serial killers. "Something's not right."

"It's the dance," Proschetta said. "Be patient. This could take hours, you know that."

She pulled out her phone and started dialing.

"Who you calling?" Proschetta asked.

"Wayne Rudnick, a friend of mine at the Behavioral Science Unit."

Two rings later, Rudnick picked up. "Karen! To what do I owe this wonderful gift that I call your *presence?*"

"Wayne, if I didn't need your help desperately, I'd find that funny."

"What do you need? You know I can't say no to you. I've had a crush on you since the first day I laid eyes on you. Wait, did I say that out loud?"

"You did. And that's sweet. But I'm in New York and the NYPD's interrogating a suspect who could be the Hades slasher."

"But you have doubts."

"Is it that obvious?"

"Simple deduction, my dear Agent Vail. You're on the phone with me and you need my help."

"Good point. I need to run this by you. It isn't adding up for me, and I know something's wrong, but I think I'm too close."

"What's the problem?"

Vail watched the interrogation a few seconds before answering. "On paper, our suspect looks dead to rights, guilty of killing ten people. Revenge killings. He has some definite psychopathic behaviors, but . . . I don't know. Others—"

"Some conditions, on the surface, mimic psychopathy. But you know this."

"I've been after this guy for nineteen years. I'm too close, I'm not being objective. I'm not seeing what I should be seeing."

"Fair enough. Let me ask you some questions, see if I can walk you through this. "What's the suspect like?"

Vail gave Rudnick a quick rundown of Dimitri's history and presumed motive.

"Okay, that all fits. So what's bothering you?"

"He seems to be nervous. He's denying killing and dissecting that squirrel. And when I accused him of murdering his sister, he got very agitated and attacked me."

"So tell me. What's his speech like?"

"You mean vocabulary?"

"Well, let's start with that."

Vail thought a moment, listened a few seconds to Dmitri's ongoing exchange with Russo, and said, "Generally simple sentences. But sometimes he can have more lengthy exchanges."

"What's he discussing when he uses more complex syntax?"

"The Statue of Liberty."

"His work as a ranger. Memorized facts. Okay, and how about the way he talks. Is it mechanical or—"

"Oh my god. Asperger's."

"Correct, my dear Agent Vail. But—point of information, if I may. We don't use the term Asperger's anymore. It's ASD: autism spectrum disorder."

"Spectrum?"

"Because there's a range, a degree to which people are affected. They can fall anywhere along that scale. At the far left end is full-blown autism, and at the far right extreme is very high functioning Asperger's; I think you know what autism would present as—"

"Yeah, I got that. I need the far right, the very high functioning Asperger's. Real-world applications."

"Asperger's, at first blush, is frequently confused with psychopathy because these individuals lack empathy and don't have the ability to bond with others. But—and this is a huge but—the predatory behavior central to a serial killer's psychopathy is lacking in Asperger's. Also, the inability to seemingly bond with others that we see in Asperger's is not of the same depth or quality as psychopathy, where people are purposeful objects to be used and manipulated by the psychopath."

This is starting to make sense.

"You with me?" Rudnick asked.

"Yeah. Yeah, I'm here. That's all really helpful."

Rudnick proceeded to give her more details on the latest research and the typical presentation of a higher functioning ASD individual. Finally Vail said, "I think we've got a problem."

"How so?"

"I think our suspect's ASD, a very high functioning individual, the far right on the spectrum."

"And that means it's pretty unlikely that he's a serial killer."

"This sucks so bad you don't want to know."

"Hades has been at large twenty years. I get it."

"It's been longer than that. His first kill was thirty-four years ago."

"Shiitake, Hades is a seriously bad dude. But I'm fairly certain your ASD guy there is not your killer."

Vail felt a physical—and emotional—deflation.

"I have to be sure, Wayne. I need to question him. Will you help me through it?

"Can you hook me up to their surveillance camera so I can watch his facial reactions? See what you're seeing?"

Vail relayed the request to Proschetta and Slater.

"Yeah, I think it can be done," Proschetta said. "Did it once for a detective who was in the hospital and he knew the suspect, and the case, real well. He was able to tell us if he thought the guy was lying. Don't see why we can't do it for your guy in DC." Proschetta nodded at Jenkins, who pulled his phone and made a call.

"We're working on getting video, Wayne. Can you talk me through this?"

"Keep the line open and use an earbud. Put it under your hair, so he can't see it."

Vail turned to Proschetta. "Earbud that'll plug into my phone?"

"I'll see what I can do."

Vail watched Russo lean back in his seat. Dmitri had started waving his hand across his face and torso again, the chains clanking with each movement.

Crossing himself. Compulsively.

Russo shook his head and then turned to the glass and looked at them. At *her*, even though he did not know where she was standing. Vail took it as a signal that he had hit an impasse.

She went to the door and knocked. A moment later, Russo was joining Vail in the observation room.

"I thought I was getting somewhere."

I've gotta tell him something, but I can't tell him that I don't think Dmitri is the killer. It would piss him off big-time.

"There may be a reason why you're having so much difficulty. Looks like Dmitri Harris has ASD."

"ASD? What the heck is that? Some kind of venereal disease?"

"Autism spectrum disorder. He has to be questioned a certain way. Mind if I take a crack?"

Russo chortled. "Be my friggin' guest."

Proschetta entered and handed Vail the earbud.

"I'm on the line with a colleague who's going to help talk me through the questioning." She seated the device and then brushed her hair over the ear. "Say something, Wayne."

"'Something, Wayne.'"

"Very funny. Okay, we're good. You have visual?"

"Just logged in," he said. "Got it."

She walked into the room and sat down opposite Dmitri. She waved Slater away with a nod, and a few seconds later the door clicked closed.

Rudnick: "Okay, Karen, let's start him off with a friendly chat. Anything you can say to calm him, make him feel comfortable?"

"Dmitri, I know you said you don't remember when I visited with my son Jonathan back in 2006. You were really good. Jonathan didn't stop talking about the tour of the crown you gave him. He said you were like a walking Internet. You knew everything."

"You have to climb 354 stairs to reach the crown. There are twenty-five windows there and you can see the Lower Manhattan skyscrapers, Upper New York Bay, and the Hudson River. Just above you, the seven spikes on the crown represent the seven oceans and the seven continents of the world. It was designed that way to show the universal concept of liberty."

"That's what I mean," Vail said with a smile. "You're very good at your job. You know so much about the statue."

Rudnick: "Ask him about someone in his life who's his anchor. I'm assuming that's his mother?"

"You know, Dmitri, your mom's very proud of you. She told us you went to Queens College and studied history."

"History is interesting. So much to know."

Vail noticed he was looking at her, making eye contact—but not really. His gaze moved from her forehead, to her hair, to her mouth.

"A lot to know, yeah. But there are other things you like too. Death is one thing you appear to be fascinated by. Why is that?"

"I like it."

"Death? Why do you like it?"

Dmitri shrugged. "I need to read everything about it. I want to know why."

"Why we die?"

Rudnick: "Did he have a loved one die recently? Or when he was young?"

"Are you interested in death because of your father? Because your father died?"

Rubbing his arm: "Not my fault. Not my fault. Not my fault."

"How come you say that, Dmitri? I noticed you like to say that a lot."

"My dad didn't die. He was killed. That's what he said when he stopped breathing. To me and my mom and my sister. Not my fault. Not my fault. Not my fault."

His errant gaze was driving her nuts: *Look at my eyes!* But he did not. He looked at her, even at her face, but not *at* her. Her nose, her chin, her shoulders. Rudnick had explained this, but it was still unnerving.

Vail nodded slowly. "I understand why you're so fascinated with death."

"I almost died too."

"That's right. I remember Detective Proschetta telling me about that. Would you like to talk to him?"

Dmitri drew back.

Rudnick: "Don't go there, Karen. Try something else. Ask him why he was crossing himself."

"That's okay, Dmitri. It can just be you and me. But tell me something. I noticed before that you were crossing yourself, when Lieutenant Russo was talking with you. Why were you doing that?"

He looked down at the table. "It's what you're supposed to do."

"You mean when you go to church?"

"I go every Sunday with my mother. We went a lot in Astoria." He crossed himself again. "The Lord be in thy heart and on thy lips, that worthily and becomingly thou mayest announce His Gospel: In the name of the Father, and of the Son, and of the Holy Ghost. Amen."

Is the cross an X? Is that the X he's been drawing? Vail thought back to one of her earliest theories of why the offender drew an X on the victim. "Dmitri, is crossing yourself kind of like an X? Is that why you like Xs so much?"

"They represent Christ. Xs are good. Christ is good."

Rudnick: "I assume Xs have relevance to your case. I'm a little blind here, Karen. But ask him about the Xs. Be nonthreatening."

"Why do the Xs represent Christ?"

"It's the Greek letter Chi. It's the first letter of the Greek word that means Christ. That's why Christmas is abbreviated Xmas."

Shit, I was right.

"You like to draw Xs, don't you?"

Dmitri nodded.

"Where do you draw them?"

Dmitri looked around, at the ceiling, the walls. "In my room. On the wall, next to my bed."

"Why?"

"It makes me feel good. Christ is good. He's near my bed when I go to sleep."

"Do you ever draw Xs on other things, other than your wall?"

"In my books, sometimes."

"What about on people?"

"On people?" He thought about that. "You're not supposed to draw on people."

Shit, Russo, are you seeing this? This is not our killer.

Rudnick: "I sense this is important to your case, that the UNSUB wrote on his victims. Try to go a little deeper."

"We found Xs written in black marker on some women, on their necks."

Dmitri tilted his head. "You're not supposed to draw on people."

Rudnick: "Karen, a quick observation here. Dmitri's got a flat tone of voice; he's not using inflections—his voice doesn't go up at the end of a question. It's a mechanical speech lacking the typical rhythmic flow. When he's not repeating back a script, he doesn't use conjunctions, prepositions, or adjectives. For the most part his sentences are simple."

Vail nodded, silently acknowledging Rudnick's comment. "Dmitri. You got your degree in history. Did you learn about the Statue of Liberty in class?"

"The statue's full name is Liberty Enlightening the World. It was a gift from France in 1886. But the statue's head was finished first and got displayed at the World's Fair in Paris eight years earlier."

Rudnick: "Educated guess here, but I bet he really cares for the statue."

"Is that why you became a park ranger? So you could work on the statue? So you could look after her?"

"Yes."

Again, the wandering gaze.

"And you grew up looking at Liberty every morning, every day. From your house, when you lived on Ellis Island." *It had nothing to do with being close to his sanctuary. It had to do with feeling comforted by the statue.*

"I want to stop the birds. They land on the crown. They shit on her. I don't like it."

"Let's talk a little more about death. You had a lot of books in your room. On killers. How come?"

"I like to read about it. I want to know all about it. I don't understand it."

"Do you ever think of hurting someone? Of killing someone, like the books describe?"

"No."

"Why not?"

"Killing is wrong. It's bad. Christ says it's bad. My mom says it's bad. Fedor told me we shouldn't hurt animals."

"Fedor's your mother's friend, right? How do you feel about him?"

"Fedor is good to me. He helps me. He goes to church with us. He and my mom are married."

Rudnick: "Come back to the animals. We both know that's significant in psychopathy. Put your mind at ease."

"Dmitri, you mentioned that Fedor told you not to hurt animals. Did you ever hurt a squirrel on Ellis Island?"

"We shouldn't hurt animals."

"Did you ever kill one?"

"No. We shouldn't hurt animals. Animals are good."

Vail gave Dmitri a big smile and then rose from her chair. "Let's take a break for a few minutes, okay? I'll be right back."

VAIL WALKED IN to find Russo red in the face—and it had nothing to do with the pepper spray.

"What the hell kind of interrogation was that? Please tell me I taught you better than that."

Vail glanced at Proschetta, who was rubbing his forehead, avoiding her gaze. Jenkins had left the room. It was just the three of them.

"He's not our killer, Russo."

Russo laughed. "You mean because he told you so?"

Rudnick spoke in her ear: "Karen, I think this is where I sign off. You need me, call me back. I'll be right here."

"Thanks, Wayne." She pulled out the ear bud and faced Russo. "My colleague at the BSU has studied this stuff for two decades. He knows his shit, which is why I called him."

"And you're telling me that with no knowledge of the facts of this case, never having touched one of these crime scenes, your *expert* knows this guy? After ten minutes he can determine, without a doubt, that he's not the killer we've been after for nineteen *fucking* years?"

"That's not what I'm saying. He told me that *before* I even went into the room, before he listened to a single thing Dmitri said."

Russo looked at her, head tilted in incredulity. "Karen, what the hell's gotten into you?"

"Dmitri's got a disorder that renders him unable to commit premeditated, calculated violence."

"Really. He did pretty well with that pepper spray. And from what you told me, he attacked you on the torch, nearly pushed you over the edge."

"I think he was probably frustrated and angry. I don't think he was trying to push me over. He probably just wanted to stop me from accusing him of killing his sister."

Russo snorted. "Lots of 'I thinks' in there, not to mention a 'probably.' Doesn't sound like you're too sure of what's going on." He turned to Proschetta. "You're awfully friggin' quiet, Protch."

"I know you want this collar," Proschetta said. "And I want it for you too. But—"

"Ah, for chrissakes. You too? This is shrink mumbo jumbo. I mean, Karen—do you know everything there is to know, or do you still see new and different things you've never seen before?"

"Every time I think I've seen it all, something new rolls across my desk."

Russo threw out his hands. "That's what I'm saying."

"But I know of no reputable research, no case studies, no *cases* where anyone on the spectrum has committed premeditated serial murder."

"How accurate is that?" Proschetta asked. "Back when Dmitri was a kid, when he was kidnapped, nobody knew what post-traumatic stress disorder was. They thought he was acting strange because of who-knew-what happened to him when he was abducted. And I gotta tell you, I got him off that track a split second before that train was gonna flatten us. I had nightmares for years. I can't imagine what the kid went through. *Goes* through."

"PTSD presents very differently," Vail said. "You know about the problems our vets have. Depression, suicidal thoughts, flashbacks, insom—"

"I did a tour in Vietnam," Russo said. "I know what the symptoms are."

"Then you know that a lot of PTSD symptoms resolve, given time. The likelihood of persisting PTSD, forty years later, is small."

"'Small' is not the same as impossible."

Vail took a breath. "In PTSD, things directly related to the trauma often trigger a reaction. He'd avoid those things—like visiting the place where it happened, going near train tracks, or confronting his abuser. ASD is a completely different syndrome. Dmitri's affect, the way he talks, his lack of eye contact, his sentence construction, it all says ASD."

Russo waved a hand.

"Tell me something," Vail said. "When you were questioning him, did he make eye contact?"

"No, he looked everywhere *but* in my eyes. And that told me he was straight out lying. I don't have to tell you that eye contact—"

"Is not an accurate cue for us when dealing with ASD. Kids with ASD often avoid eye contact, but in older people, it's different. They have odd ways of looking at you. When you and I look at someone, we subconsciously scan the face, looking for cues about emotion. We look each other in the eye, but also at the corners of the eyes, the forehead, the mouth—we gauge its shape and movement. Are you frowning? Smiling?"

"I know this, Kar—"

"But people with ASD have problems detecting facial expressions and interpreting their meaning. When they scan the face, it's not as focused, not as efficient. They look at the face, but also the hair, the shoulders, the neck. That's what you picked up on. It seemed like avoidance, or deception, because you felt that he wasn't looking at you right. You took it to mean that he was lying. But that's not what was going on."

Proschetta seemed to consider this, but said, "His mother didn't say anything to me about autism or spectrum disorder."

"It's possible he's never been diagnosed. He may just have been written off as 'odd.' Or given his history of trauma, and not knowing any better, maybe that's what they attributed it to."

Russo scoffed. "Come on. He's worked as a ranger for what, twenty-five years? How could someone like that deal with people, coworkers, without them realizing something's not right?"

"They *do* realize something's not right, but they don't know what *it* is. The Park Police officer who helped me get to the torch described Dmitri as odd, a loner. And that makes sense because people on the spectrum have social inadequacies. But to the untrained observer, these people are strange, or creepy, or eccentric, or just plain different. But high functioning people with ASD can go to college and do well. They can hold down important jobs—provided it fits their abilities and interests."

"But that crossing shit," Russo said. "If he did that in front of a bunch of tourists—"

"He's doing that because he's confused about what's happening to him and he's under duress. There's no need to do that on the job. He follows his scripted delivery of facts and information about a topic he loves. He deeply cares for the statue."

Russo faced the glass and rested his hands on the ledge, then took a long, deep breath.

"Russo, I'm telling you. This guy isn't Hades."

"You mean you *think* he isn't Hades." He kept his gaze fixed on Dmitri. "Step back and ask yourself if your ego's guiding your actions here."

"My ego? How can you s—"

"Yeah, your ego. You can't admit you're wrong."

Vail glanced at Proschetta: disbelief. Eyes squinting, she said to the back of Russo's head, "That's not what this is about. It's not about me at all."

Russo sucked in his breath. "Dmitri Harris is the killer. We've got his trophy stash. And I'll bet his prints are all over it. Everything adds up. Plain and simple."

"Everything except—

"None a those psychiatric mumbo jumbo theories count for shit. Real world, that's what counts. I've been doin' this almost forty-two years, I know when I'm lookin' a killer in the eyes."

Vail craned her neck back and stared at the ceiling.

"The commissioner and mayor are going before the cameras in a matter of minutes," Russo said. "They're gonna announce that we've caught the killer who's terrorized the city for over three decades."

"I was you," Vail said, "I'd get down there. Better if they cancel it than look incompetent after the fact. The New York media are vultures, you know that. They'll tear them apart like sharks, then spit them out."

Russo stood there, unmoving.

Vail bit her lip. "Do you remember when we were at the Crinelli crime scene back in '96? You told me I had good instincts, and the day would come when I'd know more than you, and you'd be proud of me. Like a father and his daughter." She stopped to gauge his reaction. In the glass reflection, she thought she could see a glaze over his eyes. "I'm not saying that time's come, Russo. What I am saying is that I'm coming at this from a totally different angle. Maybe the time's right to trust my instincts. I've put it all together and I'm telling you Dmitri is not our offender."

A minute passed. Russo did not move.

"You want me to go down there," Proschetta said, "be the messenger? I'm retiring, man. They can't screw me over. I'll take the blame."

"We're good, Protch." Russo continued staring at Dmitri. "Karen, always a pleasure to see you."

Vail felt her face flushing. "But—"

"But nothing," Russo said. "We don't need your help anymore. I don't need your help anymore."

She turned to Proschetta, whose brow was raised in surprise. He took her gently by the shoulder and led her outside.

Down the narrow hall, in a secluded area of the precinct near the restroom, Proschetta said, "Give him some time."

"You and I both know that once the press conference starts, it's going to be a whole lot more difficult to backtrack on this."

Proschetta folded his arms across his chest. "That's not your problem now, is it?"

"He's not the killer, Protch."

"Let me play devil's advocate. Can you be a hundred percent sure he's not Hades? Aren't psychopaths expert manipulators?"

"Yeah, but—"

"Is it possible Dmitri Harris did an A-1 sales job on you? Put on a masterful act and did a really solid sell?"

Vail thought about that. *Of course it's possible. Did I see what I wanted to see? Did I see what I saw because Rudnick told me that's what I'd be seeing? Was I objective?*

"Maybe he's studied ASD, knows the key behaviors. Shit, if an actor can do it in a movie, why not in a police station, under interrogation? Act a little off at work around his colleagues, so if he ever falls under suspicion, he's got this ASD thing to fall back on. Psychopaths can be coldhearted sons of bitches. Ice water in their blood. Right?"

Vail frowned, shifted her feet. *Is that what happened in there?*

"And maybe, just maybe, there's a case or two somewhere in the world that you and your friend don't know about, where someone with ASD did something he's not supposed to be able to do."

There's one potential case: the Newtown shooter. But is that enough?

"There's nothing more for you to do here, Karen. Go back to your hotel room. The party's in a couple of days. Enjoy New York. Go see a show or two with your boyfriend. Because I'm willing to bet it's been a really long time since you've done that without the stress of a case weighing on your mind."

She forced a half smile. "That's for sure."

He gave her a hug and she headed out of the building, unsure if she was making the right decision. One thing was certain, however: there was no way she was going to stay in New York.

57

"Y ou sure you want to do this?" Robby asked as they stood in line at Kennedy's American Airlines ticket counter. "We came for the party. For your friends Not for you to close the Hades case."

"Yeah, well, that didn't happen, did it?"

Robby took her by the shoulders. "All I'm saying is that you should be there to celebrate with your friends. You're not thinking clearly."

Thinking clearly? I've been pissed and enraged. Confused. Disappointed. Depressed. Who can think clearly?

"Next in line," the service representative said.

Vail turned and headed toward the man, pulling her suitcase behind her.

AFTER STRUGGLING WITH the decision to change their tickets and board the flight home, Vail could not leave New York without closure, one way or another. And she did not like the way she left things with Russo. It ate at her like bile burning her throat, and she did not care for the feeling.

Vail rose from her seat and argued with the flight attendant about opening the door that she had just sealed.

"I'm going to call the captain," the steward said.

"I've got a better idea," Vail said as she held up her BlackBerry. "Why don't you call Douglas Knox? He's listed on my speed dial under 'FBI director.'"

The two flight attendants looked at each other, then the one closest to the inflight phone lifted the handset. "Captain, sorry to bother you. But we've got a situation out here . . . not exactly. An FBI agent."

The pilot emerged from the cockpit seconds later and called company dispatch, which spoke to the air marshal, who in turn called his boss, and—fifteen minutes later, they agreed to open the hatch and let Robby and Vail off with their carry-on luggage.

VAIL WAS QUIET during the cab ride into the city as she tried to clear her mind and focus on the bare components of the case. In a way, having nearly twenty years of history with it was a curse. It made stepping back and looking at it with impartiality and without preconceptions—as she would with new serials that cross her desk—extremely difficult.

She wondered if she needed to hand it off to someone else in the unit, like Art Rooney or even, God forbid, Frank Del Monaco. That would require the NYPD to request that the BAU officially take the case, and she doubted Russo was in the mood to authorize that.

Moreover, she was in Manhattan and they had a suspect in custody. There was no time to take a step back and reassess, even if Russo went along. That may yet need to be done, but for now, she was it.

One of her attempts at taking a fresh look led her to wonder whether Dmitri's mother's friend, Fedor, had been looked at as a suspect. She thought about asking Russo, but instead called Proschetta; he would know if Jenkins and the homicide detective had done a backgrounder on Fedor when Dmitri's sister was killed—and what they found, if anything.

The call went straight to voice mail, so she left a message asking him if Fedor had ever been investigated, or even questioned. She was certain it had been done, but she wanted to be thorough.

"If you think this guy is a viable suspect," Robby said, "you should call Russo."

"Yeah, I know. But I don't want to."

"You can't just show up. You should call him, tell him you're still in town."

"I never told him I was leaving."

"He's known you a really long time, Karen. I'm sure he knew you were pissed and hurt, and that you intended to be on the next flight out."

Am I that transparent?

"You're right." She phoned Russo and immediately regretted it. He was not pleased to hear from her—or so she thought—and although he attempted to put her off, she told him she was trying to step back and take a fresh look at the case.

While he did not argue with her, he was unyielding in his position. "It's the NYPD's responsibility. Go home."

Vail felt Robby's stare on her face. She turned away, facing the side window.

"I—I want to help."

She heard muffled sounds—someone asking Russo a question, and then him giving orders to someone—a driver?

"Karen, I don't have time for this. I'm on the way to a scene. I'll get back to y—"

"Hang on a minute. Another vic? One of ours?"

There was a long silence.

"Russo, is there another vic?"

"Yes."

58

Vail and Robby walked into the Battery Park City high-rise apartment twenty-five minutes later. The unpleasant smell meant the victim had been killed awhile ago—and exactly when could be significant.

Ryan Chandler, who had arrived just prior to them, appeared surprised but pleased to see Vail. Russo, on the other hand, made no attempt to hide his mixed feelings.

Vail was unsure what to make of the look he gave her, but ultimately it did not matter. If the ritual behaviors on this new victim were consistent with the other Hades victims, Russo would have to admit, to himself if to no one else, that he had been wrong in his assessment of Dmitri Harris . . . unless the time of death turned out to predate his arrest.

Unless, of course, he *was* right and she was wrong.

As Vail started her analysis of the crime scene, Robby introduced himself to Russo. Russo seemed to give him a more favorable reception than he would likely give her at the moment. She pushed it aside and focused on what was more immediately important.

As she turned away, Vail saw her former partner, Leslie Johnson, across the room. Johnson had apparently made detective at some point in the intervening years and had drawn this case. Vail had not seen her since Vail bolted for gangs after her two-year probationary period ended back in '97.

After surveying the apartment and the personal effects of the victim—a thirty-four-year-old Greek woman named Katherine Stavros—Vail crossed paths with Johnson and they made small talk about what they had been doing the past seventeen years. They were having too much of a good time poking fun at themselves and their rookie days, so Vail pulled them back to reality. There was nothing amusing behind the reason for their reunion.

Vail excused herself and sought out Finkelstein, who had closed up shop and was ready to turn the body over to Johnson. "Any new surprises, Max?"

"Same old same old. You've seen it before."

"Eight times, to be exact." She looked at the body, at the disfigured eyes and the shard of glass protruding from the neck. How about the X logo?"

"No changes. Except the lowercase letter is—"

"A k."

He looked at Vail over his reading glasses. "Like I said, you've seen it before."

"When was Katherine killed?"

Finkelstein made a note on his clipboard, then clicked his pen shut. "I did a liver stick. Looks like twenty to twenty-four hours ago. Bottom line, the guy you got in custody's good for this."

"You sure?" Russo asked, coming up behind them.

He thinks his collar is still intact. He's relieved.

"Yeah," Finkelstein said, his brow knitting together. "Twenty to twenty-four hours. I wouldn't say it if I wasn't sure. You know that."

Vail figured Russo had said something to Finkelstein about placing a priority on determining the time of death.

Whatever. Just leave it alone, Karen.

Joe Slater arrived at the apartment, saw Vail, and squinted confusion. Off to the side, Chandler brought him up to speed.

"Let's find out if there's been any contact between Dmitri Harris and Katherine Stavros," Russo said. "A meeting, a phone call, a Facebook post, anything that we can use to draw a line between victim and suspect. Nothing's insignificant until we determine it's insignificant."

Does Russo sound desperate? Stop it, Karen.

"When you have a minute," she said to Russo, "I want to ask you about another potential suspect."

His jaw tensed and he glanced up at the ceiling—it was subtle but she caught it.

She added, again, "When you have a minute," and left the room before she said something she would immediately regret. The case aside, Russo was one of the oldest friends she had, almost family, and when all was said and done she wanted to maintain that. Hades had killed a lot of things; she didn't want to add her relationship with Russo to that list.

Vail moved on to a wall where framed photos were prominently displayed. Vail looked them over, and as she had so often seen, they gave a pictorial representation of the victim's life. Several exterior Facebook-style candids showed Katherine in various cities with male and female companions: people having fun, sharing a beer, or standing on a bridge with a city skyline behind them.

Posed studio portraits also adorned the wall, with what appeared to be family members—parents and great-grandparents, perhaps. By their strong features and complexion, Katherine clearly had Greek blood coursing through her arteries.

As she started to turn away, her eye caught something. She leaned in closer, then lifted the frame off the wall, examined it and—

Wait, what the hell?

Her phone rang. She answered it without taking her eyes off the photo, trying to work it through her brain. "Vail."

"Hey Karen," Protch said, "just got your message. Fedor's clean, I knew the guy back in '73 when I caught the original case with Livana's husband. A straight shooter. Nothing suspect. Jenkins said he looked at Fedor back when Cassandra was killed because it wasn't my—"

"Did Fedor have a son? Was there another sibling in this combined family other than Dmitri and Cassandra?"

"Yeah, Niklaus. Couple years older than Dmitri."

"Is their last name Prisco?"

"Yeah, why?"

"Find out where he is," Vail said. "Right now. Niklaus Prisco is Hades. He's a cop with Harbor Patrol."

"A cop?"

"Just find out where he is and call me back." She ran into the bedroom, still holding the picture frame, and showed it to Russo. "Dmitri Harris is not Hades."

"Ah, shit, Karen. Will you just drop th—"

"But I know who is."

Russo went silent. All eyes were on Vail.

"Niklaus Prisco, a Harbor Patrol officer. One of us."

They stood there, either waiting for Vail to elaborate, or unsure of what to make of that claim.

"What makes you think this guy's our perp?" Russo finally asked.

Vail held up the frame and stabbed at the picture of Katherine Stavros. "The earring in this photo. I found one just like it on the boat, when Harbor Patrol took us over to Ellis Island."

Russo stepped closer to look at the picture. "You sure?"

"It's a pretty distinctive earring."

"But so what?" Russo asked. "Even if it's the same earring, I mean, it's an NYPD boat. What's it got to do with Prisco? Anyone could've lost it."

"No, not anyone," Johnson said. "First, it's gotta be a woman. And female cops don't wear long dangly earrings like that unless they're undercover."

"Put it together, Russo." Vail set the frame down. "We got a killer who lived on Ellis Island, who kept a photo album, a scrapbook, of his kills hidden under floorboards."

"Yeah, *Dmitri's* scrapbook."

"No, those *other* books are his. The hardcovers and paperbacks. That's all we know. He admitted to that. One thing my BSU colleague told me is that high functioning people with ASD tend to fixate on things, learn all they can on that topic, to the extreme. Dmitri's fascinated with death and killers because of what he experienced as a youth. His father's brutal beating by Crinelli and his crew. Or his kidnapping and near-death experience on the train tracks. That makes sense.

"But this album, this scrapbook, it's got a photo of his sister, taken by the offender right after he killed her. Every time we brought it up and showed it to Dmitri, it upset him. A lot. Believe me, I saw the rage it stirred in him when he backed me up against the railing on the torch."

"So if it's not his," Chandler said, "why do you assume it belongs to this Niklaus Prisco?"

"Niklaus is Dmitri's stepbrother." She shook her head. "Two families came together, out of necessity, friendship. They leaned on each other, drew strength from each other. In essence, they became one family unit. Niklaus, if he is a psychopath, if he is our killer, he would've created this scrapbook of photos and news clippings as a trophy collection, pieces of his conquests. And he kept it in Dmitri's bedroom in the house they lived in on Ellis Island in case we started to connect the dots. He was basically framing his brother, making sure things pointed to Dmitri. Psychopaths don't form bonds like you and me. People are there to be manipulated, used. And Dmitri was a perfect target.

"But there was a flaw in his plan. There's no way Niklaus could know that Dmitri had a disorder that'd make him unlikely to commit murder, something that'd make it almost impossible for him to commit premeditated serial murder. And since we know Hades can't be Dmitri"—she glanced at Russo—"then the needle points right back at Niklaus. Because once you eliminate Dmitri, no one else has the connections to the victims that Niklaus has. Not even Victor Danzig."

"The Xs on the walls in Dmitri's bedroom," Russo said.

"What Xs?" Slater asked.

"This morning at Ellis Island we found all these Xs drawn in pencil on the wall next to Dmitri's old bed."

"Dmitri likes to draw Xs because to him they represent Christ," Vail said. "It's another one of those fixation-type ASD behaviors. Niklaus knew Dmitri was enamored with Xs, so he used it as a logo that he drew on each of his vics. He used it, like so many serial killers do, to claim his vics, to take credit for them. Like a painter signing his work. But he chose the X because it'd point back to Dmitri. The letters he used inside the Xs were E, I, and D. They correspond to Ellis Island and Dmitri. Again, he chose those letters so that if anyone found the lair, they'd put it together just like we did and think the killer's Dmitri."

"And you're resting this entire theory on an earring?" Russo asked.

"Chandler," Vail said, "have you catalogued a jewelry box?"

"Not yet."

"I saw one," Johnson said. "In the walk-in closet." She led Vail inside, turned on the light, and opened the sizable rosewood case.

They ignored the gold earrings and dug through the sterling silver ones and found a match. "This is it," Vail said, holding it up and showing it to Johnson. They compared it to the photo. "Got it," Vail yelled to the others.

"There's only one in here," Johnson said, sifting and sorting the various pieces.

"Exactly. The matching earring—its pair, which is missing—was the one I found on the Harbor Patrol boat."

"What happened to it?" Finkelstein asked.

"When I saw it, I picked it up and showed it to Prisco. He said it belonged to a night shift officer and told me to bring it by the Harbor office when I got back."

"But we didn't go back," Russo said.

"Right. I asked if he could do it because we had too much going on. Prisco should've been shitting bricks that he'd dropped his trophy from his latest kill and that it was in the hands of an FBI agent. He could've been discovered. Most perps would've broken out into a cold sweat. But he was so damn cool about it."

"If you're right," Johnson said, "and he's a psychopath, doesn't that fit?"

"Exactly." Before she could elaborate, Vail's phone rang. "Talk to me, Protch."

"Prisco's working the evening shift, but he's out on patrol."

"Call ESU. Have them meet us at Battery Park."

59

Battery Park was only a few blocks away, but by the time they reached the street level of Katherine Stavros's high-rise, ESU had already deployed near the park's Harbor Patrol station.

Arriving moments later was an NYPD mobile command unit, ESS-1, formally known as the Emergency Services Squad for Lower Manhattan. A white truck the size of a city bus packed with the latest communications and computing technology, it enabled officers in the field to conduct a large-scale operation on the fly.

As part of the CRV, or critical response vehicle, a dozen patrol sectors swarmed the scene, lights and siren off, to avoid a highly visible, candy-colored presence against the night sky. The last thing they wanted was for Officer Niklaus Prisco to suspect something was wrong as he navigated his boat back to the dock.

Vail and Russo waited behind an unmarked police sedan, night vision binoculars pressed against their faces as they peered out into the dark Hudson River and Upper New York Bay.

"You sure Robby doesn't mind waiting in the car?" Russo asked.

"He had some calls to make. And with all the firepower we've got, he figured he'd just be in the way, especially with a bum arm."

Vail moved the binoculars an inch away from her face. "What about an air unit?"

"Not necessary. His boat's got GPS. And we don't want him to know he's a person of interest."

Person of interest? He's a goddamn killer.

Vail stepped onto the blue stairs below the side door of the mobile command truck. She poked her head into the interior and found the ESU lieutenant, who was talking with an inspector.

"Have we got a GPS lock on Prisco's boat?"

The man glanced at one of the large wall-mounted LCD screens. "Stationary at Ellis Island."

"Of course." She turned to Russo and relayed the position.

"Part of his normal patrol?" Russo asked.

"Maybe. But I bet he's checking to see what we took, if we found his stash."

Vail poked her head back into the truck. "Where exactly is the boat stopped? New Jersey side at the dock in the back of Island 1, or near the front of Island 3, by the hospital buildings?"

"Island 3," the lieutenant said.

"There's a bridge off Island 1 that leads into New Jersey."

"Got it covered. We've coordinated with Jersey state police. They're sitting at the other end, prepared to stop any vehicle that crosses over from Ellis."

"Perfect." She thanked the lieutenant, then rejoined Russo.

He was silent for a long moment. Then, while still peering through his binoculars, he said, "That was good work. Back at the apartment. The earring."

"Nothing good about it but luck."

"You gonna argue with me again?"

Vail chuckled. "I think we've done enough of that today."

"You know, if you are right about Harris, and it looks like you are, I owe you an apology and—"

"Let's first see if I'm right. If Prisco behaves like he's guilty, we'll pretty much have our answer. But we're not there yet. And breaking him, if it comes to that, won't be easy."

"You'll be in the room with me. We'll tackle him together."

Vail smiled. It felt great to be back in his good graces. As she looked out into the restless waters of New York harbor, she realized there weren't many people whose validation she needed.

"I'VE BEEN THINKING about some of the stuff that Agent Safarik told me back in '06."

Russo pulled his eyes away from the lenses and glanced at Vail. "About what?"

"Motive. About why Prisco does what he does to these women. When I put it together with the things Prisco's done with his recent victims, it gives me a better understanding of things."

"Such as?"

Vail thought for a moment. "Remember when we were at the Monica Glavan crime scene a few years ago? I told you about MO and ritual."

"All I remember is that MO changes and ritual doesn't."

"Right. Serial killers exhibit two primary behavioral manifestations—MO and ritual, which is need-driven behavior. Since MO is all about successfully committing the crime and killing their victim, they change it to meet their needs. But an offender's ritual never changes, no matter how many years pass. Ritual is deeply rooted psychologically or emotionally.

"These ritual behaviors—like cutting off a body part, writing on the vic, posing the body, shoving things into an orifice—they come from some vulnerable or fragile moment in their lives when there was a fusion of violence, sexual arousal, and a particular act—or the use of a particular object. They may not understand why they do these things to the vics; they just know they like doing them. They *need* to do them. Ed Gein dug up graves and removed body parts from women that he made into wearable items, like a belt made of nipples and vulvas."

"Jesus Christ."

"It's hard for us to understand that kind of pathology, but the need is so deeply embedded that it manifests in some way in all their crime scenes."

"You mentioned sexual arousal," Russo said. "You think Prisco was sexually abused?"

"No. But an offender can partake in sexual activity that serves nonsexual needs or he can engage in nonsexual activity that serves sexual needs. Prisco's behaviors appear to be driven by the nonsexual activities of stabbing the vic and cutting her eyes. It's not a sexual act, but in my experience, he's sexually aroused by doing it."

"I take it that rape would be an example of a sexual act that serves nonsexual purposes."

"Exactly. Even though it's a sexual act, the offender rarely does it for sexual gratification. He does it to exert power, control, and dominance." Vail moved her binoculars left and began scanning her grid pattern again. "But I'm now certain that Prisco's motive is revenge. His need for it, and the way he gets it—slicing the eyes, stabbing the neck, posing the body—it all got fused together with some act of violence or betrayal when he was a kid. He blames all his problems—whatever those may be—on the woman who 'caused' them. In his case, a Greek woman."

"So he thinks Greek women are responsible for his troubles?"

"Yes. And this is his way of getting back at them. Based on his postmortem ritual behaviors, it's obvious he considers them to be whores. Not only is he out to make them pay for their transgressions, but he poses their bodies and hands in sexually provocative ways to show others what he thinks of them."

Russo glanced at her again. "Since we haven't been able to dig up a connection between any of these victims—other than ethnicity—it looks like he doesn't care who he kills so long as she's Greek."

"He's not angry at the victim as a person. She's just a representation of the woman he hates. His vics are surrogates, substitutes. He's targeting a class of people, not individuals."

"With the exception of Crinelli. And we know the deal with that: pure, personal revenge."

As Vail peered into the darkness, her peripheral vision caught a blur of movement. "I see something. A boat—I think it's him."

Russo pulled his face away from the binoculars. "Where?"

"We have a fix on Officer Prisco's boat," the ESU lieutenant said across the radio. "His course is directly at us, as expected. Looking good. Hold steady."

Vail, face against her night vision glasses, kept her eyes riveted to the boat with its minimal light signature as it steered toward them. "My heart's racing."

"Mine too."

"At your age, can it take the pounding?"

"Go to hell."

She wanted to laugh but did not want to risk losing the boat on the highly magnified view.

"One thousand yards," the lieutenant's voice blurted over the two-way. "Check in."

"Team Alpha ready."

"Beta ready."

"Charlie. Ready."

"Wait—" Vail said. "What the hell? He's veering off. He's veering off!"

"All units, suspect has made us, he changed course, swung left toward the Hudson."

"Shit on rye," Russo said.

"Must've been monitoring the radio."

He pulled the glasses away from his face. "Why would he think to do that?"

"Because his scrapbook's gone. He knows we took it. And maybe—who knows—maybe that earring spooked him more than I thought. He was being extra cautious and he started scanning the encrypted tactical channels."

"Still got him on GPS," Russo said. He leaned toward the command center and looked in. "We do have him on GPS, right?"

"Affirm."

"He may be monitoring the radio," Russo said.

"Not only that, he's probably figured out we're tracking him."

"And he knows all about the Domain Awareness System. Which means he's going to try to defeat it."

"Here we go," the ESU lieutenant said. "Boat's stopped near Watts Street." He turned toward his men. "Pack it up. We're moving!"

Vail started backing away. "C'mon."

"Where we going?" Russo asked.

"You heard the man," she said as she began running toward their sedan. "Watts Street."

60

They reached Russo's car and pulled open the doors simultaneously. Robby was in the act of dialing but quickly hung up. "This doesn't look good."

"Drive," Vail said. "West Side Highway."

"Yeah, can you be a little more specific? Don't know my way around."

Russo, in the front passenger seat, directed Robby and seconds later they were headed north.

"What's this domain awareness thing you mentioned?" Vail asked.

"Something the department developed with Microsoft. Hardware and software. The software's what makes it unique. The engineers built it based on months of meetings with us. Detectives and investigators. We told them the kind of stuff we needed to know and when, and they devised this surveillance system of real-time video cameras, license plate readers, radiation sensors, and nuclear detectors.

"The sensors are mounted on helicopters, boats, trucks, light posts— even officers' duty belts. They're all regularly taking air samples, giving us a pretty good reading on the state of things all over the city."

"Awesome system," Robby said.

"We're selling it to other cities, so you'll probably come across it on your DEA ops."

"But," Vail said, "if someone calls 911 and reports a suspicious package on Fifth Avenue, what does it actually do for you?"

"We can pull up that package at the command center in seconds, look at it from different angles, remotely sniff it for bombs or chemical threats, and get the correct unit over there to deal with it ASAP."

"And Prisco?"

"If someone sees him, we can locate him on the network, follow him."

"But he knows about this system," Robby said, navigating around a pothole. "He's gonna do his best to hide from it."

"We're starting to roll out facial recognition. Once we lock on his face, the system would track him automatically. And if we told the system we're looking for him, it'd scan faces and alert us when it finds him."

"But it's not quite ready?" Vail asked.

"No."

"And if he goes underground, or into a building—"

"Even without facial rec, we've got cameras all over the place, thousands of them, public, private, and ours—every single one is tied into DAS. I'm not saying it's impossible to hide, but we've got eyes on a lot of the city. It'd be tough to escape. "

Robby reached Watts Street. "We're here. Now what?"

"Pull over. We're unmarked, so we might see him before he sees us."

Russo called up a photo of Prisco on his phone and showed it to Robby.

As Vail peered out the window, she asked, "You said some officers have those radiation sensors on their duty belts?"

"It gives us a mobile presence throughout the city, 24/7."

"What about Harbor Patrol?"

"We've got a TRACS boat—and you're gonna want to know what that stands for. Uh, tactical radiological acquisition and characterization system, I think. But it's possible Harbor's officers have sensors on their belts too. Cover a lot more ground that way. So to speak. Let me make a call. The Lower Manhattan Security Initiative command center."

Russo got Chief Terrence Bradley on the line and after asking him the question, Bradley reported back a few moments later with the answer. Russo put him on speaker.

"Affirm, Officer Prisco is one of the officers outfitted with a radiological sensor."

"Chief, this is Karen Vail, FBI. Is there any way we can tap into that sensor, use it like a GPS?"

"There's no GPS device in it, so that'd be no."

"Who's your best tech guy there?"

"You don't believe me?"

Robby turned around and gave Vail a look. It said, "Careful, Karen."

"Of course I believe you, chief. But if you can connect me with him or her, I can toss some ideas out. They may all get shot down, but it can't hurt, can it?"

"Hold on."

A minute later, a man picked up the call. "This is Isamu John—"

"Isamu, Karen Vail, FBI. Chief Bradley was just telling us there's no GPS signal we can track on Officer Prisco's belt sensor."

"That's right."

"Is there *any* signal that we can latch onto to track him?"

"None I'm aware of."

"All right, thanks. Do me a favor and text your phone number to this cell in case I have other questions."

"On its way."

Russo disconnected the call.

"What are you thinking?" Robby asked.

Vail winked at him while she dialed her BlackBerry. Three rings later, just as she feared it would bounce to voice mail, it was answered by FBI Supervisory Special Agent Aaron Uziel.

His voice was drowned out by boisterous laughter in the background. "Uzi."

She curled a bit of red hair behind her ear. "Uzi, it's Karen." She put the call on speaker.

"Karen! Caught me at a good time. We're in an OPSIG meeting— Director Knox, Secretary McNamara, and about ten other intelligence chiefs and generals. So much brass the shine is blinding. We just broke for fifteen. Oh—and Hector's here."

"Hey," DeSantos's voice boomed in the background, "how's my London bedmate doing?"

Robby's head whipped around. "*What* was that?"

Vail cleared her throat but didn't answer.

"Uh-oh," Uzi said. "Are we on speaker?"

"Tell Hector I owe him a kick in the bollocks. He'll know what I mean."

"You can tell him yourself. You're gonna get pulled into this mission soon enough."

"Well, until that happens, I'm chasing serial killers and I'm hot on the trail of one I've been after for nineteen years." She explained the situation with Prisco when he stopped her.

"The DAS. Domain Awareness System."

"How'd you know?"

"Karen, should I be insulted? High-tech gadgetry like that sweet system, deployed in a major city, and you think I don't know about it? Not to mention, I'm head of the Joint Terrorism Task Force in DC. Remember?"

How could I forget? "Guess I took a stupid pill this morning. So is there a way to hack into that sensor and turn it into a GPS device?"

"Nice thought, Karen. For a second, you actually sounded like you knew what you're talking about. But you don't. If it doesn't have a GPS receiver, you can't get a GPS position."

"That's what the DAS techie said."

"And you didn't believe him?"

"I thought that if there was someone who could figure something out, it'd be you."

"And you thought right. That device is an expensive detector, so it's got RFID built in for asset tracking—that's radio frequency identification. RFID is a wireless way of using radio-frequency electromagnetic fields to transfer data. It's totally passive until a specific radio frequency hits it. If you're close enough, your tech could amp up a unit and listen for a response. There may be a number of RFID devices that could respond, but if I remember right, the unit uses a proprietary frequency protocol. Problem is, you'll have to filter an ocean of responses looking for the correct one."

"But of course you have a solution."

"Of course. They can use an algorithm to filter out all other responses and then ping the target RFID repeatedly and triangulate based on the strength-of-response signal. Sort of like sonar. No network, no hacking, no Wi-Fi nets, no special doodads, just the good guys upgrading their detectors and using a filtering algorithm to leverage a feature already built into the sensor."

"Honestly, I'm not sure—"

"That's okay, you don't have to understand. Point is, I should be able to make it so that you can triangulate a location if the sensor's within range. It may not be pinpoint accurate—"

"Uzi, I don't care. Just get us the asshole's position."

"Will do. And?"

"And what?" She waited, then said, "Oh. You're awesome, Uzi. Not sure what I'd do without you."

"You *know* it. So who should I contact at the command center?"

61

ail gave Uzi the contact info for Isamu and waited for a lead. It came nineteen minutes later.

"We've got a double hit," Uzi said. "You can log into the system on your phone and follow along with me." He gave her instructions and talked while she entered the information. "Prisco came out of the subway station on Christopher Street and got on a bus at Greenwich and West 10th. Based on that bus's route, he's headed north."

"Greenwich and West 10th," she said to Robby.

He accelerated hard, according to Russo's directions.

"Okay, I'm logged in."

"I've tagged his signal with a yellow dot. See it?"

"Got it."

"Don't freak out when it winks out—'cause it will. Remember, we're triangulating his position. Assuming he stays in range, I'll get you something."

"Coming up on 10th," Robby said.

Russo squinted ahead at the dimly lit landscape. "Anything?"

"Kind of hard," Vail said. "I'm watching the signal on my phone and trying to keep an eye on the street at the same time." She glanced down. "Looks like he just passed 12th."

"We're right behind him, couple blocks away."

"Lost him," Vail said.

Uzi made some noise—tapping keys. "Give me a sec. You know you're making me miss my meeting. Knox is not happy. Neither is Earl Tasset," he said, referring to the CIA director.

"Thought you didn't like Tasset."

"I don't. I didn't say I cared, I just said he wasn't happy. Okay, I'm triangulating. Looks like he's on Gansevoort Street. Not sure I pronounced that right."

"You got it right," Russo said. "Meatpacking district. Whoa. Meatpacking district's where Fedor Prisco worked."

Vail lifted her brow. "Maybe that means something. Maybe not. What else is there?"

"Chelsea, the convention center, and the High Line."

"The High Line," Robby said. "I read about that place. The old elevated railroad line that they turned into an above-ground park."

Vail glanced at her BlackBerry. "That's my bet."

Russo leaned forward in his seat. "Why do you think he'd go up there?"

"Fewer cameras."

Russo nodded. "And dark."

"Harder to track too." Vail consulted her phone again. "Remember, he doesn't know we've repurposed that sensor he's wearing. More importantly, he doesn't know Aaron Uziel's on the case."

"Oh," Uzi said through the speaker. "The pressure!"

"Take us there," Russo said.

Vail pulled up a map of the High Line. "Drop me at the entrance, on Gansevoort, at Washington. And then . . . Robby, get over to the end, at—" she scrolled on her BlackBerry—"West 30th."

"We're coming up on Gansevoort," Robby said as the tires rumbled on the cobblestone streetscape.

"Uzi, I'm not getting anything on his position. You?"

"He's winking in and out, probably right on the edge of our range. If we don't completely lose him, I'll do my best to keep you up-to-date. Last fix I got is that he was right where you are, at that intersection."

Vail scrolled more on her screen. "The park's like a mile and a half long. Robby, if we run toward each other we can box him in."

"Except there are a few stairway exits along the way," Russo said.

"Then let's increase our odds in case he stays off the grid. After Robby gets off at West 30th, go to 23rd. You'll be halfway between us. Get in the shadows and wait for one of us—or Prisco—to come your way."

"We're here." Robby stopped the car and Vail got out.

She made her way up the long metal staircase at the end of the steel-girdered elevated platform, where foliage flowed over the edge.

"Uzi, you still with me?" she asked as she ran up the three levels of steps.

"Here."

"Can you multitask and ask Isamu at the command center to get as many undercovers over to our area as they can spare? We need some support, but if Prisco sees a bunch of unis, he'll freak. And he's armed."

"On it."

Vail hit the top level and entered the park. Before her was a walkway maybe thirty feet wide with meticulously pruned trees, bushes, and flowers planted in a center median and along its periphery. It was lit strategically with knee-high downlight fixtures every several feet.

This is gorgeous. Why do I always find these places when I'm hot on the trail of a serial killer?

Ahead was a flat-faced ten-story building, constructed over the High Line. *Very cool. But finding Prisco on this thing is gonna be more difficult than I thought.* The center median obscured her view of the other side of the pathway, the lighting was dramatic but poor for making out faces, and there weren't many people out this time of night. That made it easier for her to pick Prisco out—but also easier for him to be aware of her presence. And he knew what she looked like.

She ducked down and tried to scan the pathway on the other side of the median, peeking through the thinly pruned tree branches.

As she jogged along the cement path and passed beneath the building, things started to fall into place: Prisco had undoubtedly dropped that letter off at her house a dozen years ago, so he had likely been following her career, keeping tabs on her to some extent.

More importantly, as a cop, he had access to precincts, records, impounds, and property rooms. The book taken from Detective Berger's mailbox before she was officially assigned the case was thus an easy haul for him: Prisco could have just walked into the precinct and snagged it without anyone questioning it. And the missing DD-5, stolen from the file by Victor Danzig, was probably engineered by Prisco behind the scenes. It was likely Prisco who paid the law firm to have Danzig go into Property and lift the DD-5. Clean and neat: there'd be no trail back to him.

Anyone questioning it would have gone after Danzig, just as we did. And if we had found him, it would've done us no good, because Danzig had no clue about Prisco's involvement.

Vail craned her neck and peered into the darkness: a man was approaching, jogging by. Her right hand covertly reached for her Glock . . . and he passed, too tall and thirty pounds heavier.

Her mind drifted back to the analysis of Prisco's actions. With things coming together, she wanted to maintain the freeform train of thought before she lost it.

Why would he bother to take the hardcover from Property only to put it back in his sanctuary, if the sanctuary was partially being curated as a failsafe to implicate Dmitri? There had to be something inside the book that could implicate him.

There could've been forensics on it from a prior crime scene. Or he'd made notes inside and if it was found, it'd ruin his cover story of Dmitri being the offender. His handwriting would be matched back to him.

Instead, he bought another used copy and planted that one beneath the floorboards. But Berger's DD-5 had included a description of "old and worn," whereas the one she and Russo had found on Ellis Island was newer. If Berger had taken the usual route of most detectives, and listed it on his report as merely "a book," without noting its condition and title—or if Vail had not read carefully, she never would have drawn the line between the dots.

Perhaps when Prisco saw the DD-5 and realized the detail Berger had included in his description, he went out and bought another one. Cheap insurance—especially considering he had no way of knowing that Vail had made a copy of the file before the original report was removed.

Prisco was one calculating son of a bitch.

And that's probably why he's survived for thirty-four years right under the nose of one of the most elite police forces in the world.

Vail hit redial and Uzi answered immediately. "Anything? I can't watch my phone and search the park at the same time."

"Still dark. As soon as I get a hit, I'll call you."

"Fine. Later." She hung up and jogged on, beneath another high-rise, and cursed—because the pathway widened and there was more foliage to hide behind.

The night was warm and humid—a typical July day in the city—and she had to keep rubbing her sweaty palm on her pants to maintain a decent grip on her phone.

A handful of people were at the railing on the other side, looking out at the Hudson. Others were seated on wood-slatted chairs sipping wine and enjoying the view.

Vail crossed to the other side, closer to the river, and saw railroad tracks embedded in the aggregate concrete; she didn't know if they were the originals, but the nod to the park's history was a nice touch. She approached another building and stopped; there seemed to be a stairway leading down to street level.

She consulted the map on her phone. *Probably West 15th.* She looked out over the railing at the city nightscape below. *Maybe this was a stupid idea. Prisco could've gotten off at any of these stairs—if he was even up here at all.*

She jogged past a bunch of people lounging on what looked like a sundeck—wood chaise-type benches, in shorts with iPods in their laps and wires dangling from their ears. A group of others waded barefoot in a shallow pool of water that ran parallel to the path.

Coming up on her right, in a well-lit area of the park, a People's Pops vendor was selling yellow plum blueberry ices that looked refreshing—and given the heat, enticing. But she ran by it.

Two minutes later, having passed a town square-type amphitheater sitting area with large windows that looked out over the avenue below, she was back in a poorly illuminated stretch of the High Line.

Fifty yards on, she saw a woman bent over a body lying on the concrete. A phone was pressed against her cheek and she was rubbernecking her head in all directions.

"What happened?" Vail yelled as she approached.

"I think he was attacked. He collapsed, started convulsing."

As Vail arrived, she saw it was Russo. And he was having some kind of epileptic seizure. *Crap.*

She called Uzi.

"Still noth—"

"Have Isamu dispatch an ambulance to the High Line—" She turned to the woman. "Where are we?"

"Twentieth St—"

"West 20th Street."

Wait a minute. It's not a seizure.

Russo moaned and stopped twitching.

"Cancel the bus," Vail told Uzi as she patted down Russo's body. "You were Tasered." She held up the hooks that had been clinging to his shirt.

"Bastard." Russo sat up. "I drew down and ID'd myself, told him not to move, but it was dark and I didn't see the Taser until—"

"Uzi, Prisco was here less than a minute ago."

"Got a hit," Uzi said. "West 20th approaching Seventh Avenue."

She helped Russo up. "You okay?"

"Fine. But when it hit me, I lost all control over my body. My Glock..." He started spreading the leaves of the bushes in the nearby planter. "You see it?"

Vail separated the reeds with her free hand. "Assuming nobody took it, it's gotta be here."

"I can't leave without it."

And in the meantime, Prisco is getting away.

"Just turned left," Uzi said, "heading up 6th."

"Got it," Russo said, lifting it out of the brush.

Vail turned toward the brightly illuminated Empire State Building in the distance. "Can Isamu use the DAS to pull him up on camera?"

"Texting him now."

Robby came jogging up behind them. "See him?"

"Yeah, he Tasered me," Russo said.

"Consider yourself lucky," Robby said, sucking in oxygen. "He could've killed you."

Russo narrowed his eyes. "He's the lucky one. I was a split second from pulling the trigger, putting us all out of our misery."

"He's moving too fast," Uzi said. "Gotta be in a car. A taxi?"

Shit. That would not be good.

"Lost him again," Uzi said. "Possible he went down into the subway at 23rd."

Robby and Vail locked eyes—and a second later, they were headed down the stairs, Russo close behind.

62

Vail flagged down a cab and Robby stood in front of the vehicle while Russo commandeered it. The Iraqi driver complained loudly, but Russo gave him a response that would've made any New Yorker proud: "Call your fuckin' congressman."

"No lights, no siren," Russo said as he steered toward their suspect's last known location. "Forgot how long it takes to get around this city, even at night."

Robby, in the front passenger seat, pushed open the Plexiglas divider as far as it would go.

"Uzi," Vail said, putting him on speaker. "Talk to me."

"Not getting any pings. But Isamu's patched me through and given me an eye into their network. I can see what their cameras see, but I can't control anything. I've got input, no output."

"There's probably a joke in there somewhere."

"Got something. Still heading north on 6th, at 33rd. And now 35th. He's either in a cab or on the subway. Switching to visual . . . but I'm not seeing anything on street cameras. No taxis moving in that direction. Wait, got one but it's well behind his location. Gotta be the subway."

"And that's a problem," Russo said.

"Why?" Vail asked. "We can use the station's platform cameras. For that matter, what about the cameras in the cars?"

"That's the problem. Not all stations have cameras. And there aren't any cameras in the cars."

"You're shitting me."

"Makes too much sense. That's why they're not there."

Sarcasm. Ah, New York.

Vail consulted her phone and pulled up the subway map. "Okay, let's parallel him, get us to 6th and West 36th, then keep heading north/northeast. Looks like he's on the B-D-F-M line. If he doesn't get off or change trains, he could end up in Queens, Brooklyn, or upper Manhattan."

"So he could really go anywhere," Robby said, "if we lose him."

"Pretty much. Unless we catch his image on a camera. And for that, we have to get lucky as far as which station he's in. Or hope he gets off."

Russo accelerated, then turned right on 30th. "Be at 6th and West 36th in a minute." He hit a yellow light, but leaned on the horn and the accelerator and blew through the intersection.

"Any unmarked cars in the area?" Robby asked.

"Already en route," Uzi said. "Whoa, wait a minute. His signal's gone stationary at 6th and 50th."

"Fiftieth?" Russo cursed, then accelerated past 55 miles per hour. "That's the Rockefeller Center station. Gotta have eyes in there." He pulled out his phone and handed it to Robby. "Press star-9 and put it on speaker. When it was answered, he said, "Central, this is Russo in a civilian car. Hades suspect Niklaus Prisco at the Rockefeller Center subway station, possibly on the train. Get Transit unis over there. Suspect is a police officer, armed, and extremely dangerous."

"And he's got a radio," Vail said.

"Right," Russo said. "Central, suspect has a police radio. Assume he's listening in. Get as many unis into the stations along that route as you can. We need him to see the cops and get off so we can get eyes on him."

"What about stopping trains and searching them?" Vail asked.

"And contact MTA," Russo yelled toward the phone. "Shut down all trains temporarily on the B-D-F-M line. Search the cars."

"Roger that," Central replied, then disconnected the call.

"Not gonna help," Robby said, "is it? I can't imagine things moving that fast in New York City."

"Probably not, not as fast as we need it to."

"He's on the move again," Uzi said. "Just hung a right and appears to be—yup, he's gotta be underground because he's cutting through what would be a body of water in Central Park. Looks like he's following the path of the F train."

"Awesome," Vail said. "Still on the subway, heading into Queens." She pulled up her contacts and started dialing. A moment later, Joe Slater answered. "Where are you?"

"Niklaus Prisco's house in Astoria. Jenkins and Johnson are with me. We're looking through his stuff, trying to find something that might give us some friggin' idea where he's headed."

"Nothing, right?"

"Nothing. Place looks completely normal."

"You probably won't find anything. He's smart and he's been doing this—successfully—for a long time. He's not going to make any stupid mistakes. And keeping shit in your house that could indicate you're a serial killer is not the kind of thing that makes you stay in the game very long."

"So, what, we're wasting our time?"

"Keep at it," Vail said. "It's always possible you'll find something he didn't think of. It'll be subtle. Call me back if you find anything, even if you're not sure. We're in pursuit. He's headed your way—or at least toward Queens."

Vail hung up and immediately considered what she had just said. He's headed toward Queens. *Why? He'd know we'd be combing his house, so he's not going there. And we already found his lair. Or did we? A lair is a place of residence, and while he lived on Ellis Island a long time, he moved thirty years ago.*

She called Slater back. "Joe—humor me. See if there are any public records of Prisco owning other property in Queens. Or anywhere else in New York State." He said he would keep her apprised and after signing off, she explained her thought process to Russo and Robby.

"You think he's got another place where he stashes his trophies." Robby turned around and caught Vail's look through the Plexiglas. "What? You taught me stuff before I got into the DEA. I was paying attention."

"Lost his signal," Uzi said. "Checking cameras."

"What if," Vail said, "the stuff we found on Ellis Island was there for us to find. Think about it. All of it was designed to point us to his stepbrother. There were photos of each victim, taken at the point of death. But otherwise, very little. What if he's got some other place where he stores his keepsakes? That could be where he's headed."

"If that's true," Russo said, "then there's no way that property's in his name."

"I agree. It's worth checking out, but he's too smart for that. So then where does he keep his stuff?"

"Coming up on 53rd," Russo said. "But I'm not gonna be able to follow the train unless I get on the Queensboro Bridge. So we gotta be damn sure he's crossing into Queens."

"Found him," Uzi said. His voice was even, measured. "No signal but I got a facial recognition hit."

"We haven't got facial recognition online in that part of the city," Russo said.

"Using my own algorithms. Didn't think you'd mind."

Of course. Vail grinned. "Where is he?"

"Got him coming out of the Lexington Avenue subway station, headed south."

Russo accelerated hard, driving them all back into their seats. "Uzi, tell Isamu to get all units—"

"Already texted him."

Vail pushed herself forward and grabbed the seat to steady herself. The cab's worn shocks were bottoming out on the potholes and uneven asphalt patches, tossing the three of them from side to side and causing Robby to strike his head on the roof.

"Uzi, can you still see him?"

"Climbing the stairs to the Roosevelt Island tram."

"Roosevelt Island?" *What the hell?* "Call MTA, shut down the power after he's on board, when his car is halfway along the cable."

"Fuckin' A." Russo slapped the steering wheel. "We got you, you son of a bitch!"

63

But, of course, they did not. Prisco timed it perfectly or he got lucky, because the tram was waiting when he arrived and he immediately boarded.

That, however, played right into their plans. That was not the problem.

The problem was that the tram, a three quarter mile span that traveled nearly 20 miles per hour at a height of 250 feet above the East River, was not run by the Metropolitan Transportation Authority. It was owned by the State of New York and operated by a private company on behalf of another corporation, which was a state public benefit entity.

In other words, bureaucracy. Getting something done quickly because of an urgent police matter took time—more than it should have. The tram was an underappreciated mode of transport in a metropolis already crisscrossed with mass transit. Its sole function was to go back and forth to the sparsely populated—by city standards—Roosevelt Island. It was not considered a high-value target, and as such it had escaped emergency planning from a law enforcement perspective.

It should have been a simple task to cut power to the span. But it was past midnight and the brass at One Police Plaza was trying to reach those who could authorize, and then implement, a full shutdown. The power had gone off only twice, several years ago, during an outage. Renovations were made, focusing on providing water and blankets to commuters trapped in-

side the car and on ensuring uninterrupted electricity with diesel backup—
the opposite of what they were now trying to achieve.

"I had a shot of him entering the tram," Uzi said, "But he put something
over the camera. Doesn't matter, I've got him triangulated, and he's tracking
over the East River. Should be hitting the other side in about a minute.
Isamu's confirmed units are waiting."

As Russo navigated the surface streets, he leaned back toward Vail's
phone. "Keep us posted."

"There's no other way onto the island?" Robby asked.

Russo shook his head. "We could take the subway, but by the time we
got to a station and waited for the F train, we'd have made it across and
back on the tram two or three times. And the Queensboro Bridge completely bypasses the island, goes right over it."

"What about ways *off* the island?"

"The F train, back into the city. And the Roosevelt Island bridge, into
Queens."

Russo called Central again and told them to get patrol cars over to the
Queens end of the bridge, at 36th Avenue, and to keep them dark so Prisco
would not see them. He also ordered all subway stations on the island locked
down.

"So what's on Roosevelt Island?" Robby asked. "Why would he go there?"

Russo slowed along Second Avenue and hung a quick right on East 60th
Street. He pulled to the curb in front of the tram. "There are very few
cameras, especially on the waterfront. And there are docks along the West
Road. If he's got a boat stashed away or if he knows of one he can steal, we
could lose him."

They got out of the car and ran along the wrought iron fence and gray
paver walkway, then up the three flights to the station's entrance. After going through the turnstile, they entered the small transit platform—twin
receiving ports for the tram cars, one on the left and the other on the right.
Large glass doors that slid apart to permit admittance to the cabin when it
was docked were mounted in fire engine red metal frames—which also
happened to be the station's color theme.

Vail phoned Slater. "Find anything? Other properties?"

"Zip."

"Keep looking, there's gotta be something. Check under his parents'
names." She clicked back to Uzi's call.

"He's almost there, Karen. Seconds till he arrives."

The returning tram was approaching on the left when Russo's phone rang.

"What?" Russo kicked the metal crosspiece, then said, "Yeah, I'm holding." He twisted the handset away from his mouth. "Cabin's empty. He's not on it."

Uzi's voice blurted from Vail's phone. "Impossible. I'm positive he's— Oh shit. Unless he took off the duty belt, which holds the sensor."

"He's onto us," Vail said.

Russo rested his head on the metal bar of the glass window. "We lost him."

64

They headed back down the stairs toward the car.

"If he's not on the tram," Russo said, "where is he and where's he headed?"

"How would he know?" Robby said. "He kept the belt on this whole time. Suddenly he takes it off?"

"Yeah," Russo said, bringing the phone back to his mouth. "You've gotta be kidding . . . A lot of good that'll do. Imbecile . . ." He disconnected the call.

"Some idiot at the DAS command center used the radio to tell ESU where they'd located him and mentioned the belt sensor."

"Would Prisco know what that means?"

"He's smart," Vail said. "I'm sure he knew he carried the DAS sensor. He wouldn't have known it was possible to repurpose the detector to make it transmit. But he's a careful SOB. He did what he's done his entire life: he took the safe way out, dumped the belt, and changed his plan."

"To what?" Robby asked.

Russo's phone rang again.

"Yeah," Vail said, "that's the question."

They arrived at their vehicle and got back in. A moment later, Russo hung up. "Mayor wants to go public with Prisco's photo, said it'll help in case he's able to avoid the cameras.

"Don't recommend that," Vail said, "not yet."

"Tough. Commissioner's on board. Gonna happen."

"Right now," Robby said, "I think we have to focus on things we can control. The key question is, Why was he headed to Roosevelt Island?"

Vail considered that a minute. "Let's assume he really was going there and it wasn't just a ruse to make us think that's what his intentions were. He probably figured he could make his way along the riverfront from the southerly area of the island where the tram let him off, north to the bridge, where he'd cross over into Queens. Not much in the way of cameras there, right?"

Russo nodded. "Assuming he wasn't going to try to grab a boat along the way, and assuming that he wasn't going to force his way into an apartment building on the island and hole up for a few days, then slip away."

"I get your point. We've gotta make a few assumptions. But right now neither of those options are still on the table because he didn't go to the island."

"So then where's he headed?" Russo asked.

"The possibilities are endless. But these are revenge killings, so there's only one logical place he'd go. Somewhere he was happy, where he lived in harmony before everything went to hell. Astoria, his old neighborhood."

Vail told Uzi she needed to make another call, then dialed Proschetta.

"How's it going?" Proschetta asked. "I don't have clearance anymore, no one'll tell me shit."

"We lost him, but I think I may know where he's headed. You remember where Prisco and his family lived before they moved to Ellis Island?"

"More or less. I remember the street, not the address. Why?"

"I think Prisco's got a hidden place where he keeps his trophies. And I'm betting it's in the house where he used to live."

"I'll look it up. Got a copy of all my old unsolved case files."

"Text me the address. And copy Jenkins and Slater."

"I'm heading toward downtown Astoria," Russo said as he turned over the engine.

"By the time we get there," Vail said, checking her seatbelt, "we should have an address. Hope I'm right." She called Slater—but Johnson answered. "Leslie, we lost him. I still think he's headed your way."

"Ready and waiting."

"Good. Isidore Proschetta's gonna text you guys an address, the place Prisco lived before they moved to Ellis Island. That's gotta be where his stash is. There may be someone else living there, but he's got a way in they don't know about, or he sublets a room under another name. Look for a hidden place, a crawlspace, an area underneath a staircase, a small storage area, or a concealed room behind a boiler in the basement."

"Okay."

"Even an alcove that was originally bricked up where he's built a way in through a hidden panel. His stuff's gonna be there. That's where he's headed. It'll be big enough for him to hide out. I wish I could give you more detail, but—"

"I know what to look for. And I just got the address. We're headed over."

"If there are other people living there, get 'em the hell out. Their lives are in danger. Prisco can't have anyone who can identify him. Media's going live with his photo any minute. If the people who live there know him or sublet to him, they'll be the first ones he takes out."

Vail hung up, then grabbed the rubber handle above the backdoor as the car swerved. "Russo, the way you're driving I feel like I'm on a real cab ride." Her phone vibrated: Uzi.

"You still headed toward Astoria?" he asked.

"Yeah. Best guess."

"No need to guess. I reviewed some security tapes on the Queensboro Bridge. He crossed over five minutes ago, driving what looks like a stolen sedan. I texted the plate and registration to Isamu."

"You're brilliant."

"Aw, you're just being kind," Uzi said. "But you should be kind more often."

"Go to hell."

"That's what I'm saying."

Vail's shoulder squished up against the car door and the vehicle tilted sharply as Russo exited onto Northern Boulevard.

"Straight shot for about a mile," Russo said, "then we'll hang a left onto 45th. Prisco can't take a chance on drawing attention to himself by speeding, so we should be able to make up some time here." With that, he accelerated, taking the car up to 70 miles per hour.

"He knows there are cameras around here," Vail told Uzi, "so I expect him to dump the sedan. Call me if you get another hit."

They sped along the wide Northern Boulevard, then Russo braked hard and squealed his tires as he turned onto 45th, which was relatively devoid of cars during the early morning hours.

The text from Proschetta arrived. Vail gave the address to Russo, who nodded.

"I know where that is."

Vail's BlackBerry buzzed again. "What do you got, Leslie?"

"Found his old place, a townhouse. We evacuated the old couple. They sublet the basement to some middle-aged guy. They said he's very quiet and respectful. Doesn't sleep there, just uses it for 'storage.'"

"I think he's en route, could be there any minute."

"We're good, lights are out and we got plenty of unmarked cars on the surrounding streets."

"Did the couple ID him?"

"Yeah, and I put them under protective custody with a couple of unis. Searched the place, concentrating on the areas you suggested. Found a hidden room, like you said, in the basement. Shitload of stuff from all his crime scenes going back to the beginning. Earrings, photos of the vics—and closeups of his X drawings on the necks. And—get this, a fake passport and a go-bag with about ten grand in Canadian dollars. His escape plan."

"He's a narcissist, Leslie. He thinks he's smarter than us cops, so he doesn't expect to get caught. He doesn't consider it an 'escape plan.'"

"Then why the fake passport?"

"He prides himself on thinking ahead," Vail said. "So that would be his 'contingency' plan."

"Yeah, well, whatever you, or he, wants to call it, I'm thinking you're right—he's headed here to pick this shit up, then cross over into Canada."

"You see a book in there? It's called *How Humans Die*."

"Now there's one that missed my reading list," Johnson said. "There's a lot of stuff—wait, yeah. Got it. How'd you know?"

"Open it up, you see any markings inside? Handwriting or—"

"How about fingerprints?"

"Be there in three," Russo said.

"Fingerprints?"

"Yeah," Johnson said. "Looks like he used blood."

"The victims' blood." *That's why he wanted the book back. It wasn't that he was afraid we'd find him because of what he wrote inside, it's because he wanted the book. It meant something to him.* "Sit tight, Leslie. This is all gonna come to a head in a few minutes." The second Vail disconnected the call, her phone buzzed. She answered on speaker. "Give us some good news, Uzi."

"He's on foot, nearing someplace called the Bohemian Beer Garden."

"I know it," Russo said. "Been there over a hundred years." He hung a left at the next street. "Huge courtyard in the back with tables and big screen TVs. Fun place to watch a Mets game."

Vail found it on her Google Earth map, then told Uzi to hold for a second while she texted Johnson:

> something spooked him, mustve seen one of
> the unmarked cars. headed away from you.
> we r in pursuit

Russo dialed his phone while driving, not bothering to hand it off to Robby. "Suspect's on foot, headed past the Bohemian Beer Garden on 24th Avenue."

"Uh, he turned left on 31st," Uzi said through Vail's BlackBerry speaker. "Found him on a post office camera."

Russo updated Prisco's location, then hung up.

"How far away are we?" Vail asked as she again consulted her map.

"Be there in a minute."

She zoomed in and scrolled. "Drop me and Robby at the subway station and continue on. See if you can spot him on the street."

Russo tossed her a quick glance. "What?"

"Playing a hunch. Stay in contact with Uzi." She texted Russo's number to Uzi and told him to call Russo with updates. She also instructed Uzi to let her know if he saw Prisco passing the subway.

Russo pulled up to the curb beneath the green elevated tracks that ran above 31st Street. He off-loaded Vail and Robby in front of a large painted mural, which ironically included a depiction of the Statue of Liberty.

They pulled their handguns and surveyed the stairways that started on the sidewalk and rose two flights to the raised subway platform.

Vail nodded at Robby's pistol. "You okay with that thing in your left hand?"

Robby waved his cast dismissively. "I'm ambidextrous."

"No, you're not."

"I am now. I'll be fine. It's the cop, not the gun, right?"

"You really want me to answer that?"

"One stairwell on the west side of the street and one on the east," Robby said. "Two of us."

"I'll take east, you go west."

"Still have something against the West Coast, eh?"

For a fleeting second Vail flashed on her escapades in California and thought about smiling—but she could not. As Robby started across the street, she walked beneath a black-and-white sign that read:

She climbed the stairs, passed the yellow step at the top of the landing, and continued up to the next level. As she hit the platform, she turned left and—

An intense jolt of electricity shot through her body, convulsing her muscles. As soon as her Glock hit the pavement, the pulse stopped.

But by then it was too late. Niklaus Prisco had his own pistol pressed against her temple and his arm wrapped around her torso—and he was pulling her toward the green metal column of the station's partial roof.

"Federal agent. Drop your weapon!"

It was Robby, standing on the opposite side of the platform, twenty-five feet of track between them, his SIG Pro .40 aimed in their direction.

"Or what," Prisco said, tilting his head. "You'll shoot? Do I have to point out how stupid that is, Special Agent Roberto Hernandez?" He snorted. "Oh, don't look so surprised. I know who you are. And I know why you're on this trip. I know everything. I know everything about you. And *you* know very little about me."

"I wouldn't be so sure," Robby said.

Vail tried to wriggle away, but Prisco had a good grip on her. The pistol's barrel did not move from its point against her skull. "This is not a very nice greeting, Niklaus. I thought I deserved better."

"Oh, come on. I could've killed you by now. Have some gratitude."

"Forgive me," Vail said. "I lost my gratitude when I dropped my Glock."

"I suppose you did. You know, when I saw you coming down the street, I thought, 'Shit!' I was hoping for a clean getaway. But maybe this worked out for the best."

"Let her go," Robby said, "and we can talk. Tell me what you want. Maybe I can make it happen for you."

Prisco slowly turned toward Robby. "Are you still here, Agent Hernandez? Really, what good do you think you're doing just standing there? You can't possibly run across the tracks. And you've got a cast on your shooting hand."

"I'm a lefty. And a damn good shot."

"You know," he said with a laugh, "I imagine you feel kind of impotent about now. Like—let me see . . . like a beautiful woman's seducing you, pushing her breasts against your face, and you feel the excitement building, and—and—you're powerless to act. You can't get it up. You're left unfulfilled, frustrated. Embarrassed.

"That's what's going on right here, right now. You've got a great big, powerful weapon in your hand. The bullets are ready to explode from the chamber. But . . . tsk, tsk, tsk . . . you can't shoot. Because you *are* right-handed, Agent Hernandez. I can tell by the way you're holding that SIG that it's not your natural side. And you desperately want to take the shot, to put a bullet between my eyes. But again, you can't. Because you know you're just as likely to hit Karen as you are me. Such a shame." He turned his back on Robby, yanking Vail to the side.

She looked down the tracks and in the extreme distance she could make out a single headlight, poking out of the darkness. "You're a coward, Niklaus."

"Me? A coward." He coughed. "Interesting psychology you're using, Karen. But I did tell you we would meet again, didn't I?"

"Too bad for you it's on my terms, not yours."

Prisco dug the barrel deeper into the muscle beneath her skin. "You're the one with the gun pressed against your skull. How is that on your terms?"

"You were on the run. I was hunting you. You were the prey. And now I've got you."

Prisco laughed. "You're either delusional or the Behavioral Analysis Unit is teaching you some real strange shit."

"You want to know why you're a coward?"

"Not really. Your opinion carries no weight."

"Because you tried to pin everything on your brother. Your brother, who wouldn't hurt a fly unless you told him to."

"Fucking retard. Useless piece of shit, that's all he is."

"You feel that way about everyone in your life, don't you? You feel that way about your father. Did you feel that way about your sister, before you killed her? What was it like to kill Cassandra?"

"She was my first," he whispered in her ear. "The first is always special."

"See, that's what I mean. She was an object. We're all just objects to you. Because you lack the ability to *feel*."

Prisco laughed. "You say it like it's some kind of disease. But it's a strength, not a weakness."

"For killing, it's a strength. I'll give you that."

"I think *you're* the piece of shit," Robby said, "not your brother. Dmitri's made a life for himself despite enormous obstacles. And you? What did you do with your life? You took the lives of others."

He swung his gaze back toward Robby. "Your point?"

Robby squinted, a look that said, "Huh?"

"There's no reasoning with him," Vail said. "He has no moral compass. He knows what's right and wrong. But he doesn't care. The rules of society don't apply to him."

"They don't, do they?" Prisco leaned back and appraised her face. "Very good, *Karen*. I couldn't have expressed it better. By the way, if you're such a great judge of character, how'd you end up with your deadbeat husband?"

Because, asshole, he turned out to be bipolar and refused to take his meds. Ignore him, Karen. He's just playing head games with you.

"So tell me something, Niklaus. The logo and letters you draw on the women. You're numbering your victims, right?"

"*They* were not victims. *I* was the victim! That was the point."

That was the point, wasn't it?

"And your assumption, Karen, is very simplistic. I expected better. I was not numbering them, I was claiming them. Keeping track of my kills."

"Like inventory."

"See?" Prisco said. "You understand more than you let on."

"Except the second and third ones—b and c in your 'inventory'—were missing. Gregor and Alyssa Persephone?"

"Score another for the Fibbie."

"You shot them to make it look like the Castiglias put out a hit on them. To make sure no one would connect their murders to you."

"Correct again. Even back then, my execution was flawless."

"And the r on Crinelli," Vail said. "R for revenge?"

Prisco laughed. "Did it take you twenty years to figure that out?"

There was a slight rumbling under Vail's feet. *The train's coming.*

Robby's gaze drifted off to the tracks.

In the same moment, Prisco's head swung left. He noticed it too. "The N train. Our carriage awaits! We're getting on that, Karen. Me and you."

"The cameras will track you," Robby said. "You've got no way out of this. Drop the gun and I won't beat your brains in. Deal?"

"There aren't any cameras on the cars," Prisco said evenly.

No rise in pitch, no hurried speech. He was not nervous. This was the type of scenario psychopaths found exciting—an emotion they craved, since they loathed boredom and lacked most other feelings.

"In fact, a lot of stations don't have cameras, either," Prisco said. "And yes, I do know which have cameras and which don't. I've got access to police department resources, remember? And I've had plenty of time to work this through. All contingencies."

"If you had this so well planned out," Vail said, "how come we found your fake passport and ten grand in Canadian cash?"

"Shut up!" Prisco jammed the gun tighter against her skull and nudged her closer to the tracks, twisting her so that her back was to the oncoming train.

The vibration in the platform was getting stronger and a gentle breeze ruffled the back of her hair.

It's coming.

"How'd you feel about your mother?" Vail asked.

"My mother died of cancer when I was a kid. She's irrelevant."

"Irrelevant? What do you think she'd say if she saw you, right here, right now?"

Robby started waving his hands at the subway's operator, no doubt trying to signal him to keep moving past the station.

"Don't do that!" Prisco said. "You tell him not to stop and I'll shoot her. Blow her brains all over the goddamn place. I've got nothing to lose. And if I'm leaving this world. I'm gonna take her with me."

Robby tensed his jaw.

"So your mother died when you were young," Vail said. "Were you close to her?"

The subway was approaching. Vail heard the rattle of the wheels.

I can't get on that train with him. At some point after we board, he'll have no use for me. I'll never see Robby again. Or Jonathan.

Robby brought his Glock up higher, lining up the sights.

Vail knew he was trying to decide if he could get off a reasonable shot. What was the right call here? What would she do? Shoot left-handed?

"Karen," Robby said, locking eyes with her. "Do *not* get on that train."

The rumble increased. The subway was yards away.

Maintaining eye contact with Robby, she jerked her chin up and to the right. Robby understood, because he pointed his SIG at the sky and fired off two rapid shots.

The moment Prisco flinched, Vail shifted her weight onto her left leg and rammed her right boot heel into his kneecap, hyperextending the joint and forcing him to recoil in pain. It gave her just enough space—and moved the barrel away from her head.

Vail grabbed his jacket and spun, turning clockwise, using momentum and all her body weight to propel him toward the tracks—much like a shot-putter spinning and then hurling the ball through the air.

Prisco tried to stop himself, but the damaged knee buckled and he went over the platform's edge at the exact instant the subway pulled into the station. He slammed against the front of the car as the operator screeched its wheels on the track, emitting a high pitched squeal as the train skidded to an ear-piercing stop.

Robby ran ahead and leaped down onto the tracks. He shielded his eyes from the headlight and peered underneath.

Vail joined him at the edge of the platform and got down on her knees. "You see him?"

"Yeah. I see him. Well, what's left of him."

65

>USS INTREPID
PIER 86
WEST 46TH STREET & 12TH AVENUE
MANHATTAN
PRESENT DAY: JULY 19

Karen Vail and Robby Hernandez stood dockside looking up at the massive attack carrier, USS *Intrepid*.
"That's one big dude," Robby said.
Vail elbowed him in the side. "Takes one to know
one."

The former World War II naval ship's gray hull was lit from below,
thick white ropes stretching from apertures in its bow and port side across
the water to somewhere below the pier.

They ascended the glass elevator to the top level, then walked across the
gangway to the flight deck. They strolled along the battleship gray tarmac
past the fighter planes and helicopters on display, headed toward the building at the stern of the ship.

The last time I was on an aircraft carrier it was the USS New York *off the
coast of England. And here I am in New York, on the* Intrepid.

"How are the heels?" Robby asked. "Still feel too high?"

"Don't be silly. They're pumps." She stopped and twirled in the middle of the tarmac. "How do I look?"

"I think you were right. About the white blouse."

Vail play-slapped him on the shoulder as they entered the pavilion and moved down the corrugated steel corridor.

"You look stunning," he said. "Seriously, they better have automatic defibrillators onboard or all these old farts are gonna be in trouble."

They emerged in a room that housed the stark white and charcoal gray space shuttle *Enterprise*, spotlit from below and above against a blue ceiling.

"Now that is the definition of cool," Robby said, craning his neck to take in the craft. "No matter how many times I saw the shuttle take off and land on TV, I never got the sense it was this big."

Wait staff dressed in black suits were wandering the floor with trays, handing out champagne flutes. Robby took two and handed one to Vail as they made their way to the front of the shuttle. After ascending the stairs, they stood nose to nose with the spaceship. It was a foot away from them—close enough to touch.

"It's very odd looking," Vail said. "In a cute sort of way. I mean, is it me, or straight-on does it look like Snoopy?"

"Snoopy." Robby turned away from the nose of shuttle and looked at Vail. "When was the last time you took a Rorschach?"

"The Rorschach test is for analyzing inkblots—"

"Whoa. Who the *hell* is that?"

They turned and saw Russo and Proschetta standing there in tuxes, glasses of champagne in their hands. They looked like they were on their third helping.

"Sorry, miss," Russo said, his eyes wandering her body from head to toe. "You must be in the wrong place. This party is for law enforcement personnel only."

"Very funny."

Proschetta nudged Russo aside and held out a hand. "I'm Izzie Protch. Have we met before?"

"All right, all right," Vail said. "Down boys. You have no idea how much foundation I needed to cover those pepper spray burns."

"I don't think they're looking at your face," Robby said near her ear.

Russo moved his head sideward, catching the light. "I'm wearing my burns as a badge of honor."

Vail pretended to admire them. "Actually, it looks like a bad day at the beach, where you only applied sunscreen to certain spots."

"This is a captain you're addressing," Proschetta said. "Show him some respect."

Robby cleared his throat, then extended a hand. "Robby Hernandez."

"So you're Robby," Proschetta said. "Much bigger than I expected."

Vail nodded. "Kind of like the space shuttle."

Proschetta looked to Robby for an explanation.

"You don't want to know," he said. "But congrats. To both of you."

Proschetta chuckled. "Karen made sure my send-off into retirement had some spice to it. None of this riding into the sunset. I went out with a bang. And a boom."

"I'm gonna miss you, Karen," Russo said, tears welling up in his eyes. "Don't take this the wrong way, but if there was one good thing about Hades, it's that he somehow kept bringing us together the past twenty years."

"Then we'll have to find a reason to meet up," Proschetta said. "I haven't been to DC in ten, fifteen years. And I've got a lotta friggin' time on my hands. I have a feeling retirement's gonna suck."

"Either way," Robby said, "I think we'll be seeing you two in the very near future."

"Oh yeah?" Russo asked. "Why's that?"

Vail lifted her left hand.

"Holy shit." Russo grabbed her wrist. "Did you steal that out of the property room? I'm gonna tell the commish—"

"Mazel tov." Proschetta moved to tip Vail's glass—and almost missed. "To both of you."

"I hope you didn't pay retail," Russo said. "Because I got a guy in the diamond district—"

"Russo, you're so New York."

"So are you, my dear. Even if you don't want to admit it."

Russo elbowed Robby. "You realize what you're getting yourself into? This engagement?"

Robby laughed. "How do you mean?"

Vail tilted her head. "Yeah, how do you mean?"

Russo shrugged. "With Karen around, life tends to be a lot more . . . I don't know . . . exciting."

Robby raised his glass. "I'm counting on it."

They talked about their plans for the wedding, which somehow degenerated into Russo telling stories of when he and Proschetta were cops in Vice.

Vail did not mind—she loved hearing these tales, even though she had heard them at least three times before, many years ago . . . in a somewhat different form. They seemed to get a little more polished, a little more impressive, with each successive telling.

But in that moment, in reflection on closing the Hades case, something that had dogged her for two decades, she reflected back on her life, the things that shaped her, the experiences that made her the cop she is. The people who made her the person she is.

She was concerned she would eventually lose touch with Carmine Russo and Isidore Proschetta, because that's what often happened with old friends when you moved away and didn't have a reason to visit. But she would have to make sure that never happened. Because when it came right down to it, cases came and went. But friends were what mattered.

Friends were forever.

Acknowledgments

The best way to understand how something works behind the scenes is to talk with those who do the jobs I'm writing about and visit their places of business: to see, smell, taste, and hear. In essence, I want to experience what they do—and how they do it. With that in mind, I have a lot of people to thank. They each helped me bring *Spectrum* to life with real-world verisimilitude:

Bennett Leventhal, MD, world-renowned expert on child psychiatry who also happens to be my cousin. Bennett helped me understand Dmitri and the nuances of his thought processes and interactions with others. In addition, his review of the manuscript and astute observations helped make *Spectrum* a better novel.

Lawrence Wein, detective, NYPD Detective Bureau, for spending months answering unending questions regarding NYPD procedure, ranks and pro-motions, precinct and squad hierarchy, crime scene requirements—everything NYPD-related—day, night, and in between. He gave me a perspective and a "look inside" of how things work and how the department thinks; it helped me envision a mind-set and a mood, as well as the way my characters should approach a situation—and one another. That was indispensable, as was his review of the manuscript for accuracy. Thanks to **Micheal Weinhaus**, special agent, Immigration and Customs Enforcement, for introducing us.

Michael Osgood, deputy chief, NYPD Special Victims Division, for his virtual tours of restricted areas and for giving me a comprehensive view of how the department operates. Mike's an outside-the-box thinker who knew what I needed to know before I had the chance to ask him.

Mercedes Brown, detective, NYPD, Bronx Special Victims Division, for her tour of the Fort Apache facility, Special Victims Squad, Major Case Squad, Robbery Squad, Night Watch, and their attendant facilities; for her contacts at NYPD Harbor Patrol, and for her two decades of knowledge regarding NYPD procedure.

The **Bronx Night Watch detectives**. Their candid, frank discussions and stories gave me an invaluable insider's view of the department.

Jon Adler, investigator for the US Attorney's office in Manhattan and president of the Federal Law Enforcement Officers Association. Jon had the unenviable task of arranging tours of Liberty Island and fighting to get me access to security-restricted areas of the statue. Jon was also my go-to guy for eateries, pubs, and other venues in New York City that are frequented by Feds and NY-PDers.

Mark Safarik, supervisory special agent and senior FBI profiler with the Bureau's Behavioral Analysis Unit (ret.), for his personalized instruction and continuing education regarding serial offenders. As always, Mark's detailed review of the manuscript was invaluable. On a personal note, we feel that it was both strange and fun to have him appear as himself in *Spectrum*.

Mary Ellen O'Toole, supervisory special agent and senior FBI profiler with the Bureau's Behavioral Analysis Unit (ret.), for her assistance with, and information on, psychopathy and its presentation relative to ASD. As I noted in the dedication, *Spectrum* is another Vail novel with Mary Ellen's fingerprints on it.

Peter Adeo, patrol officer, NYPD, for being my go-to guy regarding information on Astoria in the mid to late 1970s, on Roosevelt Island in the present, and for pointing me to the right neighborhoods in both areas to scout for my chapters.

Marina Stajic, PhD, director of forensic toxicology, New York City Office of Chief Medical Examiner, for helping me understand the mechanisms of death regarding chloroform and carbon monoxide, and the procedures used to check body tissues for their presence.

Jonathan Hayes, MD, senior medical examiner in the Office of the Chief Medical Examiner, New York City—and author of two riveting suspense novels. Despite his insanely busy schedule, Jonathan carved out time to answer my questions regarding New York's ME procedures—and to open the door for me to Dr. Stajic.

Saoud Mohammed, sergeant, United States Park Police, New York Field Office for arranging behind-the-scenes access and a personal tour of Ellis Island and **Darrell Gilliam**, officer, United States Park Police, for setting up transportation to the island.

The **United States Park Police SWAT** personnel who took me on a personal tour of the statue and Liberty Island, and for talking "operations" with me, the history of previous terrorist attacks on the monument, deployment scenarios, Liberty's arm and torch logistics, and so on. They wished to remain anonymous.

Tómas Palmer, cryptographer. Tómas and I joke that Karen Vail would be in deep donkey dung without him. This is not far from the truth. Tómas shared the theory behind the domain awareness system's radiological sensor, enabling Uzi to work his magic. Thanks to the anonymous individuals who provided information on the domain awareness system and the Lower Manhattan Security Initiative.

Henry Dunphy, Petty Officer 1st Class, United States Coast Guard Public Affairs Detachment San Diego, and **Jetta Disco**, Petty Officer 2nd Class, United States Coast Guard Public Affairs Detachment New York, for their assistance with determining law enforcement jurisdiction in Upper New York Bay.

Luis Prosper, maintenance ranger, National Park Service, for taking me on a virtual tour of the statue's arm and torch. **Doug Treem**, ranger, for introducing me to Liberty's arm and basement.

Don Mihalek, agent, Secret Service, New York Field Office, for his behind the scenes assistance. **Matthew Cippaghila**, United States Park Police officer, New York Field Office, for helping me with Liberty Island access. **John Hnedak**, deputy superintendent, National Park Service, for taking me around Islands 2 and 3, including the abandoned Ellis Island hospital complex.

Chris Schneider, assistant SWAT team leader Anaheim Police Department (ret.), and **Joe Ramos**, captain (and former SWAT lieutenant/commanding officer), San Diego Police Department, for reviewing my SWAT chapters for correct terminology, procedure, and equipment.

A. David Lerner, MD, for assistance with the medical issues involved with Vail's car accident and their impact on her pregnancy. **Andrew Gulli** for help with Greek customs, culinary fare, and terms of endearment. **Stan Pollock**, CPA, for assistance with Deacon's career requirements and accounting irregularity details.

Jeffrey Jacobson, Esq., for his usual support and assistance on a variety of legal and law enforcement related topics. **Chuck Barrett**, former air traffic controller, commercial pilot, and fellow thriller novelist for background on FAA rules governing the closure of cabin doors.

Dave Rhoden, 5.11 Tactical's director of product intelligence, **Joe Dalton**, team leader, NYPD detective task force (ret.), and **Richard Henderson**, detective, NYPD Explosive Ordnance Disposal (and former tactical/rescue/sniper, NYPD Emergency Service Unit), for their institutional memory regarding the NYPD's ESU team and the equipment they use, past and present.

To all my fellow Rosedale-ites, thanks for your recollections regarding the old neighborhood: **Michele Petker**, **Darlene Quartieri**, **Lynn Cervo**, **Robin Middleton**, **John Anthony Porcaro**, **Sheri Byrne Buckley**, **Lisa Bergenholtz Saltzberg**, **Ray Hosey**, **Michael Lang**, **Maria Panzarella-Solomonic**, **Tony Filidoro**, **Jeff Farkash**, **Ray Samuelson**, **Anthony Vitale**, **Bill Wehner**, **Linda Higgins**, **Robert Grano**, and **Jeff Glowatz** (my buddy from way back when).

Kevin Smith, my editor. *Spectrum* is our seventh book together. Because of the novel's complexity on so many levels, Kevin served as a vital sounding board and beacon throughout the planning and writing process.

Chrisona Schmidt, my copyeditor. It's simple: I love my copyeditor. Chrisona finds the things to which I've become blind, straightens up the grammar, and helps me bring you polished, crisp narrative.

C.J. Snow and **Danielle Jacobson,** tack-sharp proofreaders who have that special ability to see what most of us inadvertently skip over.

My agents, **Joel Gotler** and **Frank Curtis.** In addition to everything "literary" that they do on my behalf, Joel keyed me into the furrier business in Queens and Manhattan in the '70s, which played a key role in the story. Frank not only kept me out of trouble, but he also fed my obsession for accuracy by assisting me with the nuances of New York City geography.

The hardworking and tireless teams at Open Road, Premier Publishing, and Norwood Press for making sure my work gets into the hands of my readers in an increasingly challenging publishing landscape.

Those readers who are regular contributors to my Facebook fan group (www.FansofAlanJacobson.com): you have my sincere appreciation. In particular, I'd like to recognize **Sandy Soreano** and **Teri Landreth** for their work in administering the group and keeping the conversations lively.

Last, but really most and never, ever least: **Jill Jacobson** for being my love, my life companion, my draft editor, and my research companion. For *Spectrum* we traipsed around, across, underneath, and over New York City in the sweltering heat of July (as if that wasn't enough, we returned in August), searching for those special places to set scenes. Jill, who holds a Master's in Special Education, also gave me an early primer on ASD and made sure my depictions rang true.

Acronyms used in Spectrum

ASAC: assistant special agent in charge (FBI)
BAU: Behavioral Analysis Unit (FBI)
BSU: Behavioral Science Unit (FBI)
CI: confidential informant
COD: cause of death
CFO: chief financial officer
CPA: certified public accountant
CRV: critical response vehicle
CSI/CSU: crime scene investigator/crime scene unit
DAS: domain awareness system
DD-5:   complaint follow-up report (NYPD)
DOA: dead on arrival
EOD: Explosives Ordnance Division
ESS: Emergency Services Squad
ETA: estimated time of arrival Federal
FAA: Aviation Administration
FDNY: Fire Department of New York
ESU: Emergency Service Unit
INS: Immigration and Naturalization Service
LEO: law enforcement officer
One PP: One Police Plaza (NYPD headquarters)
ME: medical examiner
MO: method of operation
NCAVC: National Center for the Analysis of Violent Crime
PAA: police administrative aide
PBAU: Profiling and Behavioral Analysis Unit (FBI)
PDA: personal digital assistant
RFID: radio frequency identification
SWAT: special weapons and tactics
TARU: Technical Assistance Response Unit
TDU: tactical duty uniform
TRACS: tactical radiological acquisition and characterization system
UNSUB: unknown subject
VICAP: Violent Criminal Apprehension Program
Y2K: year 2000

About the Author

Alan Jacobson is a national bestselling author. In order to take readers behind the scenes to places they might never go, Jacobson has embedded himself in many federal agencies, including spending several years working with two senior profilers at the Federal Bureau of Investigation's vaunted Behavioral Analysis Unit in Quantico. During that time, Jacobson edited four published FBI research papers on serial offenders, attended numerous FBI training courses, worked with the head firearms instructor at the academy, and received ongoing  personalized instruction on serial killers—which continues to this day. He has also worked with high-ranking members of the Drug Enforcement Administration, the US Marshals Service, the New York Police Department, SWAT teams, local bomb squads, branches of the US military, chief superintendents and detective sergeants at Scotland Yard, criminals, armorers, helicopter pilots, chief executive officers, historians, and Special Forces operators. These experiences have helped him to create gripping, realistic stories and characters. His series protagonist, FBI profiler Karen Vail, resonates with both female and male readers, and writers such as Nelson DeMille, James Patterson, and Michael Connelly have called Vail one of the most compelling heroes in suspense fiction.

Jacobson's books have been published internationally, and several have been optioned for film and television. A number have been named to Best of the Year lists.

Jacobson has been interviewed extensively on television and radio, including on CNN, NPR, and multiple ABC, CBS, NBC, and Fox network affiliates.

Connect with the author through his website (www.AlanJacobson.com), on Facebook (www.Facebook.com/AlanJacobsonFans), and on Twitter (@JacobsonAlan).

The Works of Alan Jacobson

Alan Jacobson has established a reputation as one of the most insightful suspense and thriller writers of our time. His exhaustive research, coupled with years of unprecedented access to law enforcement agencies, including the FBI's Behavioral Analysis Unit, bring realism and unique characters to his pages. Following are his current, and forthcoming, releases.

False Accusations > Dr. Phillip Madison has everything: wealth, power, and an impeccable reputation. But in the pre-dawn hours of a quiet suburb, the revered orthopedic surgeon is charged with double homicide—a cold-blooded hit-and-run that leaves an innocent couple dead. Blood evidence has brought the police to his door. An eyewitness has placed him at the crime scene, and Madison has no alibi. With his family torn apart, his career forever damaged, no way to prove his innocence and facing life in prison, Madison must find the person who has engineered the case against him. Years after reading it, people still talk about the ending. *False Accusations* launched Alan's career and became a national bestseller, prompting CNN to call him, "One of the brightest stars in the publishing industry." Detective Ryan Chandler reprises his role in *Spectrum.*

The Hunted > How well do you know the one you love? How far would you go to find out? When Lauren Chambers's husband Michael disappears, her search reveals his hidden past involving the FBI, international assassins—and government secrets that some will go to great lengths to keep hidden. As *The Hunted* hurtles toward a conclusion mined with turn-on-a-dime twists, no one is who he appears to be and nothing is as it seems. *The Hunted* introduces the dynamic Department of Defense covert operative Hector DeSantos and FBI Director Douglas Knox, characters who return in *Velocity, Hard Target, No Way Out,* and *Spectrum.*

The 7th Victim (Karen Vail #1)> Literary giants Nelson DeMille and James Patterson describe Karen Vail, the first female FBI profiler, as "tough, smart, funny, very believable," and "compelling." In *The 7th Victim*, Vail—with a dry sense of humor and a closet full of skeletons—heads up a task force to find the Dead Eyes Killer, who is murdering young women in Virginia…the backyard of the famed FBI Behavioral Analysis Unit. The twists and turns that Karen Vail endures in this tense psychological suspense thriller build to a powerful ending no reader will see coming. Named one of the Top 5 Best Books of the Year (*Library Journal*).

Crush (Karen Vail #2) > FBI Profiler Karen Vail is in the Napa Valley for a vacation—but the Crush Killer has other plans. Vail partners with Inspector Roxxann Dixon to track down the architect of death who crushes his victims' windpipes and leaves their bodies in wine caves and vineyards. But the killer is unlike anything the profiling unit has ever encountered, and Vail's miscalculations have dire consequences for those she holds dear. *Publishers Weekly* describes *Crush* as "addicting" and *New York Times* bestselling author Steve Martini calls it a thriller that's "Crisply written and meticulously researched," and "rocks from the opening page to the jarring conclusion." (Note: the *Crush* storyline continues in *Velocity*.)

Velocity (Karen Vail #3) > A missing detective. A bold serial killer. And evidence that makes FBI Profiler Karen Vail question the loyalty of those she has entrusted her life to. Squaring off against foes more dangerous than any she has yet encountered, shocking personal and professional truths emerge— truths that may be more than Vail can handle. *Velocity* was named to *The Strand Magazine*'s Top 10 Best Books for 2010, *Suspense Magazine*'s Top 4 Best Thrillers of 2010, *Library Journal*'s Top 5 Best Books of the Year, and the *Los Angeles Times*' top picks of the year. Michael Connelly said *Velocity* is "As relentless as a bullet. Karen Vail is my kind of hero and Alan Jacobson is my kind of writer!"

Inmate 1577 (Karen Vail #4) > When an elderly woman is found raped and murdered, Karen Vail heads west to team up with Inspector Lance Burden and Detective Roxxann Dixon. As they follow the killer's trail in and around San Francisco, the offender leaves behind clues that ultimately lead them to the most unlikely of places, a mysterious island ripped from city lore whose long-buried, decades-old secrets hold the key to their case: Alcatraz. The Rock. It's a case that has more twists and turns than the famed Lombard Street. The legendary Clive Cussler calls *Inmate 1577* "a powerful thriller, brilliantly conceived and written." Named one of *The Strand Magazine*'s Top 10 Best Books of the Year.

Hard Target > An explosion pulverizes the president-elect's helicopter on Election Night. The group behind the assassination attempt possesses far greater reach than anything the FBI has yet encountered—and a plot so deeply interwoven in the country's fabric that it threatens to upend America's political system. But as covert operative Hector DeSantos and FBI Agent Aaron "Uzi" Uziel sort out who is behind the bombings, Uzi's personal demons not only jeopardize the investigation but may sit at the heart of a tangle of lies that threaten to trigger an international terrorist attack. Lee Child called *Hard Target*, "Fast, hard, intelligent. A terrific thriller." Note: FBI Profiler Karen Vail plays a key role in the story.

No Way Out (Karen Vail #5) > Renowned FBI profiler Karen Vail returns in *No Way Out*, a high-stakes thriller set in London. When a high profile art gallery is bombed, Vail is dispatched to England to assist with Scotland Yard's investigation. But what she finds there—a plot to destroy a controversial, recently unearthed 440-year-old manuscript—turns into something much larger, and a whole lot more dangerous, for the UK, the US—and herself. With his trademark spirited dialogue, page-turning scenes, and well-drawn characters, National Bestselling author Alan Jacobson ("My kind of writer," per Michael Connelly) has crafted the thriller of the year. Named a top ten "Best thriller of 2013" by both *Suspense Magazine* and *The Strand Magazine*.

Spectrum (Karen Vail #6) > It's 1995, the NYPD has just graduated a promising new patrol officer named Karen Vail—and the rookie cop is immediately put to the test: A young woman has been murdered. There are no forensics. No witnesses. And the manner in which she was killed is unlike anything the department has seen before. The offender shows no signs of stopping, however, and over the ensuing 19 years, the case that becomes known as "Hades" takes many unexpected twists and turns—as does Vail's career. Now a skilled FBI profiler, will she be in a better position to catch a killer who has terrorized New York City for three decades? Or will Hades prove to be Karen Vail's hell on earth?

Number 1 *New York Times* bestseller Richard North Patterson called *Spectrum*, "Compelling and crisp…A pleasure to read."

Short Stories

Fatal Twist > The Park Rapist has murdered his first victim—and FBI profiler Karen Vail is on the case. As Vail races through the streets of Washington, D.C. to chase down a promising lead that may help her catch the killer, a military-trained sniper takes aim at his target, a wealthy businessman's son. But what brings these two unrelated offenders together is something the nation's capital has never before experienced. *Fatal Twist* provides a taste of Karen Vail that will whet your appetite.

Double Take > NYPD Detective Ben Dyer awakens from cancer surgery to find his life turned upside down. His fiancée has disappeared and Dyer, determined to find her, embarks on a journey mined with potholes and startling revelations—revelations that have the potential to forever change his life. *Double Take* introduces NYPD Lieutenant Carmine Russo and Detective Ben Dyer, who return to play significant roles in *Spectrum* (Karen Vail #6).

More to come > For a peek at recently released Alan Jacobson novels, interviews, videos, reading group guides, tips for aspiring writers, and more, visit www.AlanJacobson.com.

THE KAREN VAIL SERIES

FROM OPEN ROAD MEDIA

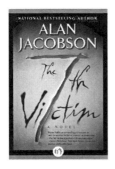

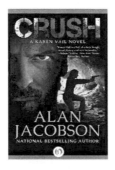

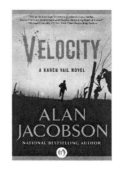

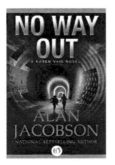

Available wherever ebooks are sold

OPEN ROAD

INTEGRATED MEDIA

CPSIA information can be obtained at www.ICGtesting.com
Printed in the USA
BVOW07s0800160914

366951BV00002B/3/P